THE LAST OF THE
TRUE BELIEVERS

BOOKS BY ANN BIRSTEIN

The Last of the True Believers

The Rabbi on Forty-seventh Street

American Children

Dickie's List

Summer Situations

The Sweet Birds of Gorham

The Troublemaker

Star of Glass

The Last of the True Believers

A NOVEL

Ann Birstein

(// (//

W·W·NORTON & COMPANY

NEW YORK LONDON

Published simultaneously in Canada
by Penguin Books Canada Ltd.,
2801 John Street, Markham, Ontario L3R 1B4
Printed in the United States of America.

THE AUTHOR WISHES TO EXPRESS SPECIAL THANKS
TO THE VIRGINIA CENTER FOR THE CREATIVE ARTS.

The text of this book is composed
in 11/13 Linotron 202 Electra,
with display type set in Antique Solid Roman.
Composition by PennSet, Inc.
Manufacturing by The Maple-Vail Book
Manufacturing Group.
Book design by Margaret M. Wagner.
First Edition

Library of Congress Cataloging in Publication Data
Birstein, Ann.
The last of the true believers.
I. Title.
PS3503.I768L37   1988   813'.54   87-31353

ISBN 0-393-02587-X

W. W. Norton & Company, Inc.
500 Fifth Avenue, New York, N.Y. 10110
W. W. Norton & Company Ltd.
37 Great Russell Street, London WC1B 3NU

1 2 3 4 5 6 7 8 9 0

For Joe Machlis

One

1

OCTOBER 27, 1951
Greenwood, Hamilton, N.Y.

Dear Sunny:

I love your name.

It's a ridiculous name, of course, for someone who aspires to be a serious writer. But you tell me you're not sure whether you have such aspirations—when will you decide? Shouldn't it be soon?—and in any case, it suits you. You are very light. Full of light, I would say if I knew you better, as I hope one day I will.

Do you know anything about Greenwood? It's a large estate, now given over to the use of writers and other artists. In residence at the moment are a young poet, not much older than you, an Abstract Expressionist painter—do you know what that is?—an elderly lady poet, an alcoholic Southern novelist, and this Jewish homme de lettres. They have given me a large west bedroom in the mansion to work in, now so shot through with sunshine that everything is a glistening yellow—my table, my chair, my French window looking out on a long avenue of pines—all the color of your hair, my dear. Even this paper I'm typing on, I see, is yellow. It's a remarkable place, full of serenity and bygone splendor, and I always come here to put the finishing touches on a piece of work, never feel right unless I do, and to restore my soul, now much bruised from a bitter divorce. One day, maybe, you will want to come and work here too.

Well, this is only to say hello, and that I've thought of you a lot, and that I'm glad we met. Have Amanda send me your book since you're too shy to do so yourself. I'm not such a dragon with first novels as I'm made out to be.

So long for now, dear Sunny.

David Harvey

OCTOBER 30, 1951
New York, N.Y.

Dear Mr. Harvey,

I was very glad to get your letter, which came as a surprise, though you said you would write when you called so unexpectedly the other day. I am glad we met too. The funny thing is that when Amanda invited me to dinner I didn't want to go. Amanda said you were a fascinating conversationalist and you certainly are. I don't think you're a dragon at all. It's just that I truly don't feel that my book is worth your while, and I'm afraid that if you read it, this will interfere with our relationship. Does that sound strange? Anyway, I will screw up my courage and send it to you personally. It's my book and therefore my responsibility, not my editor's.

Greenwood sounds beautiful. It's nice to imagine you writing in that golden room, among other things, a letter to me. Sunny is my real name, as I believe I told you. My mother was very fond of musical comedies at the time of my birth, and I consider myself lucky that I wasn't named "Nanette." I have thought of you a lot, too. In fact, that night we met, I went to sleep dreaming that in about ten years I would run into you at a party, now an important person myself, and tap you on the shoulder and remind you of the evening with the Montinis. And then, when I awoke the next morning, the phone was ringing, and it was you. Usually, I mind having my dreams interrupted. I am very devoted to my dreams. But not this time.

I hope your work goes well and that your soul is healing.

Yours,
Sunny Mansfield

NOVEMBER 2, 1951
Greenwood, Hamilton, New York

Dear Sunny,

Ten years hence. Oh, my. The carelessness—or should I say heartlessness?—of the young. In ten years I will be an old man of forty-seven and you will be five years younger than I am now. Did you mean to rub this in? But no, I can't think you are so cruel. You were laughing as I entered Amanda's living room, but it was a hearty, good-natured laugh, untinged with malice. What was the joke, by the way?

Do you know Amanda well, or does she merely function as your editor, planting copies of your novel on her coffee table for people to find as they look for a place to put their drinks? Don't misunderstand me. I like her well enough and approve of her having arranged our meeting for whatever purpose. She's a decent sort, decidedly unliterary but good at literary jobs. It's her husband I can't stand—those awful, nervous, modernistic sculptures of his adorning all free floor space, and his trumped-up opinions on all matters intellectual. So boringly anti-American, and more Italian than anyone need be. Did you know that Milo escaped army service during World War II by serving as a papal guard at the Vatican, thus eluding Mussolini by dressing in the style of Michelangelo?

I'm finishing up a project that at one point I thought might take me the rest of my life. I'll tell you about it sometime. Greenwood is very lonely. The elderly lady poet plies me with her poems and tells me of her glaucoma. In my mansion bedroom the dying light stabs me like a knife. Did I understand you to say that you were brought up in Connecticut, the daughter of a brain surgeon? It's hard to imagine you as part of a country club set. Your legs are too solid, your laughter too felt. (What *were* you laughing about with Amanda before I came in, by the way?) My own father, actual if not spiritual, is a poor little Jewish tailor. Izzy is his name, and he reads Pushkin and Turgenev. I can say for him that he never personally sought to assume the nice WASP name of Harvey. It was given to him by an immigration officer at Ellis Island.

Write again soon. Your letter was a bit stilted, avoiding contractions and repetitions, except for "dreams/dreaming." But your charm came through. Is your novel like that too? Stilted but charming? Please do, as you say, assume the responsibility and send it. In return maybe I'll send you a copy of my *Home-*

ward Bound, unless you already have one, though probably you wouldn't be interested in a study of expatriate poets of the twenties—too much before your time. I'm still glad we met. Gladder than ever.

David

NOVEMBER 9, 1951
New York, N.Y.

Dear David (?),

If my letter was stilted, it's because though I could imagine having many different kinds of relationships with you, none of them was that of a pen pal. I really hate to write letters. In fact, I hate to write, period, though for some reason I seem to have embarked on a new novel. I don't quite understand this since I am miserable sitting home alone and writing, (I am really a very gregarious person), and while I was working on *Watch for the Sunrise* swore I would never do it again. In fact, I had even applied to several graduate schools and received a fellowship to Cornell when I got the idea for this new book. And then, suddenly, I was seized with a strange kind of homesickness and couldn't bear the thought of going away. Does any of this make sense to you? Anyway, I wrote to Cornell, turning them down, and applied for an Abingdon Fellowship to France for next year instead. I hope I won't regret my rashness. (It just occurred to me that if I had accepted that Cornell fellowship, I would have been in *Ithaca* the night we met. Isn't that amazing?) Also, to make matters even more mysterious, it wasn't Connecticut or my parents or my roommate, Mary Jane, I was homesick for. It was something I couldn't name.

No, I'm not part of a "country club set," and neither are my parents. They just use the place to play golf and to have an occasional dinner. They are really wonderful people. I know that it's unfashionable to love your parents and even like them on top of that, but I do. I'm sure you would love my mother if you met her. Everybody does. Please don't hold my name against her. I think it was my coloring that influenced her more than anything else. My father is a doctor, actual *and* spiritual. What are you working on now? I mailed my book to you this morning with great trepidation. I should be very grateful to receive a copy of *Homeward Bound* in return. I apologize for not already owning a copy, not to say never having read it. But, as I believe I explained, I'm not really an intellectual. To tell the truth, and as long as I'm making all these confessions, when Amanda said you were coming to dinner, I had never even heard of you. But you called yourself a "writer" many times during the evening, and I now realize that you are a well-known poet. Well-known, it would seem, to everyone but me. I'm sorry that Greenwood is so lonely and that the female poet with glaucoma keeps foisting her work on you. How long do you intend to stay there? Please don't feel you have to say anything about my book if, after reading, it, you would rather not. It won't matter. I'm sure we have many other things to discuss.

I, too, am gladder than ever that we met. As to my dreams, I really don't mind your interrupting them. I'm sorry about that ten year business, but why do you make yourself out to be so old? I mentioned your age to my father, and he said you were in your prime.

Yours,
Sunny

P.S. Amanda is more my editor than my friend, but she has taken a very kind personal interest in me and my work. I'm afraid I like Milo, too, except when he's rude to her. But I don't think he really means it.

NOVEMBER 13, 1951
Greenwood, Hamilton, N.Y.

Sunnoo, sunnas, sunnat:

To get to what is no doubt uppermost in your mind, yes, I have read your book and, yes, within certain decided and prescribed limits, I like it. To begin with, let me congratulate you on not having written an autobiographical novel the first time around—unless you see yourself as a lame cleaning woman named Hilda living on the wrong side of the tracks in Bridgeport. I admire the evenness of your design, and its clarity, rare in one so young. And since I'm sure that more than one writing teacher, including the redoubtable George Auerbach, under whom you tell me you studied, has spoken to you of your talent, there is no need for me to tell you what you already know nor to say what I don't altogether mean. But the problem is, my dear Sunny, that you are *too* modest in your intent, too *much* in control. It's all very well to limit yourself to writing about what you know, but when there is an opportunity to write about more than you *think* you know, you lapse into generalizations, or—I'm sorry, my dear—turn cute.

The point is, what do you really feel about Hilda besides a nice middle-class, diffuse pity for all cleaning ladies, concentrated on this one abject specimen? Suffering in itself, despite what some Russians tell us, does not make one beautiful. Only transcendent suffering is meaningful, a suffering which aspires and evolves toward a higher form of truth and, ergo, beauty. I am thinking here of Jesus, yes, and I am also thinking of Rilke's definition of love, that it consists of two solitudes protecting and touching and greeting each other. (By which he emphatically did not mean two lonely hearts seizing upon each other at a social club.) I am thinking also, to bring the matter somewhat closer to home and possibly suggest areas you might think about exploring, of my aunt, Natalia Harvey (Kirschenbaum). Like my parents, born in the Ukraine, victimized from childhood on by discrimination, various humiliations, etc., etc.—all the usual Jewish experiences—she nevertheless does not perceive herself as a victim. Unlike my parents, she is never abject, nor hopelessly at sea but, on the contrary, sublime. At present, she teaches Russian at the New School, but she is a superb political thinker and I'm sure the world will hear from her. To paraphrase Faulkner in his Nobel Prize acceptance speech, Natalia not only endures but will prevail. All of this just by way of suggesting heroic materials close at hand. . . . In any case, I'm delighted you sent me your book. You're very talented, but you're also very young and have far to go. So please let's have no more false modesty about this or any of your other work. . . . Oh, yes, your title, *Watch for the Sunrise*. It's a notch higher than *Wait for the Sunrise*, but only a notch. Did your publisher foist it on you? It has that ring.

Look, I can't stick it out here much longer. I want to *see* you. That dreadful studio portrait on your dust jacket isn't of any girl *I* know. I've promised to go to a boring cocktail party next Sunday, but ought to be able to make my exit by seven. Can you meet me at the fountain in front of the Plaza? The one the Fitzgeralds jumped into with all their clothes on? I can't promise you an experience so exuberant, only dinner and talk. Pen pal, oh my.

David

NOVEMBER 16, 1951
New York, N.Y.

Dear David,

I'm glad you liked my book as well as you did, and I agree with everything you said, except the part about my undue modesty. Of course, I can't help thinking how sorry Amanda would be not to be able to use the quotable parts of your letter in an ad. Don't worry, I'm only kidding. Amanda doesn't know anything about our correspondence. In fact, she doesn't know anything about us, period. Anyway, I'm so glad the book sending part is over and we can now talk about other things. Aren't you?

Sunday at the Plaza fountain, 7:00 PM. I'll be there with bells on.

Yours,
Sunny

Oh, yes, the title of my book before they made me change it was *Hilda*.

2

"Hilda?"

"I guess I've never been very poetic."

"Evidently not."

She giggled nervously. "I must be the only person I know who's written a whole novel without ever having tried to write a poem. Even a little one."

"That's probably a good thing," David Harvey said with a deep sigh.

They were still standing in front of the Plaza fountain, bemused by each other's faces. Although he was quite short and they were almost at eye level, he seemed to be looking down at her, a dark, intense man, almost handsome except for the two lines that ran from his nose to his chin and gave him the look of a tired clown. He was also, at the moment, frowning. Out of disapproval? Disappointment? She didn't know. Was *she* disappointed? She didn't know that either. Her memory of the evening they had met was all confused with his letters. And also Amanda's laughing description of David Harvey as an irritable hypochondriac. Then in he had walked, complaining of a cold, saying that his students at NYU, where he was a visiting professor, were as bad as his students at Cole, the small upstate college where he usually taught—and what were they all laughing about? She had watched him push aside the several copies of her book that lay on the coffee table. The rest of the evening was a blur. They had had dinner very late, in a local Italian restaurant and only after he threatened to leave if he didn't get something to eat soon—"Do you have to be so Mediterranean in all your habits?" he had asked Milo—and proceeded to talk all through the meal, brilliantly, so immersed in his monologue that Sunny had had to keep plucking his sleeve from his eggplant parmigiana, murmuring apologies. Each time she apologized he had looked around, surprised to see her there. What had *she* eaten? She no longer remembered that either. Only that in the taxi going back uptown—he had given her a lift—she was glad of every swerve that threw her against him.

Dusk was falling. He raised the collar of his dark blue raincoat. "Do you want to walk? Do you like to walk?"

"I love to walk," she said, smiling and shivering. "It's my favorite thing to do."

"Good." He nodded and tucked her arm under his. They started out along Fifty-ninth Street and at the entrance to the park descended the path to the pond. Under the lamplight they stopped and looked at the ducks floating on the water. She was still gazing at the ducks when he kissed her. His mouth was closed. "Oh, Mr. Harvey," she said, forgetting momentarily that they were on a first-name basis. The closed-mouth kiss had made it all seem formal.

He took her to a little French restaurant nearby and sat looking at her seriously, as if he were about to make a major decision. Finally he ordered two Gibsons. She gingerly put her package of Philip Morrises on the table. She had just remembered something else. That first night in the restaurant the two of them had put their Philip Morrises on the table, and he had absentmindedly pocketed both packs. After a while she had asked him timidly for a cigarette and he had told her with a laugh to buy her own. "They *are* my own," she had said, and he had said, "Possessive, aren't you?" Had she made a terrible mistake? Would it have been better to keep quiet? She sipped at her Gibson, a stronger, clearer version of a martini, and surfaced in time to realize that he was saying something to her intently.

"Never shall a young man,/Thrown into despair/By those great honey-colored/Ramparts at your ear/Love you for yourself alone/And not your yellow hair."

"I beg your pardon?"

". . . I heard an old religious man/But yesternight declare/That he had found a text to prove/That only God, my dear,/Could love you for yourself alone/And not your yellow hair."

"Oh, that's beautiful," she said. "Did you write it recently?"

He sighed and ordered another Gibson for each of them. "William Butler Yeats wrote it, not I," he said. " 'To Lady Anne Gregory.' Did they not teach you to read at Gorham, only to write?"

By the main course, which he had ordered for both of them—the menu was long, the Gibsons potent—he had told her about his parents, his mother illiterate even in Yiddish, his father self-taught, both still living on the same street in the Bronx where he was born, about the horrors of growing up in the Depression, about his aunt Natalia, who had made the big breakthrough into the outside world. By dessert—he hoped she liked crème caramel, his favorite dessert—he had gone on to his marriage. "It was a mistake from the beginning, but the war kept us together by keeping us apart, on two separate continents. When Gloria was born, for all practical purposes I no longer existed at all. Gertrude wouldn't even come to the book party for *Homeward Bound* because Gloria had diarrhea. . . . Don't you ever finish what's on your plate?"

"I was distracted."

"Do you like music?"

"Yes."

"I play the violin—like all good Jewish boys. One of these days we'll go to a concert."

He paid the check, reminded her she had left her cigarettes, and took her back to the one-room apartment on the West Side, which he had sublet for the time of his leave from Cole College. Closing the door with his shoulder, he started to undress her in the dark, moving her backwards by instinct to the studio couch against the wall.

Later he said in the blackness, "Do you always come so easily?"

"Yes. No. Am I not supposed to? I don't remember."

"Remember *me*, honey girl. Remember *me*."

In the light, David was a different person. He put on his red paisley bathrobe, stuck a record on the turntable, then sat back with his hands folded across his stomach, staring at the ceiling. "Yvette Guilbert," he told her, "one of the great chanteuses of all time."

"*Plaisirs d'amour ne durent qu'un moment. Chagrins d'amour durent toute la vie.*"

"I don't believe that, even if it is in French," Sunny said from under the sheets on the studio couch.

"Ah? You believe that love conquers all?"

"Of course."

"Don't think I'm going to marry you," David said.

"I don't want to get married."

"Ever?"

"Well, certainly not now."

"Miss Prissy," David said. "Okay, Sunshine, would you like to hear a piece of what I'm working on now?"

"Is it a poem?" she asked dubiously.

"In a way. It's also an autobiography."

"But you're so young."

"Don't be so literal-minded. It's a spiritual autobiography. I call it *Ancestors*. Listen."

She listened. For an hour she listened. Oh, my God, Sunny thought, that man in the red paisley bathrobe who has just made love to me is reading me a masterpiece. Catching sight of her face, David stopped in the middle of a sentence and said, "Marry me."

"I think David Harvey was very interested in you that night," Amanda said over the phone several weeks later.

"Really?"

"Yes, I can tell. I've known David for years and the more irascible he seems, the more beguiled he actually is. Well, who knows? He may even give us a quote. The problem is no one's seen him around lately. He seems to be hiding out."

"I think we ought to forget about a quote," Sunny said. "My novel isn't very poetic, anyhow."

"Listen," Amanda said, "you could use some literary attention. The reviews are good, but that book isn't taking off."

Sunny hung up with a guilty sigh. She had lied to Amanda by omission and she was not sure why. Her love affair with David was hardly a dark secret—he was divorced and free—but somehow not a matter for public consumption either. No, not secret, just private, sweeter because it concerned only her and David. David found it sweeter that way also. Each afternoon now they met at the Plaza fountain and walked, wandered, had dinner, made love in his studio apartment, went to the movies—surprisingly, David loved the movies—dropped in at a concert at Carnegie Hall. He had introduced her to very few of his friends, and only when they ran into them accidentally. He had also refused point blank to meet her parents when they came to town—" 'Mommy, this is Dave'? No thank you." He had even balked at meeting her roommate, Mary Jane. "Young people bore me. I see enough of them in class. . . . Except you, my darling. You're not any age." And perhaps it had been a mistake to cajole him into having dinner here last night, since he had dozed off in the middle of it. Mary Jane was still smarting from the insult.

"He's too old for you," Mary Jane said. "He can't even stay awake past nine o'clock."

"Yes, he can. It's just that he gets up very early. His mind starts ticking away practically at dawn. That's the way poets are."

"You should have stuck with Howard," Mary Jane said. "You should never have broken that date with him to go to your editor's."

"She said it was time I started moving in literary circles. Howard is a sweet boy who will one day make a very nice garment manufacturer."

"Well, you're moving in circles, that's for sure," Mary Jane said. "Howard adored you, silly. He would have given you the moon."

Sunny laughed. ("I love your laugh," David said. "Have you always laughed so easily?") She *had* the moon, and the sun and the stars too. Mary Jane didn't understand, and how could she? She was a Southern girl from Kentucky, trained from birth to regard men as beaux who would ultimately turn into solid providers. "Like Candace in *The Sound and the Fury*," Sunny had explained to David, who looked dubious. Her accent waxed with men and waned with women—it had waxed horrendously with David—and she wore tacky cotton dresses and sneakers all the year round. But she was also beautiful, with curly brown hair and large green eyes that had little black flecks in them. Ironically, it was Mary Jane's own romantic life that was a mess. She was madly in love with the owner of the art gallery on Fifty-seventh Street where she worked, a married man some thirty years her senior. So how could she call David old? But there was no point in quarreling with Mary Jane. She was too happy to quarrel with anyone, and besides, she and Mary Jane had been friends and roommates too long, ever since freshman year at Gorham. Still, there were times these days when Sunny looked at Mary Jane with a fleeting sense of poignancy, as if Mary Jane represented a piece of her life that was now over.

"I understand one thing," Mary Jane said. "You've been seeing this guy every single day for over a month." Had it only been a month? Was it possible that a month ago she didn't even know he existed? "You live, breathe, and eat David Harvey. You quote David Harvey. You can't even put a cigarette in your mouth without inhaling David Harvey. But may I remind you that this same David Harvey is leaving you high and dry for Christmas and New Year's? Howard Goldfarb would never do that."

"The trip to Key West was planned ages ago, long before he ever met me. He's doing research on an important new book."

"What about *your* new book? Isn't that important?"

"Oh, Mary Jane, David couldn't love me if I weren't a writer."

"Is that what he told you?"

"Many times."

Mary Jane snorted. No, she didn't understand, and it *was* pointless to argue. Sunny went to her bedroom, carefully closed the door behind her, and sat down with her journal. She had not wanted to admit to Mary Jane that the new novel, for the sake of which she had cavalierly turned down the fellowship at

Cornell, had somehow gotten away from her lately. "Don't agonize over it. Just write *something*," David said consolingly. A clean white page awaited. She had never kept a journal before David told her she must and even presented her with this notebook as a final push. A leatherette, loose-leaf binder; it had once been his own. There was still an hour to go before she was to meet him at the Plaza fountain. She unscrewed her pen thoughtfully, wondering what the something should be today, wanting it to be great, worthy of posterity. Perhaps some pensées on the subject of music? They had gone to a great many concerts, she and David, and tonight were to hear Isaac Stern at Carnegie Hall. David, being a fiddler himself, knew a great deal about the violin. But then, David knew a great deal about everything. She had never met anyone like him in her life. There *was* no one like him. Sometimes it frightened her. Not the possibility of his no longer loving her. Even after so short a time she knew that he would always love her. But what if she should prove to be unworthy?

// 3 //

Well, my darling sunshine,

I owe you an apology, I suppose. Not for the fact of my leaving, but for the manner of it yesterday. I simply don't like long goodbyes, or people hovering over me at airports when I'm distracted by the work ahead. You do understand, don't you, that if I sometimes seem short-tempered or irritable it has nothing to do with you? That I've been under nightmarish pressures these last few months, putting the final touches on *Ancestors* that will give it an absolute ring of authenticity, trying to get a leg up on the long epic poem that I mean to write, that I must write, was meant to write, while at the same time placating my publisher, who wants to see a piece of the new book as soon as possible, dealing with Gertrude and her whining complaints, trying to penetrate the convoluted stubborn little brain of my thirteen-year-old daughter, be something of a father to her, fend off my creditors, my students, my colleagues, everyone determined to tear me to bits and shreds, while all I long to do is recover somehow, some way, the sanctity of my own soul. No, you can't know all this, though I've tried at times to suggest it. Tried to explain that, no, I have no desire to meet your parents, "nice" though they may be—and what does nice mean, anyhow?—or spend long evenings listening to the prattle of your all too adorable, loose-moraled Southern roommate. But, I repeat, this has nothing to do with you. Nothing. Only, darling, try to be patient. Be sweet, as I know you can be, as you were when you stood in the airport, smiling and waving though tears glistened in your lovely gray eyes, wishing me over and over again a Merry Christmas and a Happy New Year, holidays which simply don't exist for me, though they evidently do for you. But we, each of us, must be true to ourselves, mustn't we? For, darling Sunny, isn't that, in the end, what we're all about?

And so here I am in Key West, trying to do some leg work on that book about American poets after World War II that Ed Gaskell is nagging me about. (Caught in the old sequel syndrome: *Homeward Bound* was about poets after World War I, so why not another about them after World War II? The kind of mind that dreams up this sort of publishing scheme, if not familiar to you already, one day will be.) It's a slatternly town, a sailor's town, atmospherically more Caribbean than mainland. My hotel is a large white clapboard structure that sits on a dinky street, the same old hotel that Hemingway once stayed in. My room is white-washed. I sleep alone, alas, in a brass bed for two, and wake each morning to a palm tree sun wavering through slatted louvres. It is all clean and hot and lazy, lazy, lazy. The locals amble along, soaking up the sun as if that were all they were made for. A cactus leans against an adobe church. I had tea this afternoon with that grand old relic, Claudia Ames, who knows everyone who's anyone in this town. She doesn't like to talk to journalists (*sic!*), but I explained myself, persuaded her of my higher purposes, and we got along splendidly. The little bar adjoining this hotel is filled nightly with drifters, failed painters, minor literati, who imagine themselves expatriates although, despite its Caribbean orientation, Key West is part of the good old U.S.A. I had a decent walk on the beach but couldn't go in the water because of the lousy cold that has plagued me ever since I landed. But please don't worry about me. With enough rest and freedom from anxiety I'll feel better in a few days.

Oh, darling, how strange it has suddenly become to go anywhere without you. I did not expect to miss you as I do.

Your
David

Dearest David,

This is just a line to say hello, and that I hope you had a good flight down. Please try to relax a bit. You seemed so tired when you left. It's hard to believe that was only yesterday, since already it feels like an eternity. I know that's a trite observation, but somehow I'm not ashamed to be trite with you, or ashamed to be anything with you, who have told me so many times we must be what we are. Sometimes I try to remember back to before I knew you even existed and can't. Because, now that I know you do exist, every day has a new complexion, and there are times when I'm even frightened of so much joy. Please don't think you're therefore obligated to keep me happy. You're not. It's the simple fact of your existence that makes me happy. I've been writing in the notebook you gave me—the right book, since it came from you—and wish I had started it at the beginning of us. Growth is such a difficult thing to record—don't you think?—and one of the most difficult things to remember afterwards. But although this is not quite the beginning, it's soon enough, I suppose, because I'm growing still. It's a tangible sensation. I can feel it.

Have you met Claudia Ames yet, or any of the other people you wanted to see in connection with the new book? You are so extraordinary to be able to embark on a new project while putting the finishing touches on the old one. I'll never forget as long as I live your reading me that first time from *Ancestors*. Those beautiful portraits of all the poets and prophets who have gone into the making of you. Of course, as I said, I'm afraid I'm more attuned to Keats than to Jesus. But then it's hard for me to see Christ as that angry young Jewish prophet you portray. This is my own fault, of course, and comes from all those years of church on Sunday.

Anyway, it started to snow when you flew off and has kept on snowing. A snowy day in New York is always a good day, don't you agree? It seems to bring out the best in people and everybody becomes very friendly and villagey. This morning a policeman on Park Avenue shouted to me, "Are you going for a sleighride tonight?" And I worried about a woman caught without her galoshes. Someday, I want to describe the beauty of the city in the snow, but for the present I'll content myself with saying that people who carry umbrellas in the snow look as if they're not to be trusted.

Don't forget me, David, in all that sand and sun. I keep telling myself that you will be gone only three weeks and that if I work hard in my journal the time will pass quickly. But I must stop now. Mary Jane is laughing at me because I am laughing and crying at the same time.

Your
Sunny

DECEMBER 19, 1951
Key West, Florida

My dearest Sunny,

Where there is sun, how could I forget you?

Your sweet letter, just arrived, has moved me to tears. It is so purely loving, so unwavering in your faith in me, in us. But you do understand, don't you, that if *I* seem to waver, it is only the result of long bitter experience with fending off philistinism at every hand, of trying to keep myself intact to say what I must say, write what I must write, speak out in my own fashion? I suppose, given all this, I am sometimes bewildered by finding a pure, open nature such as yours—especially bewildering in the guise of a first novelist!—and automatically try to protect myself in the old way. Yet you are so generous about my work, especially *Ancestors*—I don't believe you ever finished *Homeward Bound*—have been from the very beginning. I keep seeing you in your slip sitting at my desk, glasses perched on your unlikely debutante nose, carefully checking my syntax against all the weight and wisdom of your Gorham College for Women courses in English. So determined to make sure my manuscript would be, as you said, "Perfect." (Are you sure about eliminating the colon and the subtitle? Just *Ancestors*? Not, *Ancestors: A Spiritual Autobiography?*)

Look, this "holiday" doesn't make any sense without you. I'm perishing of loneliness. The bloody cold refuses to go away. The pseudo-expatriates at the bar next door get shriller and shallower every night. The sun on my verandah fails to warm me because it's not *my* sun. The only sunshine I need and want. Do you think you could possibly persuade yourself to drop everything and come flying down here, if only for a few days? I can't believe your work will suffer from a quick infusion of joy, or that money is a problem to the daughter of a brain surgeon. It's cheap enough here, anyway. Or are you afraid your parents would disapprove of such nefarious goings-on? (I really don't know how much you've told them.) In which case, couldn't your roommate, as they say, "cover" for you? (Oh, the embarrassment of being involved with one so young!) Think about it, darling. We have so much to talk about in this never-ending conversation of ours. I long to see the sun on your tawny neck Christmas day, go deep inside you New Year's Eve after we've returned tipsy and tiddly from the bar next door. Unless your New Year's Eve plans involve carousing with some young swain at the Starlight Roof of the Astor. Ought I to assume that?

Come for me, darling, come, come, come.

David

Call from my editor in New York. Has read the last minute changes, considers *Ancestors* a "small classic." There's a chance the New Yorker will take a section. So maybe we have something "perfect" on our hands, after all.

Dearest David,

I've just made my plane reservations, and will arrive at 5 PM on the 24th, but as I tried to say over the phone, I hope you won't feel bound by this invitation and will feel free to cancel it, even at the last minute. I know how eager you were to get away by yourself, and I would hate you to think that I'm anything like the other women in your life, those awful grasping females whom you castigate yourself for not having truly loved, when you are the most truly loving man in the world. I know that your solitude is everything to you, so if I do come down please don't worry about me when you need to be alone with your work. You only hurt my feelings when you do, though I know you don't mean to, as if you imagined I were in competition with your work instead of its most ardent champion. It's true that I myself am, as you have often said, "hopelessly gregarious," the product of a doting family and a crowded girls dormitory. But it's a purely personal bent that I would never want to inflict on you.

Oh, David, I love you so and am longing to see you, but would rather not if you would rather not. That's all I'm trying to say. Happiness and anticipation have got me all muddled.

Your
Sunny

David's hand crept around her breast as sunlight began to filter through the slatted louvres. They had slept as they always did, like two nesting teaspoons. " 'Bliss was it in that dawn to be alive,' " he said into her ear, " 'and to be young was very heaven.' "

He flopped over on his back and laughed. "Of course, that second line applies only to you, but what the hell."

"Oh, David, I *am* so happy." So was David, despite his carping about age. She raised herself on an elbow and kissed his black brows, his long fine nose, his cheeks darkened with stubble. The clown lines had disappeared. David was suntanned, rested, and handsome.

Sunny looked at him with a proprietary air, feeling responsible for his excellent condition, responsible for keeping him that way. Was there a touch of Gertrude developing in her? No, she could never be grasping and possessive. Only David free to be himself was David, if he could only be persuaded to believe that she meant it.

They showered together in their shared bathroom—technically they occupied adjoining rooms, though she was never in hers except to nap while David was making notes—David singing all the parts of a Beethoven quartet at the top of his lungs as she soaped his back. They had breakfast outside of a little Cuban café down the street, dappled in sunlight. David was right, Key West was more Caribbean than American. She felt as if she were in a foreign country, though she had never been abroad. After their last cup of strong black coffee they kissed and went their separate ways. From the first day she had understood that David's mornings were inviolate. He wrote in his journal while she explored the town. "Don't you want to work in *your* journal, too?" David had asked the morning after she arrived. "I forgot to bring it," Sunny said shamefacedly. "Anyway, I'd rather just be, just look."

After lunch they made love, napped, took a bus to the beach. Palm tree fronds wavered romantically overhead. The air was soft, the water a bright greenish blue, totally unlike the steely Atlantic. Back in town they walked out to the end of the pier and looked at the huge turtles lazing in the water, tasted turtleburgers and key lime pie, rubbed shoulders with tourists in flowered shirts. "I keep expecting to see Harry Truman," Sunny said. "They all look like him."

"I'll bet you don't even remember Roosevelt," David said.

"Of course I do. When he died I felt as if I had lost my father. Though of course my real father didn't share the feeling, being a Republican."

David shook his head, sighing as he always did at her political naiveté. "Listen, Sunnoo," he said, "I have to have tea again with Claudia Ames today. Will you be okay?"

"Certainly. I'll wait for you in the bar."

He left her sitting on a stool, chatting gaily with the fake expatriates, and returned much sooner than expected. "They're really very nice," Sunny said as David pulled her away, forgetting until he frowned how much David hated the word nice. He was still frowning all during dinner, which they ate in their favorite restaurant nearby. They had ordered shashlik, and the waiter, actually a painter from New York, brought it flaming on the skewer to amuse them, a towel wrapped turban-style around his head.

"Oh, all the world loves a lover." Sunny laughed. ". . . What is it, darling? You seem so sad."

"It's nothing. Just a letter from Gertrude this morning."

"Another one? Why does she keep torturing you?"

"On the contrary, she's worried about me. She's heard I've been carrying on with 'a glamorous blonde.' Direct quote."

" 'A glamorous blonde'? Oh, how fabulous. Is that me?"

But it wasn't Gertrude who was bothering him. It was Gloria.

"Nothing from her, not even a postcard. The kid absolutely hates me. I take her to concerts, to museums, buy her books, and all she wants to do is go bowling. Well, I guess I'm just a lousy father."

"Don't be ridiculous, darling. You're a wonderful father. Don't your see? Because you're you. I love the idea of your being a father. I think it's absolutely thrilling. Can't I ever meet Gloria someday?"

"Someday," David said. "I don't think you're up to it yet." He kissed Sunny's hand. "Our own child would be different. She'd be blond."

"And she'd play the violin."

"Sunny, I can't promise you anything."

"Oh, David, what is there to promise? You give me so much."

New Year's Eve they found themselves in a low-down bar watching a stripper while a bunch of sailors hooted and hollered at the next table. The stripper was billed as "Miss Amazon," a tall brassy redhead whom David gravely wished a joyous year when she bounced off, holding her spangled garments. He was slightly and sweetly drunk, and tried to catch the few tired balloons that floated down at midnight.

"I hope you're not missing the Starlight Roof of the Astor and your garment manufacturer," he said, giving Sunny a wet, Happy New Year kiss.

"David, don't be silly."

"Why so serious?"

"I'm thinking. I'm making resolutions. I'm going to dedicate this year to my work."

"Oh, that," David said.

"No, truly. In fact I have a confession to make. I was a little hurt when you returned those two little stories I showed you and said they were 'cute.' I guess I didn't expect you to dismiss them so easily. I guess I thought you would say something like, 'Sunny Mansfield, you're a born storyteller.' But I see now that that's not fair. You have very high literary standards. You've spent a lifetime acquiring them. It would be a betrayal to ask you to compromise them."

"Actually your hair really isn't yellow," David said. "It's more like the color of this onion at the bottom of my Gibson."

"You demand from my work what you demand from all work you read. Only the problem is that I'm not up to it yet. In fact it may be years before I'm able to produce anything you like. So what am I to do until then?"

"Work."

"Yes, you're right. Work, work, work. It's the only answer. But if you give everything to your work, what's left for anything else?" David handed her his handkerchief and she wiped her eyes and blew her nose. "Oh God," Sunny said, as the next stripper came on. "I see a long and unending apprenticeship ahead."

The next day, New Year's day, their last, they walked back down to the pier to see the huge turtles once more. Brownish, greenish, ageless.

"You look like a heron," David said, smiling.

"I do?"

"Balanced on one leg like that."

"I'm looking out at the sea."

"I'll never forget my first crossing," David said. "It was on a troopship bound for England. It took us ten days. We were in a convoy. We left at night and at dawn there were ships as far as the eye could see." He sighed. "The next time I went over it was with Gertrude. She came accompanied by a Kodak and a weak bladder."

"I've never crossed the ocean," Sunny said.

"One day you will."

"Soon, if that Abingdon comes through. Did I tell you they've called me for an interview? That's supposed to be a good sign."

"Is it?"

"Oh, David, wouldn't that be fabulous? A whole year in France. It's what I've always dreamed of."

"I must say you're very brave," David said.

"Brave?"

"Well it's not every young woman who would contemplate leaving her lover to go abroad for a whole year."

"Are you my lover?" Sunny said. "You're my love. I can't put you in any smaller category. Are you suggesting that if that fellowship does come through I don't take it?"

"Of course not. It's very prestigious."

She thought a moment. "Anyway, if Rilke is right about two solitudes meeting and greeting each other, does it really matter where they are at the time?"

Laughing, she nestled cozily against him, feeling his chest go in and out, as David continued to gaze out to sea.

4

David, in Chicago doing more research for the book he was increasingly in despair of, had actually sent her a Valentine. She turned it over and over as if it were an artifact. It had "Yes! Yes! Yes!" written in different colors all over it. ("Yes to what?" Mary Jane asked sourly. Sunny ignored her, lost in amazement.) She had never dreamed that David would send her a Valentine. She had certainly never dreamed of sending him one, for fear that he would think her young and silly. But David was so unpredictable. He had taken to giving her little presents too. No longer notebooks, or printed books—those he lent her from his library—but a gold-colored pin, flowers, a handbag. He even spoke of buying her a black lace nightgown, which wasn't her sort of thing at all, though she hated to tell him so. He had also started to introduce her to some of his friends. Writers mostly, whose names, alas, were totally unfamiliar to her, a fact David found very hard to credit. But she had never heard such talk as when they got together. They had theories about everything—politics, art, religion, sex. Very often sex. Before she met David she had thought sex was spontaneous, something that just happened, not a subject of study. But David often spoke of a "grand seductress," whom he had met years before when he was giving a reading in California, and whose artistry in bed had inspired him to break with Gertrude. And Isaac Rosenfeld, a novelist from Chicago, sat in something called an orgone box to charge up his sexual energies. (She tried to imagine what it was—like a telephone booth?) If she had not known better she would have thought they sounded like adolescents, erudite adolescents, except that in this case they seemed not to have discovered sex but invented it. "Do you miss her, the grand seductress?" she had asked once when David sighed deeply afterward. "Don't be silly," he had said. "I just wish there were a little more of you up here to work with." And laughed. Yes, he laughed too now, made jokes, and even Amanda spoke of how he had changed, loosened up, no longer flew off the handle with Milo.

"A Valentine? David?" Amanda said one day at lunch. "Well, you've certainly had an incredible effect on him."

"Do you really think it's me?"

"Sunny, I've known this man for years. I've never before seen David Harvey relaxed and happy."

"He worries about that sometimes," Sunny said. "About what happiness will do to his work."

Amanda laughed. "You don't seem worried about what it's doing to yours. Or shouldn't I ask how the new novel is coming along? No, seriously, Tommy Job wants to know."

"I'm taking a rest from it, actually," Sunny said. "Lying fallow."

"Lying fallow? I thought you were excited about it."

"I am. But I'm exploring other forms. I want to enlarge my experience, broaden my horizons. I mean, isn't living important too?"

Amanda smiled, half editor, half female confidante. "He never did give you a blurb for the last one," she said.

From Chicago David called her almost every day and in between wrote her letters. . . . "When I think of the Midwest as one of the great literary regions of this country, on a par with New England and New York, I see no evidence that this still exists. Hemingway, Fitzgerald, Dreiser, Willa Cather—*not* Carl Sandburg—where are their contemporary equivalents? And even of this list, the ones who aren't dead are writing badly. . . ." She missed him terribly, as she always did when he traveled—he was often away, giving lectures and readings. But each time he returned the reunion was so passionate she almost thought missing him was worth it.

Happy to be back in New York, David decided to give a party.

"In this small studio?" Sunny asked. David looked around. "Why not?" He had fewer social pretensions and inhibitions than anyone she had ever met. For the party he bought a pound of sliced baloney and a bottle of Guckenheimer's Reserve. His papers he left scattered all over his desk though he made a quick stab at smoothing the blue madras spread on the studio couch. Sunny hurriedly smoothed it down again and tried to arrange the slices of baloney to look like more, then wondered if David would be angry, and stopped. But David didn't notice.

They all came at once, and within a few minutes were talking heatedly, as they always did. It was a small group but when she came out of the bathroom where she had been combing her hair and neatening herself up, they sounded like a multitude. Isaac was there with his wife, and Delmore Schwartz, a poet, and Harold Rosenberg, an older Village intellectual, and Elijah Rose, a novelist, and also a pair of David's old friends from his Bronx youth, Hymie and Lila Shapiro. Hymie was actually David's accountant, but was happy to prepare David's taxes in return for meeting David's literary friends. David's aunt Natalia was there too, a very formidable woman, and totally unlike her brother, David's dear little father, whom Sunny had met when David's parents paid a short visit to the studio apartment. She sat swathed in shawls, smoking with a long cigarette holder, showing her long discolored teeth frequently since she laughed often. "If you don't like Natalia I can't love you," David had said early on, and Sunny was trying.

At the moment Natalia was telling Harold Rosenberg with a disparaging wave of her hand that her smattering of Yiddish she had picked up only in New York; Russian was her native language. Harold, who was formidable too, a huge man with black beetley eyebrows and a stiff leg that he kept thrust out, nodded and offered his own theory on language—he was always willing to discuss his ideas with anyone near at hand. Delmore was, as usual, doleful, his protuberant eyes rimmed round with black circles—a symptom of glandular malfunction, he told Sunny. She turned with relief to Elijah Rose, who was almost Delmore's exact opposite: witty and gay, he loved to tell long jokes at which he laughed so hard he could barely say the punchline. He was also so classically beautiful, with his black curly hair and long fine nose, it was sometimes hard to take her eyes off him. ("Well, he's very gifted and he knows it," David had said with a shrug, giving her a long hard look. "I suppose any young novelist would be taken with him." It was the only time he had ever called her a novelist.) Now, perched on the studio couch, David was demanding of Isaac, who sat on the floor, "Hemingway, Fitzgerald, Dreiser, Willa Cather—tell me, where are the giants of the Midwest *now?*" Roly-poly Isaac shrugged good-naturedly, not bothering to point out that he himself came from Chicago.

How strange that a few months ago she didn't believe that such people existed, or if they did exist that they would talk to *her*. Well, they still didn't exactly talk to her, more around her and above her. And in a way she was relieved, if not exactly glad. Sometimes with David's friends she felt an uneasiness it was hard to explain. As if she would have to skip the normal stages of her development to arrive where they were.

"That girl just got an Abingdon Fellowship to France," David said, pointing to her. Only Hymie and Lila Shapiro looked around with some show of interest. Delmore said wearily that there was no point in going all the way to Europe when life in the United States was difficult enough. Natalia, with a rasping laugh, informed him that nevertheless there was no real culture in America, only in Europe. David agreed. He told about his first trip over to England on the troopship—"And at dawn there were ships as far as the eye could see"—about postwar Italy, and meeting Gertrude Stein in Paris.

When they left, Sunny started to clean up, though there wasn't much to clean up. The slices of baloney had vanished within minutes. So had the Guckenheimer's Reserve. David took the empty bottle from her hand, and led her to the studio couch. He put his hands inside her sweater. "Harold said the French will go mad for you. A natural blonde. . . . What's the matter?"

"Suddenly I'm scared."

"Scared of what?"

"Europe, all of it. Couldn't we go together? Spend the summer traveling?"

"Sunny," David said. "Applying for a fellowship was your idea. The big breakthrough, remember? Though why it has to be a literal voyage, I've never understood. Why not a voyage of the mind and heart?"

"We'd have such fun," Sunny said.

"Darling, I have not the slightest intention of accompanying you on your maiden voyage. You can't have it both ways, you know. If you're going to strike out for independence then you've got to face what comes by yourself. Alone—and stop looking so lost and hurt."

"I'm not lost and hurt."

"Oh, Sunnoo, you still have so much growing up to do, though in some ways you're a thousand times more mature than I was at your age. But you must stop fantasizing." He stopped short and laughed bitterly. "Next thing you'll be wanting a diamond engagement ring. Then no doubt a church wedding. Well, I've been married, thank you, and it was awful."

"That's insulting," Sunny said. "*You're* the one who keeps talking about marriage, not me. You proposed to me the first night we slept together, if you remember, and I said no. Anyway, why is being in Europe together such a fantasy?"

"Oh, it's tempting, I don't deny it. I'd love to show you Europe. Especially Italy. Take you to the top of the Spanish Steps and show you the little room where Keats, our Keats, lay dying, looking up at the painted stars on the ceiling and thinking that his life had been writ on water. And Venice, the Piazza San Marco, to see the pigeons fluttering at your feet. And take you in the sunshine under the cypresses, all golden, my golden Italy, my golden girl . . . Not France. I hate the French and you'll have enough of them. But perhaps Chartres."

"I've always longed to see Chartres."

"You see?" David said, snapping out of it. "You've bound me up in your fantasies again. You just don't understand the realities of the situation."

"What are the realities of the situation?"

"That I have to pay the rent and do something to earn the advance on the new book and by summer move out of this place, which is so full of you, goddamnit, and get back to Cole, where I have endless reading to do for my courses and—oh, Christ, sunshine, darling, love. Stop trying to seduce me into going with you. It won't work."

"But, of course we'll be in separate cabins," Sunny said to her mother. "So you and Daddy don't have to worry about appearances. Daddy, anyway."

"Daddy just wants you to be happy, darling."

"I know that, Mother, and I am. Oh, God, it's all my dreams come true."

She looked around the Palm Court of the Plaza, Grace Mansfield's favorite place to lunch when she was in town. They had come here so many times over the years, after shopping, before matinees, to celebrate birthdays. Now its turn-of-the-century splendor looked a bit faded. It was funny that in all the times she had met David outside of the Plaza they had never gone inside. They even had a joke abut never making it inside. She felt a bit uneasy about being inside now.

"And then David knows so much about Europe. So I'm lucky about that too. Even if he can't stay past the summer."

"From what you tell me, darling, he knows 'so much' about everything. When do we finally meet this wonder man?"

"Soon," Sunny said guiltily, "soon."

Grace smiled, tilting her head skeptically like a pretty little bird. She was so lovely, why *wouldn't* David meet her? Prettier than Sunny, which Sunny knew and didn't mind, her short blond hair, now graying a bit, carefully coiffed and curled, her features smaller, her eyes a bright blue. She was always so beautifully turned out too. Today in a black velvet pillbox with a short veil, a white silk blouse and diamond pin. Her mink stole was slung from the back of her chair, her white doeskin gloves folded carefully on top of her black suede purse. Given the chance, David would really love her, though he didn't believe it—even crusty George Auerbach had been charmed by her at graduation. But David believed that all mothers should be stayed away from as a matter of principle. And having met Tillie, Sunny understood why.

"Tell me about Mary Jane," Grace said. "How is she?"

"Mary Jane? Oh, she's fine, I suppose. We don't seem to be home much at the same time."

"And Anne and Peg and your other friends from Gorham?"

"I'm kind of out of touch," Sunny said. She picked up the menu. "What'll it be? Chef's salad, as usual?"

"But you were all so close."

"I know. But things happen . . . Is Daddy okay? I haven't spoken to him in ages."

"Fine. Busy as ever."

"He's not taking a high moral tone about all this, is he? The way he did about my apartment? I mean because David is divorced and older. And Jewish."

"Howard was Jewish, darling. He and Daddy got on very well."

"Oh, but David isn't Jewish *that* way. He has no use for clannishness. For David, being Jewish is a historical imperative."

"Well, that's an interesting idea, isn't it?" Grace said. She picked up the menu too, and agreed on the chef's salad. "Darling, you haven't told me what you're going to do for the rest of the year, as your fellowship project. Or can you work on your new novel?"

"Fellowship?" Sunny said. She had forgotten all about it.

Grace looked at her for a moment with troubled eyes as she signaled the waiter. Then she smiled, squeezed Sunny's hand, and ordered champagne.

"You shouldn't have champagne before a typhoid shot," David said, looking at her dubiously.

"I know it," Sunny said. "But she was being so sweet. You'd really—" Her eyes suddenly widened, and she flew into his bathroom. When she had finished retching into the toilet bowl she brushed her teeth and came out, smiling weakly. David kissed her on the forehead and she clung to him. Somehow, her throwing up had brought them even closer together.

"Here," David said. "I meant to wait, but—" He gave her her going-away present. A brand-new passport case for her brand-new passport. The card inside said, "Bon voyage to the little traveler." Sunny gave him the present she had bought for him at Saks Fifth Avenue after the lunch with her mother. A silver cigarette case, with a card that said, "Oh, my darling, bon voyage to *us.*"

5

The summer had passed like a dream. She waved and waved as the USS *Independence* sailed out of the Genoa harbor. Did David see her trying to be brave, as he said she must? He had his hands clasped over his head like a triumphant boxer. When confetti suddenly dripped down on her, she couldn't help it, and finally broke into tears. An Italian customs guard nearby placed his hand on her shoulder and said, "*Corragio!*" She turned away. Oh, these Italians, oh Italy, country every bit as golden as David had said it would be, oh golden summer— now over.

A few hours later she took the train to Paris, glad as she looked out the window that Paris was gray. It would have been unendurable otherwise. She checked back into the Hotel Voltaire, though David had said it would kill him to return to the hotel where they had started, and thought how gauche she must have seemed to him when they first arrived, with her prattle of how *small* everything looked, little crooked houses, tiny buses and automobiles, short people. Not to mention her constant state of astonishment at the plumbing. But he had been so patient, only once closing his eyes and murmuring, "Gertrude." And she had learned fast. (She hardly blinked an eye now, entering a WC where one stood over a hole with legs apart and wiped with torn newspapers.) In fact, she had probably learned more this past summer than ever before in her life, and probably ever would again until she and David were together. No, she wasn't "counting on" anything, as David said she mustn't— only "believing" in them, as he had said she must.

She lay down on the bed, surrounded by luggage. Tomorrow she would move to the American pavillion of the Cité Universitaire and start her life as a foreign student, but that was tomorrow. Meanwhile, the room was full of him, though David, hating the French, had moved them on very quickly to Italy. She closed her eyes, dreaming of candy-striped cathedrals and Roman ruins, of hearing *Aida* in the Baths of Caracalla, of the steely canals of Venice, of a picnic in Rapallo by the blue Mediterranean, drinking white wine, eating peaches whose juice dripped sensuously down their chins. And the fuzzy, sleepy lovemaking afterwards in the marble cool of a hotel. Of course, the war ruins in Pisa were not so charming, with those skinny little children playing in the rubble. Nor were the obsequious waiters in the empty grand hotel dining rooms, awaiting their pleasure. How sorry she had felt for them, how sorry for everyone, really. And then those few poor old Jews in the courtyard of the synagogue in Florence. Inside, all those rich carvings and the inlaid dome and the gold candelabra. And outside those few pitiful poor old Jews, remnants, waiting for a bowl of thin soup. Oh, David, she thought, and again burst into tears. What have we done to your people?

She sat up and reached inside her purse for a handkerchief, removing instead a hard flat object, David's now somewhat tarnished silver cigarette case. He had asked her to hold it for him and forgotten to take it back. She thought of his beautiful hands holding a cigarette, gesturing while he spoke, and the smoke curling upwards. Had she ever told him that he had beautiful hands, and that she loved the thought of those beautiful hands touching her? She was sure she had written it down in her journal.

SEPTEMBER 2, 1952
USS Independence

Sunshine, sunshine,

Why do people speak of a sea voyage as a rest, when in fact it is a long illness? It is dull, dull, dull without you, my radiant love, and as I write this I am still absorbed in my last sight of you, so young, so blond, so vulnerable, waving to me from the pier. Who was the soldier, by the way, who put his arm around you as we sailed off? Lucky fellow. I hope he was helpful to you in your last few hours in Genoa. I couldn't bear to think of you wandering about alone.

This ship is as American as can be. I am back in the United States with a vengeance. Terrible food, people talking about baseball scores, the waiter kibitzing in Yiddish. Dick Reeves and his wife Nancy are on board, the Ur academic couple, with two children in tow and a beloved dog awaiting them in a kennel at home. I avoid them, will soon enough find them on my doorstep at Cole, importuning me to come to one of their unspeakably boring dinner parties, and sit apart, writing to you. No, I don't miss you, only feel dead without you, my soul dark and cold as the slate Atlantic. I am writing this now, knowing it won't be posted until we dock briefly at Pompeii tomorrow, because I must somehow reach you, bask in the remembered light of your bright laughing face. . . .

Next day. . . . Still adrift, still hopelessly without my bearings. The entries in my journal have all become hymns to you, to your sweetness, your purity, your light. When I'm not writing to you, I *talk* to you, confide in you. But don't worry about me. Don't worry about anything. Have faith in our faith.

The Reeveses are quite sweet, really, full of concern. I had almost forgotten the startling ingenuousness of Americans. They tell me they have never seen me in this state. Am I ill? Has something happened? In answer, I smile, bewildering them still further, and go back to talking to you. I can't read anything, only a little poetry, and now that evening is descending—I seem to have caught a chill, but don't worry, it's nothing—must unwrap myself from my blankets and leave this deck chair to go inside. But first I send you these lines:

> Oh Western wind, when wilt thou blow
> That the small rain down can rain?
> Christ that my love were in my arms
> And I in my bed again!

With all my heart,
David

A cablegram ("Am here. Love. Dadvi.") and two more letters waited for her at the American Express. Sunny read them several times over, then held them against her heart, proof that David existed, that she had not made him up, as sometimes she wondered if she had. But David was real, realer now that he was back on land than when they had been sea miles apart. As usual too, they were of the same mind. She was also finding Americans, at least the ones she met at the Cité Universitaire, hopelessly ingenuous, pathetically terrified of offending the French. Several of the most pimply of them had already told her that Americans were adolescent. She was determined to get out of the Cité as soon as possible and find a room with a French family; she was too old, especially after a summer with David, to live student style again, share dormitory quarters, eat in a noisy cafeteria, although some of the "students," particularly those on the GI bill, were older than she—war veterans, extremely hostile to those on cushy fellowships. By coincidence, however, one of the Abingdon Fellows had turned out to be Muffy Drake, whom she had known at Gorham. They had greeted each other like long lost friends, though they hadn't been particularly close at college, and at Muffy's suggestion went together to try to find rooms with the same French family. Now, after several days of looking, they were both depressed. The potential landladies, most of them widows—not their fault though it made Sunny wonder what their husbands had gone through—had shown them around vast dark apartments that looked like mausoleums, rooms shrouded in draperies, crowded with heavy furniture, fringed lamps, and Moroccan rugs. She had never really understood what the word bourgeois meant before meeting these landladies. But the accommodations they slyly offered the two young Americans would hardly have sufficed for the lowliest *domestique*. Rent included breakfast, but baths were extra. When the matter of drinking water came up, one of them had said to drink Coca-Cola.

"Oh, God," Muffy said, who had also just collected her mail. "Paris is so awful. I'm so homesick. What wouldn't I do for a good juicy American hamburger."

"An American hamburger? But you've only been here a week."

"I know, but it's all so scary."

Sunny took Muffy by the elbow and, with a decisiveness she did not feel but that David would have been proud of, ushered her out of the American Express building. They plopped down at a sidewalk café opposite the Opéra. The unquestionable beauties of Paris were all around but, perhaps thanks to Muffy, Sunny saw them as from a great distance. Even her French had almost vanished, though it had been one of her best subjects all through school. Muffy's was better, since she had been a French major at Gorham, but Muffy was too tongue-tied with fear to use it. Muffy was also petrified of taking buses, going to museums, and making *correspondances* in the Métro. But then, as Sunny remembered, Muffy had been something of a junior miss in college too. Tiny, her face heart-shaped, her brown hair in a little pageboy, given to the same kind of plaid skirt, bobby sox, and saddle shoes she was wearing now. In fact, if she recalled correctly, Muffy also used to boast of using only Junior Tampax.

"You'll see, Muff," Sunny said with false cheer, now sounding as David had in their first days in Europe, "in a few weeks we'll be all settled down and we'll find our way around Paris like a pair of natives."

"I didn't mind that small room," Muffy said. "I like small rooms."

"It wasn't heated," Sunny said.

The two of them sighed and started to reread their letters. Muffy's little diamond engagement ring glinted in the fall sun. On the back of the envelope from her fiancé she had already doodled her silver pattern. She couldn't believe that Sunny wasn't officially engaged too.

"But why won't you tell me his name? Is he the one I saw you with at the City Center ballet? The one who was so handsome and distingué?"

"Just call him the Poet," Sunny said. "Just call him the divine Monsieur X."

Muffy giggled, more and more intrigued. Why wouldn't Sunny tell her his name? Sunny wasn't sure herself, only that it seemed imperative to keep the worlds of Muffy Drake and David Harvey far apart. She decided that as soon as she was settled she would screw up her courage and call some of the people David had suggested she look up, the expatriate couple named Silver, who were known to be very hospitable to visiting intellectuals, maybe even those Russian friends of Natalia's, though if they were anything like Natalia that would take more courage than she thought she had. She read through David's letters again, which contained more wry allusions to Dick and Nancy Reeves. He had never mentioned them before and yet these people who had popped up on shipboard were apparently old friends. It made her shiver a little to think there were whole areas to David's life she knew nothing about. She and Muffy wended their way slowly back to the Cité Universitaire. It was dusk, it was Paris, and all along the boulevards lovers strolled arm in arm. Only, *her* lover wasn't there. David had admired her for accepting this fellowship. But what if it been a terrible mistake? What if she had consigned herself to a life with Muffy Drake? No, she mustn't even think that—yet.

SEPTEMBER 12, 1952
Rhinebeck, New York

Sweet Sunshine,
Home with a vengeance, everything about me blisteringly, explosively American, except for your sweet letters, which belong to no time and no place. The talk here is all of the World Series and, in New York, where I spent several days, of the Jewish holidays. Perhaps I should send you one of those cards emblazoned with Torah scrolls. I had forgotten what a Jewish town New York is, felt more a foreigner there than in Roma. Hymie Shapiro met me at the dock and saw me through customs, looking exactly like the certified public accountant he is, though as usual he held some new chapters of his novel under his arm and as usual presented them to me with endearing diffidence. High school makes strange bedfellows, Bronx high schools stranger ones. Have never had the heart in all these years to tell Hymie

he is barking up the wrong tree. He pressed me to stay with him and Lila, but I explained it would be more expeditious to check into the Biltmore. The mention of reduced academic rates finally persuaded him. He asked after you tenderly.

Izzy and Tillie still at the same old stand, immutable, as our friend Faulkner would call them: Tillie *quvetching*—I assume you must have heard me use that word in this connection before—Izzy quoting from Pushkin. And why does Tillie cry and quvetch? Because she sees so little of her only granddaughter! I advised her that this was a blessing the way things were going with Gloria these days, which of course made her throw up her hands and weep all the more. Izzy has a special smile when he speaks of you. Have you bewitched him also, my darling? Not so, I'm afraid, Gertrude, with whom I spent an obligatory and depressing few minutes when I went out to Forest Hills to pick up Gloria. I had tickets for Town Hall in my pocket, but my daughter made a beeline for the nearest bowling alley. When I brought her back, stuffed with pizza, she was sent out of the room. Not only is Gertrude worried about my having been seduced by this glamorous blonde, but so are all my friends, it seems. I assured her that I would be attentive to the dangers, gave her the child support check and left. Oh, darling, only you and Natalia are oases of sanity in this nutty world. Natalia continues sublime. I'm so glad you like her. We had a long wonderful dinner at her apartment (she's an inspired cook), and since Fritz was away on one of his business trips there was a chance for real talk. Her mind is at home everywhere and we spoke of everything under the sun (pun intended). She approves of you, feels you have had a good influence on me, says that when I was married to Gertrude she could never reach me, I was so miserable and hostile. Whereas now I'm open to her again. You can imagine how happy her saying this made me.

What else? I had a quick drink with your mother at the Algonquin—had no time for lunch—gave her your presents, with which she was delighted. I can understand why you're so devoted to her. I don't think I've ever met a mother quite as proud of her daughter's every little achievement. Most mothers want only to see their girls wedded down within a year of their college graduation, Jewish mothers long before that. But yours positively applauds your every stab at independence. She strikes me as much younger than you in some ways, unsteadier, with something of the air of a co-ed of the twenties about her, and your unwavering eyes in a more uncertain setting. (Do you realize there is the same difference in age—fifteen years—between your mother and me as between me and you? Something to think about.) Yes, I can easily see Grace charlestoning away at parties, getting just a wee bit tipsy before her stolid husband carts her back home to suburban Connecticut. You'll forgive me if I admit I like your father less, judging from the few minutes I saw him before we sailed? Yes, I know, a pillar of society and all that. But a pillar. . . . Also popped in at your apartment to give Mary Jane *her* gifts. Couldn't stay. As you know, the young lady doesn't interest me in the least, and the sight of that apartment, devoid of your presence, was painful beyond words. I was almost relieved, finally, to return here to my little house at Cole and my tuna fish dinners and bachelor solitude.

Darling, your letters trouble me a bit. You sound so lost, so lonely, so intimidated by the French. You must learn to stand up for yourself, not let them grind you down. Are you working? It's terribly important to work every day, if not on your novel—which I've seen you grapple with as if your whole young life depended on it—then in your journal, which can serve as a place for meditation, for charting and exploring the course of your thinking. Remember, *nothing* is too trivial to put in. Make yourself a workshop. Glorious as our summer together was, you mustn't impale yourself on your memories of it, allow your mind to grow fuzzy with nostalgia. I'm thinking particularly of what you write about that synagogue in Florence. Forgive me, Sunnoo, but it reads like a piece of arrant Christian sentimentality. You don't know anything about Jews—how could you?—except what your vaguely liberal leanings have led you to imagine. France and Italy are Catholic countries, yet everywhere we traveled you shrank from discussing Catholicism. Sweetheart, all Catholics don't go around banning books. Why not read Simone Weil, a Jew who became one of the great Catholic thinkers of our age, a young woman whom Camus has called "the only great spirit of our time." A true modern saint. I read her in English, unwilling to struggle with language because I'm so on fire with her. But you must read her in French. Start with *Waiting for God*, in which she speaks of prayer as a supreme form of attention, says that in loving our neighbors we imitate divine love. And my darling, isn't this the transcendent love to which you and I are committed? A love of truth which we value even beyond our love for each other, but which we reach *through* our love for each other?

Your
David

P.S. Galleys of *Ancestors* due next week—wouldn't you like to come over for a few days, put on your slip, and help me correct them?

6

She reread David's last letters guiltily, having forgotten the confusion caused by the time lag in their correspondence. So that here was David worried about her, worried in letter after letter—three or four a week—whereas, aside from missing him desperately, many of her problems had actually worked themselves out. She almost hated to tell him so, as if she had wasted his time for nothing, especially when she reread her mother's description of their brief meeting. "So handsome, dark, brooding . . . a clean classic profile and soft brown Etruscan eyes . . . a sudden unexpected smile like sun sparkling on raindrops . . . serious, intense, but so willing to whisk you along on his intellectual flights." Mary Jane had merely reported that he had popped his head in the door, handed her Sunny's presents, looked around, said, "Painful!" and fled.

Nevertheless, her life in Paris had looked up amazingly. She and Muffy had finally found a place to live, in a large apartment near the Champs de Mars, with a good-sized bedroom for her, and a tiny one for Muffy, who was still playing it close to the chest. Furthermore, Madame Beaupain, unique among French landladies, was plump and jolly, with bright red, hennaed hair, a short wide sexy nose and flashing teeth. She was not even a widow, but lived with a little bald husband, a retired *fonctionnaire* some years her senior, and their sixteen-year-old son who was studying for his *bachot*. It was wonderful suddenly to be taken into the bosom of a real French family—though dinner, when she chose to take it *en famille*, was a stipulated 300 francs extra—bliss to be able to sign herself, as she had in her last letter to David, which he had obviously not yet received, *chez* somebody. Each morning she and Muffy went to the Cours Aux Etrangers at the Sorbonne. *Sorbonne*. The word had a lovely ring, though the lectures were actually quite boring and took place in a large amphitheater where everyone rose respectfully when the professor marched in, and after he had droned on uninterrupted for a solid hour, rose respectfully again. But as she had told herself and written David, it was all pro forma, only an excuse for being in Paris. She could probably never be a real student again, never get that Ph.D. she still thought of from time to time whenever she worried about what she would do when she returned to the United States.

Some of the students had formed the habit of having lunch afterwards at a cheap restaurant on the rue Monsieur le Prince, along with their nominal tutor, Michel Daudet, a stocky man, swarthy in appearance, very French in his attitudes. He was also an openly avowed member of the Communist party. She had never met one before, but couldn't help liking him immensely. (She did not write to David about him, however. She could all too vividly see David and Natalia shaking their heads over her dangerous political naiveté.)

Nevertheless, to keep her end up, Sunny said that day in much improved French, "But surely, Michel, you don't believe all that propaganda about Americans engaging in germ warfare. You know us too well by now."

"In capitalist countries the people are not the government."

"In the United States we are."

A few of the other foreign students looked at her pityingly. One of them, a fair-haired French Canadian with a sweet boyish face and a stammer, smiled and changed the subject to the worker priests.

"What can I say? They work among the poor and live as the poor. I know one very well," Michel said. "Would you like to meet him?"

"V-very m-much."

"So would I," Sunny said, wishing to prove to herself that she was not as wary of Catholicism as David thought.

"It's a rough quartier," Michel said dubiously.

"That doesn't matter."

Michel smiled at her bravado. They had finished their *biftek*

and *pommes frites,* their carafe of *rouge,* their *crème caramel*—
all amazingly cheap by American standards—and pushed back
their chairs.

Michel was still smiling at her. "*Quelle jolie poule,*" he said.
She stared at him, amazed and insulted. A poule? After all
their discussions was this Frenchman now calling her a *poule?*

"*Quel joli pullovère,*" Michel repeated.

"He l-l-likes your sweater," Claude said gently.

The visit to the worker priest—a rough type in a maroon
sweater, who met them in the church basement—was altogether
confusing. Claude stammered out concerned questions, Michel
encouraged him. Sunny understood almost not a word. They
had lapsed into a thick argot. Also the *priest* seemed to be a
Communist, so where did that leave her? "Oh, Claude," she
said afterward, as they walked arm in arm to the Métro, "sometimes I lie awake at night wondering what else I didn't understand. And then even my French seems to have reached a
plateau and stayed there. It refuses to budge. It's like an unrequited love affair."

"It's n-n-not unrequited," Claude said, and smiled with a
sweetness that puzzled her.

She decided that perhaps a visit to the Silvers, the expatriate
friends David had been urging her to call on, would be more
her style, and the minute she got there knew that it was. Their
apartment on the rue de Lille, crammed with Empire furniture,
the tiled kitchen with its long rubber spigots that looked like a
nineteenth-century laboratory, could have existed only in Paris.
But she felt at home immediately. The Silvers were very nice
indeed. (Except that David hated that word. She must avoid
using it in her letter about them.) Arlene, very toothy and gay,
and with an astonishingly sexy body, worked for an import-
export firm. Morty, lean, bald, handsome, and extremely intellectual, was a writer and also a complete Francophile. He
had memorized the map of Paris before he ever got there; his
French was enviable, his accent perfect. Also, the apartment

was clearly an oasis for other expatriates, since there were several already on hand when she entered the salon. She thought of the false expatriates David had so disliked in Key West, but these were *real*. Habitués, from the looks of it, who came each Sunday for the talk and the gigot: a scholar of comparative literature, who, unlike the floundering ex-GIs at the Cité Universitaire, was seriously working on a book in a cheap hotel around the corner; a British anarchist couple, who apologized for being married (it had something to do with their passports); a mannish-looking female playwright from Norway; a young Negro novelist with bulging bloodshot eyes named Jimmy Baldwin, who looked terribly tragic but laughed a great deal.

Long after the last of the gigot had been consumed and the bonne had cleared up, they sat around the long oval table in the dining room, drinking the last of the wine, smoking Gauloise Bleue, swapping Paris experiences. Poor Jimmy, who had come to France fleeing discrimination in the United States, had been locked up by the flics a couple of days after he arrived because they mistook him for an Arab. They were all broke—except for Arlene, who had the only steady job—had come to Paris, in fact, because they *were* broke, which somehow made them superior, the last in the line of a long literary tradition. (Sunny, ashamed of her fellowship, had said only that she was writing a novel, which wasn't strictly true. She wasn't even writing in her journal. All she had written so far was letters to David.) But back in the salon sipping cognac, she joined them in making up titles for articles that might sell. Jimmy, who was waiting to hear if his first novel had been accepted, came up with "A Negro Looks at Henry James," for *Partisan Review*.

Sunny walked home happier than she had been since she arrived, a long walk which took her clear through the heart of Paris. She hadn't read Simone Weil yet, though she had slit the pages of *Attente de Dieu* with the letter opener David had bought her in Florence. But she had fallen in love with a writer named Colette, whose short novel *Chéri* was being serialized in *Paris Soir*. She had assumed, from the title and the author's name too, that it would be a bit of French fluff, but she had been entirely mistaken. She had never read anything at once so sensuous and yet so meticulous in its detail. It was Paris all over, the same immutable Paris she was walking through now. . . . And, oh, how beautiful Paris was, posing for her at every turn, as if it were saying, look at me! look at me! She crossed the Pont du Caroussel, passed the palatial façade of the Louvre, cut through the Tuilleries with its lovely pastel flower beds, took a detour over to the Opéra where she stood marveling at the globes, flutings, horizontal and vertical curves, topped with draped statues—such a melange of stylistic grandeurs she began to laugh. Suddenly she wanted to write a story. Something about Paris. Something about two American students who had really nothing in common, except that the fact of being in Paris made them fall in love. She came back to the Beaupain apartment, exhausted but excited, and sat down immediately to make a few notes and then write to David—about the Silvers, about Colette.

But there was that time lag again. While she was rejoicing in Paris, David, it turned out, was plunged into the deepest despair. "Oh, Sunnoo," he wrote in black ink, unable to face his typewriter, the lines sloping downward. He was reading the galleys of *Ancestors*, so full of printer's errors that he no longer knew what to make of the book, didn't even know if it *was* a book, wondered if its very originality would not prove his undoing. Nor was there anyone to turn to except the usual backbiters in the English department, all of them writing about literature in the hopes of creating more literature about literature. His students were idiots, the girls wept in conference and he kept having to hand them Kleenex. Dick Reeves had been approached by Columbia, which was also depressing though not surprising, since Edward Maxwell, Columbia's big gun, was interested only in disciples. At night he burrowed deeper and deeper into his solitude, listened to Bach, read Saint Paul, prayed that this latest spiritual crisis would soon lift. Sunny's picture, the one he had taken on the Spanish Steps, sat like an icon on his bed table. "I know these crises all too well, there is nothing to do but suffer through them. But, darling, are we more trusting than other lovers, or what, that we've contrived to spend a whole year apart? Please don't think I'm bitter. I haven't an ounce of bitterness toward you, couldn't have if I tried. You're young, eager, vulnerable, imagine—have every right to imagine—that at every turn life waits to fill your cup of joy. Whereas I, who am caught in the grinding day to day of it, and can't promise you *anything*, know only that with all my soul I pine for you. . . ." A lousy cold made everything worse.

Reading these sad letters in her big sunny room on the rue Chamfort—there was a series of them over several weeks— Sunny wondered why poor David had been elected to suffer so much. (She didn't mean physically, though he really ought to see a doctor about these frequent colds.) But why must he always undergo this spiritual anguish? Why should David Harvey be tried and tested over and above all other men? Perhaps this God he spoke about so often wanted something from him. Could he possibly be a *saint?* The sudden thought, which struck her like a thunderbolt, would explain so much. His problems with being Jewish, so puzzling to her at first. His attraction toward the Church and yet his insistence that he was not of it. His impatience with all the little details of living that other men (lesser men?) took for granted. His feeling about marriage, and specifically his constant self-torture about not having loved Gertrude sufficiently, whereas he *had* loved her, Gertrude just wasn't up to it. Even his abiding concern with celibacy. It occurred to her that the first night they had gone to bed together David had said he thought he was really meant to be celibate.

But now that she had arrived at this explanation, she didn't know what to do with it. Was she up to it anymore than Gertrude had been? Ought she to be? She would always love David, saint or not. That wasn't the issue. But that picture of her like an icon on David's night table was disturbing. What if David wasn't pining for her at all? What if David was pining for his God?

My darling,
A saint? I opened your letter trembling. I thought, now she is giving me up. And so you were. But on a level beyond my wildest imaginings. Dearest, you ennoble me, you hallow me. And yet I also read between the lines—no, don't deny it—a small hint of resentment. But, darling, surely you understand that whatever the name of my desire—and why should we hang ourselves up on words?—you are the deepest part of it. You pain me dreadfully when you suggest otherwise, since it's you, only you to whom I can begin to speak the truth. I'm no longer interested in being "liked," can no longer play that old game of accommodation, don't give a damn about "good relationships," an easy celebrity, *The New Yorker*. (They turned down that excerpt, by the way.) Want only to do my work, speak in my own voice.

Took the train into New York for the weekend to slough off a bit of the old academic mildew, and went to the theater with Natalia and Fritz to see *I Am a Camera*, John Van Druten's "dramatization" of Isherwood's *Berlin Stories*. You can imagine the hilarious derision with which our Natalia greeted it, she who has known the Moscow Art Theater. Also had dinner with Amanda and Milo, invited for eight and no thought of food until past ten—Milo, Italian in his habits to the end. Amanda is pregnant—did she write you?—looks soft and lovely. She spoke of you tenderly, laughed when tears sprang into my eyes. She is, God forgive me, such a shikse. Don't be offended. I'm speaking not ethnologically but spiritually. Spiritually, my darling, you are no shikse at all. But aren't you meeting any French intellectuals? Or is it all silly students and impoverished veterans on the GI bill, self-styled literary exiles? (Ask Morty Silver what he's written lately. The answer is, not a line.) Yes, do send me your story when you've finished it. You're quite right not to want to talk about it in advance, which only too often ends in talking it out. Good intentions don't count, only text. I promise to read it objectively, and never once wonder what personal experience might have led you to write about "young love in Paris."

And so to bed. Oh, God, even writing to you makes me feel as if I were about to come. Do you know this George Herbert poem? Here is the first stanza, but look up the rest.

> Love bade me welcome, yet my soul drew back,
> Guilty of dust and sin.
> But quick-eyed Love, observing me grow slack
> From my first entrance in,
> Drew nearer to me, sweetly questioning,
> If I lacked anything.

Have patience with me, my darling, be there for me, be there.

David

Now she too was depressed—how could she be happy when David was so miserable? Also her command of the French language had reached a plateau again, and the Cours Aux Etrangers had become so impossibly boring she had stopped going, though she still sometimes turned up at the lunches with Michel and Claude. The Silvers too no longer seemed top drawer when she went there on an occasional Sunday. David had chided her for not meeting any French intellectuals, but the French never invited you anywhere and the nearest she had ever come to the intellectual scene was once seeing Simone de Beauvoir and Jean Paul Sartre at a rear table in the Deux Magots. She had given up on the Paris story, which was a trite and silly subject in any case. On the home front, Mary Jane had written that she was afraid she was pregnant, which was doubly depressing since the father seemed to be the other half of a one-night stand and the experience totally meaningless. When Sunny thought of what she and David had, a love that was *all* meaning, she felt depressed all over again, and guiltily wrote Mary Jane to say the word if she needed money for an abortion. And on top of that,

Mary Jane had decided that she could no longer afford their old apartment and didn't want another roommate, so she was moving into some kind of basement in the Village. Which by extension left Sunny homeless.

Paris turned cold and rainy. Sunny developed the flu and took to her bed, causing Madame Beaupain, in her brown tailleur and little hat with a veil, to cycle off to fetch a doctor. He listened to Sunny's lungs with his ear against her chest— evidently the stethoscope had not yet been invented in France— and when he had gone, with assurances of her ultimate recovery, Madame Beaupain tiptoed in with a packet of medicine that she seemed to feel was a specific for Americans. It was sulfa, and the directions were to sprinkle it over the wound and with-draw from battle.

Muffy managed to find the Herbert poem in the USIS library. Sunny read it like a message from David. It was beautiful but very ambiguous. (The word "saint" flew through her mind again.) Michel wrote her a concerned note which included the strange line—"*Anne, ma soeur Anne, ne vois tu rien venir?*"—and Claude, arriving with flowers, needed to explain that it came from *Blue-beard*, a reference that any French child would have known but that had escaped Sunny completely. When she felt a little better she began to tackle *Attente de Dieu*, though possibly Simone Weil was not quite the thing when you were sick to begin with. But there must be a difference between wanting to live like a saint and wanting to die like one. That all-absorbing humility on every page seemed particularly odd in someone bent on self-effacement. Surely true humility forgot the self entirely. Or, to come at it another way, wasn't it as vain to dwell on your ugliness as on your beauty? No, weak as she was, Sunny could not conceive of life *only* as a preparation for death. No doubt, David would say it was because she was so young— though she didn't think she was as young as he thought she was—or blithe and unfeeling, or too much of this world. But she had never been able to grasp the idea of anything except as it had to do with living people, their strivings and pratfalls, their eternal yearnings toward what they could never fully understand:

truth, beauty, love. Of course, what Weil said about *attention* being the supreme form of prayer, this she did understand. Too tired to go on, but still thinking of David, Sunny reached for the copy of *I Leap Over the Wall*, by Monica Baldwin, a former nun, which Muffy, acting on some strange childish intuition, had also brought back from the library.

Thanksgiving was approaching, her favorite holiday, but neither she nor Muffy knew what to do with it. David, spurned by Gloria, was spending *his* holiday at Greenwood, working on his big poem. He had meant to be a good father, had offered his daughter a big festive dinner at the Reeveses, good music listened to in front of the fire and a walk in the woods afterward, only to be told that Gloria didn't want to "blow the weekend." Sunny and Muffy decided that there must be turkey somewhere in Paris and came back defeated. "*Vous êtes allées chercher un dindon?*" Madame Beaupain asked in surprise. "*Ces américains,*" little Monsieur said, shaking his bald head. Yves, their sixteen-year-old son, shrugged. Nothing about these foreign spinsters surprised him. As if to make up for the turkey fiasco Madame Beaupain invited them to a birthday dinner for Yves' girlfriend. It was a happy family celebration. They all sat around the Beaupains' table, Madame, Monsieur, Yves, the girlfriend and her parents, Sunny and Muffy, exclaiming over course after course: oysters, a blanquette de veau, dry white wine, a perfect tarte aux pommes, tangerines, nuts. Afterwards, Madame Beaupain presented her and Muffy with a bill for 300 francs each.

"Oh, David," Sunny wrote, "what am I doing here, really? You are so lonely, I am so lonely. Our being apart doesn't seem to make sense anymore. I have begun to think of all time in terms of achievement, as if each day accomplished were a little miracle, a small step forward on the tightrope of time that stretches between us. I'm really so tempted to chuck it all and go home. Forgive me, darling, I know I'm whining. It's just that I miss you so and long so terribly to be in your arms and have all this homesickness go away."

DECEMBER 1, 1952
Rhinebeck, New York

My darling,
Your latest letter, which I found on my return from Greenwood, has saddened me deeply. I feel I've let you down, made you think that my occasional despair owes itself to your absence. Sweetheart, nothing could be further from the truth. No, I'm not "horrified" by your confession of homesickness, *nothing* about you could ever horrify me. But you must believe me when I say that this homesickness you think you feel is a void that no other human being, no other place can fill. We separated because we each had things to do, and because you wanted, still want, though you may no longer think so, your year in Europe. Truly, my sweet, wrenching as it is, this period of solitude is necessary to both of us.

If you're still feeling low, why not look up Natalia's friends? She's written them about you and so there is no need for you to be shy about approaching them. They will certainly be a welcome change from your other pals, such as Muffy and her silver patterns. Ran into Mary Jane on 57th Street, by the way, looking bemused and very Southern, pregnant I didn't notice. I promised to come to dinner before she moves, and probably will, in your honor, looking for traces of you in your old apartment, painful as that might be. But, Sunoo, though I'm willing to see your friends because they're *your* friends, I know this type of Southern flirt better than you do—New York is full of them, never mind Faulkner—and hope you won't waste too much compassion or too much of your stipend helping her out of this scrape, since she will only, I assure you, soon get into another, and you will spend your life bailing her out.

Yes, of course I know Colette and am happy to hear that you're reading her in the original. But perhaps you ought to give up on Simone Weil for a while. If you're older than I think you are—and I admit that in certain respects you're older than anyone I know—then you must realize that to consider SW anti-Semitic is very "provincial," one of your favorite words these days, and altogether unworthy of you. Jesus, I must remind you, was a Jew. So were Marx and Freud. Each of them in his time a voice crying in the wilderness, not a dues-paying member of the B'Nai B'Rith. Each of them scorned, reviled, attacked by fellow Jews for the worst sin of all—being an original thinker. Sunny, I know you think you're being humane when you take issue with certain of Weil's remarks, but don't let a generous heart addle your excellent brain. The greatest Jews, the only real Jews, have always stood outside the mainstream of culture, and any attempt, however well-meant, to absorb them, pity them, homogenize them, define what is or is not Jewish, can only end in tragedy, by which I mean the death of the mind.

I'm off to Gorham to give a reading and will report back on your alma mater on my return. No, Greenwood wasn't "lots of fun." It was cold, bleak, cheerless, except for an abstract expressionist painter who was there the last time, the landscape so relentlessly piny, I fled after a few days. But the "big" poem inches along, which is the main thing. I expect advance copies of *Ancestors* any day now and will send you one as soon as they arrive.

Corragio,
David

P.S. Re Weil: you got the attention/prayer thing mixed up; it's the other way around. But, as I said, why not let it go for now?

A trip to Chartres gave her fresh courage. David was right. She had been an idiot on the subject of Catholicism, had missed the exaltation, the nobility of it—though, as she turned away from the gorgeous rosette window and left the cathedral, she had horribly begun to wonder what she would do when her fellowship was over. She made herself look up Natalia's friends. Serge Beransky, a white-haired and heavy-jowled Russian writer, was, alas, almost as formidable as Natalia. But his wife, Violet, turned out to be a young American. She was also stunningly beautiful, her skin like alabaster, her jet-black hair done in a classic chignon, her gown a deep amethyst—"dress" didn't do it justice—with amethysts at her ears to match. "Ah, yes," an elderly Russian woman seated beside Sunny at the tea table remarked with a smile, "she is having a *grande saison, notre belle Violette*," making Violet seem more like a Jamesian heroine than ever. Serge asked after Natalia in a surprisingly perfunctory manner. The talk turned to other emigrés, long lost friends and world-renowned figures such as Stravinsky and Balanchine, whom they discussed in fluent French, oblivious of their heavy Russian accents.

"Natalia is David Harvey's aunt?" Violet said to Sunny in English, with a faint air of amusement. "Quite a battle-ax, isn't she?" Her amusement deepened. "Look, let's have lunch one day."

They had lunch. Although Violet was so beautiful that grand couturiers loaned her ball gowns and jewels for gala occasions, she was more interested in intellectuals than in fashion, writers particularly, though at lunch Sunny seemed oddly to interest her more than David. She invited Sunny to the opera, where during intermission Igor Stravinsky casually dropped in at the box. He kissed the hands of the ladies, rendering Sunny speechless. All the *monde* was there. Violet had surpassed herself this time—a vision in heavy topaz silk with topazes at her ears. Sunny wrote David about this gala evening. Then an Italian friend from the Cours Aux Etrangers, Paula, asked Sunny to visit her in Rome during the Christmas holidays. Violet suggested that on her way back Sunny stop in Aix, where Violet would be staying with some friends who had a villa. There was a note from Mary Jane saying not to worry, it had only been a false alarm, but that she was fed up with New York and had decided to come to Paris for a few weeks in January. Suddenly, Paris was wonderful all over again.

DECEMBER 15, 1952
Rhinebeck, New York

Dearest Sunshine,

I am so happy that you're once more enjoying Paris in your youngness. Natalia tells me that Serge enjoyed meeting you very much. Violet, I dimly remember as somewhat raffish, overly sophisticated. As to the beauty that has you completely "*bouleversée*"—oh, sweetheart, what women consider beautiful in a woman has always astounded me. Nevertheless, I'm glad that you have these new friends to take you under their wings.

My own life continues far from glamorous. I am just back from a reading at Gorham College, which was exactly what I expected, a gaggle of giggling girls—darling, were you ever really one of them?—the pound of flesh exacted at faculty parties before and after, complete with unwashed faculty children tangled underfoot, impoverished professorial types getting looped on the free drinks, leering questions about Dylan Thomas and poets in general. The one bright note was the presence of Marjorie Stewart, a painter I once met at Greenwood who's now a member of the Gorham art department and seemed as much a fish out of water as I was.

Pause to look for the mail, hoping for a letter from you. Nothing except bills and Marianne Moore's collected poems. (I showed Hymie a piece of your last and he said, "Harvey, why are you here?") Rereading your first letters to me at Greenwood, it astonishes me that we were once so stiff and formal with each other, like finding a picture of one's parents when they were young. And now, there you are, half the world away. I think I must get over to see you soon—how, I don't know. Only that I must. Has the advance copy of *Ancestors* reached you yet? I don't give a damn what the reviewers think, but for you not to have a copy kills me.

Your pal, Mary Jane, called by the way, and I promised to meet her at some point before she leaves to give her a belated Christmas present for you. Don't be disappointed. It's nothing much, since I wasn't sure what you needed. Your mother also kindly invited me to Connecticut for Christmas Day, but understood when I explained that I am too hard pressed these days to accept any invitations. I didn't further explain that Christmas means nothing to me, an unrepentant Jew, but perhaps you can break it to her gently.

Ciao, cara. Have a wonderful holiday. But remember

Your loving
David

7

She put down her bags in her room in the rue Chamfort, looking for a letter from David, very glad to be home. She had heard it said that one never knew what one felt about a place until one came back to it, and she knew now how much she loved Paris. It was the only good thing to come out of the trip, which had been otherwise a fiasco. Astonishingly, Rome had not been sunny at all, but cold and wintry. Paula had deposited her in a dreary little pension and not retrieved her until Christmas Day when she had dinner with Paula's family in a vast marbled apartment that had been clearly decorated for Mussolini. Harried servant girls ran about obsequiously deferring to Paula's fiancé, the *"ingeniere,"* and her father the *"professore."* (Even her own father and the nurses at the hospital were on more familiar terms.) Where was Vittorio de Sica in all this? . . . Afterwards, Paula had drawn her aside for a girl-to-girl talk. *"Senta,"* Paula had said, after she heard Sunny try to describe her relationship with David. "Why not marry him and end it all?"

If anything, the interlude in Aix was even worse. Another pension on a dreary sidestreet, dinner with Violet's friends in their villa, two skinny Frenchwomen with cupid's bow mouths and thin crescent eyebrows who greeted Sunny's every attempt at polite conversation with *"Comment?"* She had been forced to spend the night—there were no taxis, and clearly no one was going to offer her a lift anywhere. In the bedroom, Violet, reclining on a chaise longue, had advised her not to marry David.

"Don't marry him?" Sunny had said, still bemused by her conversation with Paula, and forgetting to add that anyway she and David had no plans. "Why not? We're already lovers."

"Believe me, it's not the same thing. I've been married since I was eighteen years old, and would never have married in the first place, if Serge hadn't been so persistent."

"Really?"

Violet had looked at Sunny with her great sapphire blue eyes. "Are you discreet?"

"Within reason."

She mentioned the name of an Irish poet. "Do you know him?"

"No, but David might."

"Then you must never repeat this to him."

The poet had a wife in Ireland, but lived in Paris. The Irish wife would understand. But there was always the problem that Serge would go mad. Still, how could Violet, so young a woman, resign herself to a loveless life, a life without her grand passion? She had read Sunny a few lines of the poet's last letter.

"He's Irish, but it's in French," Sunny had said.

"The language of love. We speak only French when we make love."

"Extraordinary."

Outside a perfumed night had fallen. Violet had handed her an ecru satin nightgown and—perhaps still under the spell of her lover—undressed utterly unselfconsciously. She had the wide hips of a woman, the chest of a boy. A flat-chested *grande amoureuse*. Was nothing in Europe ever what it seemed?

Never mind. the real question now was, when would David be coming over? She rifled eagerly through the mail Madame Beaupain had placed on her desk. But the only sign of David was a book package from his publisher. She sat down on her bed, unable to believe it. Of course, she hadn't been away that long, only ten days or so, and David had known she wouldn't be in Paris during the holidays. But he always wrote, almost daily, no matter what. Was he ill? Had something happened? She quickly read the note from Mary Jane, which said only that she would be staying at a hotel on the rue de la Harpe that Sunny had warned her was a flea bag, and put it aside. Then she opened a letter from her mother and discovered that David had spent Christmas with her parents, after all. In wonderful form, her mother said, as handsome and charming as ever, talking brilliantly for hours, utterly fascinating on the subject of Jesus, singing carols louder than anyone else. Then what accounted for this strange silence? But how stupid she was. He wasn't being silent. He had sent her his *book*. She tore open the package, stared at the cover and, forgetting her luggage and everything else, started to read. How beautiful it was, how right in every line and every phrase—even more so in print than in manuscript! And the care that had gone into the physical making of it, the paper, the typeface, the montage on the cover with a photograph of David in the center and all around him pictures of the great men who had gone into the making of him. When she finally finished, dawn was breaking. "Oh, David," she wrote to him, hastily grabbing a piece of airmail stationery. "It's here! To have your beautiful book in my hands and soon to have *you!*" And how happy she was that he had dedicated this masterpiece to Gloria. "Now she'll finally know what an extraordinary man her father is. For a long time I've had this fantasy of having a long heart-to-heart talk with her and telling her what you're really like—a version very different from her mother's—and how lucky she is to be your daughter. But now all she has to do is read *Ancestors* . . . Oh, darling, have you any idea specifically when you might be coming over?"

But a week later, still no letter. Perhaps David was busy publicizing his book, giving interviews, going to parties in his honor. Or perhaps, horrible thought, the day with her parents had soured him?

"He was all right when you saw him?" Sunny said to Mary Jane when they met in the Deux Magots. "He was all right during dinner?"

"He was fine, fine," Mary Jane said irritably. "He just wanted to give me your Christmas present."

"It's beautiful, isn't it?" Sunny said. "Have you ever seen such a beautiful blouse? He loves sheer blouses. I don't know why. It must have something to do with his early background. But what made him so sure of my size?"

"I don't know," Mary Jane said, looking uncomfortably around the café.

Paris did not seem to be making her happy. Sunny had taken her along the Seine on the *bateau mouche*, shown her the Louvre, had introduced her to the Beaupains and Claude. But her face was strained, her body tense. She looked like a cat wanting to jump, and talked of going home early. But what was there to go home to? As far as Sunny could make out Mary Jane's life was still a shambles, the new apartment in the Village a damp basement, the art dealer still unwilling to divorce his wife.

"I wish you could see Paris as I do," Sunny said. "But maybe you have to live here. I must say that when I came back from my trip the Beaupains greeted me like a long lost daughter, though I proceeded to make the most incredible gaffe at their Epiphany party. There was mistletoe all over the place and I said that in America when you catch somebody under it you 'baiser' them, which I thought meant kiss them. And Madame looked as if she were going to faint. And Monsieur was gasping, 'O, ces américains.' And I said, no, there was nothing wrong, perfect strangers did it, and children too, and parents watched. And there was poor Claude, red as a beet, tugging at my arm and trying to get me to shut up. . . . It turns out you can baiser a hand or cheek, but you *embrasse* a person. If you baiser them, you're actually—" She laughed. "God, what they never taught us at Gorham."

"What they never taught us at Gorham," Mary Jane repeated.

"I wrote David about it. I think he'll be amused, don't you?"

"Yes, I'm sure," Mary Jane said.

JANUARY 10, 1953
Paris

Darling David,
Such a beautiful blouse. And so naughtily sheer, as you no doubt realized when you bought it. Poor Mary Jane, I think,

is jealous. A funny distant look comes over her face whenever I talk about you, and since I always talk about you—there isn't really much else to talk about with her anymore—we're more or less at an impasse. I wish you liked each other better since I love it when people I love love each other, but I suppose in this case it's not to be. Anyway, she's leaving tomorrow, so for the present that's an academic question.

Oh, David, do you know when you're coming over? I need a touch of home so much, and as you can see from the above, Mary Jane isn't it. Only you. I suppose part of me—especially after my Christmas travels alone—is getting tired of being a foreigner. Have *I* become provincial—my favorite word, as you say? Is that why I haven't heard from you in so long? Or was it meeting my friends and relations during Christmas that finally made you decide not to have anything to do with me? I'm only kidding of course. My mother, who is now madly in love with you, said you were in great shape. Mary Jane says you are fine too. But please do write soon, my darling. I want to know all about your Christmas (your version) and your New Year's, and all your days and nights in-between.

Voulez-vous baiser avec moi?

> *Ta stupide,*
> *Sunny*

Muffy knocked quietly at the door, or rather scratched, as she used to at school, then came in looking rather odd and adrift. Something seemed to be on her mind these days. At the Beaupains' Epiphany party (the "fête des trois rois," for which no doubt they would be charged 300 francs apiece), she had been quite unaccustomedly quiet and sober even when she got the slice of cake with the bean in it and Madame put a gold paper crown on her head. It was unlike Muffy not to delight in toys and parties, not to have giggled about how silly she must look with a crown on top of her unregal little head. (Eng. trans.: adorable.) Was she pregnant? No, the Junior Tampax was much in evidence. And in any case she had not seen her fiancé in months.

"You never told me about your holiday," Muffy said, lounging slantwise on the bed, as usual. What was there about Muffy, sober or gay, that turned everything into a dorm?

"It was okay," Sunny said, not wanting to pursue it. "How was yours?"

"Well, I never got to Spain. I stayed here the whole time."

"Really? I thought you were dying to go."

"I was. To bone up on my Spanish, I was a split major, you know. . . . But something more major kept me in Paris."

Simpering, eyes wide, Muffy waited for Sunny to guess what that something was. "Don't you see anything different about me?"

"No," Sunny said, catching the general drift, but surprised to learn that he was a Frenchman.

"His name is Maurice—as in Chevalier?—and he's a chemist and he goes to the same restaurant as you and Claude and Michel. He says he noticed me whenever I sat with you all. He says I looked so sad and out of it, he just longed to come over and comfort me."

"And now you have a new boyfriend."

"Not *boyfriend*," Muffy said, her little mouth tight with indignation. "Maurice swept me off my feet. We're engaged to be married."

"*Married*? Muffy, what are you talking about? You hardly know this man. You have a fiancé in Boston."

"No longer." Muffy held up her bare little left hand. "Robert was very brave about it, I must say. Very gallant."

Was it really possible that Muffy, of all people, was going to abandon her silver patterns and marry some Frenchman she hardly knew? That, as she went on to say, she blandly intended to stay in France and maybe teach English, or maybe move back to the United States if Maurice could get a job there—it made no difference?

"I can't believe this," Sunny said. "Doesn't any of it scare you?"

"Oh, no," Muffy said, smiling sweetly and getting off the bed. "I've already taken him to a gynecologist."

The Beaupains were as bouleversés as Sunny. *"Mais elle est formidable, cette petite fille,"* Monsieur kept repeating. And Madame, French to the core, kept looking at Sunny as if expecting similar news.

JANUARY 20, 1953
Paris

Dearest David,
    And still no word. I'm terribly worried. Are you sick? Are you unhappy? If there is something, someone, please let me know now. I can understand. We're far apart. It's my fault that we're far apart. It's been a long time. Tell me. I can take it.
                                    Sunny

This is a lie. I couldn't understand, probably couldn't take it at all. But the silence is worse. Let me *know*.

RELAX EVERYTHING FINE WRITING LOVE DAVID

JANUARY 30, 1953
Rhinebeck, New York

My darling Sunny,
I'm sorry my silence has troubled you, but I haven't had the heart lately to write anything, not even a letter. I too have been laid low by "holiday" doldrums, by the inanity of the season, the endless parties, the glancing encounters, the conversations that suggest more than they mean. When all one wants to do is settle down, and turn one's face in the direction of the truth. (For the past several weeks I have been reading the *Epistles of St. Paul*.) Yes, your sad letters from Rome and Aix seemed to come straight from my own heart—there is nothing more bitter than to feel a foreigner among "friends"—but you must try to assert yourself in such situations, forget about hurting people's feelings and all the rest of it, insist on your dignity, even with your friend, the shrinking Violet. (Ah, how voluptuously she

must cringe whenever the beast, Serge, approaches her bed-chamber!)

In any case, although Christmas with your parents is not an event I would like to repeat, to put it mildly, it has nothing to do with my silence. So put your mind at ease about that. (I'll skip over your other suspicions. And please, *basta* Muffy.) Your mother and father were very cordial, really, did their best to make me feel at home. And what a home! My darling, I knew you were well-heeled, but not to what extent. Grinning Negro maid, turkeys, pies, puddings, gleaming silver, eggnog, champagne, an enormous Christmas tree. (Will you want a Christmas tree when we're married? Ha, ha!) Your father very much the lord of the manor—he kindly asked me to lunch with him at the Century Club where, as you may not know, sons of poor Eastern-Jewish immigrants are not altogether welcome—your mother gay as ever, particularly after a few of your father's very potent martinis. I know that women are supposed to turn into their mothers, but will you promise me anyway not to turn into your father? I'm only joking, it was all very pleasant, an easy life to fall into, so cushy I fell into it myself for that one day.

Still, darling, I see now more clearly than ever how difficult it must be for you to understand how terribly burdened I am by all my obligations, having to teach when I want only to write, having to meet the rent, food bills, electricity, Gertrude's monthly child-support check—she's decided now that Gloria ought to go to a private school, complete with private bowling alley, I suppose. Etc., etc. We never do talk about money and why should we? You have nothing to worry about in that area, evidently. But if we're ever to come together in a real way, you must understand that to most writers money is time, energy, blood. You talk so blithely about my coming over to see you—which God knows I want to do more than anything else—but how am I to arrange that, do you suppose? My leave from Cole I've already spent, from one point of view squandered. I can't take another advance on the post-World War II book since I haven't done a bloody thing with it yet, don't know if I ever will. But if I do, then I won't have time for the "big" poem,

which means everything to me, consumes me more and more
each day. Darling, I don't ask you to worry about any of this,
only to understand.

Well, something will work out. It always does. Meanwhile,
I'm glad you liked the blouse, even though the bearer depressed
you. And thank you for the letter about *Ancestors*. It is so sane,
so beautiful, so full of love, as are all your letters, and mine so
doleful and "quvetchy" (do you know that word?) that sometimes
I'm ashamed.

I'm enclosing the first two reviews. Incredibly imperceptive,
but I thought you might want to see them.

And yes, I would love to "baiser" you, the question is when
and where.

David

Oh, David. Would she ever get to the bottom of him? It was
hard to believe that he found the reviews he had enclosed "imperceptive." Surely to be told by *The New Yorker* that his book
was "well-nigh perfect," and by the *New York Times* that he
had written "a small classic," would have elated any other man.
But perhaps *she* was being imperceptive and there was more
here—or in this case less—than met the eye. (But had his
disappointment in the reviews really caused his strange silence?
Or was there some deeper source of anguish? She realized that
she might never know. That curiously she didn't want to know.)
Still there must be, even on David's exalted level, a kind of
postpartum depression when a book was finally published. She
remembered from her own experience how eagerly she had
expected the whole world to change when *Watch for the Sunrise*
came out, and how amazed she was when nothing changed at
all. At least not overnight. (Not that she compared herself to
David; she was very careful to make that clear in her letter.)
No stars rising in the East, no parades, no sudden celebrity.
Nothing. Just a few reviews gradually trickling in, a few interviews, a few letters, mostly from old school friends she hadn't
heard from in years, and that was it. She didn't even feel like

a writer. Yet now that she looked back on it, her world *had* changed, bit by bit, and then with a huge rush. Because through her book she had met Amanda, and through Amanda, David. One couldn't expect more from a first novel than that. And here was Amanda, on the other hand, retiring from publishing. She had had her baby, a little girl named Anne, and her letters were ecstatic. She was going to do only free-lance editorial work from now on, nothing that would take her away from home, and have another child as soon as possible. It was all rather puzzling and also a bit disturbing. Amanda had always seemed to be the ultimate career woman and here she was turning into some kind of earth mother, waxing eloquent on such matters a natural childbirth and breast feeding. Was it this shifting quality that bothered David?

In any case she must try to be more patient, though increasingly she felt that if she could only fix on a date in her mind when she and David would be together again, no matter how far off, it would serve as a guiding star. Meanwhile, his letters buoyed her up—they had started to arrive again, three or four a week—made her feel part of his world. Natalia had given him a party in New York, the Reeveses had given him one in Rhinebeck. The advance comments on Elijah's new novel were absolute raves and Elijah was walking around more full of himself than ever. David's own reviews, more of which he kept enclosing, continued, to his mind, idiotic—"I've always considered reviewing a mug's game and I'm now more persuaded of this than ever. No one, except in the Jewish press has even touched on my section on Jesus, the heart of my book, as you well know. And the Jewish press notices nothing else. So that I am now the arch apostate of B'Nai B'Rith, Hadassah, and Commentary, Inc." But he had also received, on the goyish side, wonderful letters from people like ee cummings and Archibald MacLeish, the lone dissenter being Milo Montini, who had told him quite frankly that either as autobiography or poetry *Ancestors* didn't work. "Finito . . . the ultimate arbiter has spoken . . .ah, Sunnoo, what does it matter? Only you understand. Only you have ever truly understood. Do you know these lines? They are from the Bishop of Chicester to his dead wife, written in the sixteenth century. Death in this case being metaphoric, and meaning her absence merely:

> . . . Thou art the book
> The library whereon I look,
> Tho almost blind. For thee, loved clay,
> I languish out, not live, the day. . . .
>
> Stay for me there: I will not fail
> To meet thee in that hollow vale.
> And think not much of my delay:
> I am already on the way. . . .

Then, literally, David *was* on the way. He had received an invitation to teach at the Kinsale Seminar in Ireland, a conference held every summer at Kinsale Castle—"yes, a real castle, my Sunnoo." The Seminar would not only pay his passage and expenses, but also make teaching worth his while for a change, since the faculty would consist of a select group of distinguished Americans, and the students would be hand-picked from all over Europe—all in all a far cry from the chumps at Cole. The conference didn't start until July, but David would set off for Europe as soon as his classes were over in June.

Summer in a castle with David! It was like a daydream. But then, from the moment she'd met him all her daydreams had come true. In fact, David himself was all her daydreams put together. Of course, the Irish, at least in America, were notoriously anti-Semitic. And, worthwhile teaching experience aside, should David expose himself to that sort of thing simply, or partly, because he wanted to be with her? She would have to put it to him, make clear that she would understand if he changed his mind. Meanwhile, April was approaching, not the cruelest month after all—they had confounded the poets!—and just the possibility of seeing David lit a fire under her. She realized that she had done very little on her new novel, putting it off from day to day as if she had all the time in the world.

Then too, new love, young love, the subject of her book, was now so far behind her that it was hard to remember its agonies, the debate over whether to call him, what to wear, the need to say such things as, "Do you like music?" Oh, David! How much she owed him. Not least the utter bliss of never having to say, "Do you like music?" again.

But her time in Paris was no longer endless. For months she had been having a recurrent nightmare that she had left Paris forever, and each time woke up sobbing. Soon the loss would be real. How curious to anticipate such sadness when she had everything in the world to look forward to. Yet with each day she felt that not only a period in her own personal life, but an entire historical era was coming to an end. The signs were everywhere: Eisenhower's inauguration—David would laugh, but she had thought until the last minute that Truman would go on being President; the death of Stalin; plans for Elizabeth's coronation, followed by the peculiar realization that she was only a few years younger than the Queen of England. Suddenly it seemed that too much history was happening, happening so as to make her acutely aware it would be history at the very moment it was taking place. It was hard to rest easy with such a changing outside world—which made her inner world, so secure and full of love, doubly blessed.

She returned to her novel with a vengeance, determined to make herself worthy of David's love, or at least be able to give him a good report. But when David announced that he was arriving on the *Liberté*, June fifth ("Our ship, darling, the same one we sailed on together, because the moment I step on board I'll be that much nearer to you . . ."), she gave it up. There was too much to do, too much to decide. Obviously she would have to vacate her room at the Beaupains. But where would she and David stay until they went to Ireland? Finding a decent hotel would be a problem, one that she could afford on her student stipend and yet be suitable to David's station in life. The Hotel Voltaire was far too expensive. She would consult dear Michel. Also, her fellowship ran through June, but if she and David left for Ireland earlier perhaps she should ask Claude to forward her check. Or maybe just give up the fellowship altogether? Yes, why not, she had done nothing to deserve it. And once in Kinsale, would they actually stay in the castle, or was that just where classes were held? And what about their passage home? If David didn't want to take a French ship back, it might be something of a problem since her grant required her to pay her fare in francs. But why wouldn't David want to take a French ship back? Ah, what a delicious turmoil! She had counted months, now she was counting weeks, but soon she would be counting days!

MAY 8, 1953
Rhinebeck

Dearest Sunny,

Whoa, darling, take it easy. I too count the weeks, the days, the hours, and last night dreamed of you in a thin nightgown. You were standing in the wind, and I could see the outline of your breasts and nipples. You haven't got fat on French cooking, have you? (Forgive this silliness. I'm just head over heels in love and wild with anticipation.) But you mustn't think of giving up your stipend for me, or your room at the Beaupains. I'll be in Paris only about three weeks or so, and any halfway decent hotel will do. How about the Hotel des Saints-Pères? You loved the look of it that morning we stumbled across it our first day in Paris, and it would be a deliciously naughty, very French pleasure to sneak you into one of its rooms at night. As to Kinsale Castle, yes, the *faculty* does live there. But Kinsale isn't Paris, and I can hardly produce a girlfriend straight off. After I've settled in, I'll look for something nearby when you want to come and visit. But until then you would make me very happy if you would concentrate a bit less on Father Coughlin and a bit more on Yeats and Joyce. As I've suggested before, like all "good" Christians you're more of a Judaophile than strictly necessary and much more of one than you would be if you were Jewish. I promise you, sweetheart, that no one will beat me up, or you either if you come.

Now, what would you like me to bring you? Toilet paper,

books, jewels? Say the word. I'll even call your parents and find out what they would like to send along. How's that for devotion? Oh, sweet. Soon! Soon!

David

MAY 14, 1953
Rhinebeck

Darling Sunny,

No letter from you for almost a week now and I am ridiculously disappointed. Somehow I had expected that up until the moment I embarked there would be great hosannas from your side of the ocean to urge me on. I arrive by boat train at the Gare St. Lazare at 2:00 PM on June 5th, incidentally, but of course there's no need for you to meet me unless you truly can't bear to stay away.

New York—where I have spent the last several days getting Ed Gaskell to see reason, arguing with Hymie about my highly original bookkeeping, explaining to Gertrude that I'm not abandoning Gloria for the second summer in a row but *need* to return to Europe—New York, when I finally grope my way outdoors, is in full glorious spring. Sunshine floods the city streets, as my own sunshine floods my heart. In Central Park trees bud, birds twitter, couples stroll arm in arm. Soon we too, for a few precious weeks, will be pressed close, two halves of a peach. At home on my bookshelves *Ancestors* and *Sunrise* sit side by side, as is fitting and proper. Please tell me absolutely freely what to bring you. Tomorrow I have lunch with your father at the Century Club and expect to come away with many gifts but not, I hope, too close a scrutiny of my character. Sunshine, 22 days, 6 hours!

I adore you,
David

MAY 21, 1953
Rhinebeck

Darling—

Are you all right? If you're ill please tell me. I had lunch with your father in his fancy club and he seemed concerned only about your financial situation, not your health. Which doesn't mean that if you were unwell you would necessarily tell him. Please however do tell *me* if anything is wrong. Your letters are so central, so passionate, so internal that sometimes I feel I know very little about your external life. If it's not an illness but a lover, the suave Michel, the engaging Claude, I'll understand that too. Why should you settle for a middle-aged hack when all Paris in the spring is before you?

A week from Thursday I sail. I am already the American dream, replete with Kleenex, cartons of cigarettes, letters of credit, bandaids, shaving cream, Koromex jelly (!), nylon stockings, aspirin. It's all a mess, pure bedlam. Yet never have I felt so sane and tranquil in my life.

Seriously, darling, I know that you're working hard, as I am, tidying up a thousand odds and ends so that we can "afford" some time together. But I am worried about you. I don't want you to feel that you "must write"—there must never be any sense of obligation between us. But a line would cheer me immeasurably.

I love you,
David

P.S. Did I tell you that I've been rereading *Watch for the Sunrise* and how much I love it, truly, and how much Hymie admires it too? You can't imagine how objectively I read it. So, please, no more nonsense about not writing well. You don't know, you can't, how fantastically advanced you are.

SUNNY ARE YOU OKAY? SILENCE PROFOUND AND TROUBLING DAVID

22 MAY 1953
Paris

Dear David,

I have reserved a *single* room for you at the Hotel des Saint-Pères a partir de 5 juin at 850 francs a night. I will, of course, meet you at the boat train at the Gare St. Lazare but forward this information in case we should miss each other.

I don't want anything at all, but Muffy would like some bobby sox, 6 pr. white, size 8½.

Your girlfriend,
Sunny

8

"Okay, okay," David said into the night air. "So I hurt your feelings again. I apologize."

"You didn't hurt my feelings," Sunny said.

They continued stiffly down the crooked, dimly lit rue Monsieur le Prince, two strangers who had encountered each other by chance, though in fact they had made love in David's hotel room only a few hours before. She had met him at the boat train, they had traveled across Paris almost in silence, David studying her intently, and then he had hauled her from the taxi straight into bed. Dinner at her old student haunt had been *her* idea, alas. She glanced at him as he began to whistle, as if he were keeping up his courage in the dark. He still didn't look like what she had remembered. He was smaller, slighter. The clown lines were back. There was a gap between his two front teeth she had never noticed before. He was wearing a red plaid short-sleeved summer shirt and khaki pants, both wrinkled from his suitcase, though the shirt was new and unfamiliar.

"Look, am I supposed to like *all* your pals," David said finally. "*All* your little 'copains'?"

"They are not my little *copains*. Claude has been a very dear friend to me and—"

"He's in love with you, for Christssake, it's all over him."

"—and Michel is *not* merely a lousy Commie."

"What do you think he is? Spouting that propaganda at me about the United States engaging in germ warfare."

"He doesn't think it's propaganda. He believes it. He believes in social betterment. He was a member of the Maquis."

"All the French were members of the Maquis to hear them tell it. It makes you wonder how the Germans managed to occupy this country so successfully."

"I wish you didn't hate France so much," Sunny said, sighing.

"I don't. I hate the French."

He gave a short laugh, and they walked a few more blocks toward the Boulevard Raspail, through crooked, winding streets now as familiar as her own hand, streets she had longed to walk on with David.

Should she have stayed in the restaurant? She had thought of it, but when David rose to leave, throwing some newly changed francs on the table, his look had meant unmistakably that she was to leave with him. The look had surprised her almost as much as the small gap between his front teeth. Had he never given her that look before? Or didn't she remember? It was all so confusing. But they were back at the Hotel des Saints-Pères again, and David was determinedly ushering her past a disapproving concierge. Afterwards, she lay beside him more confused than ever. Perhaps she had been "counting" on things too much, instead of "believing" in them. David certainly seemed happy enough now. But had he always told her to be still and let him catch his breath? Come with his eyes closed as if he had wafted off into some private sphere of his own? Even the cigarettes had changed. He still smoked Philip Morris. She had fallen in love with Gauloise Bleue.

As he dozed she looked around. Despite the romantic street façade, David's room was as grudgingly furnished as her room in the pension in Rome. A few of his clothes drooped lopsidedly on old wire hangers in the open armoire. The rest of his luggage—his portable typewriter and several suitcases full of manuscripts, notes, and miscellanea—was strewn about haphazardly. A black nightgown peeped disconcertingly out of one of them.

"Ah, Sunnoo, Sunnoo . . . ," David murmured, his arm seeking her on the bed. He opened an eye, then both. "Where the hell are *you* going?"

"I can't stay here," Sunny said. "I'm your girlfriend."

"Oh, Christ," David said, sitting up. "I knew from your bobby sox letter that you'd pull something like this."

He reached out for her, and held her close to him. She wondered if Claude and Michel had gone on to a café together.

"Sunshine, why must you take my stupid caution so personally? Don't you know that these past few months only the thought of you has kept me alive? Don't you know how afraid I am that one day my distractedness and my utter absorption in my work will drive you away? That you'll decide, and with good reason, that you're 'not up to it'? Like Gertrude."

"I'm nothing like Gertrude. That's offensive."

He released her abruptly and lay back down, one arm slung across his forehead. "I know. I know."

"Also I do wish you wouldn't keep saying that your work comes between us when it doesn't. It makes me feel like a toy."

David sighed. "Look, as soon as I get to Kinsale, I'll find you a room nearby. We'll sneak you into the castle at night. Okay?"

"David, I'm sorry. I have to stay in Paris."

"What are you talking about? Some very distinguished people will be at that Seminar."

"No."

"Sunnoo, what's come over you for Christssake? You were always so sweet, so loving. I don't recognize you anymore."

She laughed nervously. "Maybe it's the pony tail. People tell me it makes me look very French."

"Sunny, don't pressure me, please," David said firmly. "I do not wish to get married. Period."

"I don't either," Sunny said, which was the truth. And wondered why she nevertheless felt that she had seen the last of Claude and Michel forever.

But they would not be married in Paris, David was adamant on the subject, though at her urging he had let Arlene Silver find them a lawyer who would explain the legal requirements. The requirements turned out to be a mimeographed list three pages long, and impossible to fulfill. "You see what I mean about the French?" David said, his blood clearly chilled by all that blue ink. Ireland was out too—anti-Semitism aside, it was not so easy to be married in *any* Catholic country. They sat in café after café discussing the matter so earnestly she almost forgot where they were. Finally, David came up with the solution. "England, of course! London! I'll show you my London." Yes, it was perfect. David would go on to Kinsale and pave the way for Sunny's arrival while Sunny stayed in Paris to tidy up her affairs and collect her last fellowship check. They would join up in London and triumphantly get married in a registry office, just the two of them.

"July fourteenth," David said, throwing her a bone. "Bastille Day, so you won't miss the French influence. We'll meet in the morning and proceed straight to the altar."

Sunny hesitated. They were back in David's hotel room, and she was looking, bemused, at their new wedding rings, still in their little jeweler's boxes—two plain gold circles with "Yes, Yes, Yes," inscribed in each. The very tarnished silver cigarette case lay next to them. "Do you think we could meet the day before?"

"It would mean my missing classes," David said dubiously, "and the two of us wandering around London all day in a state of suspense."

"I know, darling. But I just can't get off a plane and get married. I need to take a bath first. Does that sound frivolous, compulsively American?"

"It sounds Jewish." David sighed. "Okay, Sunshine. Since I'm to spend the rest of my life indulging you, I may as well start now. . . . By the way, you haven't told anybody about this, have you? Written a loving note to my parents or anything like that?"

"Of course not," Sunny said. "We agreed. No friends, no parents. Just us. Though I must confess that the Beaupains and Muffy have guessed, and Violet, who called the other day—"

"—said don't do it."

Sunny laughed. "Anyway. I know you told Natalia because I got a letter from her this morning."

"What kind of a letter?" David said, alert and frowning.

"Oh, the usual, wishing us well and all that. Though, she

did say, 'Be careful, little one. My Duskinka mustn't get hurt. This will be his second marriage.' . . . Isn't that funny? Her thinking of you as someone *vulnerable*? And of our being together always as something that could possibly *hurt* you? I told her not to worry. That it was really your first marriage too."

"Sunny, I don't think you realize how much I had to recover, literally, when Gertrude and I broke up. And that Natalia—"

"I know, saved your life."

"Not only then, believe me. Do you have any idea what it was like for me as a kid? I mean, you've met Tillie—" She nodded sadly. "And I know you think Izzy's adorable. But that poor sap couldn't even earn a living, and I was growing up right in the middle of the Depression, which, take my word for it, was a lot worse than the war. And I've been through both."

"But David, you went to college."

"Sure, on the subway. And tutored at night and took handouts from Natalia. My god, Sunnoo, I was younger than you are now when I first met Gertrude, and I only married her to get away from home. Though I realized the minute the ceremony was over that all I had done was make myself more homeless. In fact, right afterwards I kissed Natalia instead of Gertrude by mistake. When Gloria was born I couldn't even find a place to work in my own apartment."

"Oh, David, I know. It was awful. But it's all over now."

"I won't even talk about other women because they were all so meaningless—"

"Except for your grand seductress in California," Sunny said.

David ignored her. "Pursuit and conquest. Conquest and consolation. Followed by bills on each side for services rendered. By the time I met you I wasn't even sure I was capable of love any longer because no one had ever really loved me in return."

"*I* love you in return," Sunny said. And she did. He was back to looking like David.

"But what if I fail you too, the way I failed Gertrude and the way I failed Gloria? What if I'm a bad husband, even to you?"

"You couldn't be," Sunny said. "It's not possible," and took him in her arms. She felt the wet from his bitter tears seep into her blouse.

Suddenly David lifted his head and began to laugh, wet eyes and all. Then he burst into song, "Il Mio Tesoro," which he sang at the top of his lungs all the way down in the little caged elevator. At the sight of the suspicious concierge, he defiantly changed to "Auprès de Ma Blonde." Sunny joined him in the chorus. With their arms around each other, they walked out singing into the street.

The skinny old night porter smiled at them. "*Vous avez la chance de chanter,*" he said.

"We do," Sunny said. She stopped short and looked at David. "Oh, David, we have luck in everything. Please, let's never squander it."

He had gone off in high spirits, hands clasped overhead in that old triumphant boxer gesture, all fears so immediately and thoroughly overcome, as they always were with him, that she was left with the strange sensation of still arguing him out of what he had long since forgotten. She walked along the quai Voltaire, then took the bus back to the rue Chamfort, standing on the open back platform to enjoy the view. Paris looked empty in the morning light, and incredibly beautiful. It was hard to believe that soon she would be leaving this city forever. Never to come back, she almost thought. But of course that was ridiculous. One day she and David would no doubt come back together. She would just never again arrive in Paris so young and eager, or to be honest about it, so frightened and alone.

All the arrangements for the wedding were made. David had both gold rings with him for safekeeping. Someone from the American Embassy in London would be their witness and, if they needed another, maybe a clerk from their hotel. David had seen to all of that and also to their reservations. To please him she would wear the sheer dark blue blouse David had sent over for Christmas and the pleated navy blue skirt she had bought to go with it. Though why did David like skirts and blouses better than dresses? Did it have something to do with his memories of the women in his youth? In any case there was really very little left for Sunny to do in the next few days except grow more and more nervous, suspended between one life and the next. She dropped in at the dry cleaning establishment near the rue Chamfort to pick up the blue skirt, which she had left there. She had worn it the afternoon David arrived in France and he had pulled her out of the taxi straight up to his room. There was a silvery spot on it that she saw now had not come out.

"What is this stain?" Sunny asked.

The proprietress regarded it for a long time and then looked up at Sunny. "*Vous êtes Madame ou Mademoiselle?*"

"*Mademoiselle.*"

In that case, the proprietress said firmly, it was yogurt.

Sunny laughed. She would have to buy another skirt—but oh, the French! Why couldn't David see how funny and enchanting they were? How hard it was for her to leave them? Upstairs Madame Beaupain had slipped a letter from David discreetly under her door. Sunny skimmed it. David loved Ireland and knew she would love it too. Kinsale Castle sat on the greenest of hillsides overlooking the sea. The little town below, within easy walking distance, was a charming hodgepodge of thatched roofs, quaint pubs, rosy Irish faces. Of course, the Seminar itself was taking a lot more out of him than he had expected. Classes crowded, meals at the long communal tables incredibly hectic. The European student body was rigorous-minded and demanding, but the American faculty so sweet and soft they seemed never to know what they thought. Luckily there was a good pianist on the premises, the seminar secretary, Lucy Kraft, with whom David played duets in the evening and who, poor girl, already looked desolate at the prospect of Sunny's coming. But everyone else was eager to meet her. His room, Sunny would be glad to know, contained a baronial double bed, heaped high with goose-down coverlets:

"Ah, sunshine, soon we will be together for the rest of our lives. Whatever my qualms in the past I know now that I have enough love, enough trust, enough faith—yes, even enough money for both of us. You see? Nothing good ever vanishes, nothing true is ever lost. My plane on the 13th gets into London about two hours before yours and unless something happens to change your plans or, as is more likely, you oversleep, I will be at the gate Thursday morning at 10:32. Possibly I may dawdle and be there at 10:33. I'll be the fellow whose heart is bounding to the skies. Bring the black nightgown. Oh, baby, oh, sweetest, oh, honey, oh *you*. . . ."

With a sigh, she pushed aside the manuscript of the unfinished novel that lay on her desk and began to practice writing her name, which in eleven days would be: Sunny Harvey, Sunny Mansfield Harvey, Mrs. David Harvey—or all of them put together.

London, 13 JULY, 1953
Midnight

"Dearest David, dearest darling David, dearest . . ."

Sunny tore the sheet of paper out of her notebook and threw it away in the basket with the others. It was ridiculous. David was in an adjoining room—he had been so patient and understanding about the two rooms for tonight, just as he had been patient about the extra day to allow for a bath—and there was nothing to stop her from going in and speaking to him, nothing except the fear of making a fool of herself. Of course, all brides were nervous, that was understood. But why didn't she feel like a bride?

Outside the window soft lights gleamed on Russell Square. But she had actually seen nothing of London. If she ever came back again she wouldn't know where she was. She had followed David about all day in a gray drizzle to museums, libraries, monuments, no longer even caring that she and Queen Elizabeth were almost the same age. At dinner in some Indian restaurant she had barely managed to eke out a smile when David burst into Beethoven's *Ode to Joy,* singing so lustily even the inscrutable waiter grinned. "Poor Lucy Kraft," he had said, "wait until she sees you . . . ," and looked so cocky Sunny felt sorry for her too, guilty for the pain she would inflict on the poor woman when she showed up in Kinsale. *If* she showed up in Kinsale. She tried again.

". . . Oh, David. How can I put this? What can I say? Will I ever find the courage to slip this under your door? But I really, truly don't think we should be married tomorrow. I don't mean that we should never be married. Only not yet, not tomorrow. Please don't be angry. Please don't ask how I could have put you through this, have brought you all this way for nothing. But darling, I've thought and thought—and how can marriage do anything but spoil things for us? We've always been so special, you and I, so proud of being separate and apart, above the fray. What would we gain by acting like everyone else, bending our necks to the yoke, a yoke both of us fear and despise? Even your suggestion that I wear my wedding ring on my right hand because Gertrude wore hers on her left indicates how much you want it to be different for us. And there have been a thousand other indications.

"Maybe I should be writing this to my mother. (I feel so awful about not telling her about my wedding.) Maybe she would laugh at my fears as she did when I was little and tell me all brides have qualms. But I don't feel like a bride. Why is that? Because I'm not supposed to be one? Yes, I know that marriages aren't irrevocable, especially these days, that it's a tie that can easily be broken. But I don't want anything to be broken between us, ever. . . . Oh, darling, oh love, I'm so homesick and scared right now I don't see how I'll ever find the courage to give you this. Except that, is it possible that as always we're thinking the same thing at the same time? And that right now you too are frightened, not of taking the bold step, no, neither of us could ever fear that, but of taking the wrong one? Sweetheart, can't we be bold together? Can't we be truly moral by being what the rest of the world considers immoral, and having as our only tie what we feel for each other in our hearts?

"You do understand what I'm trying to say, don't you, my darling? Forgive me. I can feel you glowering. I can hear you saying that I take all this lightly. But, I don't . . . . Oh, David, I want my mother. I want my *mother!*"

London, JULY 14, 1953

For my darling, these flowers on her wedding day.
David

Two

1

The Hudson Valley was hot, hot, hot, houses and trees shimmering in the haze as in a nineteenth-century painting. She came out onto the porch, fanning herself with a wadded diaper. Under the still branches of the copper beech Rip Van Winkle might have lain fast asleep. Instead, David's parents sat side by side on canvas folding chairs, like a pair of lawn statues. It was one of their self-invited weekends. Every month or so Tillie called, to suggest in her wheedling voice that it was time, and then they came up and sat like this for hours at a stretch, indoors or out. It had been one of the first surprises of Sunny's married life, this stony silence, since she had assumed all Jews talked a blue streak—David certainly did—joked, laughed, argued even with God. But when these two spoke it was only to blurt out a remark utterly unconnected with what had gone before: Izzy usually to pull a tattered clipping from the *Times* out of his wallet and explain to the world at large that it said David Harvey had written a "small classic"; Tillie, to corner Sunny in the kitchen and offer confidences about her dropped womb. "So I said, 'Doctor, David is already five years old, what will be?' And he says to me, 'Mrs. Harvey, you see this palm on your hand? When that grows hair, then you'll be pregnant again.' "

Hair on the palm. As often as she had heard it, the idea still gave Sunny a bad taste in her mouth. "David, does she have to tell me these things?" "What do you want from her?" David always said. "Why do you try to make me feel guilty?" Maybe if Tillie had been interested in the baby . . . but Tillie only looked at little Sarah from a great distance, as if she were some kind of sideshow. Another surprise. To hear David tell it, Tillie was the ultimate Jewish mother incarnate. But then, on the other hand, Natalia, whom David seemed to regard as his true mother, had never come to see Sarah at all. As a baby present she had sent (to David) an expensive book of reproductions from the Hermitage collection in Leningrad. Otherwise, she firmly intended to stay away until Sarah reached the safe age of two. "Isn't she curious about what you've produced?" Sunny said. "She takes my word for it." Only Gloria, an otherwise difficult and surly adolescent, seemed melted by the baby on those rare occasions when she could be persuaded to visit. Once Sunny had caught her bending over Sarah's crib with such a vulnerable and tender look she could have been a young Madonna. But as soon as she saw Sunny, all tenderness vanished.

Oh, well. In a few minutes, David's parents would be leaving—they had already packed the cardboard box tied with knotted string in which they always brought their belongings—and that would be the end of his relatives, at least for a while. Sunny left the porch and went back into the house, where it was a bit cooler. Upstairs there were sounds of David being busy with something, maybe getting ready for his trip that evening, though David was always busy with something when his parents were around. Downstairs, in David's old study, the baby was stirring in her crib. Surrounded by bookshelves, desk, manuscripts, papers, little Sarah looked like a footnote.

"Come on, sweetheart," Sunny said, lifting her up and kissing her. Sarah smiled sleepily and wrapped her arms around Sunny's neck. "Come on, Sarah. We have to take Grandma and Grandpa to the train." Sarah, Sarah, such a beautiful biblical name. Tillie had wanted her to be called Edna, after a dead sister. David had suggested the name Natalia—the first request Sunny had ever pointblank refused him. She wiped Sarah's sweaty little face with an extra diaper, pushed her damp gold hair off her forehead, changed her, put her into a clean sunsuit. The diaper pail stank in the heat, but she was nevertheless grateful to her parents for the present of the diaper service. She did not know how she would have managed without it, or without their presents of the crib and the toys and most of Sarah's baby clothes too. Strange. She had hardly married, as other young women did, to get away from her parents. Yet, here she was, in some ways more dependent on them than since she was a child. But it was so different having a baby than she had imagined. So different being married, for that matter. Yes, Violet had been right. It wasn't like being lovers, not here in Rhinebeck, anyway. Take the simple fact of meals, for example. There had been no cooking in the courtship, but now it seemed to be the cornerstone of the marriage—the cornerstone of all the other local marriages too, as David was quick to point out. Nevertheless, what with the trips to the supermarket, the hours in the kitchen, on top of the housecleaning, the laundry, and taking care of Sarah. . . . Perhaps if they could have afforded some help, not that there was any around here. Or perhaps if David hadn't been too busy and distracted to lend a hand, not that any of the other husbands did either. . . . Well, maybe she should just be happy he was crazy about Sarah.

"David," she called upstairs, "I'm taking your parents to the station now." Pause. "Aren't you coming down?"

"In a minute."

David's parents had silently entered the study. They watched Sarah take a few steps, holding onto Sunny with one hand and the bars of the crib with the other.

"So how long David will be away?" Tillie said, as usual observing Sarah from afar.

"Two weeks."

"He'll be in New York two weeks?'

"No, just overnight. He's having dinner with Natalia. Then he's going up to Breadloaf in Vermont."

"A funny name, Breadloaf," Izzy said, laughing.

"I know," Sunny said, laughing too. "It's a writer's conference."

"It's a long time I didn't see Gloria," Tillie said. "But Gertrude calls me all the time on the telephone. 'How are you, Mama?' she says. She calls me Mama."

Sunny looked around at David, who had appeared in the study. He picked up Sarah, but said nothing. The three of them followed him out of the house and across the lawn to the car. Over David's shoulder, Izzy playfully ruffled Sarah's blond curls, then gripped his own bald pate with alarm. "You stole my hair!" he cried. "Give it back."

Sarah squealed with laughter. "*My* hair. *My* hair."

"You heard that?" Tillie said to David. "*My* hair."

"A *Yiddishe kup*," Izzy said.

"How a child can have a Jewish head if the mother isn't Jewish?" Tillie asked with a bitter little smile.

Sunny again looked around at David who frowned, but still said nothing.

"Believe me, this ketzele is more Jewish than I am," Izzy said, laughing until Tillie gave him a dirty look. He picked up the cardboard box resting against the beech tree.

"Do you want to come with us?" Sunny asked David, taking Sarah from him and strapping her into the car seat. She got behind the wheel.

"He's busy. Don't bother him," Tillie said.

"He's just getting his things together for the trip."

"Why we should bother him?" Tillie said.

"You go ahead," David said to Sunny. "I'll see you later."

It was probably just as well. David was a nervous passenger, alerting her to dangers that weren't there, sometimes crying out so loudly she almost skidded off the road. There was a pause while David and his parents stood by the car in the hot hazy sunlight. "Well, goodbye, Pop," David said, shaking Izzy's hand. For a moment he seemed about to shake Tillie's too until he recollected himself and kissed her quickly on her seamed cheek. He held open the car door and they seated themselves in the back, statues once more. "And for God's sake don't get off at the wrong station," David said, smiling for the first time when Sarah waved bye-bye.

The ride to the train was the silent end to the silent weekend. Sarah kept squirming around in the car seat and then turned back, puzzled, until Izzy finally waggled his fingers at her and she giggled. A very different pair from her other set of grandparents, who took such a lively interest in her. Tillie's idea of a baby present was a dirty, shopworn snowsuit from Klein's, a wrinkled brown paper bag with crumbled cookies, a tin candy box without any candy. Lifelong poverty didn't account for it, no matter what David thought. Poor David. Seeing his mother close up explained so much about him. Tillie had probably been like this when he was a child too, mean and grudging but persuaded that she was a saint. In that case, why did David care about Tillie and not Izzy, who at least tried? Dear little Izzy, with his tan fruit-man's sweater and bald head and terrible jokes. But of course Izzy's sister Natalia didn't think much of Izzy either.

"So you won't be afraid by yourself?" Tillie asked, as they got out at the station and stood looking down the tracks.

"What's to be afraid?" Izzy said, smiling at Sunny.

The train pulled in and Tillie and Izzy clambered up, Tillie's legs square and swollen in her black oxfords. For a moment they looked around bewildered, as if they were going to New York by steerage. Would they get off at the wrong station? It had happened before. And if they did manage to emerge at the right one, would they be able to find their way safely back to the Bronx? She wished that David were there, giving them stern last minute instructions, the father of his own parents, though in the beginning it had astonished her when he talked to them like that.

When she drove back, the lawn looked no more nor less empty than when David's parents had sat under the copper beech. It was still daylight and David was still inside the house, but a Sunday night sadness had settled over her. Increasingly depressed, she fed Sarah her dinner, relieved that David would be having his in town, bathed her and powdered her against the heat. By now she had come to think of the valley as a kind of Shangri-la in reverse. Outside people were laughing and gay, here it was all stifling and still, lonely as the grave. It was hard even to remember Paris, hardest of all to remember that she had been there on a fellowship, under her own steam—she was so stuck now. David didn't understand. How could he? It was easy for him to get away to talk with his publisher, give a reading, see Gloria, help Natalia put her book on Russian history into good English, and he often did. Though of course he maintained it was all a miserable hassle and Sunny was lucky to stay put. She put Sarah back into her crib and picked up the manila envelope marked "Photographs" that lay on top of David's old desk. He had had them taken for the new book, *Selected Poems*. She slid out the top one and showed it to Sarah.

"Who's this?" she said.

"Da-dee!" Sarah cried, kissing it.

Sunny took the photograph over to the window. Oh, David. He was still so beautiful to her, so exactly the husband she had always wanted, without even knowing he was the one she wanted. He was wearing a tweed jacket and a button-down shirt, his eyes squinting a little, his smile almost rueful, as if he were musing on the joke of being photographed at all. His left hand, slightly upraised, held a cigarette, and the gold wedding ring on the fourth finger was very plain. No wonder that when he first brought Sunny to Cole his female students had looked at her with eyes large with envy, and later when Sunny was obviously pregnant could hardly bear to look at her at all. Only Jenny Abruzzi, their freshman babysitter, who had not known David as a bachelor, rejoiced over the Harveys' "storybook marriage." She looked at David's face again, and was suddenly frightened. It wasn't only Paris she couldn't remember. It was all her life before David, without David. How had he become her whole world?

"You haven't used that big suitcase since Europe," Sunny said, handing David his freshly cleaned cord suit. "It's so strange to see you packing."

"I've been away before."

"Not for so long."

"Believe me, sweetheart," David said, turning with a rueful smile. "I wish there were some easier way to make a buck."

"Your mother asked me if I was going to be scared."

David shrugged. "So she's a foolish, ignorant woman. What can I do about it?"

"I just wish she'd play with Sarah instead of staring at her.

I know, it's hard enough to have a shikse daughter-in-law without a shikse granddaughter too."

"Would it be so terrible to please her on this one point?"

"David, I can't convert simply to please your mother. It would have to be a matter of the deepest religious conviction."

David laughed. "What deep religious convictions do you hold now?"

"That's not the point. I'm enough of a Protestant to believe that the Jews *are* the chosen people, and I really don't know that I'm up to it. I'm also, quite frankly, not so crazy about the secondary role women play in Judaism."

"Baloney."

"David, it's not baloney, it's—"

"Sunnoo, please," David said. "I'm trying to do something here." Frowning, he jammed the sleeves of a jacket down into the sides of his suitcase. She wanted to help him, but didn't. It would merely irritate him. He liked to do things his own way, quickly, if clumsily.

"Sarah kissed your picture when I showed it to her," Sunny said. "You will use the one I love, won't you? With the tweed jacket and the cigarette and the wedding ring?"

"Whatever you like. It makes no difference to me."

"I don't know why you're not prouder of the *Selected Poems*. After all, how many poets your age—?

"Sunshine," David said, "I may be young for a retrospective, but I'm too old to imagine anything will come of it."

"But Ed thinks—"

"Ed hasn't had a thought since the year one. . . . *Will* you be okay when I'm gone? I'm worried about you."

"I'll be fine," Sunny said. She hesitated. "Actually I did think of asking Mary Jane up for a weekend. She's only seen Sarah that once, when she came to visit me in the hospital. And since you don't like her, anyway—"

"Aren't there enough women around here to keep you company?"

"Who?"

"I don't know. Nancy Reeves?"

"And spend the whole time on her back porch talking about Dr. Spock and boeuf bourguignon?"

"Then call some other woman."

What other woman, when all the faculty wives were just like Nancy Reeves in her dirndl, or worse? That was the whole point of inviting an old friend like Mary Jane—though David had trouble understanding why a married woman needed friends at all. He had gone into the bathroom to get his shaving kit. Sighing, Sunny looked down at the makeshift card table where she sometimes still made a stab at writing her novel. There was some old mail on it, a chatty newsletter, half in French, from Muffy, a note from Amanda asking how her book was coming along. She pushed them aside and picked up the Cole Women's Club Weekly Announcement: ". . . Wednesday: sewing. Thursday: batik. Friday: gardening. Saturday night: Couples Gourmet Dinner . . ."

"It's just that Mary Jane is so up against it," she said when David came out again. "I mean, that bastard will never leave his wife and marry her, and she lives in that little hole-in-the-wall in the Village—you know, you saw it—no, you went to the old apartment—but—"

"Look, sweetie, suit yourself," David interrupted. "But just remember that every time you see her you get depressed. Can't you make better use of this free time?"

"What free time?"

"Come on. How do the other women manage?"

"I don't know. But they're not trying to write novels. Not around here, anyway."

David went on packing, but a worried look crossed his face. He always looked worried these days when the subject of her novel writing came up, as if it were a dangerous occupation, one that could easily bring her to grief. And yet how many times in the past had he said, "I couldn't love you if you weren't a writer"?

"I don't know why you're so unhappy with your life," David said.

"I'm not unhappy with my life. I love you, I love Sarah. I love everything about us."

"Except—?"

"Oh, David, it's not us, it's this place. If only we could live in New York."

"Sunnoo, please. Not that again. I have to leave in a few minutes."

"But other people do backward commutes. And we were so happy in New York, David. We knew all these wonderful people."

"You said they scared you."

"That was just in the beginning." She did not add that the formidable Natalia still scared her. She put her hand on David's sleeve. "Oh, darling, don't you remember all the walks, and the lovely movies and dinners? We *could* be like lovers again."

"You don't like our lovemaking, either?"

"I didn't mean that. I—"

"Look, I can't discuss anything now," David said, slamming shut his suitcase. "The taxi will be here any minute."

"Let me drive you to the train. I can take Sarah along in her pajamas. It doesn't seem right for you to go off alone."

"It's better than constantly being made to feel guilty."

"I wasn't trying to make you feel guilty, I was only—"

The taxi driver honked his horn outside. David gathered up his suitcase, his portable typewriter and his raincoat, took a few steps toward the door and turned around.

"Sunnoo, what are these quarrels about?" David said. "I love you so."

"Oh, David."

They held each other fast, kissing each other's faces, the two of them in tears. David's portable typewriter slapped against her backside. He was right. These quarrels made no sense. Whatever her discontents, she was already sick with longing for him.

JULY 4, 1955
Middlebury, Vermont

Sunnoo, my love, my wife,

Yes it is funny and tender and sweet to be writing each other again after all this time. Four years—two legal!—and still to feel my heart leap when I see an envelope with your typing on it. As you've gathered from my phone calls, I miss you excruciatingly and wish there were some better way to make a buck than spending two weeks in this intellectual desert. If there is one real poet here at Breadloaf, I haven't figured out yet where he's hiding. The "she's" are all aging high school teachers from Teaneck, New Jersey, desperate to be creative, pretty young secretaries at publishing houses hoping to be discovered, or more probably laid, by the boss, simpering . . .

Sunny quickly folded the letter and put it back inside the envelope as Mary Jane came through the kitchen door, holding Sarah by the hand. They had just gone for a little walk around the backyard, and Sarah in her sunsuit was looking up adoringly at Mary Jane and babbling away. Mary Jane was laughing. It was good to see Mary Jane so happy, since she had arrived in worse shape than Sunny had ever seen her. Her black hair tangled, her eyes wild, her cotton dress rumpled. For two nights now she had drunk herself into a crying jag at dinner and had to be helped to bed, tears spilling out of her flecked green eyes. The same old story. Her lover would never be able to marry her, and Mary Jane would never be able to give him up. It was lucky that David wasn't here to see her. Still, part of the old Mary Jane charm must still have been working, since Sarah had fallen in love with her immediately, holding out her arms from the crib to be picked up whenever Mary Jane passed by, climbing on Mary Jane's lap whenever Mary Jane sat down.

"Are you two writing to each other already?" Mary Jane said, pouring herself a glass of Chianti from the big bottle on the table. "He's only been gone a week."

"David loves to correspond," Sunny said apologetically. "Also, we've never been apart this long. Only overnight sometimes."

Sarah had climbed up on Mary Jane's lap again. "You're so lucky," Mary Jane said, bouncing the baby on her knee.

"Oh, I know. The co-eds think so too. You should see them when David and I—"

"I meant to have Sarah."

"Oh. Well she's certainly crazy about *you*," Sunny said. "I don't know anyone besides my mother she's taken to so completely. Would you mind holding her while I make this salad? Watch the wine glass." She began to shred lettuce at the sink, then stopped and laughed. "Do you remember the first real meal we ever tried to make? Neither of us had a clue how to do it. And it was only a steak. What was the occasion? I forget."

"Your boyfriend, Howard, was coming to dinner."

"Oh God, yes, that's right. I wonder whatever happened to him."

"He probably married some nice Jewish girl who appreciates him."

"I suppose so. It's funny to think of us all so domesticated now."

"Not I," Mary Jane said.

"Not *yet*," Sunny pointed out. "I never pictured myself as a wife and a mother, either."

"And in Happy Valley, where the males reign supreme."

"Well, that's certainly true," Sunny agreed with a sigh. "I think the only man who ever talks to me about anything is Dick Reeves next door. Except for poor David, of course, who can never understand what I'm complaining about."

"Do you really think of him as poor David?"

"No, of course not."

"Neither do I," Mary Jane said, and poured herself another glass of wine. Sarah grabbed for it.

"Still, do you really not want any of this?" Sunny said.

"The American Dream? Are you kidding?"

"Well, it's not *all* bad. I mean, if we didn't have to live here—" She shut off the water. "Look, Mary Jane, you can tell me it's none of my business if you want to. But can't you really say goodbye to that love affair once and for all? Maybe go back to Louisville for a while? I'll bet there's some wonderful guy down there who—" Mary Jane snorted. "Okay, you may not like the wife part, but I know you'd be a great mother. Look at how Sarah loves you."

"She's an unusually friendly child," Mary Jane said, removing Sarah from her lap and depositing her in the play pen. Sarah rattled the bars, but Mary Jane took her glass and the wine bottle over to the screen door and stood staring out.

"You really can't imagine what a miracle it is to have a baby," Sunny said. "Oh, I admit I was scared to death when I was pregnant of what a baby would do to our life. You know, come between David and me. We were so free, and he had had such a lousy experience when his first child was born. But that night when I watched Sarah come out all cheesey and white and bloody and they put her on the sheet over my chest, I really could have died of happiness. Literally. Because somehow at that moment she was the thin line between life and death, and I really felt that I *understood*. And if God had said, 'Sunny, you have to die now,' it would have been okay. I mean it. And then there was David afterwards, leaning over me when they wheeled me back to my room. So worried when it was all so perfect. And I laughed and said, 'I gave you a daughter.' "

"And I'll bet he gave her back as soon as her diapers needed changing," Mary Jane said.

"Why do you hate him so much?"

"I don't hate him."

"Well, anyway," Sunny said. "All I meant was that you'd be a wonderful mother."

"Stop *saying* that," Mary Jane said. She turned around from the screen door, her eyes bloodshot and stricken.

"Oh, God," Sunny said. "Not again. What are you going to do?"

"What do I always do?"

"You can't keep putting yourself through that. You'll kill yourself."

"No, ma'am. I'll die of a peaceful old age in the poor house."

"You mean he won't even pay for it?"

Mary Jane looked embarrassed. "His wife keeps an iron hand on the bank account."

An awkward silence hung between them and Sunny looked away. She wanted to offer Mary Jane money, but David would hit the roof. And he would be right of course, considering how he struggled to support her and Sarah, teaching, giving readings, writing pieces he didn't want to. Even the Breadloaf stint was costing him much needed time and energy. But Mary Jane wouldn't understand any of that, she was so mired in her own misery. Self-inflicted misery, if one wanted to be brutal about it.

"How did you get caught this time?" Sunny said. "I would have thought that by now—"

"Don't sweat it, darlin'," Mary Jane said. "I don't want your goddamn money. And I don't want your goddamn lectures either."

"That's not fair."

"You really have turned into a smug little bitch, haven't you? Jus' mired in your cozy little domesticity and complainin' how it's spoilin' your pretty little intellect."

"Why do you get so Southern when you're drunk?" Sunny said.

"Did your husband teach you to say that?"

"He didn't teach me to say anything. You really do hate him."

"No, I don't hate David, darlin'," Mary Jane said. "And believe me, David sure doesn't hate me."

"What does *that* mean?"

"I'm celebratin' Christmas."

"You're totally drunk. It's July."

"You're wrong. It's always Christmastime where your beloved husband is concerned."

"What are you talking about?"

"Oh, you damn fool! You damn fool!" Mary Jane cried, running out of the kitchen and up the stairs.

Overhead a door slammed. Sunny looked over to the playpen. Sarah had sat down with a thump and was crying.

"Sunnoo, Sunnoo I'm home!"

She carefully closed the door of the study where she had just put Sarah down for a nap and stood there hesitantly, her heart beating fast. It was the moment she had been dreading all week, though Mary Jane had insisted afterward that she was drunk and didn't know what she was saying. "I was crazy. I was jealous. It was all crap," she had said, bursting into tears on the long awful ride to the station the next morning. "Don't hate me, Sunny, you're my best friend in the world." But what if David's face betrayed even by a glimmer the absolutely unthinkable, the thing that could make her whole life come crashing down—that Mary Jane had let slip the truth?

"Sunnoo?"

She made herself turn the corner into the hallway, and there David stood, grinning triumphantly, bags at his feet, cord suit wrinkled, his tie askew. As if he, not she, had been through hell.

"Well, home is the hunter," David said. "God, I missed you. How did it go? How's Sarah?"

"Fine."

"You don't seem very glad to see me," he said dubiously, then shrugged it off. "Any mail?"

"Just what's here on the table."

He kissed her hard, pressing his teeth against her lips, as if to establish his presence. Then, keeping a free arm wrapped around her waist, he leafed through his letters.

"Oh, Christ, galleys in a month and Ed's going to want them back the day before yesterday. . . . Did I tell you that now he wants me to do an anthology of contemporary verse? I don't know where I'll find the time or what we'll do for money if I don't. . . . Look at these bills. . . .Oh, well, the hell with it for now."

David tossed the mail aside and started to carry his suitcase upstairs to the bedroom, pulling Sunny along with him. The typewriter he had left down below to bring to his office on campus. He sat down on the bed to take off his shoes and trousers. "Are you sure you're okay?" He looked at her, frowning, then unbuttoned his shirt and gave a deep sigh. "Well, I'll never do another stint like that again, I can tell you, no matter what they pay me. It was one goddamn houseparty, with all the bigwigs racing around, trying to imprint their wisdom on every available mind. Benny de Voto is as pig-faced and pig-headed as ever, and William Sloane looked as if he cried himself to sleep every night, out of sheer sensitivity to this cruel world, I suppose. And of course Ciardi wasn't too happy to see me to begin with since he knows what I think of him. In the evenings our big moment came when Robert Frost wandered over to 'say' us some of his poems."

He had written all that in his letters.

"Craggy son-of-a-bitch, Frost, carved out of granite. Knows his own worth, though. Knew it when no one else did. For which I have to hand it to him. Otherwise it was all an absolute waste of time. Square dancing, picnics . . ."

"You square danced?" Sunny said. "You went on picnics?"

"One picnic," David said, lying back on the bed in his undershorts. "At night, in the woods. The sun went down so fast we couldn't even find the melon and the wine chilling in the goddamn brook, much less our way out of there. Then it began to pour. Luckily, this gifted young poet, Lauralee Haines, managed to lead us out. But I went to bed drenched. For a few days I thought I had pneumonia."

"I thought all the 'she's' were supremely untalented."

David laughed. "Well, there always has to be an exception to everything. . . . Hey, Sunnoo, come over here."

"Sarah will be up in a minute."

"You always have so many goddamn excuses," David said, and closed his eyes. "Okay, forget it. Any phone calls?"

"The Reeveses are back from the Cape."

"We ought to have them to dinner."

"Why?"

"Because they've had *us* over a million times," David said wearily. "Dick's my colleague, for Christ's sake. . . . Anyone else?"

"Your mother."

"What did she want?"

"From me, the usual."

"You know, Natalia thinks you're making a mountain out of a molehill with this conversion business."

"Does she?"

"Come on, Sunny. I don't give a damn whether you ever light a candle or do any of that mumbo-jumbo afterward. You'll always be my big blond beautiful shikse, you know that." She walked over to the card table.

"You never wrote me about the weekend with La Bixley," David said, his eyes following her.

"There wasn't anything to write."

"Let me guess. She's in trouble again, am I right? Look, sweetie, with all my other burdens I am not going to finance your pal's latest abortion."

"I didn't ask you to."

"Just so long as you don't give me that routine about old friends. She's not your friend. She hasn't been your friend for years."

"David, let's get out of here," Sunny said, impulsively sitting down beside him on the bed. "It's no good for us. Please—let's move to New York. I could get a job. It would pay for a maid. In another year or so Sarah could go to nursery school."

David bolted up angrily. "Goddamn it, I've been home two minutes and you're already at it. Don't you know that rents in New York are sky-high? Don't you realize that commuting would take three working, which is to say three *writing* days from my week? I don't understand you. You were so happy to come here, to live in the country, to be near a campus again."

"My only connection with this campus is that I walk around it pushing a stroller."

"Really? Well, what do other women—?" He pulled her down as she started to get up. "Okay, forget I said that. But Sunnoo, listen to me. Aside from finding this great maid to whom you'd be willing to entrust Sarah, you've never had a nine-to-five job in your life and, I assure you, you'd hate it. Your job is writing, and it's about time you got down to it again seriously. Nobody's asking you to bring home the bacon, that's my department. Meanwhile, you have what most writers would die for. A place to live and a place to work and, though you don't agree, enough *time* to work too. Not to mention a husband and a baby who adore you . . . Sunny, what's really wrong? I know you. New York is a red herring. What's really bothering you?"

She didn't answer.

"Look, if it's a maid you need, go visit your parents in New Hampshire for a while. The maid will take care of Sarah."

"Why do you always try to send me off to my parents?"

"You like them. I like them too. Your mother, anyway."

"If I went, would you join us?"

"Sunny, you know how much I have to do, how—okay, I'll try to fit in a long weekend." He looked into her face, troubled. "You're still upset. What's up? Did Mary Jane give you a hard time?"

"She drank a lot," Sunny said.

"I'm not surprised."

"She said things."

"What kind of things?"

Sunny turned her face away. "She talked about Christmas—"

"Christmas? Why Christmas?"

"—but the only Christmas I can think of is when I was in Paris and you went to her apartment for dinner to give her my wedding blouse. . . . Oh, David I feel very sick."

"Did she say anything else?"

"No."

"Because there isn't anything else," David said, gripping her by the arms. "Look at me. There isn't anything else."

He laid her to rest against his shoulder, as he did with Sarah on those rare times when he burped her. "Baby, baby, don't cry," David said. "I'm home."

2

Yes, David was right. Getting away was all she had needed, and being gathered up bag and baggage and baby by her parents and Willie Mae. This month at the summer place in New Hampshire had totally restored her perspective, banished her awful fears and imaginings, the turmoil caused by Mary Jane's visit. (He had been right about Mary Jane too, who certainly *wasn't* her friend.) Here at the lakeshore with Sarah, who squatted, brown and naked, near a lily pad, it was all serenity: tall jagged pines rising in the near distance, behind them the Monadnock mountains echoing and re-echoing in gradations of blue. When she swam out to the middle of the lake she felt like a small stone casting endless ripples. Now she watched Sarah carefully inspect a waterlily, wipe her little sandy fingers on her chest. Watching Sarah was like watching herself as a child, like being her own mother and her own daughter at the same time, a sweet feeling. Even David had enjoyed his few days here last week, submitting cheerfully to a party in his honor, charming the locals.

Halloing, her parents came drifting down the path from the house. They were in great shape, her father very tan and handsome, though a little stouter around the middle, her mother brown as a berry, hair a bit grayer but eyes sparkling like aquamarines.

"The sun's over the yard arm, sweetheart," William said. "Don't you want to come back up for a drink?"

"You'd better hurry," Grace added, laughing. "We're already one ahead of you." Grace held out her arms to naked little Sarah, who ran into them, and carried her up the path to the house. William and Sunny followed behind, smiling at each other. The house was really only a rustic camp, though David liked to refer to it as her ancestral manse, with old comfortable chairs and a big flagstone fireplace in the timbered living room.

A beaming Willie Mae, in her clean white uniform, met them at the door and took Sarah off to be bathed and fed. William poured a round of martinis from the chrome pitcher. "I ought to change too," Sunny said, flopping into an easy chair and accepting a drink anyway. She wondered suddenly what Willie Mae did on her day off in New Hampshire, a question which, curiously, had never occurred to her before. Had David asked it when he was here?

"Well, your handsome husband certainly made a great hit in these parts," Grace said. "Everyone at the post office was still talking about him. The ladies especially, I need not add. What an intellect. I'm impressed that you keep up with him, darling. But then he said you're the most brilliant person he knows."

"That's impossible," Sunny said, laughing. "I know the people he knows."

"It's a very intelligent race," William said. "There's no doubt about it. I'm thinking of proposing him for the Century Club. It may be a bit sticky, but I'm sure Jock would second him."

Jock. *Jock, Rock, Felicia, Muffy, Buffy.* After the party David had cheerfully recited the litany of names like a line from a comic poem. "Let me guess. It's a secret society. Regulation uniform is old school blazers and plaid slacks for the gentlemen, pink and green flowered shifts for the ladies." "But, David, they're really very nice," she had said. "Nice? Every one of them is an Eisenhower Republican." But David had moved among them easily, courtly and charming with the women, serious and knowledgeable with the men, a little dark handsome Semitic rooster in a barnyard of overgrown WASPs. She could hear David hooting with laughter at the idea of being proposed for the Century Club. Still, the suggestion should scotch forever Natalia's insistence that her "country club set" was nothing but a bunch of anti-Semites.

"That's awfully sweet, Daddy, but since we don't live in New York—"

"But David is in New York frequently from what you say,

darling," Grace said. "I think he'd enjoy having a place to meet with other distinguished men."

"Well, maybe, but—"

"Too bad he can't come back for Labor Day."

"He has to work. He's under tremendous pressure."

"He seems to work very hard," William said approvingly.

Grace laughed. "Well, I hope Sarah picks up some virtues from being half Jewish."

"Actually, she's not half Jewish," Sunny said. "According to Jewish law, you're not Jewish at all unless your mother is. . . . I'd have to convert."

"Convert?" William said. "Has there been talk of your converting?"

"Not exactly," Sunny said.

"Whose idea is this, his aunt's? I hope Mrs. Kirschenbaum isn't bullying you to—" From the first her parents had totally accepted Tillie and Izzy. It was Natalia whom they found offensive.

"No, Natalia has nothing to do with it, Daddy, honestly." She did not add that Natalia thought that she should submit to all the "mumbo-jumbo" anyway. Her parents would have found that even more offensive.

"I wouldn't think," Grace said cheerfully, "that among artists and bohemians any kind of formal religious affiliation was necessary."

"David isn't bohemian, Mother."

"But he's an artist. A poet. The highest form of artist."

Her father frowned but dropped the subject. As they sat there sipping another round of martinis, raucous voices rang out from across the lake. Children from one of the summer camps swimming at the public beach? No, probably a group from the Monadnock artists colony down the road. Adults who behaved like children, no, worse than children, as if being "artists" gave them free license to booze it up on the beach, splash around so crazily in the water no one else could swim. Maybe Greenwood, as David insisted, was more serious and staid. But the one time Sunny had driven over to the Monadnock Colony to take a look the place had scared her, she wasn't sure why. She had been told about the studios deep in the woods, lunches delivered in baskets to the door so that the creative work would remain uninterrupted. But there was an overall wildness that still bothered her whenever she thought about it.

"I'd better go up to change," Sunny said.

"Hurry down, darling," Grace said. "Willie Mae's making her sweet potato soufflé." She graciously accepted yet another martini from William.

Sunny looked in on Sarah, who in diaper and bib, was eating happily in the kitchen under Willie Mae's eye, then went up to her old room with its two narrow bunk beds. Here she had slept as a child, and here she and David had made love last week. It had been funny, awkward, wonderful, especially the night they were still wet from their midnight swim in the lake. "My sleek, glistening porpoise," David had said, "oh the slithery, thithery feel of you." For once they had wanted each other at the same time. For once David had not lain heavily on top of her, told her not to move, to let him catch his breath. Something new had come over David, something wonderful, free, ardent. Suddenly she wanted him terribly, ached for him. And knew instinctively when the phone rang that it was David.

"Sunny, your husband!" Grace called.

Sunny, who had already raced downstairs, took the receiver breathlessly.

"David? Oh, David! I was just thinking about you, dying for you."

"I'm dying for you too," David said.

They spoke for a few minutes and then she went upstairs and looked out the window. Suddenly the sky went gray and dry leaves skipped across the raft. Tomorrow was the first of September, the start of Labor Day weekend and the cocktail parties and the socializing that David hated. She shivered, remembering his voice on the phone, wanting him more than anything else. It was time to go home.

She had called him back immediately to tell him she was returning the next morning, but there was no answer. Probably

David had walked into town for a bit of supper at the local diner. He had said with a sad chuckle that he was getting very tired of canned tuna fish. It didn't matter. It would be more fun to surprise him. William frowned at her change of plans and worried about the Labor Day traffic. But Grace smiled understandingly and found it all terribly romantic. Early the next morning Sunny packed up herself and Sarah and drove hard all the way home, with the same breathless urgency as when David was her lover—better than her lover now. She ran into the house calling his name. "David? David!" Sarah trotted around searching for him too. There was no answer. No one was home. Strange. How sure she had been that David would know she was coming, just as he had known she was longing for him yesterday when he called. But she was being silly. It was a holiday weekend and therefore David would be hard at work in his office on campus precisely because everyone else was taking the day off. She decided not to call him there. She still wanted to keep her arrival a surprise.

Sarah seemed as happy to be home as she had been happy in New Hampshire. "Daddy? Daddy!"

"He'll be home very soon, darling," Sunny said. "Here, look at your books in the playpen while Mommy unpacks."

The house was a mess, bachelor quarters again, but she had expected that. She made the bed, cleared the dishes piled up in the sink, made herself some fresh coffee. The grounds in the pot were dried up and old. Evidently poor David had been going out to breakfast too. Well, why not call him at his office, give him the happy news that she and Sarah were home? The phone rang and rang, but he didn't answer. Which didn't mean anything. Often when David was hard at work, he didn't answer. It had been difficult to reach him by telephone from New Hampshire too, but he had so frequently called and written it didn't matter. Still, she was beginning to feel a foolish panic. It was strange to travel such a long way and then walk into an empty house, strange not to really know where David was. She always knew where David was. Even when she was in Paris, separated from him by an ocean, she'd always known where David was.

The phone rang, and Sunny went weak with relief. But it was Tillie. Wheedling, whiny Tillie.

"Hallo, Sahnny?"

"Oh, hi. David isn't around right now. I'll have him call you back later, all right?"

"Why should I bother him?" Tillie said. "So how are you? You're back from the country?"

"We're fine. Yes, we just got back."

"So how's the baby?"

"She's fine too. Not such a baby anymore. She's walking much better."

"Oy, such a head," Tillie said. "It's a long time I didn't see her."

"Look, David will call you back later," Sunny said, cutting her short.

As she spoke she had been looking around the kitchen for a note. But there was nothing there, nor on the desk in David's old study, nor on her card table in the bedroom. On impulse, Sunny looked into the bathroom medicine cabinet. David's shaving kit was gone. So also, she realized, after an inspection of the closet and their bureau, were his cord suit, his bathrobe, a pair of pajamas, some shirts.

She went back into the kitchen and called New Hampshire.

"Is anything wrong, darling?" Grace asked.

"No, no, I just wanted to tell you that we arrived safely."

"It's hard to hear you." Grace laughed above the cocktail chatter in the background. "Love to your darling husband."

"Yes, I'll tell him," Sunny said.

On impulse she dialed the Biltmore, where David stayed when in New York on account of its special academic rates. Mr. Harvey? Yes, he had been there earlier in the week, but had checked out. Checked out? What had he been doing in New York in the first place? And where was he now?

Out of habit, trying to create some order from the chaos forming in her mind, she went to take the mail out of the mailbox, which was crammed full. She stood outside on the sidewalk, leafing quicky through the letters as if they held some clue to David's whereabouts. But most of it was the usual junk.

Should she call Gertrude on the off chance that David had gone in to consult her about Gloria? No, there was no point in upsetting Gertrude if David wasn't there, though she was hardly the hysteric David claimed she was. Only a nice sentimental woman, who could never understand David's perpetual exasperation with her. Sunny leafed through the mail again. There was a letter from Gorham College, probably about alumnae dues or something, though they had addressed it to *Mr.* David Harvey by mistake. Or was it a mistake? She looked at the envelope uneasily. The typing wasn't quite right.

From inside the house the phone rang and she ran into the kitchen to answer it. But it was only some woman looking for David, probably to ask him to give a reading or a lecture for a ladies club. She wouldn't leave her name. David would be annoyed. He hated it when messages were vague. He was edgy about his mail too, and always felt that somehow it would choke the mailbox or get returned if he didn't fish it out in time. Then why had he left it to pile up?

Giving Sarah some more picture books to look at, Sunny opened the envelope from Gorham College. Inside was a short handwritten note. She scanned it quickly and then sat down and read it quite calmly over and over again. Suddenly, numbness gave way to pain. Her heart literally hurt. It was a thousand times worse than the night with Mary Jane. She put her head down on the kitchen table and started to cry. This is the way the world ends, this is the way the world ends . . . "Mommy sleeping?" Sarah said.

Behind her the screen door creaked open. She wiped her eyes quickly and looked around.

"Hi," Dick Reeves said. "I saw your car outside. Welcome home."

"Thanks. David isn't here. I'll tell him you stopped by."

"That's okay. Can you spare me a cup of coffee?"

She hesitated. "Sure."

If Dick noticed she'd been crying, he had the good grace not to remark on it. "Nancy's off on a picnic with the kids," he said, settling down cheerfully. "They won't be back until evening. I suppose I should be more like David and seize this opportunity to work, but I don't know. It feels too much like a holiday. Did you have a good time in New Hampshire?"

"Yes, it was wonderful."

"You look great," Dick said.

"I do?"

It was really Dick who looked great: lean, blond, boyish in his chino pants and pale blue shirt. A sweet man. Always smiling, always relaxed. What would it be like to have a sweet husband?

He picked up the copy of *Notes of a Native Son* that she had been reading before she left. "Did Baldwin send this to you?"

"No, the publisher sent it to David."

"But you knew him in Paris, right?"

"It was so long ago I've almost forgotten. Probably he has too."

"David missed you," Dick said. "He talked about you all the time."

"Did he?"

"You've made a terrific difference in his life, Sunny. I remember him from before."

"Want some more coffee?"

"Sure, why not?"

He stayed a while, talking of this and that, playfully teasing Sarah, helping Sunny stave off the moment when she would be alone in a desolate world. When he kissed her goodbye, it was a longer kiss than usual, and then he held her off by the shoulders and looked hard at her. "Take it easy, Sunny, okay?"

"Sure, Dick," Sunny said, trying to smile. Take it easy, take it easy. Wasn't that what David would say too?

David came home late the next morning, smiling cheerfully as he got out of the taxi. He waved to Sunny, who was sitting on the porch steps with Sarah in her lap, feeding her milk and cookies.

"Hello, Sunshine! You look beautiful!" David called as he paid off the driver. "You too, baby girl."

He put down his bag and took Sarah in his arms, looking at Sunny over her head. "Did you miss me?" he said, jouncing Sarah up and down.

"I missed you! I missed you!" Sarah cried.

"You did? I have a present for you in my suitcase."

"How did you know we were back?" Sunny said.

"Your mother told me. I called you in Hancock."

"Oh? From where?"

"Ed Gaskell's place in Croton."

"Really?"

"Yes, *really*," David said, laughing. "The galleys came in early and I was going to hole up with them at the Biltmore, but then Ed called and said to bring them to Croton. So I thought, why not? The city was a sweat box, and you were in New Hampshire, so . . ." He waited for her to answer, lifted a quizzical eyebrow, and put Sarah down on the porch. Sunny walked into the house, leaving Sarah to try to open David's bag. David followed her.

"I still haven't finished them yet, believe it or not. Anyway, I wanted you to look them over before I send them back. You can't believe how these idiotic printers set poetry. They justify the margins! Muriel Rukeyser used to attach a card to her manuscript saying, 'Please believe the punctuation.' I think I'll try that the next time."

"Some woman called who wouldn't leave her name," Sunny said. "That's the only message. Also, you'll want your mail." She handed him the envelope from Gorham.

David glanced at it without opening it. "You're being ridiculous."

"Am I?"

"Marjorie Stewart means nothing to me. I told you about her years ago. She's a painter I met at Greenwood. She's an old friend."

"Do most of your old friends write you letters beginning, 'Carissimo, I think I lost my earrings at the Biltmore but it was worth it.'?"

"Why did you open this letter, anyway?" David asked.

"It's from Gorham. I thought it was addressed to me."

"Horseshit."

"Like the friend part? Though even if that were true, the very idea that you could conceal such a 'friendship' from me all these years would make me sick. And I am."

"I haven't concealed anything!" David protested. "I ran into the woman in the Biltmore lobby. I hadn't even seen her for years. We got to talking. She told me she was broke. She needed to borrow some money."

"Borrow money?"

"A few bucks. It was nothing."

"You actually lent her money, when all you do is tell me how every penny comes out of your hide? When we can hardly afford to go to a restaurant or hire a babysitter? When I even have to accept handouts from my parents? Though come to think of it, why is there always money for you to stay at the Biltmore? And please don't say anything about the academic rates, or I'll scream."

"You'll scream anyway. You've probably already gone crying to Mother and Daddy with this crazy story."

"You're wrong. They admire you. I'd be too ashamed. I'm already ashamed enough over how stupidly I've believed you all these years. Believed there was nothing between you and Mary Jane. Believed that when you rushed into New York it was to see your aunt or your daughter or your publisher or whoever. Believed that whole fairy tale that we would always be open and honest, tell each other the truth no matter what it cost."

"I'm telling the truth."

"Not to mention the particularly sickening fact that in this case your 'friend,' your artistic and impoverished and no doubt supremely untalented 'friend,' teaches at Gorham, *my* school, *my* alma mater, so that the real shame is on *my* head, as usual, not on yours."

"What shame? What is this high school sarcasm? Angel, listen—"

"I'm not your angel. And I'm not your sunshine, either."

Sarah was still outside on the porch, trying to open the suitcase, crying because she wanted her present. David went out and gave it to her, a souvenir bracelet with "NEW YORK CITY" spelled out in dangling letters. He took out his galleys and, giving Sunny a bitter backward look, stalked off with the flapping sheaf of them. "I'll be at my office—" he called over his shoulder—"you know the number in case you want to make sure I'm there."

For the rest of the day, Sunny went through the motions of ordinary life though feeling, as she had said, quite literally sick at heart. She unpacked David's suitcase, put his dirty clothes in the hamper, played with Sarah in the yard. The supermarket was closed, but there was a stew she had cooked and put in the freezer for an emergency. Was this an emergency now? It felt like one. Over and over again she reached for the phone and stopped. She longed to hear David's voice, to be lied to, comforted any which way. And then the sick feeling would be back and she would put down the receiver. But what if David didn't come home for dinner? What if he stayed away another night? She couldn't bear another night of not knowing where he was.

David did come home for dinner, however. And, after one look at her face, sat at the table eating silently. Only Sarah chattered away, played with her new bracelet in her high chair, pretended to know the letters, "X, Z, Q!" Said, "Water lily . . . Puddleduck . . . Willie Mae." David looked at Sunny warily, and each time Sunny turned away. When Dick Reeves called later that night, it was astonishing to hear David talk in his normal voice, even laugh. David settled down in the living room, reading Frost, making notes. He said nothing more about his galleys, and wanting her to see them. After a while, he went to bed. She waited as long as she could, smoking cigarette after cigarette in the kitchen, and then went upstairs too, and undressed in the dark. David was snoring lightly, and when she got into bed reached out for her in his sleep. She stiffened and moved miserably to the edge of the mattress. But when she awoke in the morning, she was lying pressed against his back with her arms wrapped around him. A pair of teaspoons. She slipped out of bed at once.

David didn't speak at breakfast, except to Sarah, but came home again for dinner. Again she avoided his pleading eyes.

"Sunnoo, please," David said finally, after he had stood with her as she tucked Sarah into her crib for the night. "Won't you please come to your senses? You know I can't live without you. You know you're the most important thing that ever happened to me."

"Am I?"

"Marjorie Stewart means absolutely nothing to me. I told you. You're the only woman I've ever loved, ever will love, ever want to love. Can't you believe that?"

"I don't know what to believe anymore. That's the awful part of it. I just wish the earth would swallow me up."

"Look, her brother died. She needed money for funeral expenses. That's the whole story. Actually I think you'd even like her. She's a very motherly type."

"Another mother? Well, she doesn't sound motherly," Sunny said. "Maybe she looks motherly."

"If you want I'll write her and tell her never to get in touch with me again. I'll even show you the letter first. I'll let you mail it. All right? Will that satisfy you?"

"Since I never want to hear that creature's name again," Sunny said, "it would hardly give me any satisfaction to be a party to your continued correspondence."

"All right, so I won't write to her." David sighed. "But why are you so determined to destroy everything we have together?"

"Destroy what?" Sunny said. "Don't you see, I *want* to believe you've never been unfaithful. Because if you've been unfaithful, what are we all about?"

"I haven't been unfaithful," David said.

"And if we're not about anything, what's the point of us?"

"This is a nightmare," David said, gripping his head. "I feel utterly homeless, wifeless, childless."

"David," Sunny said imploringly. "Don't you see what I'm getting at?"

"No, leave me alone. Get the goddamn hell away from me."

For a moment she had a crazy desire to take him in her arms, console him for being married to her. But David, blowing his nose, trudged off to bed.

At noon the next day, however, David came back from his office, his face wreathed in smiles. "Sunnoo, listen! I've got great news for you. NYU wants me again for the spring term."

"Really?"

"Yes, really. Well, naturally the bastards didn't offer me anything permanent. But I swallowed my pride and accepted. How's that? We can spend the whole spring in New York, even the whole summer, if you really want to, though the city's a hell hole in the summer, and you'll probably be pleading to come back."

"I won't," Sunny said.

"All right, so you won't be pleading. But isn't it great?"

"No."

"What do you mean, no? I thought you were dying to get away from here."

"I am. I've been dying to get away for two long miserable years—"

"Come on, don't exaggerate."

"—twisting myself into a pretzel here to please you. Even feeling guilty because I don't type your manuscripts like 'the other women.' Crying myself to sleep at night out of loneliness. Wondering what ever became of Sunny Mansfield. And all of this when I've never had a single reason to be here except that you're here."

"So?"

"So I can't do it any more. I can't predicate my entire existence on yours any longer. I've been too frightened by what's happened."

"Nothing happened."

"David, it's no use. Sarah and I will go to New York with you in the spring, if you like, but we're going to stay there. If you like, I'll find a big enough apartment for all of us, and when the NYU term is over, you can commute from there to Rhinebeck."

"And if I don't like?"

"I guess that's it."

"Are you crazy? What are you doing to us? I love you."

"I love you too, David. But I can't turn back. I'll truly die if I do."

"You won't die. I'm the one who's dying, you foolish bitch."

"David, please."

"Oh, Christ," David said, weeping. "You're my girl. Why can't you just be my girl?"

3

"Splendissima, I'm off to the Century Club to have lunch.
See you later. Your mother called. I luv you. Bessie Cohen
said she'll meet you in the Park. I still luv you. *D."*

David must have stuck the note on the refrigerator door while
she was back in the little maid's room, working. Sunny laughed
and put it in her pocket—funny that she could never throw
away the smallest scrap written by David. She was glad that he
was in such a good mood today, though he usually was on the
days he spent in New York. Of course, being David, he continued to grumble about his weekly commute, and the rent on
this big West Side apartment, not to mention the growing demands of their social life. But his complaints weren't serious.
Sometimes she still trembled over the chance she had taken,
over how close they had come to breaking up in Rhinebeck.
But moving to New York really had changed everything. Even
David was forced to admit that all their troubles and misun-
derstandings had come from living in that awful place, and that
now that his wife was happy he was happy too. Naturally she
had never dreamed that one expression of his happiness would
be to join the Century Club (proposed by Ed Gaskell, seconded
by William Mansfield), much less spend so much of his time
there. But what did it matter? They were all happy now, not
least Sarah, whom it was suddenly time to pick up at nursery
school.
    She walked the few blocks over to the pretty Dutch townhouse
on West End Avenue, golden and dappled in the September
sun. Sarah was already sitting on a bench in the noisy anteroom,
bedraggled but smiling when Sunny came in. "Mama, Mama!
Look what I did!" Sarah cried excitedly, waving a sheaf of

fingerpaintings. Sunny hugged and kissed her—what a *big* girl she was getting to be—admired the paintings, and tucked Sarah's blouse into her plaid suspender skirt before she led her back out onto the quiet leafy street. They walked over to Riverside Drive through the solid, Jewish, residential neighborhood, where many other intellectuals had also settled, attracted by the huge old apartments at reasonable rents. She had loved it from the moment they moved in, even the tacky doormen, even the elderly "allrightniks," as David disparagingly called them, the bleached-blond grandmothers and white-haired gentlemen in sportscoats, who strolled along the Drive taking the air. One of the gentlemen bent to pinch Sarah's cheek and tell her she was a little doll. How wonderful Jews were with children. She had never realized it before they came back to New York.

They entered the park and Sarah ran ahead into the playground, where Bessie Cohen was already sitting on a bench, reading an issue of *Commentary* while the two little Cohen girls played in the sandbox. Bessie tucked a strand of her lank brown hair behind an ear, pushed her eyeglasses back up her nose with a forefinger and looked around.

"Bubbeleh!" she cried.

They kissed each other on the cheek. Sarah clambered happily into the sandbox and Sunny settled down on the bench. "Anything good in this issue?" "Rabbi Binder has a piece on Judaism and the intellectuals." "Really? I must read it." Or perhaps try to show it to David. For the moment, though, Sunny contentedly closed her eyes and raised her face to the sun, listening to the boats hooting on the Hudson, thinking, as always, how nice it was to sit here with Bessie instead of being trapped in Nancy Reeves's backyard. In fact, she had met Bessie on this very bench the first week they were back in New York, and immediately discovered that Bessie and her husband, Manny, a fund-raiser for a Jewish organization, knew David from way back—a discovery, alas, that had left David far from thrilled. She didn't care. She had needed a friend and Bessie was the best one she could ever have found.

"How lovely this is," Sunny said.

"Watching your kids destroy each other in a sandbox is lovely?"
Bessie said, getting up to redistribute pails and wipe noses.

Sunny laughed. "Oh, Bessie, you know what I mean. Or
maybe you don't. You can't imagine how awful it is to be stuck
in the country with a bunch of babified women, while the
husbands—"

"You think the situation here is so different?" Bessie said.

"Of course it is. Just to give you an example, there are so
many places to take Sarah that both of us enjoy—museums,
restaurants, movies . . ."

"Maybe you should write a piece about it," Bessie said.
"Bringing up a kid in the city. Why not? All the anti-New York
crap is just another form of anti-Semitism, anyway."

"Do you really think so?"

"Listen," Bessie said, laughing. "Do I have to preach to the
converted?"

Sunny laughed too, but a bit uneasily. Well, maybe Bessie
was right. She had been right about so many things. Zabar's,
the part-time cleaning lady, Rabbi Binder for the formal in-
struction in Judaism. It was Bessie, too, who had stood by her
during the conversion, countered her arguments about Abraham
and Isaac—"I mean, Bessie, what kind of God would make a
test of faith the murder of one's child?" "The kid was never
sacrificed. We call it the *binding* of Isaac"—all matters that
David refused to discuss, though really she had been doing it
for his mother, and caused Natalia to hoot with derisive laughter
whenever they were raised. Above all, it was Bessie who had
assured her that in the end it was all just a matter of "being
welcomed to the fold, bubbeleh"—easy to believe in New York.
Still, now that it was all over, could she honestly say she felt
Jewish? David had immediately forgotten the whole thing. And
besides, the conversion would not be complete until Sunny and
David were remarried in a Jewish ceremony—which coinci-
dentally also meant his getting a Jewish divorce from Gertrude.
Rabbi Binder, for all his liberalism, had stated firmly that it was
necessary, and Tillie would never be finally mollified until it
was done. But when she mentioned it to David, he hit the roof,
said to leave him out of it.

"What's the matter, kid?" Bessie asked. "Is he still giving you a hard time?"

"I'm afraid to bring it up again."

"Maybe it's not the Jewish wedding that's bothering him," Bessie said, laughing. "Maybe he just doesn't want to get a Jewish divorce from Gertrude."

Sunny looked at Bessie blankly, momentarily fazed by Bessie's thick eyeglasses.

"I'm only kidding, doll. Don't worry. He'll come around. Doesn't he always?"

It was true. She thought of how much he had already acquiesced in, a lot of it for her sake. But this was different, this went to the very heart of his convictions.

"I know," Bessie said. "It's hard for you. First you had to give up Jesus, and now—"

"Well, actually," Sunny said, "the point is that David has always been much more attracted to Jesus than I was."

"He thinks they're two only children."

Sunny glanced at Bessie to see if she was kidding again, and then looked at her watch.

"Oh, my God, I almost forgot. We're going to a cocktail party. I'd better get going."

"*Another* party?" Bessie said.

"Do you think we go to too many? They're just so different from the ones at Cole. You can't believe all those dreary conversations over all that dreary boeuf bourguignon—"

"What are you apologizing to *me* for?" Bessie said. "Go ahead, enjoy. I'll call you tomorrow."

As a special treat, and to make up for tearing her away from the sandbox, Sunny took Sarah over to Irving's candy store on Broadway for an egg cream, though it was very near Sarah's dinner. Some of Irving's other young customers were lined up on stools, ordering water.

"I'm not giving you this soda until you tell me how old you are," Irving said to Sarah.

"I am three," Sarah said, holding up three fingers.

"Okay," Irving said. "You're on." Next to his cash register was a display of Jewish New Year's cards. They were prominently displayed in Levy's stationery store too, and all over the neighborhood. The sight of them suddenly made her sad. Away from Bessie Cohen she could never really believe she had been welcomed to the fold.

David was already home when they got upstairs, working in his study. He swiveled around in his typing chair, and Sarah ran excitedly into his arms. "What did you do in school today?" David asked, planting her on his lap.

"We fingerpainted and we cutted and we pasted."

"Good," David said, putting her down again. "You'll make a first rate academic."

Sarah ran happily off to her room to color.

"Well," David said, turning back to his typewriter, "I'd better finish this review of *Homage to Mistress Bradstreet* before I go back to Rhinebeck. The *New Republic* wants it last week. What time are we having dinner?"

Sunny hesitated, looking at David's booklined walls, and then out at the shining river. "There's that party at Ed Gaskell's."

"Oh, Christ. I forgot. Well, I'll just have to call him and say—okay, okay, don't sulk. I'll work when we get back. But just out of curiosity, sweetheart, what would happen if you missed a literary party?"

"David, he's your publisher."

"You don't care whose publisher it is."

"Well I love the conversation, the intellectual excitement."

"And there's not enough intellectual excitement for you at home?"

Sunny laughed. "You're twisting my words. Why can't you just admit that we're all happy? Look how Sarah's thriving. Bessie Cohen says maybe I should write a piece about it, the joys of bring up a child in the city—as opposed to the country, I mean. Maybe I could call it the 'City Mouse,' or something like that."

"Hey, Sunnoo," David said, smiling. "Remember that I still have to live in the 'country.' "

"I didn't mean it to be an exposé or anything like that."

"Anyway, what does Mrs. Bessie know about the joys of growing up in New York? She spent her entire youth in her father's delicatessen in Brooklyn, making potato salad. I can't understand the magical effect this woman has on you. I thought you hated Manny's politics."

"I do. I hate that kind of virulent anti-communism, or virulent anti-anything. But Bessie's so nice and she—"

"Bessie thinks the same way as her husband, believe me, Sunnoo. I know all about Bessie Cohen's famous niceness. I grew up among 'nice' women like that, and they can eat you up alive if you're not careful." David sighed and picked up his review. It was typed on yellow paper and very much crossed out. "Well, let me work for a little while. It's an exciting book. Maybe Berryman's best."

He put in another yellow sheet and immediately began to type. She stood smiling at him for a moment, thinking how generous he was being to a fellow poet, especially to a fellow poet he often called "the meshuganah." And most especially since David's own *Selected Poems* had received such terrible reviews. But David had appeared almost to welcome the attacks, had seemed more comfortable with them than with the praise for *Ancestors,* as if they confirmed his view of himself as one man against many.

She kissed a now totally absorbed David on the top of his head, and went into the bedroom, where she opened the closet and tried to decide what to wear that evening. She finally settled on the black with pearls, though she had recently worn it twice already. But she really couldn't let her mother buy her any more clothes when they went shopping together, even if Grace insisted it was her pleasure. She had let her mother buy too many things already, though David never questioned where they came from any more than he had the baby clothes. Still, it was a problem. Clothes had never mattered at Cole, where the women made a point of honor in looking like something the cat dragged in. But in New York the wives of intellectuals dressed well. Though why was she thinking of herself as the *wife* of an intellectual, she wondered. Maybe because she didn't think of herself as an intellectual. Maybe because in the circles in which she and David moved, very few novelists were considered intellectuals, only providers of raw material for deeper minds to analyze.

She finished dressing and went back to the maid's room to look at her manuscript one more time before the sitter came. The room was dark and cramped, its only view the brick wall across the court. But at least it was her own, and a big step up from a rickety card table in a bedroom. She turned over the last pages she had written that morning. No, it just wasn't jelling. Somehow lately the subject of young love didn't seem *important* enough to write about. Perhaps she could work in some of the Paris material from that old story? She wished that Amanda were still at Job and Job, an editor whose opinion she could rely on. But Amanda, occupied with her two children, was now working at home as an occasional free lance—oddly Amanda didn't mind this at all—and Tommy Job, not the brightest man in the world but heir to the company, was technically her editor. Maybe she should give up writing for a while and look for a job, as she had first intended. In fact, she had made one stab at it by calling Cyrilly Abels at *Mademoiselle*, where she had been a college guest editor the summer of her senior year at Gorham. But, as Cyrilly had delicately explained, the *Mademoiselle* readership was well under thirty and Sunny was already twenty-eight. Cyrilly had laughed politely when she said it. Still, after all these years of David telling her how young she was, it had come as a shock to be told she was too old. But Cyrilly did say she would be glad to look at anything Sunny wrote that she thought might be suitable for the magazine. Should she suggest the "City Mouse" piece? It was a possibility, though maybe not quite as bright a one as when she and Bessie had first discussed it.

The doorbell rang and she went to let in the sitter, a pretty Barnard undergraduate—the Barnard sitters had also been Bessie's suggestion. Sarah raced in and flung her arms around Susan, just as she had once flung her arms around Jenny Abruzzi. Poor Jenny had wept bitterly when the Harvey family left

Rhinebeck, and for some time afterwards had written Sunny letters so illiterate that David said she ought to be a critic. But all of that was now history. Even the Reeveses no longer suggested staying with them for a weekend. The one time they had, it was a disaster, David somehow embarrassed to have them around, Nancy making a lot of provincial cracks about how awful it must be for children to grow up in New York, though Sarah was clearly blooming (was Bessie right about the anti-Semitism?), Dick trying to get Sunny into a corner and talk to her earnestly. But David rented the Reeveses little top floor apartment the two nights he spent at Rhinebeck and so she had been nice to them. She was glad, though, that they had never suggested another weekend.

"David, Susan's here, the sitter's here!" she called. In a few moments, David emerged, all spruced up and very handsome in his new navy blue blazer and striped rep tie. She threw her arms around him.

"Hey, what's this?" David said, laughing.

"I'm just glad to see you."

She put her arm through his and posed them head to head in front of the hall mirror: she in her black with the pearls, David with a touch of gray at his temples. "Oh, what a handsome couple we are, we are," Sunny said, her heart lifting as it always did these days whenever she went out with David.

Everybody was there—"the whole *mishpocha*," Bessie would have said—Jimmy Starrett's new book of essays more the pretext than the real reason for the party. They milled about in the beautiful twin drawing rooms of Ed's East Side townhouse, sampling the elegant hors d'oeuvres, lifting drinks from the trays circulated by the waiters, greeting each other, hugging, kissing. But no, *mishpocha* wasn't really the word. Often as she had seen them by now they weren't family but stars, each of them as striking as a book jacket photograph. Handsome Saul Bellow, in from Chicago. Ralph Ellison, very much the man of distinction since the amazing success of *Invisible Man*. Curly-haired Norman Mailer, the latest darling of the intellectuals—even David was fascinated by him—though it was hard to figure out why, since despite the fake Texas drawl and the palaver about sex and drugs, he seemed to be a quite ordinary nice Jewish boy, like Howard, the garment manufacturer. She waved to Elijah Rose, still so beautiful and charismatic she had spotted him immediately in the crowd. It was a shame that Elijah and David had drifted apart over the years, but it wasn't David's fault. Elijah seemed to disapprove of David these days. She also ran into Violet Beransky, who was just back from Paris and recently divorced. Serge, it turned out to Violet's horrified astonishment, had been having his own secret love affair all along, with a Romanoff princess to whom he was now married. How did people get involved in such Byzantine betrayals? She and Violet agreed to have lunch, though even after all this time Violet still appeared dubious about Sunny's marriage to David. And then there was Gertrude, of all people, David's ex-wife, chubby, friendly, and distinctly out of place.

On her way to get another drink, Sunny sidestepped the two editors of *Partisan Review*, little William Phillips and gross Philip Rahv, who never paid attention to her anyway, except for the times Rahv tried to pinch her in the backside, and also steered clear of Hannah Arendt, who stood smiling arrogantly. Sunny had told Bessie that at Cole only the men counted, which was true. Nevertheless, the women most highly regarded in New York literary circles always seemed to be women like Arendt: ugly, opinionated, hostile to other women. Why did all the male intellectuals, David included, admire them so enormously? ("That's who they admire," Bessie had said, laughing. "Who they screw is another story.") Well, maybe. But didn't that raise more questions than it answered? She took a drink from a passing waiter, and to her surprise bumped into Hymie Shapiro, David's old accountant, and his wife, Lila, both of them beaming away. "Ed's just taken my novel," Hymie said proudly, light bouncing happily off his eyeglasses. Amazing. David had never thought anything of that book.

Where was David, anyway? Oh, yes, over there, surrounded

by several admiring females. She looked at him with an amused sense of proprietorship. She wasn't jealous. The escapade with that dreadful, untalented painter was as much past history as Rhinebeck. No, not even an escapade. "Just someone to talk to," as David had explained many times, because Sunny had been so miserable he could hardly approach her. When the party petered out, she gaily plucked David from his admirers and persuaded him to join some others who were going on to dinner at La Rochefoucauld, including Jimmy Starrett and his latest wife. David worked so hard it was important for him to relax occasionally. All through the meal in the fancy French restaurant she looked at David, bursting with pride over his wit, his fluency, the touch of gray at his temples, his Semitic good looks, the fact that everyone seemed to defer to him. It was almost like that first night with Amanda and Milo, except that much as she had desired David then, she desired him even more tonight. It was delicious to anticipate the moment when they would come home alone.

As David paid off the sitter and took her downstairs to find her a taxi, Sunny checked on Sarah, who was safely asleep with her crumpled finger paintings. She went into the living room and made herself another drink, just a little one and only because she didn't want the party high to end. "How handsome you look," Sunny said, when David came back. He raised a dubious eyebrow and went into the bedroom. After a moment she followed him. David was already undressing. David always took off his good clothes as soon as they came home from anywhere. She wished he wouldn't. It always put a damper on the evening.

She sat down on the bed beside him anyway, kissed his ear, and the tender place below it, where his hair met his collar. David twisted his neck a little, as if he were being buzzed by an insect.

"God, I want you," Sunny said.

"Did you know Ed was taking Hymie's book?"

"Not until tonight. Did you? Does it matter?" She pressed her mouth against his, trying to open his lips with her tongue.

David pushed her away gently. "Ed wanted to surprise me. Big deal. But why didn't Hymie tell me himself? Well, I suppose he'll come to me when he needs a blurb."

He slid off his trousers and stood up in his shirt and shorts and socks. She still wanted him though he did not look nearly as appealing as at the party. She began to undress too, slowly, peeling down to her black lacy bra and garter belt and sheer black stockings. All during dinner, she had imagined David carrying her off to bed like this, stripping away the bra, the garter belt, the sheer black stockings, touching, licking, kissing every part of her bare skin. But David had already gone off to the bathroom in his baggy pajamas. When he came back he smelled toothpasty.

"Aren't you coming to bed?" David said, lying against the pillows, propping his head up behind with linked fingers.

She stripped quickly and slipped in beside him, naked.

"I mean, after all these years," David said. "And after all the help I gave him with that manuscript . . . No, don't, not yet . . . By the way, what were you and Gertrude chatting about so cozily?"

"Nothing," Sunny said. "She was just being friendly." Friendly enough to approach about a Jewish divorce? "I didn't expect to see her there."

"Now that she has that low-level administrative job with the B'Nai B'Rith, she thinks she's a big muck-a-muck. I wonder how the hell she got Ed to invite her."

"I think Hymie and Lila brought her along." She snuggled closer and reached between David's legs. He was still soft, flaccid. She bent over him.

"Sweetie, I'm tired," David said. "I have to get up early and finish that review tomorrow. Don't you want to work tomorrow too?"

"Isn't it enough just to be happy?" Sunny said, lifting her head.

"No writer's happy unless he's working," David said. "What's the matter? Isn't it going well?"

"It's fine. It's just going very, very slowly."

"Why don't you show it to me if you're having trouble?"

"I don't want you to read it. It's just going slowly."

"I'm a pretty good critic, you know, even if Hymie Shapiro doesn't think so."

"I know that, darling. But critic's such a big word. It raises the ante. Sometimes I wonder if the ante isn't going up too much all around."

"What's that supposed to mean?"

"Nothing." Sunny laughed and cuddled closer. "It means that the last time I was in Saks with my mother, I saw a gorgeous mink hat, but it was too expensive."

"A writer's wife doesn't need a gorgeous mink hat," David said.

Did a writer? David said it was chilly and advised her to put on a nightgown. In the middle of the night it was up around her neck, and David was on top of her, panting with passion, and telling her not to move so much.

4

The long Sunday afternoon was almost at an end and with it Tillie's and Izzy's March visit—they had narrowed it down to one Sunday a month. It had begun badly. Tillie and Izzy had managed to arrive in the service elevator, surrounded by garbage cans, which enraged David, though they had done it before. Natalia, whom he had urged to come, had begged off on account of overwork, though she was never too overworked to come to one of their parties, and Gloria, whom he wanted his parents to see, and who had broken date after date finally showed up two hours late, when Sunny's carefully prepared lunch had long gone cold. "How can she do this me?" David said, though it was poor Sarah who cried out of disappointment. Now they all sat in the living room while Sarah, the afternoon's entertainment, pranced about singing a song she had learned in nursery school. "Who stole the cookie from the cookie jar? *I* stole the cookie from the cookie jar." Izzy clapped his hands in rhythm and Tillie smiled stonily. Against the other wall Gloria sat on an ottoman like a cornered animal, her hair wild, her prune eyes, so like David's, squeezing shut every time David spoke to her.

"Listen, Gloria, I asked you a question. Why can't you answer me?"

Silence.

"Why Bennington, for Christssake? With all the great universities in this country, why Bennington?"

"I told you. I want to be a dance major."

"What the hell kind of major is that?"

"The right kind of major if you want to be a dancer."

"Terrific. And what are you going to do for your Ph.D.? Choreograph your dissertation?"

"You never want me to do what I want to do."

"I want you to use your mind, provided you still have one. All this anti-intellectual crap is just a way of spitting in my face, and you know it."

Gloria burst into tears and ran out of the room. Sarah, stopping in mid-phrase, followed her.

Sunny looked at the fancy layer cake sitting in the middle of the coffee table—David's mother always expected a fancy cake on their Sunday visits—thought of offering everyone another piece, glanced at David, and changed her mind.

"Well, what are you all looking at me like that for?" David said. "I'm the source of all her misery. She's been trained by her mother since birth to hate me and there's nothing I can do about it."

"Gertrude calls me all the time on the telephone," Tillie said. " 'How are you, Mama?' she says."

"You know, David," Izzy began tentatively, "sometimes with a young girl—"

"Don't *you* start to tell me how to raise children," David said.

"Gertrude says she wouldn't mind about a divorce," Tillie said. " 'Mama,' she says, 'whatever David wants, whatever makes you happy.' "

"Enough about that divorce. That's all I ever hear about around here. Why doesn't anybody think about what makes *me* happy for a change?" David said.

Sunny excused herself and went into Sarah's room. Gloria was sitting hunched up in Sarah's rocker, holding Sarah's teddy bear. Sarah was smoothing Gloria's black unruly hair. Someday Gloria would be a great beauty, Sunny was sure, though no one believed it yet, least of all David.

"They'll be leaving soon," Sunny said. "Don't you want to come out and say goodbye?"

"Why should I? Everything I do is wrong, anyhow. I hate that fucking bastard."

"Oh, Gloria, he doesn't hate *you*."

"Yes, he does."

"No, he loves you. He worries about you, that's all."

"It's a shitty way of loving people, making them feel guilty all the time."

"Gloria, Gloria, help me do my puzzle," Sarah said, dumping the pieces on the floor at her feet. Gloria crouched down beside her and began to sort them out carefully. The last of the March sun flared up and caught her full in the face. She looked so vulnerable, so defenseless, it broke Sunny's heart. Why didn't David ever notice that vulnerable look? Or was it that look that drove him crazy?

"Okay, so I'm the heavy again," David said as they were dressing to go out, this time to a buffet dinner up near Columbia. "The villain in all directions."

"Darling, that's not the point."

"My feelings don't count for anything anymore?"

"Of course, they do, David, but—"

"I don't want to talk about it," David said.

They finished getting ready for the party, each one nursing private grievances, and tacitly put them aside when the taxi dropped them off at the Claremont Avenue address of Howard Fisher, a professor of comparative literature at Columbia, and something of a West Side bon vivant. As usual, once inside the door, they automatically went their separate ways, easy in that big apartment which, like their own, had long dark corridors leading to back bedrooms and a general air of being hastily furnished. She did notice, however, that David, frowning, avoided the corner of the living room where Edward Maxwell was having a discussion with a few colleagues in the English department. She avoided that corner, too, not because she disliked Edward— on the contrary, she found him courtly and charming—but because it would merely set David off to see her there. He was still persuaded that Maxwell alone was keeping him off the Columbia faculty. In another corner, Norman Podhoretz and his overeager wife, Midge, were talking to Lionel and Diana Trilling. Nearby, Sylvia Maxwell, Edward's wife, was holding court as usual, a tall, absurdly pretentious woman, wearing a black velvet picture hat that flapped about her head as she made a series of emphatic pronouncements to a small group of listeners. As far as Sunny knew, Sylvia had never written anything but a few feeble essays. So it was hard to know why anyone took her seriously, but people did. The *Times* invariably printed her letters, most of them denouncing someone's Stalinoid tendencies, and at a recent political conference where Sylvia made an anti-Communist speech in front of a banner that said, "One World or None," only Sunny laughed to see Sylvia Maxwell planted firmly under "None." No, no matter what Bessie said about the screwing, Sunny still couldn't understand why the women who commanded respect in intellectual circles had to be so dreadfully unappealing. In line with which, there was Natalia with her own small circle. She looked very happy, in her fashion, showing many long yellow teeth in laughter, and waving her cigarette holder here and there. Her impending appointment to the history department of NYU appeared to have made her even more self-confident than usual. Not a big appointment but at least a permanent one. Ironically, David had helped her get it, just as he had helped her put her book on Russian history into decent English and found a small publisher for her. Was he rueful that NYU had never offered him anything permanent for himself? If so, he never mentioned it.

Natalie had begun to wave the cigarette holder at Sunny, indicating that Sunny should go over and join her husband, Fritz Kirschenbaum, who sat on a sofa by himself. Sunny ignored the signal. She liked Fritz well enough, who was perfectly pleasant on those rare occasions when she saw him, but not Natalia's habit of linking her and Fritz together, as if they were members of the same sub-species, just as at Cole she had been sent to sit with the wives. Who else was there? The usual Upper West Side crowd. Both Irvings, Howe the socialist, Kristol the now English-style conservative. (Ever since they had come back from London the Kristols constantly used words like "flat" and "lorry.") Also, nice Richard Hofstadter who was doing one of his famous Lou Holtz imitations for Bessie and Manny Cohen, and the host, short, bald Howard Fisher. Bessie comfortably put her arm around Sunny's waist. They hadn't seen each other much lately. It was too cold for the sandbox, the husbands didn't get along. But they still spoke on the phone and Bessie was still relaying messages from Rabbi Binder. Remembering the unpleasantness of the afternoon, Sunny looked for David— was he still in a black mood?—and found him talking to still another female admirer. The sight was hardly surprising. Once she had been literally pushed against the wall by a beautiful woman determined to get at him. But beautiful women or talented women never worried her. What worried her was the type David had singled out for his attention now, bending his head intently, almost solicitously. A dark, plain little thing with a plaintive expression, and clearly a spiritual twin of that horror who had inadvertently almost broken up her marriage. There seemed to be more and more of such types around him these days. "Pathetic professionals," she called them in her own mind when David told her their sad stories: poets manqués, or un-published fiction writers, or unexhibited painters, always fail-ures, always on the fringes of the arts. Tonight Natalia seemed to be nodding approval in the near distance.

"So I came to Chicaga for my brother's daughter's wedding . . . I open de suitcase and de jacket is, de west is, de pants ain't . . . "

"Hi, cutie," Bessie said to Sunny when the joke was finished and Dick Hofstadter was professorially beaming at their laughter, "welcome to the Kibbutz. I forgot to ask you this morning, what are you and David doing for Pesach?"

"Passover?" Sunny said. "I don't know."

"So come to my seder, the second night if you can't make the first."

"Really? I'd love it. I'll ask David. I've never been to a real seder. I mean, David's father is the dearest man in the world, but he's an old Socialist and David—"

"David—" Bessie began, breaking off as David approached with a continental-looking gentleman.

"—oh, darling, here you are. Bessie's just asked us to—"

"May I present Arturo Milano," David said formally.

"*Piacere, signora.*"

He bent over to kiss her hand. With a "*Ciao,* bubbeleh," Bessie Cohen drifted away and so after a dirty look in Bessie's direction, did David. The name Arturo Milano suddenly rang a bell. David's Italian publisher.

"You did such a beautiful job with *Ancestors,*" Sunny said.

"A beautiful book. You must be very proud to have such a distinguished husband."

"I am."

"Though it's not easy to be married to a writer, eh?"

Sunny laughed. "He is, too."

"Ah, you write a little? You were his student?"

"No, I was never David's student," Sunny said. "Actually, my first novel was written before—"

"*Scusi, bella signora,* my English is very poor."

There was a diversion in another part of the room. She looked around and heard Edward Maxwell very clearly say, "I don't like you, David. I never have." David was smiling, triumphantly defiant, the way he had smiled over the unfavorable reviews of *Selected Poems.* People moved in quickly to separate them, as if there were about to be physical violence, which in these circumstances was ridiculous. Nevertheless, some kind of violence was in the air. "Dinner!" Howard Fisher suddenly called. "Dinner!"—fortunately diverting them all to the dining room. They clustered around the buffet table exclaiming at how wonderful everything looked. Howard Fisher stood by proudly. Sunny looked into the big casserole. It was only that tired old academic standby, boeuf bourguinon. "Cheer up," Bessie said wryly. "This time a guy made it."

"Arturo was very smitten with you," David said in the taxi going home.

"Really? He seemed to think I was your student."

"That's because you look so ridiculously young," David said. "We ought to give him a party while he's here."

"Must we?" It wasn't giving the cocktail party she minded, which would certainly be easier than a big sit-down dinner, but David's old way of presenting it as an obligation rather than a pleasure.

"Sweetie, he's my Italian publisher—though he's still hedging about *Selected Poems*, the bastard. You don't need to do anything elaborate. Just invite all the Irvings and the Normans, and Dwight, maybe Delmore, that son of a bitch—and Natalia, of course."

"Of course," Sunny said. They always invited Natalia anyway, Sunny wondering whom Natalia would manage to antagonize this time. But if well-known literary people were around, Natalia was curiously subdued, even coquettish, amazing since they were the same people she scorned and reviled behind their backs. "By the way, who was the woman who was smitten with *you?*"

"Which woman?"

"The dark little pitiful one."

"You know, Sunnoo, you ought to have more compassion for women who . . ." David sighed and gave it up. "Christ, what a day." She tensed and looked at him sideways, assuming that he was about to talk of Edward Maxwell, and the injustice of being excluded from Columbia, the triumph of having finally forced a crack in Maxwell's polished marble facade. But for the moment he seemed to have forgotten Maxwell completely. "That powwow with Gloria absolutely drained me. Tomorrow I'm going to call Gertrude and give her a piece of my mind."

"It's not Gertrude's fault."

"Are you on her side now?"

"I'm not on anybody's side, darling. I just think you take Gloria too seriously, that's all. It's hard for a girl that age to be taken so seriously. Anyway, I've always found Gertrude very reasonable."

"I'm sure."

"Well, she's been pretty decent about everything, hasn't she?" Sunny hesitated. "Even about the divorce. Not that she'd really have to be involved. I gather a group of rabbis just present this parchment to her and—"

"Listen, Sunny, for the last time, nobody's going to present Gertrude with anything, so get it out of your head. I will not have her served with divorce papers by some derbied messenger with wings on his shoes like a character out of a Malamud story."

"We can't be married otherwise."

"I thought we were already married, or have you forgotten?"

"It was only a civil ceremony."

"Only?"

"I meant it was private. I mean it was lovely, but just us and the attaché and that clerk from the hotel."

How frightened she had been the night before, trying to screw up her courage to write David the letter calling it off. And how he had laughed when she gave it to him, trembling. And then the next morning all her fears had vanished and the whole world was perfect. Could it be that David, never mind his convictions, was frightened now? She remembered an old conversation with Bessie.

"Sunny, sometimes I think you have the soul of a chameleon. In Paris you dreamed in French. In New York you're more Jewish than Chaim Weizmann. For what it's worth, Natalia thinks the whole idea of a Jewish wedding is insane. Why don't you call her sometimes when I'm away? An evening with Natalia would be a lot more worthwhile than being instructed in *yiddishkeit* by your pal Bessie Cohen."

"Bessie invited us to her seder," Sunny said.

"Absolutely not."

"She said the second night if we couldn't make the first."

"Absolutely not."

She stared straight ahead, and David touched her arm in a surprisingly placating gesture. "Sweetie, I need to spend the spring break at Cole, catch my breath, get a leg up on the epic poem, do something about that anthology. You understand, don't you?"

"I see . . . Well, would you like Sarah and me to come up

for a few days? Jenny could sit for us. I know Sarah would love that."

"Jenny won't be there during the holidays," David said. "Listen, why not just go to Bessie's seder by yourself?"

"Oh, no, I couldn't," Sunny said. "I'd feel so out of place alone. I mean it's not a cocktail party, after all. It's a family occasion, a Jewish—"

"Sunny, don't start with all that crap again."

"David," Sunny said, taking a deep breath. "Do you not want a Jewish wedding, or do you not want to get a Jewish divorce from Gertrude?"

David said nothing. The taxi stopped in front of their building. She waited, whipped by the March wind as David paid off the driver and the doorman held the door open. "Between you and my mother—" David began. He rang for the elevator and then looked at her long and hard. "Okay, tell Gertrude I'll trade her in for a camel."

"Oh, David, do you really mean it? Rabbi Binder said we could be married between Passover and Shevuoth."

"Spare me Shevuoth," David said. "Just keep it small, that's all I ask. They tricked me out in a monkey suit the first time and I swore it would never happen to me again. No Cohens, no professional Jews."

"All right."

"You may as well ask Natalia."

"Natalia?"

"She might be amused."

Natalia was amused all right. She came in laughing heartily and since there were no literary celebrities around to suppress her, laughed right through the ceremony. Though she had laughed hardest when Tillie and Izzy arrived via the service elevator as usual, along with the garbage cans. "Why the hell can't you two come in the front door like normal people?" David cried. The two of them looked at him, frightened, while Natalia hooted. It was too bad that Fritz was away on business since, in family situations at least, he could sometimes tone Natalia down. But now she sat on the sofa in a state of hilarity, all done up in her shawls and combs, with a glum David standing to one side of her and Sunny's parents sitting on the other end, polite and stiffly smiling and edging away. It was all very hard for Grace and William, though they did not show it and no one seemed to take their possible discomfort into account. The conversion had been offstage, and therefore more easily acceptable. ("They're just relieved you haven't turned Catholic," David had said.) But actually to see their daughter married by a *rabbi*, go through this pagan rite. . . . And yet Sunny had wanted her mother at this wedding, had never gotten over missing her the first time. Without being told, Grace understood. She had taken Sunny to Bergdorf's for the white silk tailored suit, the small hat with the white veil, a pink organdy dress for Sarah. And she and William had insisted on providing the champagne, the wedding cake, the flowers. (There had been no question of David remembering flowers this time.) Poor Sarah, also edging away from Natalia, scratched uncomfortably at the back of her neck where the organdy rubbed it and dropped her little nosegay so often Grace offered to hold it for her. Sarah leaned against Grace's knees for solace, looking around for Gloria. But Gloria had refused to come to the ceremony, which enraged David further, though given the choice, he wouldn't have come either.

Rabbi Binder called them politely to order, giving William and Izzy the handles of the portable wedding canopy to hold. It was strange to see William in a yarmulke, even stranger to see David in one. Izzy had merely stuck his old gray fedora on his head. As he had promised, Rabbi Binder made the ceremony short and sweet, so short that Sunny didn't realize it was over until she saw David crushing the glass underfoot. She waited for him to kiss her. But he kept fiercely grinding the glass with his heel until Natalia came up and thrust her arm through his. "Dushinka," she heard Natalia say. For a moment she wondered if he would kiss Natalia by mistake this time too.

"*Mazel tov!*" Izzy cried. Grace, and then William, followed suit almost inaudibly. Shaking hands all around, Rabbi Binder folded and put away the canopy in his suitcase. At a signal from Sunny, the cleaning lady emerged from the kitchen with the champagne, then followed with the elegant white frosted fruit-cake. Grace had offered them Willie Mae for the occasion too, but David had put his foot down.

William, dignified and serious in his role as father of the bride, proposed a toast to the happy couple. "*L'chaim!*" Izzy said loudly before he had quite finished, upending his glass. "Where are the birthday candles?" Sarah cried, and had to be comforted by Sunny. "Well, we missed our children's wedding the first time," Grace remarked to Tillie, who immediately turned to stone, corsage and all. "Isn't it lovely to be here now?" Izzy immediately pulled the tattered review of *Ancestors* out of his wallet. "Maybe you never saw this?" "Oh, I'm a great admirer of David's work. I think your son is brilliant."

Sunny stood by, holding Sarah tightly by the hand while David glowered from across the room. Natalia had kept her arm through his. The only other person he had spoken a polite word to was Grace, not as her son-in-law—he seemed too old to be her son-in-law—but as if he and Grace were Sunny's sane parents. She wished she had been allowed to invite the Cohens, have Bessie at her side, making wisecracks, easing the tension between all these warring factions. She wished that Bessie hadn't waved away her nervous apologies so understandingly.

"Will you come and swim in my lake this summer?" Grace asked Sarah, whom she had given a sip of champagne as a consolation for the lack of candles.

"Actually, Mother," Sunny said, "we're going up to Wellfleet."

"Wellfleet?"

"It's on the Cape, near Provincetown. A lot of writers go there. Amanda says it's beautiful."

"Oh, yes, do you see much of Amanda these days?"

"No, just at an occasional lunch. She has these two children."

"I know. And Mary Jane? I was hoping to find her here today."

"I told you. We're out of touch."

"And you were such good friends," Grace said, pouring herself another glass of champagne.

Rabbi Binder asked Natalia if she would give a speech at his synagogue. He had already asked David, who refused. Natalia laughed heartily, glancing around at David. "Believe me, Rabbi, you don't want a speech from me. You wouldn't like what I'd say."

"Well, that would make it more interesting, wouldn't it?"

"What? That I have only contempt for your temples and your synagogues? That they're the enemy of reason? The real oppressors of Jews?" She turned to Grace. "You're surprised? You thought all Jews wrapped themselves in prayer shawls, waiting for the Messiah to appear?"

"Not at all," Grace said.

"You're too 'liberal' for that?"

"Yes, I suppose so."

"Liberal what? Republicans?"

"Well, yes."

"A contradiction in terms, my dear. Americans are political idiots."

"Natalia, let's first talk about Debs—" Izzy began, but Natalia waved at him to be quiet.

"I can hardly agree with you that Americans are idiots, political or otherwise," William said with an icy smile, appearing at Grace's elbow.

"But you voted for Eisenhower?"

"Indeed I did. Twice."

"You see?" Natalia laughed uproariously.

"I think Eisenhower has had a very good effect on this country," Grace said, reaching for more champagne.

"And I think you must be drunk," Natalia said.

Rabbi Binder stood listening intently, as if he were privy to a brilliant intellectual discussion. Sunny looked to David, but he had retreated miserably to a corner and was glaring at his feet.

William suggested to Grace that it was time to go. Looking at his watch, Rabbi Binder offered Natalia a lift, still eager to pursue the matter of the speech. Tillie and Izzy set off for the subway to the Bronx.

"Please, Mama, may I take my dress off now?" Sarah said, when the cleaning lady left too.

"What? Of course, darling." Sunny helped her, and Sarah raced off in her underwear, trampling on her forgotten nosegay. There were empty champagne glasses everywhere, plates with half-eaten slices of wedding cake, a wilting bridal bouquet in Sunny's hand.

"What the hell are you crying about?" David said.

"It was awful."

"What did you think it would be?"

"Wonderful. I thought it would be wonderful. I thought we would all be so happy. Everybody wanted to be happy." Sunny put down the bouquet and poured herself some champagne. "Except Natalia."

"You don't know what you're talking about."

"What right had she to laugh in my parents' faces just because they said they were Republicans? How *dared* she say my mother was drunk because she said she thought Eisenhower had a good effect on this country!"

"Your mother *was* drunk. So are you."

"Well, for your information, this country happens to have been founded on political division. It has thrived on a two-party system, something your ex-Bolshevik, ex-Socialist friends and relatives don't always seem to understand. Furthermore, the Declaration of Independence, the most beautiful political document in the world, was conceived and written by WASPs, not by some ex-Stalinist bedraggled hangers-on of *Partisan Review*. In fact, if not for the Declaration of Independence those terrible people wouldn't even *be* here!"

"Oh, Sunny, for Christssake."

"I keep remembering how you wanted us to name Sarah after Natalia. I keep remembering how before that when we first met you said you couldn't love me if I didn't like Natalia. Well, I don't care. This time she's gone too far. *She's gone too goddamn far!*"

But David had already walked out of the apartment, slamming the door behind him.

5

Wellfleet *was* beautiful, as beautiful as Amanda said it would be. Everyone thought so except Natalia, who came up for a weekend to visit a former student, looked around scornfully, and announced that she preferred Hagersville, a seedy village in upstate New York that reminded her of Russia. Sunny had been obliged to be civil, even give a little dinner party in her honor, so as not to air dirty linen in public. (David, of course, had typically put all the trials and tribulations of the Jewish wedding behind him.) Besides, it was hard to remain offended with someone who had so little idea she was offensive. "Why must you take Natalia's every little remark so seriously?" David said. "She likes you." "Likes me?" It was possible. Natalia was so much a law unto herself she probably even thought Sunny liked *her*. Nevertheless, for all his apparent indifference, the afternoon Natalia was leaving, when they had dropped Sarah off at the Montinis and were making passionate love in a deserted hollow in a dune, David had suddenly leaped up and raced into town to say goodbye.

But, Natalia aside—David was right, why take her so seriously, even if *he* did?—Wellfleet was a glorious setting for a holiday, an unspoiled Cape Cod fishing village, white and clean, bounded on one side by the ocean, on the other by the bay, with pure fresh water ponds in the scrubby woods that lay between. It was hard to say which she loved best, probably the great wild outer beach, which stretched out infinitely, the ocean red and silver when they walked there at sunset. "I think that when God created the world it must have looked like this," Sunny said. "Read Thoreau about this beach," David said, kissing her, happy that Sunny was so happy. Sarah had turned into a little water child, tawny-skinned and platinum-haired, running in and out of the small waves that lapped on shore and squealing with pleasure. Sometimes at night she wet her bed and cried in confusion, but Sunny told her that was only because she was dreaming of water. Sunny dreamed of water too after she and David made love, submerged in sex, floating in sex. But then why had he abandoned her in the dunes to run after Natalia? She sat up on her blanket in the dazzling sun.

"You look as if a little goose has walked over your *grrave*," Elena Wilson said, smiling kindly. "Is anything *wrrong*?"

"No, no, I'm fine."

Sunny smiled back, reassured by the presence of the tall patrician lady who had become her friend here—truly a lady, which Natalia for all her absurd pretensions could never be—before her marriage to the great writer Edmund Wilson, a Mumm, as in champagne. Of course, Sunny was very fond of Edmund too, though he could certainly be awesome, especially when he appeared on the beach, a rare event, looking like Sidney Greenstreet in his white suit and white Panama hat and a walking stick. She wondered what it must be like for Elena to be married to such an imposing figure; it was hard enough to believe that some people actually called him Bunny, his old college nickname. Naturally, it went without saying that he had reduced Natalia to a pussycat. And in spite of David's denials she was sure that David was awed by Edmund too, since he always laughed heartily at Edmund's smallest witticism and offered one of his own with the proud upright bearing of the smartest boy in the class, enunciating clearly as if Edmund were deaf, which he wasn't. His parents had been and so he tended to bark. But there was no harm in it. Like Elena, he was one of the least pretentious people she had ever met. Last night at the Wilson's dinner party, after David had mentioned Sunny's conversion, he had boomed at her amiably across the table that he himself was reading Genesis in Hebrew, and what did Sunny think of the diacritical markings of the Masoretic text? Edmund's version of small talk. Still, if she had worried about the ante in New York going up, in Wellfleet it had skyrocketed. There were so many intellectuals everywhere that a story had circulated all

summer about one mother telling the children who played outside to keep quiet because Katherine's daddy was writing a review. "And I'm sure all your daddies are too."

Actually, nobody's daddy was here yet. It was too early. The
beach population was still all women and children—in the
immediate vicinity, Elena offering Sarah some flowers from her
garden, Geraldine Marx, part of the Harvard contingent, mea-
suring Sarah with her eye. David was all for having Geraldine
sculpt Sarah, since her little clay heads of children were all the
rage in Wellfleet. But Sunny didn't like the woman, who was
rude and bitter, probably because Rufus, her husband, a hotshot
historian, was mean to her. She had most especially not cared
for Geraldine's remark when the Marxes came to the dinner
party for Natalia: "Well, we all know you're a glamour girl.
Now let's see if you can cook." Naturally, Natalia had burst
into appreciative laughter.

She was glad when the men finally began to trickle onto the
beach, though they grouped themselves a little apart. Rufus
Marx, David, Dick Hofstadter, handsome, genial Edwin
O'Connor, who had practically become the mayor of the place
after his success with *The Last Hurrah*. Immediately the atmosphere became electric, as if uneasy in the anonymity of
their bathing suits, which were hardly flattering in any case,
the men had brought their public personae with them. Soon
David was twitting Rufus, whom he liked and disliked simultaneously, bitter that he had never been asked to teach at Harvard. And Rufus parried indirectly by telling affectionate stories
about Edmund, which indicated that Rufus had known him
better and longer than David. And Ed O'Connor launched into
some anecdotes about the Kennedy family and Mayor Curley,
catching the Boston-Irish accent perfectly. Dick Hofstadter, a
peaceful type, shook his head over Norman Mailer's latest run-
in with the Provincetown police. Provincetown, touristy and
overcrowded, was only for rainy days. Sunny had heard that
Jimmy Baldwin was there too. But the rainy day she and David
had taken Sarah to Provincetown to cheer her up with pebble
candy, Sunny had hoped they wouldn't run into him. Somehow

it would have been awkward, one part of her life confronting another, though flanked as she was by Sarah and David, he probably wouldn't even have recognized her.

She ran down into the ocean, diving into the white cresting waves until she was out of breath. "You look like a beautiful mermaid," Rufus said when she came back, ignoring plump Geraldine in her flowered dressmaker bathing suit. Other people had come drifting down meanwhile, including Amanda and Milo Montini and their two children, who were living in a ramshackle Quonset hut at the top of the dunes, exactly the sort of place that would suit a self-styled bohemian like Milo. They all watched Elena leave the beach, with her nice smelly old dog bounding behind her. She needed to help Edmund get ready for his annual trip to his ancestral home in Talcottville, which he made every year, claiming that in August Wellfleet was "the fucking Riviera."

Sunny understood what he meant. It was certainly crowding up. The next to arrive were Hymie and Lila Shapiro, who were staying at a bungalow colony for a week. The galleys of Hymie's novel were circulating to much advance praise. "Oh, I've known Hymie for years," David always said when the subject came up. "We both got B's in high school English." He had finally been asked for a blurb, but the fact that it had taken so long still rankled him. Sunny had read the galleys too when David finished with them—it was an interesting novel, a surprisingly surreal treatment of a Jewish theme—but she could not understand why it was creating that much of a stir. Hymie still looked like an accountant, bald head, glinting eyeglasses and all, but there was already an incipient aura of the celebrity about him, especially when the men took him into their circle. She made room on her blanket for Lila, wishing it were Bessie Cohen instead. But Bessie was far away in the Catskills with Manny and the girls, and the few letters they had exchanged were awkward and stiff, as if the wedding for which Bessie had been so largely responsible had come between them.

Novelist to novelist, Ed asked Hymie what he was working on now, and then the other men began to discuss their own work. Ed O'Connor, his new novel about an alcoholic priest, Rufus, his latest volume on Jefferson, David, his epic poem. On another blanket she saw Arthur Schlesinger and Abe Burrows similarly engrossed.

"How's *your* book coming along?" Amanda asked Sunny, startling her. She had almost forgotten that Amanda was once her editor.

"I'm getting there, I think."

"I loved your first one," Milo said unexpectedly.

"Really? I didn't know you'd read it."

"Amanda showed me some of the galleys. I loved it."

Ed O'Connor turned around curiously, then turned away again. Actually, they had become good summer friends, such pals that he had shown her several chapters of his new novel, eager for her opinion. But now that she thought of it, he had never asked to see hers.

Suddenly it was getting late and chilly. Sarah, though her lips were already turning blue, had to be coaxed away from the water's edge, where she was playing with the Montini children. Sunny rubbed her down with a beach towel, and asked David, who had been on the verge of picking a quarrel with Rufus Marx, to carry Sarah home to their little cottage through the path in the woods. Wearing heavy sweaters, they had supper together by the fire, both of them glad not to be going out, for a change.

"Edmund's right," David said. "It *is* the fucking Riviera."

"I know," Sunny said. "Dinner parties, cocktail parties. Even the beach is a cocktail party. It's like the opening of *Tender is the Night*."

"Hey, don't start complaining. You can work if you want to. After all, you have a sitter to take Sarah off your hands three mornings a week."

She looked at him surprised. She hadn't been complaining. In fact, those three mornings when the local baby sitter led Sarah off and Sunny cleared the dining table and settled down, she had a wonderful new feeling about her work, a joy she had never experienced before. What accounted for it, she wondered.

Her anonymity as a writer here, freeing in its way? The sun, the sea air, the sweet sex which made it easy to remember young love? Her passion for Wellfleet, similar to her old passion for Paris? Whatever the reason, she could hardly speak of joy in this context to David, who would only think she was nuts, since writing was always such a terrible burden to him, an awesome responsibility. Still, how astonishing that she had forgotten, even momentarily, that Amanda was once her editor. She decided that as soon as they were back in New York she would show Amanda what she had done, fortify herself with Amanda's opinion before she took on Tommy Job.

Oddly, David made very little fuss about going to the Montinis for dinner the next night, though of course he forgot all about it until Sunny reminded him. He had always liked Amanda, anyway, and despite his quoting Edmund Wilson, he had become as sociable as everyone else in Wellfleet. In his tan linen jacket he looked wonderful, suntanned, his hazel eyes shining. Unfortunately, when they drove through the woods and parked at the top of the dunes a pair of police dogs were the first to greet them, which meant that Heinrich Stadtler, an arrogant German art historian, was among the guests in the Quonset hut. The dogs leaped up and down, menacing, snarling, much like their owner, who was already inside with his mild and stupid wife. The dogs refused to stay behind the screen door, though David tried bravely to keep them there.

"Goddamn it, Heinrich," David said, as one of them put its paws on his shoulders. "Why can't you keep these beasts tied up?"

"Don't you like animals?" Amanda asked, stirring something elaborate in a huge battered pot. She was wearing jeans and a man's blue workshirt.

"Jews are afraid of dogs," Heinrich said, laughing. "Didn't you know that?"

Sunny looked at David, whose jaw had tightened grimly. It was her fault for bringing him here.

"Oh, get them out," Milo said to Amanda before David had a chance to speak, "and let's end this stupid discussion."

Amanda stopped stirring, wiped her hands on her jeans, and obediently wrestled the dogs out.

It was an unfortunate beginning to a very unpleasant evening. Milo was nastier than ever to Amanda, who paid no attention, or seemed not to. The ocean roared and pounded until the very foundations of the shack seemed in danger. Heinrich got drunk and sneered when David had doubts about the new Guggenheim Museum.

"You don't know anything about museums," Heinrich roared. "You're just a peasant stumbling through the sacred corridors of art."

"What do *you* think, Sunny?" Milo said. "Of the Guggenheim?"

"I—?" She looked at Amanda, who sat smiling and insouciant.

"Come on, Sunny, let's get the hell out of here," David said.

Sunny rose. How could Amanda sit there and let David be insulted right at her own table? No, she would never show Amanda the new manuscript, never show Amanda anything. It was true that Amanda and Milo were the only ones on the beach who had thought to ask about her work, but all that would change. She would send the novel directly to Tommy Job, and some day when she and David were back in Wellfleet and the other writers talked about their books, it wouldn't require Amanda to—some day . . . some day. . . . She suddenly realized she was back to square one, thinking as she had that first night she met David.

6

It was hard to believe that the sick little girl sleeping fretfully in her pink flannel pajamas was the same child who had cavorted at the ocean's edge on the Cape that summer, brown as berry. In fact, after the past six weeks tending Sarah in the dead of winter, getting sick herself, it was hard to believe that the Cape had ever existed at all. She blew her nose on a tattered Kleenex. Naturally it wasn't Sarah's fault that she brought back all those colds and worse from school and passed them on to Sunny. (Oddly, David, once so susceptible to colds, rarely caught anything.) But there were days, like this one, when Sunny wondered if it would ever end, if she would forever see the world, like Sarah, with her face pressed against the window pane.

For a moment, she did press her face against Sarah's window pane just as an Orthodox family, all dressed up, emerged from the entrance of the building down below. It was a Saturday morning and they were all dressed up because they were on their way to the synagogue. They were also clearly Orthodox because, as Bessie Cohen had pointed out early on, the women didn't carry pocketbooks, which at that moment made them seem touching and vulnerable, as if they were naked in their faith. A quality which, she realized more and more, was distinctly lacking in Rabbi Binder. The memory still rankled her of Rabbi Binder trying to cajole Natalia into speaking at his synagogue. She had never felt quite right about him since, though, of course, David had insisted from the start that Bessie was all wet, that the man was just a phony. But what was faith anyway? She musn't think of God as a tooth fairy, leaving spiritual rewards under her pillow if she were good. No, this was just a season of discontent and she would have to muddle through it on her own: Sarah sick, David testy because he had stopped smoking, Gloria miserable at Bennington, herself rejected and defeated, with a cold to make her even more depressed.

She felt Sarah's forehead, which was still hot and dry—Sarah would need more aspirin when she woke from her nap—and sat down in Sarah's little rocker to glance at the back pages of the *Times*. Her eye fixed on an item: Hyman Shapiro had just been nominated for the National Book Award. She laid the newspaper down with a jealous pang. Well, there it was, final proof that Hymie, who had started way behind her, was now way ahead. As to the four publishers who had turned down her own novel, Tommy Job didn't get it, Hiram Haydn had sworn that he loved it but that unfortunately his partners at Atheneum had no taste, and the other two spoke of the market place and asked pleasantly at the end of their letters of rejection what her husband was up to. And to think that she had once associated that novel with joy. To think that she had once imagined she could take on the whole Wellfleet male powerhouse with it.

She heard David puttering about in the kitchen, and disconsolately went to join him. He was standing at the stove, heating leftover coffee. She lit a cigarette and took a cup from the drainboard.

"Would you mind putting that out?" David asked, waving away the smoke. "I don't know how the hell you can go on smoking when you have a cold." He was wearing an old tweed jacket over a heavy sweater, since to add to all their other troubles, the landlord had unaccountably turned off the heat in his study.

"David, you're getting more pious than a reformed whore. It's one of the few comforts remaining to me these days."

"Smoking is an obnoxious habit, extremely expensive and dangerous to the health. It is the main cause of your recurrent respiratory infections." Many of David's speeches on the subject of smoking these days were peculiarly formal, as if he had learned them from someone.

"I have all these colds because Sarah brings them home from school."

"Oh, Sunnoo, you couldn't wait to send her there."

"I know. But now I'm wondering what she'll bring back from the first grade. Not that I know where she'll be in first grade. Ethical Culture? Brearley? Thorndike? We'll be lucky if any of them accept her. They're harder to get into than Harvard."

"And just as expensive." David had poured out his coffee and was wandering back into his study with his cup.

"Did you know that Hymie was nominated for the NBA?" Sunny said.

"So what?" David said, stopping short. "I know Hymie from way back."

"That's right, you both failed freshman composition."

"We both got B's in English at Chester B. Arthur High School. Look, Sunnoo, Hymie Shapiro has nothing to do with you. Neither does any other writer. Why don't you listen to your husband for a change? Don't let those bastards grind you down. Stop wallowing in self-pity. Forget about novels for a while. Try a story."

"A story? Why a story?"

"Well, because, frankly, sweetheart, the novel requires a much greater breadth than you have at the moment."

"How are you spelling that?"

"Both ways. . . . Look, I have to get back to work. We'll talk later."

"I always thought that when I got to be thirty I'd be somebody."

"Thirty's ridiculously young. Wait until you get to be my age, then you'll know how tough life can be."

"I wish you wouldn't keep saying I'm so young. Why is it all right to tell people that they're too young but not that they're too old?"

Exasperated, David reached for her package of Kents, caught himself, and jammed his hand into his pocket. "Okay, I'm too old for you. I'm also too old to be living in a graduate student apartment and being asked by the Reeveses how my wife is enjoying New York. I'll tell you frankly, Sunny, that if that

Guggenheim hadn't come through for next year, I don't know what I'd have done."

"Well, at least the Reeveses won't be there when you come back."

"Great. Rub that in too. Of course a slick operator like Reeves gets invited to Princeton. Even that meshuganah Berryman. I'm too passionate and Semitic for Cleanthe Brooks and that gang, don't you realize that? Or doesn't your shikse mentality take that in?"

Sunny started back to Sarah's room.

"Oh, Sunnoo, I'm sorry. I apologize," David said, catching her by the shoulder. "It's the nicotine deprivation. You'll see, sweetie. Everything will work out. Maybe we'll even get to Europe this summer. Return to Paris in triumph. Wouldn't you like that?"

He reached under her sweater and amiably tweaked her nipples. Return to Paris in triumph? What kind of a triumph would it be if she couldn't even get her novel published? But she did not mention this to David who would say that her goddamn novel was all she ever thought about these days. And he would be right. It had become an obsession, darkening her waking hours, causing her to bolt up at night in a sweat, dread going to literary parties. Not the novel itself, nor her old grandiose dreams for it, but the idea that no one wanted it at all, that no one would *ever* want it. Sometimes nothing else mattered, not David, not even Sarah. But what kind of a woman did this make her, what kind of a wife and mother? David, fingers still toying under her sweater, was giving her a familiar smile. In a spirit of atonement, she let him lead her into the bedroom, hoping poor Sarah would nap a while longer.

Afterwards, David turned on the television set, which they had gotten ostensibly for Sarah, and lay watching in his old red paisley bathrobe. Since it was Saturday morning what he was watching was an animated cartoon. Once she had come home to find him absorbed in "The Lone Ranger." But he didn't seem to care. He was now as fascinated by television as he had always been with the movies, though, being David, he claimed he was merely keeping abreast of popular culture—the same excuse he gave when he said he was going to work and she caught him lying on the couch in his study reading the *New York Post*. Still, there was something endearing about David watching children's cartoons on TV, also a little lost and lonely. She realized again how much her obsession with her novel had caused her to neglect him.

"You shouldn't let Sarah watch too much of this crap," David said finally, turning off the set.

"I won't," Sunny promised, though in fact Sarah hardly ever did. She snuggled closer and rested her chin against his shoulder. "Darling? It's really wonderful about your Guggenheim."

"Well, I'm glad you think something about me is wonderful," David said with a rueful smile. "Lately I haven't been too sure."

"I know, I know. But you were absolutely right. The summer in Europe. Paris, London, Ireland. Oh, we could have a second honeymoon."

"Hey, wait a minute," David said, turning. "This Guggenheim is supposed to provide me with a breather from teaching, not a honeymoon."

"Oh, I realize that, darling."

"I'm going to have to work my tail off if I want that poem to get any bigger instead of staler."

"I know that too. I just meant—"

"Do you know what a whole summer in Europe would cost? We're still in hock from the Cape."

"We could do it on the cheap, just like old times."

"Sunnoo, we don't do anything on the cheap anymore. Don't kid yourself. You may think you're the girl you once were, but believe me, you've developed quite a fondness for good living. Not to mention the extra expense of taking Sarah."

"We're taking Sarah?"

"We aren't?"

"Well, when I spoke to Mother, who sends you many many congratulations, by the way, she said that she and Willie Mae would always be glad to—"

"Sunny, I don't know anything about family retainers because we didn't have them in the Bronx—though yours seems pretty old and off her chump by now. But would you really trust Grace to lay off the martinis for a whole summer?"

"What are you *talking* about?" Sunny said, sitting up. "Really, David, for God's sake, ever since Natalia made those insulting remarks at our Jewish wedding you've acted as if my mother were the star of the *Lost Weekend* or something. Maybe she *was* a bit squiffed—as who wouldn't have been under the circumstances? But do you really think she'd drink while she was taking care of Sarah? I mean, when I consider that the author of those nasty comments refused even to go near Sarah until she was two years old, whereas my mother. . . . Or are you saying that Jews don't drink—though judging from some of the *Partisan Review* parties I've been to I'd challenge that—whereas all the goys—?"

"Goyim."

"Goyim sit around swilling martinis. Well, you can think what you like. But I can assure you they're just as responsible toward their children as some Jews I can mention, especially those high and mighty 'Russian' Jewesses who wouldn't have any children if you paid them. When I think of a real lady, like Elena Wilson—"

"Sunnoo, calm down. What are you going off half-cocked about? It's just that you seem so devoted to Sarah—"

"*Seem* devoted. Who do you think I've been taking care of all these years? My god, the night she was born, I was so happy I would have willingly died at that moment."

"I know," David said. "You've told me. Many times."

"Yes, and you told *me* when I was in my ninth month that you had to go to New York and help Natalia with her book, even though Sarah could have been born any minute. A remark that chills my spine even now when I remember how pregnant I was."

"You have a very selective memory," David said. "Do you also remember that in point of fact, I didn't go anywhere?"

No, he didn't, did he? She slid down in bed again. "Oh, God, how guilty I feel now, how torn. I just wanted to be alone with you again, to be just us again. Is that wicked? Does that make me bad?"

"Sunshine, stop torturing yourself. Do whatever you think is right."

"But anything I do now will be wrong, don't you see? Oh, David, I love you so much."

"Then why are you crying?"

"Because I also *miss* you so much," Sunny said.

In fact a few weeks later a miracle occurred. Suddenly there was springtime at the end of her tunnel. Nothing to compare with David's Guggenheim, of course, but enough to set her heart singing.

"Oh, David, David!" Sunny cried, running to meet him at the door the next time he returned from Rhinebeck. "Do you remember that story I was revising? The one you said was cute when I showed it to you years ago, about the little rich boy I used to play with who lived on the big estate next door? Well, *Mademoiselle* just took it! And Cyrilly Abels said she hopes it's the first of many!"

"That's terrific, congratulations," David said as she followed him into the bedroom. "How much are they paying you?"

"A fortune. Three hundred dollars."

"Well, that will certainly help," David said, dumping the dirty shirts and socks from his suitcase.

"I can't tell you how this sets me up. I mean, of course it's only a short story—though you were the one who said to try going back to them—and you probably won't like this version, either. But to have something accepted again!"

"Why do you always take my smallest criticisms so much to heart?" David said. "There were just a few small places where— look, would you rather I weren't honest with you? Pulled my punches as if you weren't a professional?"

"No, of course not," Sunny said, gathering up his laundry. "Anyway, now I don't have to agonize anymore about whether to take Sarah to Europe."

"Why not?"

"Well, don't you see? I feel so strong and happy now. And I've just earned her fare."

"Selling a story makes you feel more of a mother? Shouldn't it make you feel more of a writer, which is what I've been hoping for you all along?"

"You don't understand."

David shook his head, laughing. "I just hope Grace doesn't think you're crazy. Ah, good old Sigmund was right. We will never know what women want."

Sunny dropped the laundry into the bathroom hamper and followed David to the study, where he stood at his desk, looking over the mail which had accumulated in his absence.

"Now we'll definitely need an apartment," she said. They had worked it down to three weeks in Paris, where David would give several readings, courtesy of the U.S. Information Service, plus a long sentimental side trip to Kinsale. "And probably a bonne also. I'll call Violet. She still has strong Paris connections. And I'll write to the Silvers. Maybe they'll know someone who can take care of Sarah when we go to Switzerland. I wonder who else is still around—"

She tore herself from a sea of plans as, with a dark frown, David held out a letter.

"Sunny, did you tell Gloria she could quit Bennington and come to live with us next year?"

"Oh, that. No, not really."

"Not really?"

"Well, she's so miserable there—"

"Miserable? Gloria would be miserable anywhere. I told her not to go to that place, but she wouldn't listen to me, of course. Look, Sunny, are you nuts? If you aren't now, believe me, after a few months of Gloria you'd be a prime candidate for the booby hatch. I know, I've lived with her. Anyway, where would you put her? You do agree that I need a study in my own house? Or do you see us both working in your maid's room?"

"She could move in with Sarah."

"Sarah doesn't need to acquire a filthy vocabulary at this

point in her life. And what about Europe? Or are you proposing to drag Gloria along too?"

"I wasn't proposing anything. Gertrude and I just thought that maybe for a while—"

"Oh, yes, Gertrude and I. I and Gertrude. That's one of the things about you that's always mystified me, your eagerness for 'good relationships'—even with my worst enemies. Don't think I didn't see you last week at William Phillips's party cozying up with Berryman. And after what that bastard said to me about my review. Delmore had a field day, leering."

"I wasn't cozying up. We were just talking."

"Never mind. I told you what I thought about that."

"Oh, David, not now. I'm so happy about *Mademoiselle*. Can't you be happy for me the way I was happy about your Guggenheim?"

David gazed at her glumly, as if happiness had just joined the list of cardinal sins.

Paris was the same. Paris was still heartwrenchingly beautiful. It was she who was dull. She sat with David at a table outside the Deux Magots on a late August afternoon, both of them sipping Cinzano, both of their wedding rings faintly glinting in the sun. Soon it would be time to return to the borrowed apartment on the rue de Verneuil and their *bonne à tout faire*, who was presently in the Luxembourg Gardens with Sarah. Meanwhile they watched a strange new generation stroll by on an overcrowded Boulevard St. Germain. The truth was they no longer knew many people in Paris. The old copains were gone, either on holiday or permanently departed: the Silvers on vacation in St. Tropez; Jimmy Baldwin in seclusion in Marrakesh—she had steeled herself to inquire; Violet in the United States; the Beaupains retired to Provence. Claude was back in Canada. It had not seemed wise to look up Michel. Muffy, who taught at a provincial lycée and whose chatty newsletters appalled David, was out of the question. Perhaps if she and David were going off to Ireland, she would not have felt so stranded. But that plan had abruptly been canceled.

"Why don't you join me in Rome, then?" David said, not for the first time. "What will you do with yourself here?"

"I have nowhere to leave Sarah."

"Where would you have left her if we were going to Ireland?"

"That's different. That was the whole point of this trip."

"The point of this trip was to be together."

"Was it?"

"Come on, Sunnoo, you know I didn't ask Arturo to arrange those lectures."

"I didn't say you did."

"Okay," David said. "So maybe I was a bit hasty in accepting.

But it's a man's *business* to seize such opportunities—something you never fully take in. . . . Sunnoo, don't be so hurt all the time. Fly over for a weekend. Take Sarah, if you have to. Somebody in the hotel will look after her."

"That hotel costs the earth, don't you remember?"

"All right. I was foolishly worried about there not being enough money for all of us. Now I think we can manage. Why hold me up on every small thing? What am I supposed to do by myself in Rome for a week?"

"You should have thought of that in the first place."

David angrily threw down a few francs for their aperitifs. Out of old habit, the two of them headed for the quai Voltaire and a Seine turning rosy in the sunset. Down below, in the shadow of the Pont du Carrousel, a pair of lovers embraced. Was she, as David insisted, being foolishly stubborn about nothing? Was her hurt pride obscuring all that really mattered? She already missed him terribly, as she knew he would miss her. But she missed most of all the time when they were lovers too.

"Il est parti comme ça, sans vous?"

"Oui, sans moi."

"Ah, ces hommes," Renée said, shaking her head, and flicking a feather duster here and there.

The woman-to-woman sympathy made Sunny feel better. In the first excitement of her arrival in Paris she had told Renée, in French gone sadly rusty, about the romantic honeymoon in the castle, the plans for a romantic return, and Renée had sighed blissfully. Now she was almost as disappointed as Sunny. The woman truly was a gem, missing teeth, black brassiere under her white blouse and all. Sarah, who had almost at once begun to chatter in French, adored her. Renée's own daughter, whom she sometimes brought over, was Sarah's age, but looked no more than two, a white-faced, wizened little thing in a shrunken pink sweater and brown sandals slashed off at the top to make room for her toes. Yet Renée never bore Sarah any resentment for her strapping good health and exuberance. Like so many of her compatriots, she simply loved children, though David never believed that they did, nor that waiters in cafés worried about whether an egg or an orange were fresh enough for *la petite*.

Renée continued to commiserate over David's defection. Guiltily, Sunny felt she had misled her, but would any French woman grasp her real disappointment—that the trip to Ireland was to be for *both* of them, whereas Rome was merely another place where David's presence was required and Sunny's an afterthought? How, in the course of their marriage, had they managed to reverse themselves so thoroughly? It was hard to believe that David had once sailed to France only because Sunny was there. Now, wherever they went, Sunny was there only because of David.

And what would Madame do by herself all week, Renée wanted to know. Well, to begin with, Sunny would take Sarah on a little excursion this afternoon. Paris was Paris, after all. Renée agreed, planning to whip up a little custard for her *ange* on their return, a tiny chop browned to a turn. Nevertheless Madame should not languish in the evenings. What about her friends? Renée was right. Sunny tried the Silvers again and discovered that they had returned from St. Tropez a week early.

"Come to dinner on Sunday," Arlene said, delighted she had called.

"David is away," Sunny said. "I'm here alone with my little girl."

"Then bring your little girl," Arlene said. "Unless she doesn't like rare gigot?

"Oh, it will be like old times!" Sunny said, happily.

She hung up. Renée, grinning from ear to ear, soon presented her with a Sarah who had been carefully washed and combed for the promenade with Maman. The two of them set out together, Sarah skipping along. Sunny told her about the old friends they would visit on Sunday whom Mommy had known long before Sarah was born. "Before I was born!" Sarah cried, and pretended to read the signs in shop windows. They took the bus to the Right Bank and descended at the rue du Rivoli. Just beyond, in the famous apartment in the Palais-Royale,

Colette had lain on her divan, writing under her blue paper lampshade. Someday she would tell Sarah how she had first discovered Colette, and walked across Paris seeing her everywhere. Now the elegant arcades, deserted by Parisians, were full of other strolling Americans. One of them hailed her. It was Dick Reeves.

"Sunny! Well, I'll be damned! Is this Sarah? My god how big she is. What are you doing here?"

"What are you?"

He had come over from London, it seemed, to do some research at the Bibliothèque Nationale while Nancy visited friends in the Lake Country. So for all practical purposes, for the rest of the week anyway, he was a lonely bachelor.

"Where are you off to?" Dick asked eagerly, looking boyish and handsome and very American in his chino suit and blue polka-dot bow tie. "Let me buy you both a drink."

Sarah was prancing up and down in her joy at seeing him again, though she couldn't possibly have remembered him. "Dick, Dick, Dick!" she cried. "What are *you* doing here?"

They sat down outside a café on the rue Saint Honoré and ordered vermouth for themselves, a *citron pressé* for Sarah into which Dick kept pouring sugar while she squealed with delight.

"Dick, you'll spoil her."

"Little girls need spoiling," Dick said. "Even big girls." Their eyes met. Sunny looked down into her drink as Dick said, "How's David?"

"He's in Rome. He was asked to give some lectures."

"And you didn't want to go with him?"

"Mommy wanted to go to Ireland," Sarah said. "Mommy cried."

"I decided to stay in Paris. I love Paris."

"I know. You once lived here. I'll bet your French is terrific." He laughed. "The only word I understand is '*comment*,' which is what they say to me everytime I open my mouth."

"We're going to the Silvers to have gigot on Sunday," Sarah said. "They knew Mommy before I was born. Mommy, make him come too."

Sunny hesitated. "Well, if you're free . . ."

"Hell, I'm free every day," Dick said cheerfully, an admission that would have horrified David.

"Are you looking forward to Princeton?"

"Sure." He raised his glass to her. "But I'll always have some great memories of Cole."

Sunny told Sarah it was time to go. She gave Dick her phone number so that they could make plans to go to the Silvers.

"Listen, if you have any free time before then," Dick said, "maybe you could show me your old haunts. I'm really helpless in this town."

"Show him your old haunts, Mommy," Sarah said.

Sunny looked at Dick and Sarah, both of them waiting for her answer. "Okay, why not?" she said, suddenly lighthearted, carefree. "But don't be disappointed in my French. It really hasn't held up very well."

"I won't know the difference," Dick promised.

She and Sarah continued their promenade to the Tuilleries, where they sat down on wire chairs in the sun and watched a pair of fin de siècle children roll their hoops on gravel paths. In the background, the black and white lithograph facade of the Louvre loomed behind beautiful pastel flowerbeds. No, Paris never changed.

When they came back to the apartment on the rue de Verneuil, Renée, with a tight little smile, held out a cable from David. "Heartsick. Please come. Stick with me." Sunny cabled back, "Staying in Paris."

She had forgotten how easy it was to be with Dick, how much fun. Renée, anticipating a new amour in the person of the handsome American, insisted on babysitting, though it meant sleeping in a big armchair with her skinny little daughter in her lap until Sunny came home. "*Mais non, ça ne fait rien, Madame. Paris, c'est pour s'enjouir*—at the suggestion of enjoyment she raised her eyebrows significantly—"*et puisque vous êtes ici pour si peu de temps . . .*" and waved them off. The first evening

Sunny took Dick to the old student restaurant on the rue Monsieur le Prince, where Dick enthusiastically ate the thin, rubbery *biftek*, and drank the rough *vin rouge*—surely the food and wine hadn't always been this bad, or had her tastes changed, as David insisted?—impressed with Sunny's fluency in French, which had unaccountably improved, and with what he called her savoir-faire. Afterwards he followed her willingly through the old familiar labyrinthine streets of the Latin Quarter, not in the least self-conscious about gawking like a tourist. "Listen, I'm the quintessential American hick," he said, laughing. The next evening they went to a small excellent bistro on the rue Vaugirard which Morty had recommended as known only to Parisians, and the next to a three-star restaurant near the Opéra that Dick had found in the Michelin. Sometimes they met in the afternoon, strolled along the grand boulevards, talked long hours in cafés. She introduced him to the Louvre, the Orangerie, and her favorite, the Cluny. As a lark, they went to the top of the Eiffel Tower, where she had never been before. "Look at it," Sunny said, "all Paris spread out before us." The wind blew her hair. "Hey, Sunny, you're nice," Dick said. "You're so nice." Nice, nice, nice. What does nice mean, David always said. "Dick, don't." "Don't what?" Dick said, kissing her. She went back to his hotel with him, sat on the bed talking, then suddenly got up and left. It was too beckoning, too sweet, too perilous. She mustn't let the charms of Paris go to her head.

Almost every day there was a letter from David. "Darling, Rome baking in the summer heat isn't worth any anguish, and I'll be back before we both know it. But you could have relented and come, you know. Why does so much anger and misunderstanding have to arise between us? Why must you always insist that things go only one way? I miss you terribly. Without my golden girl all the hot sunshine in Rome leaves me cold. Yes, cold, cold, cold without you. At least write and tell me that you're happy in Paris."

His lectures, once they began, were a great success, amazingly well attended. Paula, Sunny's old Sorbonne friend, had shown up at one of them, much to Sunny's surprise. According to David, she was now a stout gray-haired Roman matron, looked ten years older than Sunny—though of course Sunny looked ridiculously young—was the mother of *five* children, taught American literature, now all the rage in Italy, had translated many American writers, and knew some of David's work by heart, which she proved by reciting whole stanzas of it to him. In a few days David would be having dinner with her and *l'ingeniere*. Meanwhile she sent Sunny her tenderest regards and expressed her surprise and disappointment that Sunny wasn't in Rome too. They were also meeting for lunch. Had Paula turned into one of David's pathetic professionals? No, probably not. Five children would tax even David's predilection for long-suffering women.

In his next letters he described Moravia, Silone:

"I had a drink with Moravia at the Café Greco. He is sullen, full of himself, blurts out the end of a paragraph that has been forming in his mind on the assumption that one will know what has gone before, departs abruptly when he is finished speaking. He is married to a novelist very much his junior, Elsa Morante. I understand that they maintain separate establishments in the same apartment building, an arrangement that would cause even the most emancipated of American women to raise an eyebrow. . . . Silone much the same, a saintly paisano with a long nose, rugged features, gentle eyes, rough corduroy jacket, a serenely spiritual aura despite his political confusions. Since my Italian wasn't up to an entire evening, his Irish wife, an enormous powerhouse of a woman, took it upon herself to translate, but since her accent is exceedingly strange, the consequence of long years of living in Italy imposed on a heavy native brogue, much of the time she was incomprehensible also. . . ."

Sunny put the letter aside, breathing a small sigh of relief when Dick walked in to take her to the Silvers. So often David's letters didn't read like personal letters anymore, but more like travelogues, notes for his journal. And in fact a piece by David had not long ago appeared in the *Hudson Review*, "Journal of a Poet," much of it taken from old letters to her. Or perhaps her letters had been taken from the journal.

"My last day in Paris," Dick said on their way to the Silvers, slipping his arm through hers.

"I know," she said, looking up at him. In a sense, her last day too. David was returning tomorrow. Had she made the wrong decision in the hotel?

The Silvers' apartment on the rue de Lille, an apartment with heavy velvet portieres and Empire furniture that could have existed only in Paris and nowhere else, had not changed one iota since she had last seen it years ago. Nor had the Silvers, Arlene still toothy and gay, Morty saturnine and intellectual. The femme de ménage was still the same, and so was what she brought to the table for the Sunday dinner: a gigot running with pink juices, haricots verts. Among the guests were an angry male black novelist, a lesbian poet from Holland, a smooth-talking American who ostensibly worked for the Institute of International Education, but, as the black novelist whispered in Sunny's ear, was known to be a CIA agent. Different players, slightly different parts, but the old familiar scene. If she had dipped a madeleine into tea, Sunny could not have felt more instantly at home. Dick fitted in easily too, much more easily than David ever had. "Hey, grab him," Arlene said, nudging Sunny and giggling. "He's *cute*." "He's also married," Sunny said, "and so am I." Arlene lifted an eyebrow and gave an extremely Gallic shrug.

They had moved away from the table, congratulating the femme de ménage on the gigot, and now sat in the salon. Sarah and her little mastery of French had been exclaimed over, and they were all chattering away in their various foreign accents, when some late guests arrived. Arlene led them in from the foyer. A short, bald, middle-aged man with a mustache entered, smiling. Behind him, also smiling until she saw Sunny, was Gloria.

"Oh, my God," Sunny said. Sarah was jumping up and down with excitement.

"Allow me to present Jean-Louis Gauthier," Arlene said to the group. "And this is—I'm sorry. I didn't catch your name."

"Gloria," Sunny said. "Gloria Harvey."

"Harvey? Is she related to—?"

"She's David's daughter."

"Oh, how funny. Yes, I see the resemblance now. She has those same huge hazel eyes."

"Gloria," Sunny said. "What are you doing in Paris? Does your mother know you're here?"

"Certainly. And there's nothing she can do about it."

"And who is he?" Sunny said, looking over toward the middle-aged gentleman, who was greeting Morty with a handshake. "This man you're with?"

"You mean you've never heard the name Jean-Louis Gauthier? He happens to be an extremely well-known composer," Gloria said, adding a bit less proudly, "He was my music teacher at Bennington." She raised her head again defiantly. "But he's not going back there. Neither one of us is going back." "Don't go back!" Sarah cried, wrapping her arms around Gloria's waist.

In her defiance Gloria was beautiful. Her black hair was frizzed out around her head in the French style, her liquid amber eyes outlined in black. Her dress was black too, with a v-neck that revealed her slender throat and the thin gold chain that encircled it. The transformation was astonishing.

"You're Dick Reeves," Gloria said. "I remember you from Cole." She looked around, puzzled. "Where's Daddy?"

"In Rome. He's giving some lectures."

"And suffering horribly in his aloneness, no doubt."

"He's coming back tomorrow," Sunny said. "What do I tell him?"

"I couldn't care less," Gloria said with a toss of her head.

"Where can we reach you? Where are you staying?"

"At the Lutétia—until Jean-Louis' wife vacates his apartment on the Ile St. Louis. I suppose Daddy can come and see us if he promises to remain calm. . . . We'd better go now, darling."

With a rueful shrug, Jean-Louis paused to kiss Sunny's hand. Gloria started to sweep out, then suddenly bent down to give Sarah a big, long hug.

"Where has David been hiding her?" Arlene said, when they left. "She's a beauty."

"And he's married," Sunny said.

"Married, married. Oh, la, how provincial you've become,"
Arlene said. "All the men are married, it's a Catholic country.
He's also very charming, very chic. And he clearly adores her.
The girl looks radiant."
"Do you think so?" Sunny frowned. "David will have a fit,"
she said to Dick.
"She did look very happy," Dick said. "And very beautiful."
And raised Sunny's hand to his lips.

David came home with many gifts. A beautiful gold watch and
an elegant red leather handbag for Sunny, a little purse and a
bracelet for Sarah, embroidered linen place mats, even a Flor-
entine wallet for Renée, who accepted it with many thanks,
giving Sunny a wry conspiratorial smile.
"All this must have cost so much," Sunny said.
"Well, they paid me a bit more than I thought they would.
And worked me to death too." David sat back on the divan with
a deep sigh. "God, I'm happy to see you both. You didn't write
me."
"You weren't gone very long."
"Come on, Sunshine, stop being bitter. Let's let bygones be
bygones for the rest of the time we're here."
"David, listen, there's something I must tell you—"
"Oh, shit," David said. "A man can't even go away and be
sure of a welcome in his own house."
"David, please—"
She told him about Gloria. David leaped up enraged. "Where?
Where is that little bitch staying?"
"The Lutétia. David, be calm," Sunny just had a chance to
say before David charged out of the apartment. In an hour he
returned, depressed and defeated.
"The Silvers say he's very nice," Sunny said. "Very chic."
"The Silvers."
"They've known him for years."
"So have I. I know that jerk's music too. Pure cacophony.
It's just another one of Gloria's asinine attempts to get my goat.

Well, she's torn it this time. Believe me, not another penny for her support. Gertrude can take me to court if she wants to. Why the hell didn't she do anything to stop her?"

"He seems very devoted to her."

"Don't you understand that he's only using her to get to *me*? He makes a habit of meeting well-known poets so he can set their work to music, God help us. And now he's got my daughter locked up illicitly in that hotel room."

"We weren't married either the first time we were in Europe together," Sunny said.

"How the hell can you compare them to us?"

Sunny sat down on the divan next to him, patting his hand, smoothing his hair.

"What did you do while I was away?" David said finally, sighing.

"Nothing much. Saw the Silvers. Did a bit of sightseeing."

"Why you would want to spend your time in Paris in the company of Americans beats me. Nothing else?"

Sunny hesitated. "Dick Reeves was here for a few days."

"*That* slick operator," David said disgustedly, taking himself off to bed.

She had never dreamed that one day she would be glad to return from a trip to France, but nevertheless she was. Too much had gone awry. It was a relief to stop feeling like a foreigner, stop lying awake at night wondering what *bêtise* she might have committed during the day, stop fretting about currency and postage stamps. She disembarked from the *Liberté* without regret, knowing that the next time they returned to Europe they would fly. It had been a wasted sentimental gesture to sail there and back. Sarah had needed to be watched every moment on shipboard, amused with puppet shows, trotted endlessly around the deck. They had dined in the first sitting along with other families, then taken turns watching Sarah in the cabin the rest of the evening. It was all past history, that first crossing, she and David alone and in love on a moonlit sea.

David almost immediately went off to see Gertrude. "Well, I'm glad you're both so sanguine about Gloria's situation," he said when he returned, "so blithely able to decide between you what's good for her. But then I realize that fathers have no rights anymore." He made a quick call to his mother to say that he was back but busy, and a longer one to Natalia, voice changing to honey. Then he closed the door of his study and went to work.

The copy of *Mademoiselle* was waiting in the back mail, along with a pile of bills. In print her story looked skimpier than it had in manuscript, the illustration for it was silly. And on the desk in the little maid's room the cardboard stationery box containing her novel waited to be sent out again. (And again and again? No, she would have to take a hard look at it first, find out what went wrong.) Meanwhile summer was only technically over. New York was scorching and Sarah's school would not start again until Monday. She decided to take Sarah to visit her grandparents in Connecticut for the weekend. David, quickly closing the journal in which he had been making notes, looked up and said it was an excellent idea. "But don't mention Gloria," David told her.

Grace seemed unwell. She sat on the flowered chintz sofa with William, pretty as a bird in her bright blue sleeveless shift, trying to talk gaily to Sarah. But her heart appeared to be elsewhere, and her eyes kept closing as if she were about to doze off.

"*Vous êtes ma grand-mère,*" Sarah said. "*Ça c'est est mon grand-père.*"

"Angel, you sound like a native."

"I'm sorry the presents weren't more elaborate," Sunny said, embarrassed. She had wanted to do better than perfume and men's linen handkerchiefs, particularly considering all that her parents had given them, but at the last minute David announced that they had run terribly short again.

"Darling, I know what traveling costs these days," Grace said. "Anyway, they're lovely. It was sweet of you to remember us."

"I don't understand why that place can't pay David an adequate salary," William said.

"Daddy, we're on a Guggenheim this year."

William looked skeptical. He was proud of David, pleased to have him as a son-in-law, glad to have his books displayed on the living room bookshelves, see David's name in print in various journals, perfectly willing to lend a helping hand whenever necessary. But he had never understood why, given David's literary distinction, the Harveys led a life so rocky financially. Neither, sometimes, did Sunny. But that was unfair to David, who worked so hard. Still, why was David always able to give elaborate presents when *he* felt like it, with an air of distributing largesse? Such as the gold wrist watch and the expensive red leather handbag from Rome, neither of which she had been able to bring herself to wear.

"Well, ladies," William said, rising. "I'm off to the hospital. Enjoy yourselves. I'll see you this evening."

"You're going to the hospital today?" Sunny said with surprise. "It's Saturday."

"Things need Daddy's attention, darling," Grace said. And added gaily to Sarah, "We don't need any men to amuse us, do we?"

"No! No men," Sarah said emphatically, shaking her head.

But though Grace laughed, her brilliant blue eyes suddenly filled with tears. Last night she had gone to bed very early.

Grace cheerfully suggested a pre-lunch martini. For a moment, Sunny heard Natalia's jeering laughter and was immediately angry with herself. No, clearly, her mother just wasn't feeling well. In which case, why hadn't her father mentioned it? Probably because he didn't want to worry her. She longed to ask her mother what was really wrong, but couldn't. They had never intruded on each other's private feelings, a form of mutual courtesy. "Typical WASP psychology," David called it, who preferred to go for the jugular.

"Well, it sounds like an old-fashioned crying jag to me," he said. "Maybe your father's cheating on her."

"Oh, David, really. My father's often needed at the hospital. He's a doctor. A healer."

"A healer who says no one's sick?"

"Any calls for me?" Sunny said irritably.

"Just your usual crew. Amanda, Bessie, Violet, etc. . . . Oh, yes, Dick Reeves wanted to know if he could 'sack up' next time he's in from Princeton. Your Paris encounter seems to have revived the friendship."

"We were always friends."

"Yes, that's right," David said with a little smile. "By the way," he added casually, "I read your story in *Mademoiselle* while you were gone."

"And?"

"It's very nice."

Nice. His unfavorite word.

"I also read your novel while I was at it."

"You *what?*"

"You're so tied up in knots about it, I thought a fresh eye would help," David said. "My word, you do write about sex freely. I'm lost in admiration. Somehow I assumed that your hero would be your old friend, Michel. But he reminds me more of Reeves. 'Callow, bow-tied, boyish.' And, oh yes, 'that long lanky build' you dwell on so lovingly in the bedroom scenes. . . . Don't you think that as a married woman you go a bit overboard? Or am I to assume that as a married woman you did go overboard?"

"Are you crazy?" Sunny cried. "Not only did you read my manuscript without permission. You read it looking for *dirt?*"

"Calm yourself, for Christssake. I was only trying to help you."

"*Help* me? My god, what am I supposed to do now, go rifling through those journals you always slam shut the minute I walk into your study?"

"Everything I do is wrong," David said.

In tears of rage, she walked down the hall to the maid's room and slammed the door, pushing aside the bulky cardboard box of manuscript on the little desk. Even the sight of her typewriter made her ill, the symbol of everything gone amok. But how

could David have done such a thing? How could he have so
totally betrayed her, betrayed *them*? Worst of all, how would
she ever be able to write anything again when she knew David
was looking over her shoulder? She could feel him looking over
her shoulder often enough as it was.

They were coldly polite for the next few days.

"Sunnoo," David said finally. "I was only trying to help you.
Why do you never let me help you? Whatever I felt about those
sex scenes I got over."

"Great," Sunny said. "Fine."

"In fact," David said cheerfully. "I called Tommy Job this
morning and we're having lunch at the Century Club next
week."

"You're having lunch with Tommy Job at the Century Club?
Why?"

"I want to find out why he turned down your book."

"Have you gone totally mad?" Sunny said. "Are you determined to humiliate me? Is that it? What could you possibly
accomplish except to make both of you feel better at my expense?"

David looked bewildered.

"Oh, shit, David! Stop trying to legislate my life!"

He turned on his heels and left the apartment, slamming the
door behind him. Always in the past, their quarrels had flared
up and died quickly, ending in such passionate reconciliations
she sometimes thought they were merely a prelude to bed. These
days David just walked out, often not returning until long after
midnight. It frightened her not to know where he went. Had
she been too hard on him this time? Reacted too violently to a
simple, if misguided gesture of concern? She remembered his
look of utter bewilderment. What if one day she pushed him
too far? What if one day he never came back?

Three

⟨ // ⟨ //

1

"Happy about it?" Sunny said. "Of course I am. I'm ecstatic.
I miss you, that's all."

"I miss you too," David said, his voice over the telephone
sounding tinny and remote.

Cordial enough, but tinny and remote. Generally when David
spoke long distance he tended to shout, blurting out his sen-
tences like an immigrant eager to make a good connection—it
was probably a hangover from his early background. Now he
was almost inaudible. Perhaps he was embarrassed to be speaking on the public telephone at Greenwood, which was right
outside the dining room where anyone could overhear him.
More likely he was just tired. As his letters had explained, using
almost identical language each time, he was working his head
off, was absolutely on fire with the long poem, had understood
in a blaze of excitement the shape, the scope of it—perhaps it
had taken the huge white room yellowed with sunlight to bring
on this epiphany—meant to work until he dropped, or his month
there was up, whichever came first, hated to break off to do the
piece on Pasternak for the *New Leader*. But at home when
David was working hard he was thin-skinned and vulnerable.
Not remote.

"Must you, darling?" Sunny said. "Break off to do the piece
on Pasternak? I mean, if you're so on fire with the poem—"

"Sunnoo, Pasternak is a major writer insufficiently understood outside of Russia," David said, his voice suddenly strong,
his sentiments suspiciously reminiscent of Natalia. "Why do
you ask me such questions?"

"No reason. I just thought, if you're taking a break from your
poem anyway, maybe I could leave Sarah with my mother for

the weekend and come up and visit you. We could check in at a motel for a night or two, you know, that sort of thing."

"You hated Greenwood when you drove me up here. You said it was haunted. Anyway, with Sarah at day camp, and me off your hands, isn't this a good time for you to work too?"

"It's hard, David, I'm too distracted."

"I thought you were ecstatic."

"That's what's distracting me."

"Sweetie, why don't you just call your mother or one of your girl friends?" David suggested before his voice faded away completely. Then, ". . . look, I have to go now. I'll see you in a couple of weeks."

"But we'll talk before then," Sunny said anxiously. "I love you."

"Likewise," David said. His voice faded again. ". . . What? Oh, okay . . . Howard Moss and Ned Rorem send you their regards."

Sunny slowly hung up the receiver and lay back in bed. She had been ashamed to tell David that late in the morning as it was, she had been calling him from bed; she would have been more ashamed to tell him that now that the call was over there didn't seem to be much to get up for. Sarah wouldn't be back from day camp until the afternoon, Bessie was off in the Catskills, Amanda was in southern Vermont where she and Milo had bought a house—and besides Sunny had made a point of resisting all of her overtures—Grace, still in a rocky state, though maintaining she was fine, had visited in town only yesterday. Work was also out of the question since, no matter what David said, it was impossible to do any serious writing when you had a book coming out. Charlotte Burns, the novelist, whom she'd met at a party recently, said it took her months to get back in harness, a year before she got over the paranoia of thinking everyone she met hated her book but didn't want to say so. And Charlotte's husband was a psychiatrist, which showed how deep-grained the problem was. Nor did happiness have anything to do with it. Of course Sunny was happy. She had been happy ever since George Auerbach ran across her story in *Mademoiselle* and showed it to Eleanor Reed of Dunbarton and Farber, and Eleanor Reed had written asking her if she had a novel up her sleeve. It was certainly not a big publishing house, and the advance had been miniscule, but Eleanor more than made up for that in enthusiasm. They had spent days going over the manuscript together. But there were galleys yet to come, and reviews to be nervous about after that.

For the moment, though, here she was idle, and David working feverishly. Funny how life between two writers so often seemed a matter of two yo-yos going up and down at different times. This winter, the situation had been altogether reversed, she walking on air because her book had at last been accepted, eager to do revisions, David so miserable that his poem had suddenly gone cold he had then and there applied to Greenwood, for the first time since they were married. Now, in summer. . . . The strangely tinny quality of his voice struck her again, and she automatically reached for her cigarettes on the night table, only to remember that last night she had decided to stop smoking. It was meant to be a gesture in honor of her book publication and to get herself in trim for what lay ahead. Maybe the craving for nicotine was what made her suddenly so edgy. David had been even worse when he quit. Still she wished he would stop telling her to do what it was only up to her to do anyhow, e.g., call her mother, see a girlfriend, get back to work. In short, stop taking over what was hers and then handing it back as if it were a gift. Thinking about cigarettes reminded her again of how David had absentmindedly pocketed her package of Philip Morris that first night they met, and called her possessive when she asked for one back. For some reason the incident had been a good deal on her mind lately, and had even come up at her last session with Dr. Brill, the psychiatrist recommended by Charlotte, who was very helpful in every way— Charlotte had even talked of reviewing Sunny's book when it came out. But it remained a knotty problem. Which was to say, if someone took your cigarettes and you wanted one back, did you say they were yours in the first place or forget about it? Dr. Brill had also found it interesting that though Sunny remembered exactly what David had ordered that night—eggplant parmigiana; she had kept needing to remove his sleeve from the tomato sauce, he was talking so earnestly—she had long since forgotten what *she* ate.

She closed her eyes, suddenly giddy, and decided to stay in bed a while longer, maybe even until it was time to meet Sarah's camp bus downstairs. Red-faced and sweaty, Sarah would clamber out, happily holding whatever it was she had made in arts and crafts that day. Yesterday, the day Sunny had thrown away her cigarettes, it was a lumpy brown clay ashtray, the day before that, a painted stick. "Now you may think that these colors are found only in nature," Sarah had said proudly. She was doing so well that soon she would be able to go to a sleepaway camp. How wonderful that would be. Sunny and David alone again. Maybe they could even go to Greenwood together, as other writing couples did—though it really had seemed overgrown and spooky. Meanwhile, she missed him terribly. (Why did he sound as if he didn't miss her?) Especially now on this late summer morning as she lay in the cool dark bedroom with the blinds drawn, naked between the sheets. On such summer mornings long ago, before they were married, before Sarah, they would turn to each other in the semi-gloom, laugh with the sheer pleasure of being together, and make beautiful sweaty love. No longer. She wondered why sex was so much on her mind now, when, as David said, it should be her work. She had written about sex but that wasn't the same thing. She passed her hands idly over her body and closed her eyes, wondering why work and sex couldn't come together in real life too.

Bessie Cohen looked terrible. She sat sunk in a corner of Sunny's living room couch, totally exhausted, as if she had just peeled all the potatoes in her father's delicatessen, her black hair lank and dull, her myopic eyes small and red-rimmed behind her glasses. A far cry from Charlotte Burns in her chic white suit, who had come in from Easthampton for the day and invited Sunny to lunch. A gay lunch at an East Side restaurant with lots of local gossip about the Long Island literati. They had become such good friends in the course of it that Charlotte realized with a laugh that now the *Sunday Times* would never let her review Sunny's book. "They never give your book to your friends, darling—it's a policy—only to your worst enemies." Sunny had just walked in the door, slightly tipsy and highly amused, when Bessie called hysterically.

"Bessie, are you sure I can't get you anything? You really look awful."

"If you think I *look* lousy," Bessie said, "you should know how I feel. God, I want to throw up."

"Oh, Bessie, maybe it's not as serious as you think."

"Are you kidding? I catch him with his hands up the baby-sitter's skirt and it's not serious? In the kitchen yet? Behind the open refrigerator door?"

"I just can't believe it. It doesn't sound like Manny."

"Well, it looked like Manny."

Sunny sighed helplessly, wishing she knew what to do, wishing that at that moment she didn't miss Charlotte in her cool white suit. If only Bessie weren't taking it quite so hard. Not that Manny hadn't behaved abominably—he had—but Bessie had always seemed indifferent to matters of the flesh. So had Manny, for that matter, who was almost a caricature of a Jewish intellectual, stoop shouldered, with kinky hair and eyeglasses, a man apparently immersed in social problems to the exclusion of everything else.

"Look, Bessie, you don't know what really happened. And Manny denies everything. Why not give him the benefit of the doubt?"

"Men always deny everything. Doesn't David?"

"David has nothing to do with this," Sunny said.

Bessie laughed for the first time since she had come rushing over. She had sent the infamous sitter packing and left a still-protesting Manny in the Catskills with the children. She had also made two appointments, one with Rabbi Binder, the other with a lawyer.

"Oy, bubbeleh, the capacity of the human heart to believe

what it wants to believe—what do you think David is doing at Greenwood right this minute?"

"Working," Sunny said irritably. "He's on fire with his long poem. That's all that's on his mind at the moment. You don't know David."

"And you do?"

"Look, Bessie," Sunny said, trying to conquer a sudden little flurry of fear. "All I'm saying is that you can't destroy a whole marriage over a small incident. Can't you try to forgive and forget?"

"Listen, maybe in your fancy circles it's a 'small incident' to catch your husband with his hands on the babysitter's ass. But not to me. I don't want to forget. And why should I forgive? Who wants to live with a man who could stoop to such a thing?"

"Stoop to what? You can't be sure he slept with her."

"You can't be sure unless you're watching," Bessie said. "But believe me, you always *know*."

Exasperated, she gave Sunny a kiss and went off to see Rabbi Binder, but with no thought of his patching things up. All she wanted of him was to talk Manny into a Jewish divorce, then let the lawyer handle the civil end of it. (Oddly, David's Jewish divorce, to which he had been so opposed, had gone off very smoothly.) No doubt Rabbi Binder would attempt to mediate, anyway. But what could he tell her that Bessie would believe? And why did Bessie, normally so easygoing and wise, insist on going off half-cocked, impelled by principles so rigid it meant throwing away her marriage? (Sunny thought uneasily of that awful woman painter. But that was different. Nothing had happened. David had sworn nothing had happened.) And what about Manny? Why hadn't his faith as a Jew prevented him from sinning? Did keeping kosher have nothing do with keeping moral? Or was there some special blessing to recite on the occasion of adultery?

She shook her head to rid it of these stupid thoughts, and found that she had wandered into David's study and was staring at the two green filing cabinets that were lined up against the wall along with his books. For some reason, he had taken his violin, which usually rested there too and which he rarely played anymore, along with him to Greenwood. The keys to the cabinets dangled in the locks. "Believe me," Bessie had said, "even if you're not sure, you always know." If she wanted to know and also be sure, all Sunny had to do was open one of the metal drawers where David's journals, the passionate, internal records of year after year of his life, rested against each other. She stared at the cabinets as if she were staring at a cache of radium, seemingly harmless, but one touch of which could poison her for life. She quickly walked out again. No, David might read her manuscript behind her back—for which he had apologized many times. But no matter how Bessie had frightened her, that was no excuse for looking into his private journals.

"Eleanor wants to give me a book party," Sunny said, glancing up from her letter. They had just collected the mail at the Wellfleet post office and were sitting on the rickety deck of their latest rented cottage. Sarah was still at the beach with the sitter. "But whom would I invite?"

"Anyone you want."

That was easy for David to say, but for her? Ed, Elijah, Ralph, Hymie, Norman—they would hardly come rushing to celebrate her book, especially since not one of them had even acknowledged receipt of the galleys, much less sent in a blurb. A particularly embarrassing situation since Eleanor had repeatedly stressed "word of mouth" as the best advertising. Of course it was still early on, and maybe she was already being paranoid, as Charlotte had predicted. But even if they did show up, as a favor to David, the literary celebrity machine would only say "tilt." She looked through the rest of the mail—there were no other letters for her, as usual it was all for David—and went inside to put away the Portugese bread and the bag of overpriced groceries they had picked up on Main Street after the post office. She looked unhappily around the kitchen. It was impossible: primitive, permanently ingrained with grease spots, and so cramped there was hardly room to turn around.

In fact, the entire cottage was awful, the worst that Renée LeBlanc, the mean-spirited local real estate dealer, had ever rented to them—the walls cardboard, chairs and tables cheap maple and chintz, the stain and smell of mildew everywhere. If only they could have a house of their own, if only David would understand her distress at having to start her summer dealing with other people's dirt, her sorrow at the end of it in having to abandon all the things they had acquired—kites, rubber rafts, portable barbecues, jars and bottles of condiments—everything they would have to acquire all over again the next year. But David, horrified by the thought of owning property, insisted they couldn't afford a house, even though Grace and William had offered to advance them a down payment, and though Sunny had explained that in the end owning would be cheaper than renting, would be an excellent investment, in fact. Unfortunately, the word investment horrified David even more than the word property.

She went back out on the deck, where David was still going through his letters, tossing most of them aside, frowning intently over others. He was still remote, but no longer the happy man he had been when he came back from Greenwood. Somehow, in the intervening weeks, he had lost the blazing excitement of the epic poem; the Pasternak piece still wasn't finished; it drove him crazy that Delmore had won the Bollingen. If he sang in the mornings now it was more to keep afloat than celebrate life.

Sunny looked at the letter from Eleanor Reed again, then dropped it on the rusty wrought iron table.

"I must know *some* writers on my own besides Charlotte Burns. Maybe I'm blocking on this. Maybe I should ask Dr. Brill."

"Sunnoo, what is it with you?" David said. "First a rabbi, now a shrink. What's next, an Indian guru? Won't your husband do?"

"Not if I have problems about you," she said, half joking. David didn't laugh.

"Sunny, you have absolutely no problems that you can't solve for yourself. You're attractive, talented, intelligent," he said, listing her attributes as if she had won a lottery. "You also have a husband to take care of you. So what are you always agonizing over? Women far less fortunate than you do very well in this world, believe me."

"Oh?" Sunny said. "Have you met any of them lately?"

"What's that supposed to mean?"

"Nothing." But she had a feeling that there was a pathetic professional somewhere in the picture, maybe someone he had met at Greenwood. But it was only a feeling, never mind Bessie, not even a suspicion. David was taking his mail inside.

"Don't you see, David? The way you look at it is that somehow I'm not supposed to have any problems at all. Because if *I'm* worried, *you're* worried. And then I feel guilty about worrying you. And then you feel guilty about *me*, and off we go. If only you wouldn't take my problems as a personal insult, if only you'd see them as *my* problems."

"Did Dr. Brill sell you that?"

"Kind of."

David shook his head, let out a soft whistle, and went back into one of the cardboard bedrooms to struggle with his work.

Later, at Ed O'Connor's cocktail party in the woods, he perked up considerably. There was a new excitement on the Cape now that Kennedy had been elected. It was as if the President of the United States was now one of them, or that one of them was now the President of the United States. After all, didn't photographs of Kennedy show him walking along the Cape Cod beach, just as they did, pants rolled up, barefoot? Ed O'Connor, of course, had known the Kennedy family for years, from Joe on down. But Harvard too had joined the charmed circle, and Rufus Marx as well as Arthur Schlesinger had taken a leave to work at the White House. In fact, if she had worried about the skyrocketing ante before, now it was in the stratosphere. The talk was no longer of art and books but of Cuba, nuclear disarmament. The Montinis and other oldstyle bohemians had vanished from the scene altogether, Norman Mailer, having stabbed his wife in the back at a drunken party, was no longer a fit subject of discussion. (David had conveniently forgotten that he had once admired him.) Dwight MacDonald, with his high-pitched laugh and billygoat beard was still around, but most of the older generation was on the wane, including Edmund and Elena Wilson, who had put in the briefest of appearances. Poor Edmund was getting more and more solitary these days. Elena said he spent mornings in the dead of winter planning the Hebrew inscription on his tombstone: *"Chazak, chazak, v'nit chazek* . . . strength, strength, and yet more strength"—the prayer that Jews recited every year, when they finished reading the Torah and started all over again. Meanwhile, a new generation was already taking over, clever young editors like Jason Epstein, clever young speechwriters like Richard Goodwin, a special assistant to the president, who had come up to visit from the Kennedy compound in Hyannis.

Sunny wandered out on the deck to look at the sunset. The scrub pines were darkening into silhouettes against buff dunes and a silvery ocean, the salt air losing its sting in the dusk. Well, in some ways Wellfleet would never change. Or would it? She noticed a curious movement in the woods and looked more closely. Several men in dark business suits were positioned among the pine trees. Secret service? Here in Wellfleet? Was that possible? She went inside to tell David, and found him deep in conversation with Rufus. The two men, both small and slight, wearing summer jackets, looked very pleased with themselves, very distinguished. She put her arm through David's. Rufus Marx smiled as he always did, with his mouth turned *down* at the corners, like Donald Duck—and confirmed that yes, indeed, there were secret service men in the woods. They had come up from Hyannis with Richard Goodwin.

"Incredible," Sunny said. "And do you really work right in the White House?"

"In a far distant wing of it," Rufus said with amusement, maximizing his position by seeming to minimize it. "Why don't you both come and visit me there? I'm sure the President would enjoy meeting you."

The President would enjoy meeting them. The phrase was as astonishing as the secret service men in the woods. But why not? Everything seemed possible these days. Maybe she and

David would be invited to a state dinner for a Nobel laureate, maybe even be pushed into the pool at a wild party at Hickory Hill. She could already hear Charlotte Burns laughing, relishing every juicy detail.

"Rufus asked us to meet the President," Sunny said to Ed O'Connor when they were leaving. He had been telling a funny story about Joe Kennedy and Cardinal Cushing to Renée Le Blanc, who, uncomprehending and extremely French, drifted away.

"What do you mean, us?" David asked, laughing. "Who invited *you*?"

"Rufus."

Ed gave her a charming but embarrassed smile.

"But he did," Sunny insisted. "He said both."

Or had she misheard him? She realized that it didn't matter, that whatever Rufus had or had not said to be polite, the outcome would be the same: David might meet the President, but not she. No, Wellfleet never changed. She had been foolish to worry about the book party, foolish to have resuscitated the dream that she would one day come back here as a successful writer, respected by her peers. No one, in fact, had even asked about her book. Not even Ed, her summer pal, who only yesterday had walked into one of the cardboard bedrooms where she was taking a nap and left a pile of manuscript for her to read when she awoke, so eager was he for her opinion—of *his* work.

They headed out of the woods and onto Route 6 toward Truro and the restaurant, a remodeled barn, where they usually had dinner after a cocktail party. Ed and some of the others would wind up there too, sooner or later.

"What are you brooding about?" David asked.

"Nothing. I was just thinking that one of these summers maybe I ought to go to a writer's colony too."

"Greenwood?" David said dubiously. "Well, it's harder and harder to get into, but maybe I can—"

"I wasn't thinking of Greenwood. I was thinking of Monadnock.

"Traveling incognito?" David said with a wry laugh. "Well, why not? You've already used a pseudonym for your book."

Sunny turned from the wheel. "*Pseudonym?* Sunny Mansfield is my real name."

"Other married women aren't ashamed to use their married names," David said.

"You mean like Mary McCarthy? Hannah Arendt? All your other intellectual heroines?" She did not mention Natalia *Harvey*, (not Kirschenbaum). They had already had too many foolish quarrels about Natalia.

"Forget it," David said. "I don't care what name you use."

They drove on for a while in silence, the purple moors on either side turning black in the deepening night. A streak of oncoming headlights was suddenly blinding.

"Did you know that George Auerbach was leaving Gorham?" David said, when the headlights had safely passed.

"Really? How do you know?"

"President Michaels offered me his chair."

"You're kidding. George's chair?"

"It would certainly solve a lot of our money worries," David said. "You could even have that house in the country you're always talking about."

"On the Cape," Sunny said automatically, "though I'm not so sure anymore . . . But, David, you're surely not thinking of accepting. Gorham's much farther away than Cole."

"I wasn't thinking of commuting."

"You mean for us to live there? David, you can't be serious."

"It's your alma mater. I thought you loved it."

"I loved it when I was an undergraduate. What would I do there now? Everything's breaking for me in New York. Whom would I talk to?" Her mouth tightened. "You certainly don't expect me to make friends with—"

"Goddamn it," David said. "Marjorie Stewart doesn't even teach at Gorham any longer. She's at Smith. But am I supposed to turn down every decent job that's offered to me because of my wife's irrational jealousies? I don't keep bringing up Dick Reeves, or what so obviously happened in Paris."

"Nothing obviously happened in Paris."

"Oh, Sunnoo, come off it. I don't care. I really don't. I only wish you'd admit to yourself that what you're really jealous of is people who scare you intellectually, men and women both. That it's the range of Natalia's *mind* that bothers you, not what you take to be personal slights. And that those 'sad sacks,' or whatever you call them, are women with whom I have—oh, the hell with it." David sighed deeply. "I knew you'd have a fit if I told you about that job. I just wish that sometimes you'd realize how tough it is for me to keep us afloat."

"Maybe my novel will make a lot of money," Sunny said, not too convincingly, as she turned off into the restaurant parking lot.

"That would be nice," David said, with even less conviction.

"Or maybe *I* could apply for a Guggenheim."

"No, don't do that," David said quickly. "Henry Moe told me privately that if I apply for another. . . . Well, it's better to bet on a sure thing, isn't it, than—? Look, maybe when you have a large body of work behind you . . . Come on, Sunny, don't look like that. First you were miserable because no one wanted your book, and now you're miserable because it's coming out. It's all going to be great. You'll see."

"Will it?"

"Sure, it will," David said, brightening as other people from the party started to pull up. Ed, the Marxes, Arthur and Marion Schlesinger, Abe Burrows, Gilbert Seldes, the young Epsteins. He looked at her with her hands still tight on the wheel and laughed. "Sunnoo, cheer up—I already wrote and told Gorham I didn't want Auerbach's lousy job."

2

Curiously, David's prediction turned out to be right. Life *was* great, so great she could hardly believe it, as if she had awakened from a long nightmare. Naturally, *Paris in May* wasn't the success that *Ancestors* had been, certainly not the *success d'estime*: there was no lead review in the *Sunday Times* pronouncing her book "a small classic," nor one in *The New Yorker* saying it was "well-nigh perfect." But the reviews were all very good—amazingly so when she considered by how many publishers *Paris in May* had been rejected—and more and more kept pouring in from across the country each day, almost all of them praising her deft touch, her quiet humor, her witty use of the young lover's stammer. Almost all of them, alas, also identified her as the wife of David Harvey, though she supposed it couldn't be helped. ("On my next book jacket," she told Charlotte, who was highly amused, "it's going to say, 'In private life, Mrs. David Harvey is Sunny Mansfield, the novelist.' ") The few comments from "the chaps," as she now called them to herself, were better left unsent. Ed O'Connor wrote directly to her publisher, explaining that fond as he was of Sunny Mansfield personally . . . ; Rufus Marx sent her a witty little note inquiring when she was going to write about grown-ups; it was Jimmy Starrett's latest wife, not Jimmy, who sent her a long scrawl about how much she loved Sunny's book. Only Hymie, in his meticulous handwriting, wrote a short, carefully reasoned appreciation—though not for publication. But none of that mattered anymore. The people she really cared about had rallied round, Charlotte with a series of ecstatic phone calls, Bessie, who had divorced Manny twice and who would have divorced him a thousand times if she could, with a very long, intelligent and generous letter. Best of all, was Sarah's excitement, her

jumping up and down when she saw Sunny's novel in a bookstore window on Broadway, her boasting of it to her new classmates at Thorndike—had they been right to send her there?
The school was so pretentious and arriviste—Sarah who delighted in all the press clippings, and whom Sunny told in simple
words, feeling foolish, but Sarah insisted, about the invitations
from the PEN Club and the Authors Guild, the announcement
that she had been included in the next volume of *Who's Who
of American Women*, no purchase required.

"Though I am tempted to buy it," Sunny said to David with
an embarrassed giggle, "which is ridiculous, of course."

As usual they had encountered each other in the kitchen,
David walking down the hall from his study to get some coffee,
Sunny emerging from the maid's room when she heard him.
He looked woebegone and depressed, as he often did these days,
the one shadow over her new happiness. The second Guggenheim had come through but he was working his head off on
the new anthology and doing pieces for magazines to make
some money, with no time for the long poem. As always, she
felt guilty and wished there were some way she could make it
up to him.

"Of course, if I wanted to teach," Sunny said, "being in a
reference book might look good on a resume."

"*You* can't teach," David said. "You hate the academy."

"I don't hate the academy. I was an excellent student, in
fact. I hated being a faculty wife."

David looked even more unhappy.

"How about a sandwich?" Sunny said.

"That would be nice," David said wistfully.

"Is baloney okay? Sarah loves it."

"Anything," David said, and settled down at the table in the
dinette to wait. Sunny brought him the sandwich, kissed him
on the top of the head as he took his first bite, then sat down
opposite him with her elbows on the table.

"Would you believe that the reviews are still coming in?"
she said after a while. "Red Oaks, California. Rocky Mountain,
Colorado. Smithfield, New Jersey. Places I've never even heard

of. It's so strange to imagine people I've never met, thousands of them, reading what I worked on so long in such solitude."

"Is there any mustard?" David said.

She got it and sat down again. "Of course, the reviews are almost all reprints of the daily in the *Times*—I didn't realize it was syndicated. And a lot of the others are just rewrites of the flap copy—when they even bother to rewrite it, that is. The state of reviewing in this country is really quite deplorable, don't you think? Oh, well, Charlotte says it doesn't matter what they say as long as they spell your name right. And Eleanor says that in terms of a paperback sale—of course we don't expect a big one, not the way paperback houses are blowing their money on million-dollar advances these days—but still, it would keep my book alive in the public eye, which is all that matters. At least for now. Not to mention increasing the possibility of a movie option, wouldn't you say?"

"Sunny, I'm *working*," David said, and walked away, carrying what was left of his sandwich. She retreated to the little maid's room, and looked through the accumulating pile of clippings. Should she buy an album to paste them in? Sarah would enjoy it. No, that was as stupid and vainglorious as buying a big reference book just to see your name in it. Of course there was a *Who's Who*, which listed David, sitting prominently on a bookshelf in the living room, but that was different. That was the regular *Who's Who*. She heard David come back into the kitchen to heat himself some more coffee. The phone rang.

"Oh, hello, Peter," David said in a suddenly strong and lively voice. It was one of his new young colleagues at Cole. "Yes, I'm finishing the Kennedy piece now. . . . Oh, yes indeed, it was a fascinating meeting. Yes, Rufus was there, but only as a major domo." Sunny put down the clippings. By now she had almost forgotten that Rufus had invited them *both* to meet the President. Undoubtedly by now Rufus had too. "Well, it's not hard to be charmed by him. . . . He's got the grace and ease of a man who's been very rich all his life. . . . No, I couldn't take him seriously as an intellectual, though he clearly wanted me to. Kept referring to the Frost performance at his inauguration. But it's clear that he reads only for the gist not for the art, and sees his Catholicism as a political instrument rather than a spiritual . . ."

Sunny tuned out. She had heard all this before, many times. It was David's set piece at dinner parties. He would go on to the fond husbandly jokes the President had made about Jackie, and how, as a result of the French trip, Malraux was now Jackie's favorite writer.

"No," David concluded, "I can't believe that he takes Rufus or Dick Goodwin very seriously. He's merely making use of intellectuals because we're chic at the moment. Well, maybe a few more years in office will deepen him, take that Irish playboy glint out of his eyes. We'll see."

David finally hung up. She heard him pouring himself another cup of coffee, then heading off to his study. It was early, only one thirty. Sarah wouldn't be back from Thorndike for a couple of hours. From what Sunny could see of the sky above the brick wall opposite, it was a bright beautiful winter's day.

She walked across the apartment to David's study on the river. The door was slightly ajar. Sunlight streaked the couch on which David lay reading.

"Can I interest you in a walk?" Sunny said.

He was clearly about to protest that he was working when he realized that what he was reading was the *Post*. "Well, just a short one," David said, as if she had nevertheless seriously interrupted him.

They put on their heavy coats—David had taken to wearing a pea jacket and a knitted cap pulled down to his eyebrows; so, for some reason had Norman Podhoretz, whom they sometimes encountered on Broadway—and once outside their building stood for a moment breathing in and out the frosty air. At a break in the traffic they darted across Riverside Drive and entered the park amid leafless wintry trees. She thought of the old sandbox days with Bessie. She had invited Bessie to dinner several times. But it was uncomfortable. David's presence had made it uncomfortable, though less so than when Bessie was happily married. Beyond the playground, the river was white gold in the sunshine, gulls swooped and cawed overhead. Now the smell and the sound reminded her of the Cape and of Sarah playing on the beach in her little pouter-pigeon, blue bathing suit. (The little head done by Geraldine Marx was now in the hall closet, since it had made Sarah cry.) Then she pictured Sarah bundled up in a winter coat and woolen scarf, bravely riding across town on the school bus to Thorndike every morning. Maybe too bravely.

"I hope we did the right thing sending Sarah to that school," Sunny said.

"She'll be okay," David said. "As long as she doesn't turn out like Gloria."

"Oh, David, Gloria's in great shape. She and Jean-Louis are practically an old married couple by now. And wasn't that a sweet letter from her about my book? I was so particularly pleased by what she said about the Paris sections. I mean, she ought to know."

"Gloria doesn't know anything."

"Thank you."

"Sunny, do we really have to talk about your work twenty-four hours a day? Must not a minute go by without a discussion of your editors, your reviews, your god-knows-what else? There's a world out there. You used to care about it."

"I still do."

"Oh, shit, why can't we even take a simple walk without a blowup?" David said. "Why can't we just have a normal home life?"

"You don't think our home life's normal?"

"Of course it isn't," David said, walking rapidly on ahead.

"Why?" she said, almost running to catch up with him. "How have I failed you? Or is it that I'm not 'like other women'? If you wanted someone like other women, why did you marry *me*?"

"Great. Now start talking about a divorce."

"I'm not talking about a divorce."

"The truth is you're ashamed of having been married only once. It embarrasses you in front of your friends."

"That's ridiculous," Sunny said. "Oh, David, I know this is a hard time for you, but why must we keep having these silly quarrels? Even Sarah wants to know why we quarrel so much. Maybe we do need some kind of cooling off period, some kind of separation."

"Listen, Sunny," David said, stopping short under the naked trees, and grabbing her by the arms. "Divorce is nothing you try on like a hat, and discard the minute it no longer suits you. Neither is a separation. I know, I've been through both. People don't come together after they separate, even if they imagine it's only temporary. Nothing's temporary that tears your heart out bleeding by the roots."

He was hurting her.

"I only meant that since we're together all day long—"

David released her abruptly, and started walking again. "We're not going to be together all day long any more."

"What do you mean?"

"I've found a studio. A friend has found me a studio in the Village."

"A studio in the Village?" Sunny said, hurrying again to catch up with him. "What friend?"

"Nobody you know. An artist I met at Greenwood. Okay? Are you happy? Now you don't have to be miserable in your maid's room. Now you can take over my study. You can take over the whole apartment."

"I don't want to take over the whole apartment. I don't want your study."

"You don't know what you want," David said. "That's your problem."

David's piece on Kennedy was published many months later in *Partisan Review*. After it had been brought to his attention, the President called in Rufus Marx and asked him to please not introduce him to any more of his friends. Rufus reported the conversation, laughing, to David, who did not see the humor in it. He also did not see the humor in the dinner for André Malraux, to which President Kennedy invited Robert Lowell and other writers and intellectuals, but not David Harvey. He seemed to be amazed at Kennedy's ingratitude, feeling as he did whenever he criticized anyone, that it was for their own good. The Kennedy assassination affected David deeply and personally, like a death in the family. He was distraught for days. Nothing could tear him away from the television set now. Over and over he watched the smiling, sunlit couple in the open car in Dallas, the coffin descending from the plane in Washington, the caissons, the riderless horse with the boots turned backward, the cortege of dignitaries.

For weeks afterward he refused to go to parties, even to the movies. "David," Sunny pleaded, "we *all* feel it. The entire country is reeling." "You don't understand. He showed me Ike's cleat marks on the floor," David said, "we were the same generation." And so too, Sunny realized, were she and Jackie, who was now a heavily-veiled widow with two little orphaned children in short blue coats. David based a eulogy on his original piece on the President, adding his thoughts on the assassination and sent it to the *New Republic*, which printed it in a black border. Several months later President and Mrs. Johnson invited Sunny and David to tea, having evidently inherited some old list of intellectuals, but the invitation came on the same day as the tea. David, off to his new studio, told Sunny to deal with it. She called the White House and found the number had been changed. "Why don't you-all take the shuttle and come on down, anyway?" a Southern lady said when Sunny finally got through. It was too late, Sunny explained politely. . . . Yes, much too late. Camelot, or whatever you wanted to call it, was all over, though very soon at parties there was a lot of intense and self-important argument about how far to support Lyndon Johnson in Vietnam. The bombings widened the split so much that after the White House Arts Festival, to which Robert Lowell first said he was coming and then publically renounced the invitation, and where Dwight MacDonald went around circulating a petition against the government, President Johnson remarked dourly, "Some of them insult me by staying away, and some of them insult me by coming."

"Okay, Dwight's eccentric," Sunny said. "But how could the others have accepted? We can't go around bombing other people's countries." "You don't understand. Your generation is apolitical," David said, refusing to discuss the matter further, though he listened attentively to Richard Goodwin, now Johnson's assistant, knowingly inform the guests at a Podhoretz party, "Little wars prevent big wars." On the other hand, up on the Cape, Rufus Marx was gravitating toward Bobby Kennedy, who so far hadn't come out on one side or the other. Shaking his head, David began to turn more and more to literary criticism—he was now talking with Ed Gaskell about a volume of his selected *essays*—and also very graceful and deeply felt pieces on the deaths of Robert Frost, Theodore Roethke.

"Poets die," David said, gripping his temples. "Poets die."

"People die. David, what about your own poems?"

"What about them?" David said, and got on the phone with the editors of *The New York Review of Books*. Sometimes, coming home after an excursion with Sarah, Sunny would find one of them, a plump young Jew named Bloom, who had a fake British accent, talking intently to David in the living room. She would wave to the men and continue on to the kitchen, but Bloom never even bothered to look up. A whole new generation of New York intellectuals, and she still didn't seem to exist.

"Can't that man even say hello to me in my own house?" Sunny said to David when it kept happening. "Who, am I, Gracie Allen?" David said he didn't know what she was talking about. But the next time she saw Bloom, deep in conversation with David and Natalia at a party at Jason Epstein's house, Natalia gave Bloom a nudge and the chubby editor brightly called out, "Hullo!" That was all. Evidently, David and his aunt hadn't instructed him beyond hello.

"Oh, sweetie, I *know*," Charlotte said during one of their now daily morning phone calls, which one of them made to the other as soon the husbands left the house. "We'll never get to first base with these guys. Why do we keep knocking our brains out?" "What's the answer, then?" Sunny said. "Darling, how do I know?" Charlotte said, laughing. "Maybe to leave this ghastly New York literary scene altogether. Go to California, where everyone's deliciously laid back." "California?" Sunny said. An interesting thought. She had lived in Europe but never even seen California, which was surely a kind of inverse provincialism. They went on to other things, having come to depend on these phone calls, which Charlotte had initiated, though it no longer mattered who called whom. It was their way of making contact with the outside world before they submerged themselves in their work, where no outside world existed. The subject could be anything. The insane loneliness of writing a novel, the venality of publishers, editors, agents. Their passion for Jane Austen and Colette, whom they discussed almost as secret vices—no, no man would understand. More rarely, their children, Charlotte's son whose upbringing her psychiatrist husband had more or less taken over, Sarah's problems with the snobby rich kids at Thorndike—a somewhat delicate subject since Charlotte herself was very rich. Occasionally Sunny raised the matter of her conversion to Judaism, but it wasn't like talking to Bessie about it. Charlotte, also Jewish, but a Vassar graduate with a very high polish, tended to laugh it off as a lark, much like the sexual escapades she sometimes hinted at, of her past— and possibly present? (It was hard to tell, Charlotte was so discreet.) More and more though they talked about husbands. It was very liberating to discover that no matter how things seemed on the surface, all men at bottom were selfish and self-absorbed, that there were no perfect marriages. But where would it all end, they asked each other each morning. (She thought of Bessie again, now struggling with some menial job trying to support herself and her two children, with very little help from Manny.) And hastened to assure each other that David and Steve were very decent guys, really.

On that morning while Charlotte was still on the phone, David poked his head forlornly into his former study, now Sunny's. There was a wet handkerchief tied around his forehead, Indian style. He had stayed home with a sick headache.

"Can I do anything for you, darling?" Sunny said, putting her hand over the receiver.

"Do we have any aspirin?"

"I'll get them for you right away."

"He's there," Charlotte said on the other end.

"That's right."

"I'll call you back in a half hour."

"Tomorrow."

"Got it," Charlotte said, like one prisoner sending a signal to another.

But something more than a headache was bothering David. Gulping down the aspirin, which had been clearly visible in the bathroom medicine cabinet, David handed her a letter and watched, frowning and wary, as she read it—an invitation from Mark Schorer to teach the spring term at Berkeley.

California. How funny. Charlotte would be so amused. But why not? It could be the solution to everything. Or at least time out from everything—including Natalia and other pernicious influences—she had still not forgotten that nudge in Bloom's side, as if Sunny were some kind of meshugunah.

"This is wonderful, darling," she said, handing him back the letter.

"Wonderful?" David said suspiciously. "What about your faculty wife phobia?"

"First of all, Berkeley's not some small college. It's a great university with fascinating people. And I understand California's gorgeous. Oh, Sarah will be so excited."

"Well, don't expect *too* much," David said, a bit taken aback by her enthusiasm. He had clearly been planning to argue, precipitate another quarrel, tell her how hard it was for him to keep them afloat. "It's not the pot of gold at the end of the rainbow, believe me. I know California, you don't." He reminded her that he had often given readings there, though he omitted the part about the grand seductress. Sometimes it seemed that David had already done everything before she had, including get married, have a child—she almost thought, be divorced.

Sarah *was* excited. She could not wait to boast of the trip to her classmates at Thorndike, who alas were unimpressed. Most of them were going to such place as Gstaad, Bermuda, the Antilles. "And Michael's going to Africa on a safari," she told Sunny, shoulders slumping. She cheered up again. "But *we're* not going to kill any animals."

Sunny consulted with Charlotte. "David, we really must have a beautiful house," she said afterwards. "That's the whole point of being in Berkeley."

"The whole point?"

"Everyone who teaches at Berkeley is beautifully housed," Sunny said firmly.

Everyone was, except David Harvey and family. Gorgeous California was the golden land at the end of the continent, the reward for having come clear across it, and the Berkeley faculty lived high on the heights with stunning vistas spread out before them, each house more beautiful than the next. But somehow she and David and Sarah had landed down in the flats, in an ugly little avocado-colored row house, made even uglier by the absent landlady's pseudo-artistic paintings hanging on every wall. She wrote Charlotte a wittily rueful letter, and Charlotte wrote her a wittily sympathetic letter in return. (To Bessie, she merely sent a cheerful postcard; poor Bessie was so haggard these days, so lacking in her usual savvy and wisecracks.) Each day after Sarah had walked off to the local public school and she had driven David up to his office on campus, Sunny put some more of the landlady's terrible paintings away in a closet and tried to settle down in the bedroom, perched on the edge of the bed and typing on the vanity table. How had this happened to them when the rest of the faculty lived so well? "I really shouldn't be speaking to you," she said to Mark Schorer one day, laughing because she had grown very fond of this small, charming man. "Didn't David to tell you we wanted a beautiful house?" He looked puzzled. "All David said was to find something with a low rent."

If only David would *try* to overcome his background. Well, it was just for a few months. Why not regard it as an adventure? ("What is this passion for housing?" David had said uncomprehendingly.) And Berkeley was certainly an impressive university, with a distinguished and gifted faculty, a far cry altogether from Cole. Up in *their* beautiful house on the heights, reached by a private little funicular, the Schorers gave big parties, to which they invited all the visiting and local celebrities, writers, actors, politicians. Sometimes, while Sarah played happily at home with a college sitter, she and David and the Schorers would drive over the Bay Bridge to San Francisco, straight into a fiery red sinking sun, to have dinner on the wharf, hear Lenny Bruce in one of the clubs. (Surprisingly, David laughed along with the Schorers, whereas Sunny found Bruce distasteful. Had David become more laid back than she?) There were young people everywhere, flower children, clustered in the parks of San Francisco, flopping on the sidewalks in Berkeley, dressed from rag bags, smiling weirdly, but somehow seeming harmless in a setting so benign. And when working at the vanity table had given her a backache, Sunny could always sit in the little patio garden and write in her notebook, trying to describe the lush vegetation, the camellias, gardenias, huge scentless roses. The air was soft and balmy, the sun bright as a beach sun except when the gray fog came seeping in from the sea. Snails left silvery tracks on the brick floor of the patio. The shade of eucalyptus trees dappled Sarah as she came home from school.

"I could really get to love California," Sunny said dreamily.

"I could really get to love California," David mimicked her bitterly.

"What's wrong with what I just said?"

"Is your husband supposed to provide everything for you?" David said.

She realized that the English department at Berkeley had not asked him to stay on. Their old quarrels sprang up again, uglier in the beautiful surroundings, growing wildly in the hot house atmosphere.

"Why do you and Daddy quarrel so much?" Sarah asked fearfully one evening. She was thinking about Bessie Cohen, and also about so many children at Thorndike whose parents were divorced.

"Oh, darling," Sunny said. "People who quarrel care too much about each other to get divorced. It's people who don't quarrel who don't care."

"Really, Mama?"

She smiled confidently at Sarah's upraised face, and wondered if she had just told this trusting child a lie. The quarrels grew worse and worse, compounded by her and David's isolation. Anything could set them off, a chance remark that wars were worse than depressions, that America had no business being in Vietnam, that Mark Schorer had said yesterday that he loved Sunny's novel.

"And I don't?" David cried. "Is that what you're saying, you bitch!"

"Oh, David, leave me alone."

David slapped her hard across the face.

"*David!*"

He slapped her again, smiling defiantly.

She stood there, stunned, hand to her cheek, then ran into the bedroom where David tried to drag her out by the arm. Suddenly the doorbell rang. It was the sitter from Berkeley; she had forgotten that they were going to the Schorers. She and David stared at each other. "Come with me to the party," David said stupidly. She pushed past him, and when she had sent the sitter away and come back down the hall was sickened by the sight of David on the edge of the bed by the vanity table, head in hands. She walked out into the little patio garden, surprised that it still looked so calm and beautiful in the night. Why had she imagined that the garden and the flowers would turn ugly too? She touched her cheek again. Oh, it was awful. She couldn't believe that he had actually hit her. Suddenly she was not only angry but ashamed. Ashamed of David for behaving like a monster—could she have been so blind all these years to what he actually was? Ashamed of herself for abetting him. My God, what had they sunk to? There was the sound of sobbing from Sarah's room. She went to sit on the bed, and stroked Sarah's damp hair. "Don't cry. Why are you crying?"

"You know why," Sarah said, turning away from her.

In the morning, David got up early from the living room couch and made breakfast, talking eagerly to a silent Sarah, then phoned for a taxi to take him to the campus. In the evening he walked into the little living room with a bedraggled bouquet, which he held out shyly to both of them. Oh, David—where had he managed to find such pitiful flowers in Berkeley? Sarah walked off to her room. For a moment David looked like the poor idiot in *The Sound and the Fury,* holding out his jimson weeds, not knowing what havoc he had caused. She started to walk out too.

"Sunny, wait, please. I apologize. I don't know what happened to me last night. I swear it won't ever happen again."

"I know it won't. I'm leaving."

"Oh, Sunnoo, come on," David said, with a cajoling smile. "You can't live alone. You don't know how."

"I guess I'll have to learn."

"Damn it, I *need* you! Why won't you stick with me? Help me get through this."

"Help you get through what?"

"Can't you understand?" David said, "I've never been in such despair."

He gave her the pathetic bouquet and went into Sarah's room, where she heard him talking quietly for awhile, then finally Sarah answering. The next day he took Sarah on a tour of the campus, introducing her proudly to his colleagues while Sunny nodded everytime Sarah looked behind. She gave in and nodded too when David suggested a trip to Hollywood to a still uncertain but potentially ecstatic Sarah. He stood by, grave and patient, while she and Sarah gazed at the footprints in front of Grauman's Chinese, and afterwards, equally grave, insisted on taking them to the Brown Derby to look for movie stars in person. On their way back north they stopped at Stanford, where David had been asked to give a lecture. The campus was large, sparklingly clean, and extremely sedate, a blown-up California version of Gorham. "I'm going to shake them up and talk about Alan Ginsberg and *Howl*," David told her, suddenly coming to life. David spoke brilliantly. In the audience next to Sarah, Sunny watched and listened intently, more bewildered than ever. How to reconcile this handsome, fluent, polished speaker with the man who went absolutely beserk when they quarreled? Which was the real David, the one she had fallen in love with? Neither. *Her* David was actually tender and vulnerable, heartbroken if he hurt her, the one who needed her. Was that why she always stayed? After his lecture, which had been greeted with polite applause, and loud clapping by Sarah, David was given a reception by the English department. A few of its members referred with some amusement to the poet Leon Levine, who, during his stay at Stanford, had found himself miserable and uprooted, three thousand miles from home. The chairman expressed the hope that the next time David found himself in the area, if he ever did, he would favor them with another lecture.

"The bastards," David said, beginning to seethe.

"It's not the place for you anyhow," Sunny said quickly, reaching for Sarah's hand. "They're all so smug and territorial."

"Are you comparing me with Leon Levine?" David said.

They were dressing for the Schorers' farewell party in their honor, when the door bell rang. The sitter was early. "Goddamn it," David said, looking for a clean shirt, "who the hell wants their party?" Sighing, Sunny put on a robe. She had no interest in going to the Schorers either, and was just as eager to get back to New York as he was. The experiment, or whatever California had been, was over. With a deeper sigh, she opened the door. A different sitter stood there from the one she had expected, very different, even weirder if possible. This one wore a head-band with feathers drooping from it, a huge baggy blue work shirt, a long paisley dirndl, heavy brown leather thong sandals on dirty feet. The ultimate flower child except that the face was familiar.

"Gloria," Sunny said.

Smiling happily, Gloria walked into the living room where she shook her head at the landlady's few terrible paintings that had remained on the walls.

"Boy, are they lousy," Gloria said. She flopped down on the sagging sofa, spreading her legs wide. "Well, aren't you glad to see me? Aren't you going to give me a kiss?"

Sunny gave her a kiss. Her neck was dirty too. And she had been so chic, so beautiful. "What are you doing here?" Sunny said. "Where's Jean-Louis?"

Gloria shrugged. "In Paris, I suppose. Doing the same old thing in the same old scene. Do you have a joint?"

"A what?"

"Never mind. Why are you standing there with your mouth open? I've left my lover. It happens. I've moved to Berkeley."

"You're going to finish getting your degree?" Sunny said.

"Nope. Just take a few courses, maybe. I'm here to paint."

"Paint?"

"And to find myself."

"I didn't know you were lost," Sunny said.

"You don't know that you are, either," Gloria said with a laugh. ". . . . Well, what's up? How's Sarah? How's—" Gloria's face suddenly froze, except for her big amber eyes which looked pleadingly over Sunny's shoulder.

Sunny glanced around. David was standing in the doorway, necktie dangling. His own eyes, so like Gloria's, were squeezed shut in pain.

3

Back in New York, David refused to talk about Gloria except to call Gertrude and remind her that he had predicted the worst from the beginning. "Maybe she *will* find herself as a painter," Sunny said, as David slammed down the receiver in the middle of Gertrude's answer. David gave her a look of total despair. "David, she only wants you to love her. You're her father." "What's her idea of a father? 'Daddy, gimme'?" David said, and went downtown to his studio, where he often worked far into the evening, missing dinner. She envied him his ability to concentrate no matter what else was happening around him. It was better anyway than seeing him frustrated and angry, lashing out in all directions. Certainly better than being isolated with him in Berkeley. About one thing he had kept his word, however. There had been no more physical violence. Perhaps he had frightened himself as well as her. It didn't bear thinking about. In any case, before *she* got down to work, there was a lot to do: clean up the mess which had been left by their subtenants, get Sarah ready for camp, then try to get over missing Sarah. In August Charlotte Burns called to invite them for a long weekend in East Hampton, and to Sunny's surprise David accepted.

It was a pretty enough place, though nothing to compare with the wild beauty of the Cape, and full of a New York crowd with New York habits. People stood around on the beach in their bathing suits, holding drinks, Charlotte Burns among them. Charlotte's house, for which she laughingly apologized many times—"Oh, sweetie, I know it's an awful cliché"—was immense, white, and pseudo-colonial, with a swimming pool in the back. Her attitude toward David was equally light and gay, as if she and Sunny had never discussed him. Only good man-

ners, of course, but the absolute smoothness of Charlotte's façade—the way she threw back her hennaed hair and laughed—
was a bit surprising, even a bit shocking. Still it was just as well
that she kept it on this level and that David was willing to play
along, exchanging wry husbandly comments with Steve about
"the girls." Despite their intimate conversations, she had never
told Charlotte all of it. Had she ever told herself all of it?

A few weeks after they were back, David announced proudly
that there had been feelers from Harvard.

"Harvard? But it would mean uprooting ourselves again."
She did not add, also isolating themselves again. "It would mean
finding another school for Sarah."

"She'll be all right. She's not complaining."

"But that's the point. Sarah—"

"What about Sarah?" Sarah said gaily, coming into the kitchen
with her book bag and blazer, and grabbing a piece of toast.
The summer away at camp had increased her self-confidence.
She was determined to do better at Thorndike this year, make
new and truer friends.

"Darling, wouldn't you like to live in Cambridge?" David
said. "If Daddy's invited to teach at Harvard?"

"Yes, Daddy," Sarah said, looking anxiously from one to the
other of them.

When the invitation came to lecture, a sure sign Harvard
was seriously looking him over, David insisted that Sunny join
him for a few days. It was all picture perfect, a calendar illustration of autumn: gold and russet trees, brick walks, venerable
buildings covered with ivy. Even the names of the students who
came to his lecture were venerable—Lowell, La Farge, Pinck-
ney. In the quiet streets surrounding the campus the faculty
lived in large frame houses from which issued invitations to tea,
lunch, dinner. "We could dine out here every night, like Henry
James," David said delightedly. It was certainly a civilized life,
an antidote to what Rufus Marx contemptuously referred to as
the "New York rat race." He had returned to Harvard and a
household very different from the ramshackle one on the Cape.
Dinner, for which Rufus had told them with formal informality,

not to dress, was served by two uniformed maids, and afterwards the ladies rose with Geraldine to "powder their noses." When the men joined them at the fireplace in the living room, Rufus sounded more infatuated than ever with Bobby Kennedy and the goings-on at Hickory Hill. People didn't understand Bobby, he insisted, who was in fact even more dedicated and intelligent than his brother Jack. If anything ever happened to Bobby, would Rufus switch over to Teddy with that same knowing smile, mouth turned down at the corners?

"Nevertheless, I see where you could lead a really nice cushy life here," Sunny said, flopping down on the hotel bed after the Sunday cocktail party at the Galbraiths'.

"I could?" David said.

"One. I meant one could."

"Don't count your chickens," David said, angrily undoing the knot of his tie.

"I'm not counting anything," Sunny said with a sinking heart, realizing what was to come.

"Reginald Epstein's terrified of me. Didn't you see his tight little smile at the party?"

"Terrified? Why?"

"Come off it, Sunny. I'm the uncivilized Jew. I'm all the things Epstein's afraid will come out of the woods to haunt him."

Perhaps David was right, but she didn't think being Jewish had anything to do with it. Mark Schorer had told her that he was at Harvard for five years and then they had let him go too—not that this was the moment to bring up Mark Schorer. She watched David pour himself some vermouth from the bottle on the hotel bureau. After California he had sworn off hard liquor.

"You know, you ought to have an affair," David said out of the blue, looking at her speculatively.

"An affair?"

David poured himself another drink and laughed. "No, I guess you'd better have it with me. You'd be nervous with a stranger."

"Oh, David," Sunny said, falling in love with him all over again.

Trying to settle back into the routine of work, Sunny realized how little she had accomplished in the past year. She called Eleanor Reed to tell her that nevertheless the manuscript of the new novel was well under way, that with a month or two of uninterrupted work . . .

"Mrs. Reed isn't here," someone, not her secretary, said.

"Isn't there *now?*"

"We'll get back to you."

It was vaguely ominous. Where was Eleanor? And in fact, come to think of it, where lately were the usual little notes, phone calls, friendly nudges about the work in progress? She asked to speak to Joe Farber. There was a long impressive wait before the call was switched and his secretary finally put him on the line. Eleanor Reed and Dunbarton and Farber, it seemed, had come to a friendly parting of the ways.

"Does this mean I have no editor?" Sunny said.

"Now, Sunny, I promise you that when you have something to show us, someone at Dunbarton and Farber will look at it."

Ice around her heart, Sunny called Eleanor at home. The friendly parting of the ways, translated into plain English, meant that Eleanor had been fired.

"But why? You're a marvelous editor."

"No editor is marvelous these days whose books don't bring in a huge profit," Eleanor said.

"We had a paperback sale."

"We did not have a *big* paperback sale. Look, when things settle down with me, let's have lunch."

In a panic, Sunny called David at his studio.

"What are you worried about?" he said. "There are other small houses."

"I can't go through it again, I really can't. I almost died trying to find a new publisher the last time."

"Take it easy. Dunbarton and Farber hasn't turned down this book yet."

Yet. Sunny sank down on the bed and closed her eyes while David continued talking.

". . . Well, isn't that great?" David said. "Doesn't that cheer you up?"

Didn't what cheer her up? She hadn't been listening.

"It's been in the works a long time, but I didn't want to tell you until I was certain. I'm starting next fall."

Oh, no, not again. No another college which, in the end, would prove to be anti-Semitic, anti-poetic, anti-anything that would possibly persuade them to offer David a place on the faculty. Not another sublet, another upheaval, another school for poor Sarah, who *ought* to have been complaining. It took a few moments before she realized that in fact David was talking about NYU. NYU had finally come through. David had been offered a permanent appointment.

"Oh, David, that *is* wonderful!"

"Natalia wanted to give me a party," David said, laughing. "But I told her it would be easier in our house."

Natalia. She had forgotten Natalia. Now, in addition to everything else, she and David would be colleagues.

She set herself to work in earnest. *Bread and Roses,* her first foray into the subject of domesticity. Would anyone be interested? Maybe a sensitive woman editor like Eleanor Reed, but her slick boss Joe Farber? It was petrifying to imagine showing him the manuscript, paralyzing to imagine what would happen if he didn't like it. But she had already wasted too much energy following David around like a vagabond, thinking each time that this place was it, that here they would finally find perfect happiness. ("Don't show him *anything,*" Dr. Brill warned repeatedly, though David no longer asked.) Perhaps she should seriously consider applying to the Monadnock Colony. Sarah had become more and more self-sufficient, setting off determinedly each morning for the fifth grade at Thorndike, book bag slung over her back, and coming home late in the afternoon, talking of new friends. David was away all day too, either at his studio or NYU. Sometimes he stayed downtown late for a meeting. Or sometimes they met in the Village, almost never at the studio, which he was only too glad to get away from by evening, but at David's favorite Italian restaurant, where he told her about the girlfriends he used to take there when he was young and how in those days there was still sawdust on the floor. Then maybe they would walk around the old narrow streets or drop in at the Waverly to see a movie, as if they were boyfriend and girlfriend too. But the next night there David would be, reading the newspaper at the dining room table, until she put dinner on. Afterward, while she and Sarah did the dishes, he would go back to the little maid's room behind the kitchen, which had now become his personal retreat, and read or write in his journal—his violin he played in his studio—until he emerged again to watch television for a half hour or so before he went to bed.

He no longer liked going to parties. He was too old, he said— and for a moment he did look surprisingly old—too harried and pressed for pointless socializing. Though, of course, there was nothing to keep Sunny from going.

"Me? Alone?"

"Why not? You know a lot of people."

A few times, with Dr. Brill's encouragement, she tried it. In fact she did know a lot of people; more surprisingly, people she didn't know seemed to know her. Evidently, being married to David had given her a high degree of visibility. The old guard was still present and omnipotent. But there were younger people about also: editors who flirted with her and made mildly irreverent remarks about David, though invariably pudgy Bloom popped up to say "Hullo!"; a new gay set, including Bill Gould, a Jewish poet very different in style from David Harvey and his generation. Once Charlotte showed up with Steve. ("He *insisted* on coming," she whispered with a helpless laugh, still the co-conspirator.) And once Violet, who had suddenly and astonishingly married a black activist. It was unhinging to see Violet in her chignon and lovely silks next to this dark man in his dashiki and Afro, as if she had been lifted from a French Impressionist painting and put in the wrong picture.

"Where's David?" Hymie Shapiro said, finding Sunny alone.

"Working. Parties only distract him these days."

"That's right. Nothing must be allowed to distract David Harvey."

"I thought you were old friends."

"When I did his taxes we were old friends," Hymie said, smiling ironically at his wife Lila.

She came home to find David watching the news on TV. Nelly Sachs and S.Y. Agnon had just jointly won the Nobel Prize for literature. He turned off the set.

"Pure politics," he said, with a cynical wave of his hand. "It has nothing to do with literature. Do you realize that Tolstoy never won the Nobel Prize?"

She didn't know if David was right about the politics—"Your generation is so apolitical," David always said—but in its anti-Semitic overtones, and the reference to Tolstoy she heard the unmistakable echo of Natalia. The two of them were now thick as thieves. Hardly a day went by when David did not mention Natalia's honors and achievements, the high esteem in which she was held by her colleagues, the tremendous response to her latest unreadable article in *The New York Review*, as if he were determined to prove that Sunny had been wrong about her all along. When Natalia was awarded a prize by the Institute of Arts and Letters, he was as pleased as if he had won it himself, almost forgetting that he *had* won one himself, years before for *Homeward Bound*. The presentation would be at the Institute's annual meeting in May.

"She wants us to come to the ceremony," David said. "She's shy about going alone."

"Shy? Natalia? What about Fritz?"

David shrugged. "I don't know. He'll be at his business, I suppose."

The day of the award, they made their way into the crush inside the marble halls of the Institute. Distinguished artists with familiar faces floated in a sea of hangers-on. Natalia, trailing fringes, pounced on them from behind a pillar. "David!" she cried. "Why so late?" And started to pull him through the crowd into the auditorium. Sunny followed as well as she could. David turned around once or twice, and finally so did Natalia. "Sunny, go sit in the balcony," she ordered.

"What?"

"Go sit in the balcony," Natalia repeated exasperatedly. "I have only one extra ticket for downstairs."

The two of them disappeared. Sunny climbed upstairs, found an unoccupied seat, and looked into the auditorium below. A beaming David and Natalia were making their way down the crowded aisle to the front row. Then the members of the Institute filed in from the wings, looking, when they had finally filled the chairs onstage, like the picture on a box of Dutch Masters cigars—though a few of the "immortals" were almost too drunk to sit upright. Speeches began and droned on. There was a tap on Sunny's shoulder from the row behind. It was Bill Gould, the poet she had met at one of the parties recently. He whispered an introduction to his friend, Nolan, a sad-faced young man with bleached blond hair. "Couldn't David make it?" "He's downstairs." Bill looked puzzled, as if he wondered in that case what she was doing up there. What indeed? How the hell had she landed in the balcony while Natalia appropriated David for her own? Whose husband did Natalia think David was anyway? Furious, Sunny sidled past a startled Bill, and took a taxi home.

"Where were you?" David said, when he came back. "There was a big party afterwards. Everyone was looking for you. Hymie and Lila and—"

"Hymie was there with Lila?"

"Of course he was with Lila. Who else should he have been with?"

"I don't know. Only that *your* wife had been exiled to the balcony."

"You're nuts," David said with a laugh. "Natalia had only one extra ticket for downstairs."

"Really? Well tell her for me that the next time she wants to borrow my husband, she'd better ask my permission."

"Your *permission?*" David said. "She's my aunt, for God's sake."

"And also, evidently, the absolute dictator of every aspect of your life. Don't you realize that an insult to me is an insult to you?"

"Oh, cut it out," David said wearily. "You've hated her from the beginning. This is just an excuse. You're jealous because she got a prize. You can't even bear the thought of other writers existing. Much less being admired."

"Natalia isn't a writer. Not of English, anyway."

Sarah, coming home from dinner at a friend's house, entered the living room smiling brightly. "Hi, people!" she said, then, looking at the two of them, went off to her room.

"Don't you understand that she really doesn't care about you?" Sunny said, after a moment. "That she's never cared about you? That she uses you the way she uses everyone? Your mother, your father, Fritz—"

"Shut up!"

"I won't have her in this house anymore."

"She won't *come* to this house! She thinks you're crazy. Everybody thinks you're crazy. Don't you know that, you stupid bitch?"

David grabbed her by the arms and shook her furiously. "*Crazy, crazy, crazy!*" He raised a hand, then with a look of disgust let her fall on the couch, and marched into the room which was now Sunny's study. Weeping with rage and pain, she heard him dialing the telephone on her desk. "Hello . . . Yes, darling, it was wonderful. Very impressive." Pause. "Listen, Natalia, I'm afraid you hurt Sunny's feelings . . ." There was another longer pause, and then the sound of the receiver being dropped back on its cradle. Natalia had hung up on him.

David passed by the open archway of the living room and continued on to the front hall, slamming the door behind him.

He would probably spend the night at his studio. Good, at the moment she couldn't stand the sight of him. She listened to the silence from Sarah's room, thought of knocking, and instead took herself off to bed. In the middle of the night she awoke with a start. Still enraged, she dialed David's studio number and waited until he had said "Hello, hello" several times before she slammed down the receiver. Why had she done that? It was crazy to do that. ("Crazy, crazy, crazy," David had called her.) Why couldn't she even stay angry without hearing his voice, without knowing where he was?

4

The taxi sped off down Monadnock Road, and Sunny stood waving goodbye until the back of David's head was no longer visible through the window, his hair gray above the collar of his seersucker jacket. When had David turned so gray? From the back he might have been her father. It was only when he veered around, with a last wave and a rueful smile that he became her husband again. She had come here to escape their quarrels, but now she couldn't even remember what those quarrels were about. Nothing, actually, which made them so awful. And, to be fair, David had been terribly kind to insist on driving up here with her yesterday to make sure she was properly settled in, kind to insist on taking a taxi to the airport so that she would have the rest of the morning to work. They had spent last night with Grace and William, a loving poignant night, as if Sunny were about to enlist in the army. No, it was like that night years ago before he sailed from Genoa. And now once again he was gone.

She went back inside Main Hall, a converted barn, and climbed the stairs to her tiny, airless, country bedroom, a trap for the noise and heat from the kitchen just below. The communal bathroom was outside, off the large center hallway. In the evening, no doubt, a hub of activity, but now deserted, all the "colonists" off at work. She quickly unpacked—anxious, she had brought far too many clothes—and went out again, determined to start work immediately in her studio in the woods, not to brood or stall or wonder why she had come, though the studio had looked dreadfully dark and forbidding when she and David had left her typewriter and manuscripts there a while ago.

"Sunny Harvey?"

"Mansfield," she said automatically, and turned around. It was Bill Gould, of all people, no longer pale, as he had been that day at the Institute, but suntanned and dapper in white duck trousers and an Irish fisherman's sweater whose sleeves were tied around his neck. Her heart lifted.

"Bill! How wonderful to find you here. How long are you staying?"

"Until the end of July."

"Me too," Sunny said. "If I can stick it out that long." Had she seen him since the awards at the Institute? Ironic that Bill's question about where was David had brought her here in the first place. "How's your friend, Nolan?"

"He's up here too," Bill said.

"Really?"

"Look, why don't you come and have a drink in my studio one of these days. Okay?"

More than okay. The breath of home, in the person of Bill Gould, even if Bill seemed unwilling to talk of home and was now hastening to his studio, had definitely revived her spirits. So had the casual invitation to a drink. The last man who had invited her to have a drink with him had been Dick Reeves, and that was years ago in Paris. Sometimes she still thought ruefully of that missed chance with him. But it was all water under the bridge by now. He had become an important person at Princeton and never called about "sacking up" anymore, though David, oddly, had spoken of having lunch with him recently at the Century Club. She consulted her map, skirted a great open meadow, and found her studio easily, not forbidding after all as it had seemed when she peered inside with David, just a small rustic cottage furnished with all she or any writer would really need: a large work table, a gooseneck lamp, a cot covered by a green army blanket, a big blackened fireplace. There was even a distant view of the blue Monadnock mountains. She had assumed she would be frightened and lonesome, waste her time sharpening pencils, making notes. But after she had tacked up a photograph of David, and one of Sarah, and one of them both together, had stared through the window at a yellow warbler hopping from branch to branch of a spreading pine tree, she started work immediately on the final revision of her novel.

Dinnertimes were hard, however. Each day she looked forward to the cowbell that clanged at 6:30 and brought everyone trooping into the dining room at Main Hall. But by 6:55 it was all over, and only Sunny, it seemed, was still trying to talk to her right and to her left. The others had already drifted back to their studios in the woods, or sat sprawled listlessly in the cavernous recreation room, which resembled the inside of a hunting lodge, moose head and all. That was the moment when her heart sank. There had been no drink with Bill and his friend Nolan, the sad-faced composer with the bleached blond hair—they seemed to have entered into a tacit agreement not to let on that they knew each other in the outside world. Each evening that David called, she had to struggle with the desire to say she had made a terrible mistake and wanted to come home. Sarah, who hated camp this year, wanted to come home too. A crazy arrangement. But the days were glorious. The feeling of joy in her work that she had once known on the Cape had come back multiplied a thousandfold. Her characters were finally coming alive. She was making surprising connections. The tone was right. She was on to something. No, she couldn't give up those glorious days however grim the nights.

She said goodbye to David, and emerged from the phone booth with a bright smile, like a Gorham girl who had just heard from a date. But there was no one around to care. Bill Gould was sitting in front of the fireplace with an aging and tremulous blond female named Babette. Nolan had skulked off to bed. Others were sunk in shadows around the huge room: an angry black painter, a married couple who were working on a play together and who smiled a great deal, an Indian lady in a sari, a pretty Southern boy in a maroon velour pullover who every evening played pool by himself.

"We are all still strangers to one another," Babette was saying. "It can still be a terribly enriching summer."

"Oh?" Bill said. "How many summers here have you been enriched by?"

"They all blend together. I forget."

"David sends regards," Sunny said to Bill.

"Such an attentive husband," Babette said with a wistful smile. "Do you have children?"

"One. A daughter."

"Is she beautiful?"

"Yes, I suppose you'd call her beautiful," Sunny said, looking over to the pool table. The pretty Southern boy had laid down his cue stick and seemed to be sauntering over. "She has beautiful coloring, long blond hair, lovely peachy young skin."

"Why do people make such a fetish of youth in this country?" Babette said.

"She's twelve years old."

The Southern boy asked Sunny if she wanted to play ping pong. "Ping pong?" Sunny said, glancing at Bill. Bill shrugged and looked away. Shrugging too, she got up and played three games and lost them all. She always lost with David too, but only because it frightened her when she was winning. Leander, however, cut and sliced and chopped, watched with pleasant equanimity as she scrambled for missed balls under the radiator, his bland smile at variance with his cold blue eyes.

"Okay, then let's go have us a beer," Leander said, when she had refused a rematch. She persuaded Bill to come along too. Babette invited herself. They drove to a nearby motel in Leander's red convertible and entered the cocktail lounge cautiously, like newly released inmates. When the drinks came, Sunny said too soon and too loudly, "Please, I'll pay for mine." Bill gave her a peculiar look. Babette began to speak tremulously about a novel that Hiram Haydn liked but couldn't get anyone else at Atheneum to agree to publish. (Did he do this to *everyone*?) Leander, who had just published a novel, said he should have gone to Greenwood, where the food was better.

"But if you've just *published* a novel," Sunny said, wanting

to change the subject—had Leander ever run into David?—
"why come to an artist's colony at all?"

"It's a summer," Leander said, ordering another beer, then
another. The more he drank, the thicker his accent became
until he sounded like Mary Jane when she was drunk, except
that Leander seemed to have been raised in some mountainous
region in North Carolina. On their way back to the Colony,
he launched into a series of hounddog, coonskin stories, with
such gleeful chuckles at each punchline that Bill kept wincing.
The men went off to their rooms in a red clapboard farmhouse,
the women upstairs to the bedrooms in Main Hall. "I'm fifty,
you know," Babette said with a smile, as if she were confiding
a great and amazing secret, "I have a married daughter." Through
the open door, Sunny saw into Babette's room. A large flowered
bathing suit was slung from the back of her chair. On top of
her bureau were a bottle of Scotch, a bowl of fruit, jars of
cosmetics, bottles of perfume, a portable radio. As a result of
her "enriching" summers, the poor woman had certainly learned
how to make herself at home.

"*Awful*," Bill had said of Leander the next morning, and it was
certainly true. But then why was Sunny suddenly seeing him
everywhere, like a newly learned word leaping out of a page?
Wolfing down his breakfast in the morning, leafing through the
Colony copy of the *Times* in the recreation hall (strange that
she hardly ever read the paper here), speeding off to town in
his ridiculous red convertible, after dinner at the pool table,
white teeth gripping an empty pipe, intently studying a shot, in
profile a male model. Except that even his good looks were
strangely spurious and dated: the jutting jaw, the pipe, the short
wavy hair, were all out of the twenties, like the convertible.
David in his evening phone calls and frequent letters was pleased
that Sunny's work was progressing well. "Though the evenings
are pretty ghastly," Sunny said, "the people are awful." "Well,
it's always like that. It's the work that counts. You're not there
for the social life, are you?" "Of course not, darling. Tell me

what's doing in New York." "Nothing," David said quickly, "you're lucky to be out of it."

But if she was not there for the social life, why was she so looking forward to the absurd Colony party on Saturday night? A party which had arisen for no reason at all and would be held in Nolan's studio on account of the piano. She arrived with a bottle of Scotch. Everybody else came with bottles too, which they stuck on Nolan's work table with an experienced air, mostly vodka, though Leander brought two six packs of beer with his name on them. Babette had gotten herself up in a tight, flower-splashed cocktail dress, Nolan was wearing mascara. As Nolan began to play old musical comedy songs on the piano, other "colonists"—would she ever get used to calling them that?—gathered around singing. Leander sang loudest, making up lyrics when he didn't know them. Sunny left the piano to get herself a drink of her own Scotch, stepping over the angry black painter, who had fallen asleep near the fireplace, his head buttressed by an andiron. On the way back the drunk Irish writer made a lunge for her, and so did the husband half of the smiling married couple. She hurried back to the piano, and placed herself securely beside Bill while Nolan's hands flew along the keys. Where was Leander? Had he gone already? Then Leander reappeared through the screen door, making a last little adjustment to his fly. Of course, the beer. Her heart filled with a strange happiness. She had *missed* him!

Somehow the party had petered to a halt, and somehow she was riding back through the deep dark woods with Leander in his open convertible. He stopped in front of Main Hall and she made only the smallest of moves to get out.

"Such a beautiful night," she said.

"We could go for a drive," Leander said.

"Yes."

He made a swift turn around the gravel circle then headed back toward the woods and the empty studios. Overhead, the stars were brilliant and distinct. Her hair felt free in the wind. They stopped in front of his studio. She pulled her sweater over her shoulders.

"Leander?"

"Ma'am?"

"I'm thinking about my reputation."

Leander nodded agreeably—she looked at him in profile—
and quickly turned the car around again. Only a small night
light shone above the entrance to Main Hall, barely illuminating
the white columns, the twining ivy. Resting his hands on the
wheel, Leander turned to her with his bland smile. She flung
herself at him and they kissed passionately for a long time. (How
sweet he was.) "If it's your reputation you're worried about,"
Leander finally murmured into her fevered ear, "in about two
minutes you're not going to have one."

Right. She pulled herself together, remembered her sweater,
failed to resist kissing him one more passionate time, raced
inside. Upstairs Babette was unhooking her garters, pulling down
her girdle. "Why, Miss Mansfield—" she said with a wistful,
and bitchy smile. "Or, now that I know who you are, Mrs.
Harvey—have you been *necking* with that young man?"

"David, I think I'd better come home," Sunny said. She had
just realized that though she had been sleeping on only one
pillow she had now slept on both.

"Okay," David said with a sigh. "Do you want me to come
up and get you?"

"No . . . I'll stick it out."

"Why don't you spend a few days with your parents?"

"Okay, I will," she said, though her parents seemed farther
away than David. She telephoned Sarah, who came running
up from the lake. "Oh, Mama, I think I'm in love," Sarah said,
in a breathless, tinny voice.

She slogged off to her studio. She would not let that hillbilly
Lothario become an obsession, there was too much at stake.
Not just in terms of her marriage. ("You'd be nervous having
an affair with a stranger," David had said, and Leander was
certainly a stranger.) Anyway, she didn't *want* to have an affair.
An affair wouldn't solve anything, only lead to more compli-

cations. More to the point, she didn't want any distractions from her work. That morning glancing surreptitiously over Leander's shoulder at the Sunday *Book Review* after breakfast, she had glimpsed a big ad for Charlotte's new novel. (Charlotte had already sent her a witty letter about paranoia.) Imagine introducing Charlotte to Leander, imagine Charlotte listening to the hounddog-coonskin stories. No. She adjusted the pictures of David and of Sarah and of them both together, and tried to concentrate. *Married* love was the subject, she told herself, *domestic* love—not careless rapture. Nevertheless, she had a distinct sense that all around her in the Colony people were going to pieces. Bill was suffering from a slipped disc. The Indian lady had been found passed out in her studio clutching an empty bottle of vodka, sari and all. Nolan had locked himself in his bedroom and refused to come out, while a sweetish acrid odor seeped through the door. Babette was making scenes. The other night in the dining room she had burst into tears over some remark Leander had made, and stomped out with a sloshing glass of red wine. What had Leander said to hurt her, and what did it matter? Sunny rose from her desk, looked at the small wooden board propped on the mantel on which previous occupants of her studio had signed their names—"tombstones" the boards were called, on account of their shape—and failed to recognize any famous signatures, though other colonists had claimed to find Willa Cather and Thornton Wilder.

She dragged her green army blanket to the small clearing outside and lay down. It was hot. She undid her blouse. What if Leander came passing by and saw her, breasts bared to the sun? A wave of desire swept over her. She buttoned up again quickly and decided to take a walk. Why not? It was Sunday and she really had seen very little of the Colony besides her own studio. A few hundred yards down, there was Babette through the trees lying on a beach chair in her caftan. "The sex act diminishes you," Babette was murmuring to the Irish novelist, who was stretched out at her feet. She crossed the meadow and in spite of herself went down a short dirt road. At the end of it stood Leander's studio, disappointingly prosaic by daylight. There was no red convertible parked outside. She peered through the window—it was large and barren, actually a painter's studio, Leander had once complained—and stepped cautiously inside. Leander's familiar maroon velour pullover was tossed on the army cot, along with a pair of ankle sneakers and some skimpy white lastex bathing trunks. In the bookcase, half a dozen copies of Leander's novel, *Carolina Balladeer* were lined up alongside *Manchild in the Promised Land,* and the *Viking Portable Faulkner.* She looked at Leander's book jacket and at his ridiculously idealized photograph complete with pipe, not particularly surprised to learn from the caption that Leander was nearer thirty-five than twenty-five—though still a few years younger than she. Several letters were scattered beside his typewriter, and also a dim color snapshot of a little girl. She started to walk out, strangely sad, then stopped and looked at the names on Leander's "tombstone." Painters probably. *Marjorie Stewart.* Her heart jerked. She left quickly and kept walking until she saw Bill Gould on the porch of his studio, rocking back and forth for therapeutic reasons. He was no longer natty, poor man, but strained and hunched.

"Have you seen Leander?" Bill said.

"Leander?"

"He promised to pick me up some stuff in town—oh, there he is."

She turned around. Leander was sauntering across the field, hands in the pockets of a navy blue windbreaker, the pipe jutting out of his mouth. Tall wheaty grass swayed around him.

"You forgot," Bill said.

"Forgot what? Oh, hell, did I promise to go into town for you?" Leander said, his voice breaking. "Damn, I just came back from there."

"I'll go," Sunny said. "I have a car."

"No need, ma'am," Leander said. "A promise is a promise. Come on, honey, I'll take you along."

Sunny gave Bill a silly smile. Then head down, like a Chinese woman, she followed Leander back through the ripe singing fields.

"My, my, my," Leander said, carrying several large brown paper bags out of the general store and stowing them in his convertible. "You certainly do know how to domesticate a man."

"You know very well most of that's for Bill," Sunny said curtly, nevertheless obscurely flattered.

Across the street, Nolan was standing forlornly outside of the closed post office, looking around for a lift. His khaki shorts were creased in the crotch, his legs knobby. She got into the convertible beside Leander, looked over at Nolan, hesitated, and said nothing. Leander started the motor and sped off. At the fork in the road, he looked at her, then headed away from the Colony, out toward the open highway, taking himself a drive as casually as a city person like David might take a walk. He slowed down when a lake appeared on their left, easing his long legs in their jeans. His shiny blue windbreaker opened on a white T-shirt stretched taut across his chest.

"Pretty part of the world, isn't it?" Leander said.

"Yes, beautiful. Actually, I know this region. My parents have a summer house near Hancock." But suddenly she felt she didn't know this region at all.

"Is that so? . . . Could you reach me my sunglasses, honey, right there in the glove compartment?" She handed them over, realizing too late that she had automatically polished them with her kerchief. Leander gave an amused nod of thanks, and struck the glasses on top of his head like an aviator in a biplane.

"I drive around here most every day," he said. "These hills remind me of home. Except of course that we have *real* mountains. Craggy. Hell, my grandaddy and I, we used to climb up and down them like a pair of billy goats. I remember one time—"

"You're really being awfully nice about everything," Sunny said.

"Nice about what?"

"Well, I mean after the stupid way I behaved—"

"Honey, are you losing sleep over that?" Leander said with

his usual disconcerting smile. The smile traveled down the length of her, stopping at the v of her shorts. She shifted on the sticky red leather seat.

"Leander, since you're so Southern, couldn't you also contrive to be a gentleman?"

"No ma'am," Leander said, a touch nastily.

"Look, I don't blame you for being annoyed," Sunny said. "In fact, maybe I shouldn't be in this car at all. I mean, we're both adults and—would you mind watching the road? . . . That is, of course I like driving around with you like this. But—maybe you ought to take someone else."

"Certainly," Leander said, resting his elbow on the window frame. "Who?"

"I don't know. Babette?"

"*Darlin'*," Leander said, turning around, "are you trying to make yourself look good bringing up that ruin?"

"That's cruel. It's not her fault she's fifty."

"Maybe pushing sixty? Maybe with a dozen grandchildren stashed away somewhere?" Leander shook his head and chuckled.

"But all women age. What are you supposed to do when that happens?"

"I don't know, sweetheart. Maybe make sure you have a husband around when it does."

Leander stuck his empty pipe into his mouth and began to whistle around it. They had circled the lake and now it appeared on Sunny's side of the car, blue and sparkling in the sun, easy to imagine black and silvery by moonlight.

"I have a husband *now*," Sunny said.

"I know that, darlin'. David Harvey." Leander pulled up by the side of the road. "Well, what do you want to do? Sit under a tree and drink beer, or go home?"

"Go home." But it wasn't her home. Home was David and Sarah. Not some artists colony where desperate females like Marjorie Stewart came for cheap adventures, latching onto people like David.

"Are you sure now?" Leander said, obediently shifting gears

and driving on again. Why was he so compliant? "Because there are an awful lot of pleasant things we could do."

"Such as?"

"I don't know. Take a chair lift up a mountain. Swim across the lake. Go see some summer stock on Saturday night. Bring some beers back to my studio, make a fire . . . do you really want me to spell it out for you, darlin'?"

"There's Mount Monadnock up ahead," Sunny said. "Let's drive up to the top."

Leander nodded, shifted gears, and expertly negotiated the sharp curves up the narrow, leafy road. Parking at the flat open space at the top, he sprang out of the car and whirled around, so that the two halves of his shiny blue windbreaker swelled and flew apart. Then he bounded down a steep stony path between the trees. She emerged cautiously, smoothing her shorts. The view was spectacular, a vast panorama of the echoing blue mountains she could glimpse from her studio, now repeating themselves endlessly through wispy clouds, patches of sunshine. Little wet silver lakes gleamed in the valley. Leander hove back into sight a short distance away, leaping agilely from one rocky ledge to another. He was holding his blue jacket over his shoulder by a thumb, and his body looked as hard and narrow as a dancer's. She took a few steps toward him, and started to slip and slide down the pebbly dirt.

"Leander! I need help."

He turned around, frowning, and reluctantly climbed back to her. "It's my sandals," Sunny said, reaching for his hand.

"Take 'em off," Leander said and, as soon as she had, plunged off again, jumping from crag to crag, from rocky ledge to rocky ledge. A billy goat. A faun. Awful, awful, awful. On the highest ledge, he stopped and beckoned to her. Go on, Sunny, she told herself. Jump, make a break for it. A break for what? She had already turned back toward the car.

"Follow me! Follow me!"

Oh, Leander. Leander, darling, I can't.

5

Joe Farber had taken her to lunch at the Four Seasons to celebrate. She had never been there with Eleanor Reed, a mere
junior editor whose expense account would hardly allow for
such elegance. But Joe Farber, in his beautifully cut gray English suit, his impeccable striped shirt and tie, his dull gold
cufflinks, had been shown immediately and deferentially to his
own table. (She had a fleeting memory of Leander in his shiny
blue windbreaker. What had that been all about? Midsummer
madness.) To her surprise, Joe loved the new manuscript. Or
rather, the women in the office to whom he had passed it
around, including the lady at the switchboard, had loved it,
which from his point of view was even better.

"Yes, you've definitely struck a chord. Captured the drama
in the daily life of the ordinary housewife."

"I have?" Sunny said, almost persuaded that this was what
she had had in mind in the first place.

"Women. They'll respond. See themselves. Identify with
your heroine. Think they're all heroines too. Buy it. Women
buy novels, not men, you know."

"Yes, I realize that," Sunny said. It was not a literary conversation of the highest order, certainly not the conversation
that when she was young she had imagined having with her
own Maxwell Perkins. Nor would the novel that Joe was describing cause pudgy Bloom of *The New York Review* to commit
himself to more than "Hullo." But she had been snubbed by
the New York literati, old and new, for so long—and no doubt
would be as long as people thought that she had got the idea
of becoming a writer from being married to David—that it no
longer mattered. As Charlotte said, "Why knock our brains
out?" Still, she was glad that David was away in Israel at the

moment, to write "A Poet's view of the Six-Day War" for *The Saturday Review* and that she would not have to face him right after this lunch.

"Women," Joe said. "The hottest new subject. You'll see. In a few years women's books will be all anyone in publishing is talking about. You've struck a chord."

What chord Joe Farber struck with women was another matter. He didn't exactly have a hand on her knee at the moment, in fact he hadn't touched her at all, except to steer her to his table by the elbow. But despite his clipped English style, his ruddy squire's face and graying hair, his degagé air of being the completely successful man of business cum letters, a sensation of hand-on-the-knee was unmistakably there. To be honest, the longer she sat there, the more attractive Joe became. His manner was formal, but there was also an amused glint in his eye which suggested that once Joe got you in bed he would throw formality to the winds. She brought herself up short. Why was she thinking such things? Nevertheless, at the end of the lunch, refusing a cab, she walked away feeling that in the case of Joe Farber there was much more to come. The feeling worried her. She wanted it to be all business, no hanky panky, nothing that would jeopardize her book. (Again she thought fleetingly of Leander.) No, she had mixed apples and oranges once already, confused her professional life with her personal life when she met David, and look what had happened. It had become *all* personal. Bessie would probably understand—poor Bessie, she must give her a call soon—but Charlotte would no doubt think she was nuts. Charlotte had had an affair with her editor and when it was over, calmly walked away and found a new publisher. Never mind. That was Charlotte. Still, she could not wait to laugh with her about the "chord."

"How'd it go, Mama?" Sarah said, handing her an airmail letter from David.

"Wonderful, darling. Wonderful." She had spent the after-noon wandering in and out of elegant shops on Madison Avenue, unwilling to come down from her high. "He's going to send out three thousand bound galleys for comments. He's talking about a big advertising budget."

"Oh, *wow!*"

"Maybe we're counting our chickens . . . ," Sunny said dubiously. "No, the hell with it. Let's celebrate. Let's go to dinner and a movie." They hugged each other.

While Sarah voluntarily went to change in honor of the occasion, Sunny glanced through David's letter. Before his trip she had found him immersed in the Old Testament, whose imagery had suddenly gripped him profoundly. Now his enthusiasm for Israel transcended fine points of language. His letters were long, frequent, packed like fruitcakes with personal impressions. The Book of Exodus forgotten, he sent accounts of Syrian tanks hastily abandoned in the desert, expeditions to the Golan Heights with Israeli soldiers, whose toughness, burliness utterly astonished him. His letters to Sarah were practically identical. Ironic that after all these years and all their quarrels David had turned into a Jewish chauvinist. Perhaps in his letters to Natalia, David stressed Israel's importance as an ally against the Soviet Union. That is, if indeed he wrote letters to Natalia. He never mentioned her anymore, nor did she come to the house. Had David and Natalia had a falling out that he hadn't admitted to Sunny? She seemed to have won that round. But too easily?

Shaking off her misgivings, she took Sarah gaily off to Marvin Gardens, one of the new stylish restaurants on Broadway which had supplanted such old "allrightnik" standbys as Tiptoe Inn. They pored over the menu. She glanced at Sarah, who was such a big beautiful girl now, so tender-hearted and generous. ("Well, we must be doing something right," David always said.) "Listen, don't worry about the price," Sunny said, "the sky's the limit," and for some reason thought of the time she and David had celebrated David's first Guggenheim. Had they quarreled afterwards? Probably. But she and Sarah never quarreled. Despite all the stereotypes of early teenagers and the running complaints of the Thorndike parents, Sarah was a most pacific child. Even when her best friend, Daniel, told her that her first lipstick looked like a suppository, she had conceded philosophically that it did. It was so easy to be with her, such a joy. She was describing excitedly, words tripping over each other, her gym teacher at Thorndike, who all last year had been a total ape woman, and this year had turned strangely frilly and feminine. They were to fold their bras or undershirts neatly away in their lockers, bring in a little light powder or deodorant. Bras. There were little bumps on Sarah's chest.

"How do you put on deodorant?" Sarah asked.

Sunny told her.

"May I have some for home use?"

"Oh, Sarah," Sunny said, and took her off to the movies.

The two weeks alone with Sarah was like a vacation. David came home in high spirits, bringing them such souvenirs as spent bullets. When Sunny took Sarah to the peace march in Washington, David, immersed in his piece, waved them off as if they were going to a party. It was a beautiful fall day. The immense quiet crowd spread all the way over to the Washington Monument like multicolored autumn leaves. She held Sarah's hand tightly, afraid to lose her. There were tears in Sarah's eyes. Would Sarah always remember this afternoon? She wished David could have been persuaded to come; she wished she did not hear Natalia in the back of her mind pooh-poohing this peaceful horde as "canaille." In fact, a small group of poets finally did go to Washington to protest the war, but David decided not to join them. He was delighted when he heard they got only as far as a Presidential aide, who thought that Muriel Rukeyser was somebody's wife, and told the story with relish over and over again. It all had a strangely familiar ring, until she realized he was dining out on it, just as he had on his meeting with President Kennedy.

Joe Farber, in his elliptical way, had been professionally astute; her portrait of an ordinary bourgeois housewife did strike a chord. There were many favorable reviews, a few good-sized ads—the "huge promotion budget" had been hyperbole, and she had agreed that the outlay for a party would be better spent on advertising—an assortment of interviews. (Sarah carefully clipped and saved them all). *Publisher's Weekly* asked her to contribute to a symposium on women writers, *Mademoiselle* wondered if she would care to review for them on a regular basis, the dean of the New School asked her if she would like to come in and discuss a course. On what, though?

"You don't want to teach," David said.

"Why not?"

"You're a novelist."

What David made of the husband in her book, whom she had meant to be a sympathetic character, beleaguered, confused by his aspiring wife, she would never know. She had given him the first copy, inscribed with all her love. (She had dedicated the book to Sarah.) He took it off to the maid's room—he had stayed home with an attack of bursitis in his left shoulder—and spent the morning reading it, turning page after page with an unfathomable expression. To kill time, she went downstairs and wandered around Broadway, forgetting what she needed in the supermarket, then sat in the public library on Amsterdam Avenue, leafing witlessly through a stack of magazines. Why did it still matter so terribly what David thought? (She had even sent away the superintendent who had come to fix a leak in the kitchen so as not to disturb him.) Why was she still waiting for David to say, "Oh, Sunnoo, now I see, now I understand"? When she came back David was sitting in the living room rubbing his shoulder, *Bread and Roses* closed on the sofa beside him. "It's painful," David said.

"You ought to see the doctor," Sunny said, torn between awful disappointment and sympathy.

David looked at her, bewildered. She understood that he had been talking about her book. Had she reached the bottom with him, unable to distinguish between his criticism and his bursitis?

"You write good," David finally said, mustering a bleak smile.

"You write good." Hardly what she had hoped for but, looking back, the last cheerful, or even semi-cheerful words, David seemed to have spoken to her all spring. Each day, he grew more restless, more despondent. He had certainly always been given to bouts of despair, but now there was no reaching him at all. Even Sarah, usually the one bright spot in his gloom, failed to coax a smile. What was it this time? Surely not just the reception of his anthology of contemporary American poets, which was doing well and had been adopted as a text in many colleges, but had caused a lot of resentment, both about who had been included and who had been excluded—the most vociferous complainer being Bill Gould.

On a Saturday morning in May, when David's mood appeared to have softened, she and Sarah got him to take a walk, strolling uptown along Riverside Drive. The grass in the park was a tender green, cherry trees had burst into a filigree of pink blossoms overhead. On Claremont Avenue they crossed over to Broadway and abruptly left spring behind. The Columbia campus loomed up ahead of them. She waited for David to begin his litany of complaints against Edward Maxwell, and instead, like him, stared openmouthed. Students were swarming all over the lawns and buildings, carrying signs, shouting slogans, sitting in windows with their legs dangling over the ledges, catcalling. "Hey, hey, LBJ! How many kids did you kill today?" There was talk in the growing crowd around them that the cops would be called in, though that seemed impossible. They were only children, but children who had been asked to die in Vietnam. On the other hand, should children be allowed to destroy a great university?

"Mama?" Sarah said, pulling her by the sleeve. Sunny quickly put a finger on her lips and veered David in another direction. Like Sarah, she too had thought that one of the catcallers on a window ledge looked an awful lot like Gloria.

The interview was going very well. Usually she was a bit nervous beforehand, but Mary Clark, a friendly young woman from a

Cleveland paper, seemed actually to have read—and liked—Sunny's book. They sat in a new restaurant on the ground floor of the CBS building, a modernistic melange of chrome, pale furniture, and smoky mirrors, a far cry altogether from Sunny's first interview long ago, which had taken place at the old Murray Hill Hotel amid potted palms, martinis, heavy steaks, and Tommy Job at her elbow to act as guide and mentor. She and Mary smiled at each other pleasantly as they broke off to finish their white wine and salad.

"Well, you seem to be one of those rare women who have everything," Mary Clark said.

"I guess I've been lucky," Sunny said.

Lucky. The word made her nervous again. ("*Vous avez la chance de chanter*" . . . "Oh, David please let's not squander it.") Friendly as Mary was, she suddenly wished that the interview were over, weary of the canned picture of herself—early publication, successful marriage—that she gave to the press. Though, as Charlotte often consoled her, "It doesn't matter what they say, sweetie, as long as they spell your name right."

"Oh, one more thing," Mary said picking up her pencil again. "Is your husband supportive?"

"Supportive?" Sunny repeated warily.

"But I guess there's no competition, is there?" Mary said, laughing. "I mean he's a poet and you're a novelist."

"Yes."

Mary nodded, and made some small note. "And your daughter? Does she resent having a mother who's a well-known author?"

"Sarah?" Sunny said, breathing easier. "Oh no, Sarah's wonderful. She's totally on my side."

"Does she plan to become another Sunny Mansfield?"

"I hope not," Sunny said, laughing.

Sunny Mansfield. She had been foolish to worry. It was definitely Sunny Mansfield who was being interviewd, not Mrs. David Harvey. A far greater change than chrome for potted palms, and part of what Joe Farber had predicted, an entirely new perspective on women. At the interview's end, she and

Mary cordially shook hands. Sunny Mansfield. Feeling very professional, Sunny Mansfield looked at her watch and took a taxi to the New School, where she had an appointment with the dean to discuss a course on women writers.

"Or rather the female protagonist in women's fiction. I'm not sure whether I'll find heroines."

"Do you think there'll be an interest in such a subject?" the dean asked dubiously.

"Definitely. It will strike a chord."

She left him and stood on the corner of Fifth Avenue and Twelfth Street enjoying the sweet balmy air. Had she been right to try to talk the dean into such a course, quote Joe Farber at his most incoherent, or had the successful interview gone to her head? The dean had looked extremely leery, as only academics could, and it would mean a lot of reading, over the summer, too, when she had promised herself and Joe Farber to make some real headway on a new novel. But perhaps a nonfiction book would come out of it. Other writers moved back and forth between genres, why not Sunny Mansfield? She had intended to go back uptown, but instead kept walking down toward the heart of the Village, telling herself that she would soon reverse direction and go home and make notes on some characters already in her head, maybe get started on the piece she had promised *Mademoiselle*: "Then and Now." But in the window of the Eighth Street Bookstore, there was *Bread and Roses*, a whole display of *Bread and Roses*, in fact. By Sunny Mansfield, Sunny Mansfield, Sunny Mansfield. Suddenly, she felt lightheaded and gay all over again. On impulse, she called David at his studio.

"You're downtown?" David said. "Okay, I'll meet you in the bookstore. I'm finished anyway."

"Oh, David, I don't want to be trapped in a bookstore on a beautiful day like this. I'll come and get you."

"Trapped in a bookstore?"

"I'll pick you up," Sunny said, laughing.

David reluctantly agreed, and she walked the few blocks over to Bleecker Street with her heart in a sudden flurry of excitement, as if she were truly on her way, no, not to a date—something a bit spicier—an assignation. Inside the broken-down building where David had his studio, the corridors and stairway were brown and sour-smelling, the steps shaky. As always she wondered how David faced these flights of stairs every day. Didn't his spirits sink at the prospect? Yet when, hearing her footsteps, he opened the door for her and she finished climbing up, she once more understood. It was bright white behind him, the studio flooded with light, the ceiling high, the moldings around it elaborately carved and fluted. David stood in a shaft of sunlight like a photograph of himself.

"It's so sexy here," Sunny said, laughing as she came in.

David raised an eyebrow.

She sat down on the edge of the narrow daybed, which was covered with a rumpled blue madras spread. David remained standing. He was dressed to leave. Very formally dressed, in fact, in a light gray suit and white shirt and maroon tie.

"Aren't you going to offer me a drink?" Sunny said.

"I'll buy you a drink downstairs."

"I'd rather have one here."

"Sunny, what's on your mind? What did you come here looking for?"

"David, I just feel good, I told you. The interview went well. I talked the dean at the New School into a course—almost. I'm with my handsome husband in his private pad. . . . No drink?"

David fished a bottle of vermouth from under a very dirty kitchen sink and poured some for her into a little Dixie cup.

"Yes, I can see why you love this place," Sunny said. "Would you like me to send Margaret down to clean it up a bit? I could give her some extra dishes too."

"Don't bother. It's not worth it."

"It's no bother, darling."

"I won't be here that long," David said, splashing some vermouth into a Dixie cup for himself too, and then sitting down across the room next to his typewriter. "I'm losing this place."

"Oh, David, no!"

"Oh, David, yes . . . The landlord wants it back for a nephew."

"How awful. Is it certain?"

David nodded glumly. "What will *you* do?"

"I?" Sunny asked.

"When I'm back in the house."

"I don't know. I haven't had time to think about it yet."

"Don't worry," David said. "I'll work in the maid's room. I won't ask for my study back."

"No, David, it'll be okay, really. It will be fun to have you home again." She meant it. It would be like when Sarah got sick and had to be kept home from school, cozy, like a holiday, like being caught indoors in a blizzard. Cozy and sweet for the first few days, anyway.

"Meanwhile," Sunny said, leaning back on her elbows and swinging a leg. "You're here, and so am I."

"Don't," David said. "I don't feel like it. Let's go home."

"I don't want to go home," Sunny said. "I just got here."

Sighing, David rested his cheek on his palm. She got up and put her arms around him, laughing when he quickly reached out a hand and closed his notebook. His journal was the furthest thing from her mind. No, it was what she had told him. The atmosphere in the studio *was* very sexy, nothing like home where David's lovemaking had become prosaic, perfunctory. (Lately he even yawned, waiting for her to come.) Was it Shaw who had said of marriage, "From the hurly burly of the chaise longue to the deep, deep peace of the double bed"?—one of David's favorite quotations. Well, there was no boring double bed here. Only that narrow exciting daybed. Suddenly she wanted him terribly. She would seduce him, if necessary. Be his mistress, his wife, his lover all in one. She slowly undid the knot of his tie. To her amazed delight, David yielded. Reluctant at first, then fiercely passionate, he tumbled her onto the daybed. . . . Oh, David, David, there had never been anyone else, *never.* When David loved her like this, she did have everything. . . .

They had come together, and she felt giddy with happiness. Now they lay pressed against each other as they used to in David's old studio apartment, Sunny on the inside against the wall, David holding her from behind, two sticky nesting teaspoons. She dozed off, awakening once or twice in a sweet erotic haze to realize where she was. She dozed off again, and awakened this time to a sudden thump. She sat upright, flustered and confused. David was sprawled on the floor, naked. "Oh, darling, you fell, I'm so sorry."

"You threw me out of bed, you bitch!"

"David, are you crazy?"

"You threw me out of bed!" David cried. *"Bitch! Bitch! Bitch!"*

6

Why? What had come over him? What did he think she had done? David apologized and stonily shook his head. He had had a bad dream, that was all. A few weeks later he moved his stuff home—books, typewriter, violin, filing cabinets—and insisted on occupying the maid's room behind the kitchen. No amount of persuasion could get him out of there. Sweltering in an early heat wave, sweat staining his shirt, he sat glowering and miserable—every once in a while she would walk back and find him in tears—while she tried futilely to settle down to work in the study. They couldn't go on like this. It was a pressure cooker ready to explode. She began to dream of the country, of a quiet shady house where each of them could go for time out from each other.

In a way it was a godsend when Amanda Montini called to say she loved *Bread and Roses*, and to invite them up to Vermont for the weekend. Sunny had forgotten how pleasant it was to talk to Amanda, forgotten also what had led to the rupture in the first place. She chose a date when David would be off giving some readings—he would not have wanted to go anyway—and persuaded Sarah to come along. It would be their last chance to spend time together before school was over and Sarah went to camp as a junior counselor. "She was my first editor," Sunny said, almost neglecting to add, "and she introduced me to Daddy." Relaxed for the first time in weeks, she strolled down the leafy country road with Amanda, while the two girls, Sarah and Amanda's daughter, Anne, walked on ahead, their heads shiny and golden in the dappled sunlight. It was clear why Amanda had given up the wild beauty of the Cape for these quiet Vermont foothills, why she preferred her big farmhouse on its woodsy rolling acres to a rented tumbledown beach shack exposed to the sun.

"It's so solid here, so peaceful," Sunny said, sighing. "But you've always had a genius for real estate. "You're the one who first suggested the Cape, remember?"

"Do you still go there?"

"Sometimes, but it's so damn intense." They had not seen each other in ages, but it was easy to fall into the old rhythms of friendship. "I bet David would like it here too, though he's so adamant against owning property. Still, it feels so far away from New York, though it's quite near. He could go into town whenever he felt like it. It's very hard for two writers to live and work together, you know. Sometimes I think, impossible."

"It or he?" Amanda asked.

"He," Sunny said, and realized that it was Amanda, not Charlotte or Bessie, to whom she could speak frankly about David, the person who knew him the longest, the one who had introduced him into Sunny's life, had openly called him an irritable hypochondriac. Still, she hesitated before she took a deep breath and went on.

". . . Oh, Amanda, who am I kidding? I'm really at my wit's end these days. I don't know what's going on anymore. He's so unhappy. And then these awful quarrels blow up out of thin air. Like summer squalls. And he—" No, not even to Amanda could she mention the rest of it. "I don't know what I'm doing wrong."

"Maybe nothing," Amanda said.

"No, I must be, because—"

"Sunny, he has some one," Amanda said.

Sunny stopped short. "What are you talking about?"

"Someone he met at Greenwood. An artist."

"Oh, that one," Sunny said, walking on, laughing, weak with relief. "I know all about *that* one. She haunts Monadnock too. But that was years and years ago. I can't even remember her name." It was a lie. She did remember her name. She just couldn't bring herself to say it.

"I meant the last time he was at Greenwood."

"The last time? You must be mistaken. He was working very hard on his poem, and then he came right up to the Cape afterwards, and he—"

"I guess I am mistaken," Amanda said. "It's just a rumor in the art world."

The art world. If Amanda only knew how much David despised the current art scene, how often, particularly lately, he vociferously attacked it as mindless and opportunistic. But she could hardly say so without insulting Milo and Amanda too. She was glad when Amanda dropped the subject and they walked faster to join the girls.

Milo and the Montini boy had decided to stay in New York, leaving them for the rest of the weekend to be two mothers and their daughters, bringing vegetables in from the garden, cooking together in the big country kitchen, talking around the fire at night. Amanda's daughter, five years older than Sarah and in college, had made a pet of her. She watched Sarah's eager upturned face, reflecting the firelight. Under Sarah's T-shirt, the bumps had turned into breasts. For the time being she did not want to think about it. Nor did she want to think of the growing inner turmoil that had shattered her country serenity, though Amanda was careful not to mention David again. What was it Bessie had said about the capacity of the human heart to believe what it wanted to believe?

"I beg your pardon?" she said to Amanda.

"I was complimenting you on *Bread and Roses,*" Amanda said with a wry smile.

The next day she and Sarah drove back to town. They were eating cold cuts they had bought at Zabars, when David called to say he would be back tomorrow, a day earlier than he was supposed to.

"Oh, that's wonderful, darling," Sunny said with surprise.

"Wonderful?"

"Of course. You didn't have to call, though. You could have just come home."

"I didn't want to disturb you," David said.

A strange remark, but men who were having affairs didn't

come home sooner than expected. Or did they? Sarah kissed her goodnight and went to bed early. The house was quiet, too quiet. Restless, Sunny roamed the apartment, from bedroom to study to living room to kitchen, and then down the back corridor to the little maid's room. It was a tight squeeze. The old green filing cabinets were set against the wall, the violin resting against them. She sat down at her old small desk, ignoring the pages of manuscript beside David's battered Royal, and stared at the filing cabinets through the open door. They were still poison. But why would Amanda have said what she did if it weren't true? She had never lied to her. Why should she? Amanda had always been on Sunny's side, even when, ironically, she had introduced her to David. Then wouldn't it be better finally to *know*, to take the poison and be done with it? Better than to die by inches as she was doing now?

She got up and resolutely pulled open a top drawer, weak with a sense of reprieve when it turned out to contain nothing but old bills, receipts, cancelled checks. The next drawer was crammed with business correspondence, letters from editors and fans, old book contracts. In the third were personal letters dating back to the forties and old family photographs that David sometimes took out to show Sarah: a sepia print of a six-year-old David wearing high-button shoes, knickers, and a Cossack blouse; Tillie in pince-nez and a long satin skirt; Izzy in a stiff collar and bowler; a glamorized studio portrait of Natalia draped on a divan and wearing a sheer blouse; a cracked black and white snapshot of David in a v-necked sweater holding baby Gloria and seeming not to know what to do with her. She took a deep breath and opened the top drawer of the next filing cabinet.

And there they were, as if they had been waiting for her all along: David's journals. Her heart pounding, she took out a notebook at random and opened it. It was recent, the first entry, February 4, 1968. She skimmed a few pages. They were difficult to follow: a helter-skelter collection of random notes and jottings, lines of verse, longer passages in a practically illegible handwriting. There was no continuity, nothing about Sunny, nothing about Sarah. She was about to put it back when a phrase caught her eye. "My poor slender psychoanalyst's wife, who calls me when she misses my lovemaking." Then another, "She came! She came!" Then, further along, ". . . Oh, my *Virginian*." Was this someone new, or the other? She retreated to the maid's room, turning the pages more rapidly.

An hour later, she emerged, too dazed and numb to go on, her mind a blur, all she had ever believed about David shot out from under her. She didn't even recognize the David Harvey of the notebooks, part Sammy Glick, part Don Giovanni, part madman for whom the outside world hardly existed. Journal after journal, a jumble of fragmented poems, quotes from his reading, hymns to himself, to his aloneness and to the greatness he yet meant to claim. And in between a list of infidelities so long and diffuse they melted into one raging river of conquest, names of women sticking up like stones. But they weren't real names. (Was this to keep her from knowing who they were?) No, he had given them names of places, names of attributes, names of goddesses, all so exalted, so metaphoric, that the women might never have existed outside of his head except that oh, how he enjoyed writing and underlining, "*fuck . . . prick . . . cunt. . . .*" How many? When, where, how? She couldn't even tell them apart. She couldn't even figure out who the current one was. Maybe a former C student named L'Italiana who also seemed to be the psychoanalyst's wife? Maybe a present student at NYU? Maybe what seemed to be a bank teller who wrote poetry on deposit slips? (The teller at their own branch of Manufacturer's Hanover? The stupid looking one with the brown bangs and pale eyeglasses?) No, he had met whoever it was at Greenwood. Then perhaps the "sad, wicked Empress Carlotta"? Strangely, it almost didn't matter. It was no longer David's life she wanted to know about, but her own.

"All right," Sunny said, calling Amanda the next day for details. "Tell me about this one."

Amanda told her. It was a middle-aged, frumpy, phenom-
enally ungifted watercolorist, who had latched on to him his
last time at Greenwood and who, Milo said, should have stuck
to cups and saucers. They had had a brief fling, parted, and
now were together again. She had found David his first studio
and was trying to find him another one. They had been seen
at parties together. "Parties?" Sunny said. In fact, the creature
had separated from her husband on the strength of the affair.
She told people she and David were getting married. "*Married!*"
Sunny said.

"Maybe I shouldn't have said anything," Amanda said. "But
you were blaming yourself. You were so bewildered and miserable."

"No, you were right."

David came home at midday with presents. Grinning from
ear to ear, very tired, happy to be home. The readings had taken
a lot out of him, the English department faculties . . .

She couldn't bear to look at him.

"Okay, what is it this time?" David said, wearily putting his
suitcase down on the floor, the badly gift-wrapped packages on
the foyer table. "I haven't been home two minutes when I see
you're ready to start in."

"I'm not starting. I'm finished."

"Oh, come on, Sunnoo, you always say that."

"How *could* you make my life so miserable over some piece
of garbage? But then you always have, haven't you? Weren't all
those filthy little affairs bad enough? Did you have to bring
them home to me?"

"I forgot," David said. "You spent the weekend with Amanda."

"Whom did *you* spend the weekend with? No, don't tell me.
I don't give a damn anymore."

"It's over," David said. "I was lonely when you—it never
meant anything."

"I believe you. That's what's so disgusting, the utter frivolity
of it. She can never be *me* to you, none of them can. I know
that. And yet you've used her—used all of them—to crucify
me. Oh, get out! Get the hell out of here."

Sunny went into the bedroom and slammed the door. She cried until she fell asleep, and woke to Sarah scratching at the door to ask if she wanted dinner. She said no, and fell back to sleep. After a while she got up and turned back when she saw David and Sarah talking quietly in the living room. Hours later she got up again. In the little maid's room behind the kitchen, David sat head bowed, sweat staining his blue shirt. She paused, and then went back to bed. In the morning David was gone.

He called very politely a day later to ask if he could come over and get some things. He had checked into the Hotel Regal. She said yes, and left the house to go to a movie, crying through the whole thing. When she returned she looked in the bedroom closet and knew exactly what David had taken: the light blue cord suit and the brown Italian loafers, a few shirts, a couple of ties. Not very much. Also the typewriter from the maid's room. The violin still rested against the filing cabinets. Sarah, watching her come back down the corridor, did not mention him. All during their supper in the dinette, Sarah sat smiling anxiously, and then went off to do her homework. The next night she was agreeable to going out to a Chinese restaurant, the next night to Tony's Italian Kitchen, the night after that to the movies, though she had a final math test first thing in the morning. In fact, she was agreeable to everything, and gave Sunny gentle little kisses out of nowhere, as if Sunny were in the midst of a long illness. On Friday, seeking to reassure Sarah that things were fine—they weren't, every night Sunny woke in a panic, hysterical because David wasn't there—Sunny said cheerfully as she glanced through the *Times*, "Let's see what's wonderful that we can do over the weekend."

"The weekend?" Sarah said, her face full of doubt.

"What's the matter?"

"Nothing."

"Tell me."

Had Sarah made some appointment with David that Sunny didn't know about? Why did that hurt her so terribly?

"I was supposed to have a sleepover at Diana's," Sarah admitted reluctantly. "But it's okay. I'll just call her and tell her I can't."

"Oh, darling," Sunny said, absurdly relieved. "Of course you should go. I want you to go. It's about time I went to see Grandma and Grandpa, anyway."

"Are you sure? Will you be all right?"

"Sarah, please," Sunny said.

She drove out to Connecticut the next afternoon. Sarah, off to Diana's, had hugged her very hard when she said goodbye, and made Sunny promise to take care of herself. But the leafy trees along the highway, the back lanes and country houses were painful—painful, David's favorite word—a reminder of the visit to Amanda, and the talk that had sent her life into a tailspin. Had Amanda been right to tell her, she wondered now? Would she have been better left in ignorant bliss? But she could not fool herself that her ignorance had been blissful. Amanda had only wanted to relieve Sunny's misery, stop her from castigating herself for what wasn't her fault. What if the shoe were on the other foot and Milo were cheating on Amanda? Would Sunny tell *her*? Cheating. As if it were all a game.

In spite of the fine weather Grace was not outside reading a novel in the chaise longue on the patio, nor in the garden, pinching, pruning, a basket on the grass beside her, the ribbons of her big straw hat tugging against the breeze. The garden itself looked unkempt, bedraggled, unloved. "Mother? . . . Mother?" She entered through the kitchen, which was cold and empty. Willie Mae had recently retired and gone back to live with relatives in South Carolina. "Mother?" Sunny called, coming out into the front hall.

"Oh, darling! I didn't hear your car!"

In a few moments, Grace descended the stairs with a bright smile, holding tightly to the bannister, wobbling a bit on each step. She was trying to seem okay, but she wasn't okay. From the look of her she had been sleeping when Sunny arrived and quickly scrambled out of bed. Her hand was still fussing with the gray curls at the sides and the back of her head. Her pink summery flowered shift was wrinkled.

They went into the living room, where Grace immediately fixed herself a vodka on the rocks. "A *very* dry martini," she said, laughing. "Are you sure you don't want anything?"

"No, thanks."

"Well, how are you, my darling? It seems ages. Is adorable Sarah all right? And your wonderful husband?"

"My wonderful husband," Sunny said, "is not so wonderful."

"Oh, sweetheart, he's handsome, brilliant, charming, I don't know what else."

"Mother, please. I need to talk to you."

"After all these years his mind still amazes me," Grace said, finishing the first drink and fixing herself another. "The scope of it, the range. I thought his article in the *New York Review of Books* on—Robert Lowell, was it?—was absolutely brilliant, didn't you? And so long too, it went on for pages and pages."

"That article mentioned Robert Lowell exactly twice. The rest was about David Harvey. A tribute to David Harvey's profound feelings and insights."

Grace laughed uncertainly. "Felicia wanted to know where he learned all those big words."

"Mother," Sunny said, "I'm really very unhappy."

"Unhappy, darling? But why?" Suddenly all sympathy, Grace took Sunny's hands in both of hers. Tears welled up in her beautiful blue eyes.

"David—"

"What's this about David?" William said, coming in with his bag of golf clubs. He put them down to give Sunny a kiss. Grace quickly got up, smoothed her skirt, and went over to the bar. "Nothing's wrong, I hope. I saw him the other day at the Century Club sitting at the big table with Walter Lippmann, and—Robert Lowell, I think. He looked well then."

"So handsome, so brilliant," Grace said, tears still spilling from her eyes.

"Grace," William said. Grace murmured something about having to lie down for a few minutes, and walked crookedly out of the room.

"Oh, Daddy," Sunny said.

"She'll be all right," William said. "What is it, baby?"

"It's David. We're separated."

"Permanently?"

"I don't know. I just don't know."

"It's not a thing you want to do lightly, Sunny."

"Oh, Daddy, you don't understand. He's betrayed me in every possible way."

"In what way?" William said sternly. "Financially?"

"No, he's having an affair. And not just one, but—"

William's stern, dignified face broke into a smile.

"Daddy, it's not funny. You mustn't minimize the awfulness of it. It's as if our whole life together has been writ on water."

"You literary people certainly bandy words about, don't you?" William said. "Look here, Sunny, you can't throw away a whole marriage on the basis of one—or, all right—several indiscretions. A distinguished man, a man who's known to be tops in his field, is bound to feel himself under pressure, need to unwind. And if that sometimes leads to imprudent behavior, regrettable though it may be—"

"I thought you'd be on my side," Sunny said. "I thought you'd want to go out and horsewhip him."

"I am on your side," William said. "That's why I'm taking this tack. Sunny, you know that we've always indulged you, even when you wanted to leave home and be a writer, which I never thought was a sound idea in the first place. But you can't destroy a marriage on a whim. Now, sit down and have a drink and we'll have a nice dinner at the club. Your mother hasn't felt up to cooking lately."

"I don't want a drink. I have to get back," Sunny said. "Daddy, Mother needs help."

"She's fine," William said.

Fine. The healer, as David had once remarked, who refused to see that anyone close to him was sick. But what was to be done if William, as well as Grace, maintained there was no problem?

She had meant to spend the night, foolishly be comforted like a child. Now she opened the door to a big empty apartment, emptier and more cavernous without Sarah. Her father had even healed over his original dubiousness about David. Now that William saw David at the Century Club, he perceived him as distinguished. "Male bonding," was that the latest phrase for it? They were gentlemen together, though the thought of David passing as a gentleman after all his open scorn of the gentry, ought to have struck even William as odd.

Pausing at the foyer table, she began to stack David's mail in a neat pile, for when he next came for it. He had said he didn't want it forwarded to the hotel. She opened the book packages in case there was anything of interest. One book, a new biography of Colette, she put aside. The others were the usual pretentious junk sent to David by small university presses. She shook her head over what looked like the worst of them, *Eternity Must Go: Epistemology in Emily Dickinson*. The author was Jennifer Schultz, Ph.D., whose face in the book jacket photograph began to look strangely familiar, fuzzy, unfocussed, with blank eyes and thick eyebrows. She lived in Syracuse with her husband, a psychoanalyst, and their two dogs. "My slender psychoanalyst's wife who calls me when she misses my love-making. . . ." Could it be? Yes, it was—Jenny Abruzzi. *L'Italiana!* He had been fucking the old babysitter all these years. Shades of Manny Cohen. But even better, since Jenny had been so untalented a poet David had urged her to take up criticism. It was all so ludicrous, it hardly bore thinking about. She went to answer the phone. It was Amanda calling to find out how Sunny was doing.

"I'm fine, I'm okay," Sunny said, not wanting at that moment to be the object of Amanda's sympathy. And what had Amanda to be sympathetic about? Was Milo any better than David? Were any of them?

"They've broken up," Amanda said. "I thought you'd want to know."

"It doesn't make any difference," Sunny said. "There'll just be another hopeless bitch after this one. The more hopeless the better."

"I thought you'd want to know."

But when she hung up, she felt relieved. Why? Because

David had told the truth for once? Oh, why had Amanda ever said anything? And why had she snooped in David's journals, learned things she had no business knowing?

Early in the morning the phone rang again and it was David. She looked over at the undented pillow.

"I'd like to come up and get some more of my things. If it's agreeable to you. Also my mail."

"Of course. Tell me when. I'll arrange to be out again."

"Oh, Sunnoo—"

"What?"

"This is crazy. We have to talk. Meet me for dinner—please?"

"Dinner?"

"There's a place called Le Moulin down the block from the hotel."

"We've never been there," Sunny said thoughtfully.

"But it's French," David told her with a laugh.

But what did you wear for a date with your own husband? She thought about it foolishly all day, rejecting the idea of a sheer blouse—David's favorite, but Natalia's studio photograph was too fresh in her mind—and finally decided on her white summer suit: simple, tailored, and neutral, it would do as well for lunch with an editor. But what to go under the jacket? Maybe the sleeveless, v-necked green silk to add a touch of color. No bra— she didn't need one. No stockings either, her legs were tan. A pair of high-heeled sandals that she could easily kick off bare feet. Stop it, Sunny, she told herself as she was thinking how easily the green top would slip off too, the skirt slide down. This isn't a real date, some possible prelude to seduction. It's an appointment with your husband to talk things over, bring back a level of civilized behavior to a relationship that's gone haywire. Nevertheless, as she was putting on her makeup— more makeup than usual—she nervously smeared her mascara, and peered anxiously into the mirror to assess the damage. When she straightened up, she realized that Sarah stood watching in the doorway. She had come back from Diana's early in the afternoon, full of concern. Sweet pacifist Sarah in her battle fatigues.

"You didn't say you were going out tonight," Sarah said.

"Didn't I? Well, I'm just having dinner with a friend."

"What kind of friend?"

"Please, Sarah, stop prying. And no innuendos, please. It's none of your business where I go. Thorndike's filled you with false ideas of sophistication."

Sarah turned sharply and walked away. Abandoning the stupid mascara, Sunny went to find her. Sarah was in her room, standing by the window and staring out at the dusky Hudson. There were tears in her eyes.

"Sarah, I'm sorry I was rude."

"Forget it."

"Oh, baby, don't cry, what's the matter?"

"You know what's the matter. You always know what's the matter."

"You mean you're jealous because I'm having dinner with an old friend?"

"I didn't know Daddy was your friend. You usually act as if he were your worst enemy."

"What makes you think it's Daddy?" Sunny said gaily.

"Oh, Mama, please." Sarah turned to her, dry-eyed now, and exasperated. "Why don't you finish getting dressed? I have homework to do."

"Sarah, listen—"

But Sarah wasn't listening. Sunny went back to the bedroom and finished dressing, soon thinking again how easily the green silk blouse would slip away from her breasts, ashamed to be having such lascivious thoughts with Sarah in the next room. But it wasn't Sarah's business—or had she made it Sarah's business? She couldn't help herself anyway, she was suddenly too excited by the prospect of meeting David, too eager to look attractive for him, to have David see her at her best, wearing her bright public face, not her private disheveled misery. Whatever else happened, at least they would have that between them again, mutual respect, courtesy.

"Goodbye!" she called to Sarah on her way out. "There's stuff in the fridge. I won't be back late."

Sarah came and stood in the doorway, watching Sunny ring for the elevator and then step back, impatiently tapping her foot.

"Are you sure you know what you're doing?" Sarah said.

"*Please*, Sarah," Sunny said, and then, presenting a smiling face to the elevator man, stepped into the car.

He was already waiting inside the restaurant at a corner table. A small dark handsome man, wearing a light blue cord suit and staring at a vase of red carnations. There was a drink in front of him. He had come early. In the old days he had always come early when they were to meet, shamelessly eager to see her. "I have no pride where you're concerned," David used to say with a laugh. He stood up formally as she approached the table. "Do sit down," Sunny said, and took the chair he pulled out for her.

She looked around. It was a romantic little restaurant, decorated like a French bistro. Other couples were seated intimately at other small tables. He asked her what she wanted to drink, and she said firmly white wine. No Gibsons for old times sake, no martinis to threaten her self-control. It already seemed unbelievable that she had thought of her green silk blouse falling away from her breasts. David ordered another vermouth for himself.

She sat with hands primly folded until the drinks came. David looked very neat in one of the clean white shirts he had taken from the bureau drawer. His dark blue tie was carefully knotted. Both ends of his collar had stayed down.

"Are you all right?" David said, as she took a small sip of her wine.

"Yes. Are you? . . . Oh, I forgot your mail—"

"It doesn't matter. . . . Well, I'm lonely as hell, but I'm okay."

"Sarah doesn't know I'm seeing you," Sunny said. David

nodded soberly. "I didn't want to say anything to her until we talked. I suppose we'd better start talking."

"Oh, Christ."

"David, please."

"All right, what do you want to talk about?"

"Well, what did *you* want to talk about? I mean, what do other couples in our situation talk about?"

David shrugged. "I don't know. Money. You still have enough blank checks, don't you?"

"Oh, yes, plenty." She took another sip of her drink. She was determined to be brave. "David, should I get a lawyer?"

David shook his head. "No, no. Not yet."

"All right."

If it had been a real date, Sunny would have looked around again, observed the other couples in the restaurant, wondered what they were eating, eavesdropped on murmured conversations. But by bringing up the lawyer she had frightened herself. She could not take her eyes off David. He was actually there. If she could only save the moment, memorize him before it all fell apart.

"I'll have to pick up some more things at the house. I need another suit."

"Of course. I'll arrange not to be home."

"I could see Sarah at the same time."

Sunny nodded. ". . . David, is it awful at the Regal?"

David shrugged. "It's a hotel. I need to find some small studio apartment. I put an ad in *The New York Review.*"

"Really?" Sunny said. "Were they surprised?"

"The people in the advertising department don't know me. . . . Sunnoo, you look lovely."

"So do you."

He touched her hand. She had always loved David's hands, small but so capable. She loved to see them turning the pages of a book. She finally looked around. And there were the other couples, eating, sipping wine, smiling, telling each other about themselves.

"Oh, David," Sunny said, heartbroken. "Do you like music?"

It was an incredibly cheerless, dingy room. They had walked through the hotel lobby laughing, Sunny making jokes about her wickedness. But one look into David's room turned her sober with dismay. How had he endured it this past week? How had he compressed his life into this small squalid space? The light from the street brought from the shadows peeling plaster, a rumpled bed, his portable typewriter on a maple dresser, a door ajar to an antiquated bathroom. How high off the hog they had lately been living, she suddenly realized. Big West Side apartment, cleaning ladies, child in private school, parties, summer houses, trips to Europe. And David had without complaint reduced it all to this one dreadful little hotel room. It was the side of him she least understood, never remembered and most admired. His demands were not physical, but psychic. Loneliness he had spoken of, not squalor.

He moved her backward toward the rumpled bed. The date was almost over. She slipped off the green silk blouse by herself, slid down her skirt. David wouldn't take the trouble, didn't have the patience.

"David," she said in the darkness as he hunched over her, while a neon sign flashed across the street as in a B-movie, "this doesn't mean . . . we mustn't think . . ." He was weeping on her breasts, his hand found her below. "Oh, David, *oh* . . ."

On the way home, David looked distractedly out of the taxi window, one hand on his portable typewriter to steady it on the seat. His briefcase was wedged between his legs. He had temporarily left his clothes at the Regal, he was so eager to get out of there.

"Oh, darling, it will be all right now," Sunny said, turning his head to kiss him. "From now on everything will be all right."

He put his tongue in her mouth, stuck his hand up her skirt. They stayed that way until the taxi stopped in front of their building, and he released her to hand over the briefcase while he reached for his wallet. The elevator man greeted them with a polite, indifferent smile. He was used to David being away. It was only to Sunny that David's week-long absence had felt like a lifetime of separation. Once inside the apartment David put down the briefcase and typewriter and picked up the mail on the foyer table. With his other hand he was already undoing the knot of his tie.

"You'll see," Sunny repeated. "Everything will be all right now." She followed him into the bedroom, where David removed his jacket, then sat down to take off his shoes. "Do you want me to make us something to eat, darling? We never got to eat."

"That would be nice."

The two of them looked up. Sarah, in the sweatshirt she slept in, was standing in the doorway. "Hi, sweetheart," David said. Sunny grinned sheepishly.

"Grandma Tillie called," Sarah said to David. "It sounded urgent."

"Let me get you something to eat," Sunny said.

"Also Aunt Natalia."

"Natalia?" David said. Sunny put a restraining hand on his arm but he was already reaching for the telephone. He paused. "When?"

"About a half hour ago." They all looked at the clock on the bedside table. It was long past midnight.

He dialed Natalia's number quickly, listened, heard, asked curt questions, jotted down a name, an address. "He's had a stroke," David said, putting a hand on the receiver and looking up. "Izzy's had a stroke."

The three of them crowded into Izzy's half of the hospital room in the Bronx—Sarah had refused to be left behind. Tillie, a ghost in carpet slippers, had been led away by Natalia, who would spend the night with her. From his cramped bed, Izzy searched them out with stricken eyes. A flat, fecal smell pervaded the room, no air came in through the open window. But Izzy was fortunate to have even half of a room such as this. Other patients were stretched out moaning in the corridor, tangled in sheets, like battle casualties.

A young doctor poked his head in the door and David followed him into the corridor. Sunny heard the words insistently repeated: "Nursing care . . . Medicare . . . therapy." David came back in, shaking his head with exasperation. "Where the hell's Ma? Why did Natalia take her home? I have to know what kind of insurance he has. They can't keep him here very long. He'll have to go to a nursing home. Though it would be just like Izzy not to be covered at all. Leave me holding the bag, as usual."

"David, please," Sunny said. "He can hear you."

"He doesn't know what's going on," David said, and darted out into the hall to find the doctor again.

Sunny and Sarah remained backed against the wall in the little half-room, partitioned by a white curtain. They looked at each other helplessly, and then Sarah reached down and touched Izzy's hand with amazing gentleness. How long ago that turbulent lovemaking in the Hotel Regal seemed now. How frivolous the trial separation before that. Real sickness and real misery had entered their lives—poor mute Izzy the messenger and the message. Outside she could hear David haranguing the doctor, cornering still another nurse, frantic. Oh, they *had* squandered their luck.

Four

1

There was no clock, but she should probably be getting up. She sank back again when Ricky turned his handsome blond head on the pillow and gave her a ravishing smile. She was always surprised by how young his face was, how utterly unlined and untroubled. He probably wasn't even bothered that he had practically no furniture except this bed. But then his little East Side walk-up was just a pad anyway, where Ricky, when he wasn't making love, crammed for his bar exam. They had met at a dinner party given by his parents, both literary lawyers, and hadn't exchanged two words all evening. But the next morning Ricky had blithely called her—somehow knowing that David had just left for his studio—and persuaded her to come dashing over. It was a style, a generation she knew very little about, but then she had never had a lover so much younger than she, either. And he was so surprisingly tender in bed, so attentive to her wishes, though she turned out to have very few.

"Sweetie, how delicious! It's pure Colette!" Charlotte had cried, when Sunny first let it slip out about him. But Charlotte was way off base, as she often was lately. Colette had nothing to do with it, nor did aging French courtesans. In fact what Ricky made her feel was young too, very young, as if she had gone back to the time before she met David. There was never any guilt to it, not even that first evening when Sarah looked at her peculiarly. But there had been no guilt over her other lovers in the past few years either—the two architects, both wonderful with their hands, the manic composer, the suave Israeli stud. Not really lovers of course, just stray passions like Ricky, which had seemed briefly the solution to everything. And after the sex there was nothing, so what was there to be guilty about?

"I really must go," she said, finally looking at her watch. It was very late in the morning.

"Stay a while. Your old man won't be back yet."

"Please don't keep calling him my old man."

"That's the way he comes on."

"Ricky, I truly don't want to discuss David. Anyway, I have things to do. So do you, I think."

Ricky ruefully eyed the law books piled up on the floor. She laughed, got up and took a quick shower, watching Ricky take his while she dressed. He came out through the steaming curtains with his bottom half wrapped in a towel, and immediately plugged a hairdryer into an outlet over the bathroom mirror. Before Ricky she had never seen a man blow dry his hair. The sight always unnerved her—imagine David doing such a thing—and also Ricky's total absorption in the flow of air and the brushing.

"Well, goodbye," she said, kissing him quickly. He turned off the dryer and came out to wrap her in her mink coat.

"I'll call you," Ricky said, nuzzling her neck.

"Or I'll call you," she said, touching his face.

She let herself out. At the foot of the brownstone steps, she wrapped the mink coat more tightly around her, a soft sweet indulgence that had cost her plenty—at Dr. Brill's urging she had opened her own bank account—and cut over to Madison Avenue. It was bitter cold, too cold to walk, but she didn't really want to go home. Still, where else could she go? She had made no advance appointment for lunch, an absolute requirement in New York. Anyway, Charlotte, who just might have been available, was in Palm Beach with her husband; Sarah was at school; harried Bessie had no free time except over the weekend. (Funny that after that first dinner party she and Ricky had never had another meal together. But, really, what would they have talked about?) For a moment, she had an urge to call Joe Farber, but he would be booked for lunches weeks ahead.

No, the only sensible thing to do was go home and try to work up some enthusiasm for a new novel, though her last book, *Bittersweet*, had sapped her dry—steel herself against the moment when David walked in the door. Thank God for his new studio anyway. She didn't even care what pathetic girlfriend had found him this one. Ever since Izzy's stroke, he had become so impossible that poor Sarah was always running off to her room and slamming the door. "Guilt and depression," Dr. Brill said, though it seemed like pure hysteria. After more than two years, he was still running from one nursing home to another, trying to install Izzy permanently before the insurance ran out, dashing off to the Bronx to check up on his father's savings account. He had even asked William to pull a few strings, though William was based in Connecticut, and made respectful phone calls to William almost every day now besides referring to him at dinner parties as his "father-in-law, the distinguished brain surgeon." And meanwhile Izzy sat in the latest nursing home babbling the same Russian words over and over again, clutching David's wrist, smiling eagerly as if he expected David to be proud of him. "I think it's from Pushkin," David said wearily, "or maybe Turgenev." What would become of the poor man? And what about Tillie, who had been sent to live with a cousin and forbidden to carry on, who no longer called but waited humbly to be invited? "Don't worry about your mother, Dushinka," Natalia said. "Worry about yourself." When they ran into each other at a nursing home, she and Sunny never spoke. But all of them had come to regard David as the sick one, not Izzy.

She finally took a freezing hand out of her pocket and hailed a cab, looking through the window at bare winter trees as they crossed the Park. Out on the West Side the scene deteriorated badly, the streets cracked and dirty, doorways full of junkies. It would have been nice to move, but David wouldn't hear of it, even though she pointed out that when Sarah went away to college they would no longer need that huge old apartment. Too bad. It would have given her something to look forward to. Otherwise the thought of Sarah going off was too dreadful to contemplate. Ironic that the time she had once dreamed about, when she and David would finally be alone together, should loom as a nightmare. She burrowed deeper into the smooth silky fur, telling herself she was still the woman who had everything. Then why was she so cold suddenly, so bone lonely? The answer was ridiculous. She missed David. Not the David who would come through the door exhausted and irascible, but that passionate David who had swept her off her feet so many years ago, whose delight in her had seemed to justify her very existence.

Gloria, who had surfaced soon after Izzy's stroke, sat on the living room sofa talking about the 1968 Chicago convention while Sarah sat rapt at her feet and David paced the room. She was wearing her now usual camouflage outfit and army boots, a curious getup for one so vehemently opposed to war. Then again, though the Vietnam war was over, to Gloria it seemed still to be going on, since if she wasn't talking about Chicago, she was telling about her part in the busts at Berkeley and Harvard and Columbia—yes, she had been the jeering girl on the ledge—though the time of the busts was long over too. These days she was living, or rather camping out with her mother in Queens, though what she actually did with her time was unclear. Whatever it was seemed often to bring her to Manhattan on Sundays, when she would drop in unannounced, sometimes letting herself be persuaded to stay for a meal, more often raiding the refrigerator and then taking Sarah off on a ramble to parts unknown. They had probably seen more of Gloria lately than they had ever had when she was growing up.

"And then those motherfucking pigs broke into the pad when we were all asleep and started to rough us up. There was some dog shit in the corner and they stuck their toes in it and smeared it all over our sleeping bags."

"I don't want to hear any more," David said, turning angrily. "You were interfering with the democratic process. It's bad enough that you and your bunch of hopheads tried to destroy great universities all over the country."

"What great universities—Kent State? What democratic process? The one that brought us Hubert Humphrey and Richard

Nixon, and is going to bring us Richard Nixon all over again?"

"You don't understand the first thing about it," David said. "Your generation is totally apolitical."

Apolitical? Was Gloria's generation apolitical too? Had there never been a political generation except David's? How old was Gloria anyway? Probably older than Ricky, embarrassing thought. Still, she wished Gloria would stop baiting David—sometimes it seemed that was all she came over to do—while Sarah sat, face upturned with admiration, except for an occasional apprehensive glance at David. Couldn't Gloria see how beaten he looked these days, in certain lights the image of Izzy?

"You mean because we weren't in the big Depression, Daddy? It's your outmoded ex-radicalism that's apolitical. The war's still on and you'd better believe it."

"You don't know anything about war, either."

"Neither do you, father dear. You were never even near a war."

"What the hell do you mean by that?" David said, reddening. "I was in England, I went over there in a—"

"I know, a troopship, with a convoy spread out as far as the eye could see. Which was probably the only dangerous part of your cushy job pushing pencils around for the OSS."

She had hit a real sore spot now. It had taken Sunny years to realize that for all his talk about England in World War II, David had never been near any action. Even the blitz, as Gloria was quick to point out, had been over by the time he got there.

"There's nothing to discuss here," David said, stalking out.

"Oh, Gloria," Sunny said.

Gloria laughed. "What's the matter, stepmother dear? You look upset. What I said to the great man was true. If you're not part of the solution, you're part of the problem."

"Actually, I was thinking about the dog," Sunny said irritably.

"What dog?"

"The one who had to relieve himself in the corner. Why didn't someone take the poor thing out? Why didn't someone at least clean up after him?"

"I don't know. It wasn't my dog," Gloria said. "Come on,

Sarah, let's go for a walk." She looked back at Sunny, shaking her head. "Never trust anyone over thirty."

Sunny went into the bedroom, where David lay with an arm wearily slung across his forehead. "How old is Gloria?" she said.

"I don't know. Thirty-one?"

She went over to the mirror and began to comb her hair and put on lipstick, wishing that Gloria hadn't come, and especially that she hadn't taken Sarah off. David was always at his worst on Sundays anyway, even without Gloria's visits.

"Your hair's getting darker," David remarked gloomily. Then, "What are you getting all dressed up for?"

"There's a fundraiser at Charlotte's for a women's history archive."

"I thought Charlotte was in Palm Beach."

"She came back early, she was bored," Sunny said, surprised that David had remembered. Charlotte would be bored at the fundraiser too. She had simply, with a helpless laugh at her own generosity, lent her large Park Avenue apartment for the occasion. It was pointless to ask David to come along, though there would be other men, husbands—not "faggots," as David always maintained. The one time David had attended such an event, yielding to Sarah's entreaties, had been an absolute disaster, a symposium at Barnard College on women writers, at which Sunny had been one of the panelists. From the platform, she had seen him asleep in the audience, mouth slack, brow furrowed as if in pain. Only Sarah's bright eager face had kept her going. Still, he really did look worn to a frazzle by Gloria's visit.

"Look, I don't have to go to this thing," Sunny said. "We could go to the movies. Maybe there's something good at Loew's 83rd."

"Why do we always have to go to the movies?"

"Because we love the movies. We've always loved the movies."

"People only go to the movies," David said, "when they have nothing to say to one another."

Sunny turned from the mirror—was her hair really getting darker?—and considered David's remark. Untrue, it nevertheless had a strangely familiar ring. Yes, it was the kind of thing she and her girlfriends used to say when they were about fifteen, imagining they were very sophisticated: "I only go to the movies with a boy when we have nothing to say to each other." But the movies were one of the few pleasures she and David had always agreed on. He was quoting someone, she realized, another pathetic professional no doubt, with a pathetically ordinary mind. But this time, for some reason, she smelled danger. She wished Sarah would come home soon so that they could go to the party together.

She walked into Charlotte's apartment, with a Sarah at her side who beamed with pride every time someone recognized Sunny's name, or told her how much they admired her work. In a minor way, Sunny supposed she had become famous. Ironic, since *Bittersweet*, a semi-autobiographical account of her childhood in Connecticut—had not been a critical success at all. Too vague, too noncommittal, reviewers said, having expected something more along strictly feminist lines from her. But the same reviewers now called her simply Mansfield—and younger women writers marveled that she had kept her own name through a long marriage, professionally at least. Maybe in the end all success really amounted to was sheer staying power. Maybe that explained why David now occupied a chair of his own on the platform at the Institute of Arts and Letters, though he hadn't, God forgive her for even thinking it, written anything worth reading in years. (The epic poem was a receding dream.) But why hadn't he ever done anything to compare with *Ancestors* and some of the early poems? Was it that big "I," as Virginia Woolf put it, that cast too great a shadow over the rest? (An "I" that in *Bittersweet*, she could see that now, she had grappled with unsuccessfully.) But without *his* faith in that big "I" would David have been David in the first place? Giving it up, she steered Sarah over to the wine and cheese, introducing her to a current crop of feminist luminaries along the way: Lois Gould, Susan Brownmiller, a young poet named Erica Jong. "This is my daughter, Sarah," she said each time, wryly aware that she was suppressing the Harvey part. Except for the truncated introduction and the preponderance of women, it was like one of Charlotte's usual bashes, since as she had expected there were lots of husbands present too. It gave Sunny a pang to see them. Yet even she didn't know quite what to make of them, had trouble believing any man who told her he was a feminist. David had certainly brainwashed her.

"Sweetie!" Charlotte said, running up and grasping both of Sunny's hands in hers. "You're finally here. I'd almost despaired of your coming."

"David wasn't feeling very well. I wasn't sure I could get here at all."

Charlotte gave a little sardonic moue, about to commiserate further until she saw Sarah. The stay in Palm Beach hadn't relaxed her. She seemed a bit too hectically gay, her hennaed hair metallic from the sun.

"Oh, God, how did I get roped into all of this?" Charlotte said, looking around with her usual helpless laugh. "How do I get roped into anything? And now we have that awful panel on Channel 13 next week."

"You were the one who roped *me* into that," Sunny said. "Remember?"

"Oh, sweetie, I know, but you always know what to say, and I—"

"Carlotta!" someone called, and with an apologetic shrug Charlotte turned away. *Carlotta.* She had never heard Charlotte called that before. Why did that name strike a bell?

She found herself smiling at a young woman with big eyeglasses.

"Arlene Simmons."

"Sunny Mansfield."

"Oh."

The young woman extended her hand, suddenly seemed tonguetied, smiled harder, and finally drifted off.

Sarah looked around at Sunny. "That little '*oh*,'" Sarah said.

The speeches began, boring, almost inaudible, but blessedly

short. Sarah listened to them attentively. She was becoming quite a feminist herself, actually more of one than Sunny. It was a shame she couldn't come to the TV panel on women in the arts next week, but it would be televised late and Sarah had explained apologetically that she had a test the next morning. Charlotte came threading her way back through the crowd.

"Sweetie, could you *bear* to make a little speech?" she whispered urgently. "We need you."

"But, Charlotte, I don't know a thing about women's history."

"Sweetie, I'm sure you'll think of something," Charlotte said, pulling Sunny along by the hand. Suddenly she found herself standing in a cleared space in Charlotte's living room, being introduced by a woman whose name she hadn't even caught. She felt like a fool, an imposter, could see in her mind David shaking his head scornfully and turning away. Not to mention hearing a big hee-haw from Natalia, whose motto vis-à-vis women had always been, as it was about everything: *after me pull up the ladder.* Well, the hell with Natalia. Even though David no longer brought her up except in connection with Izzy, she still thought about her too much. She cleared her throat and began to speak, heard herself say that if the world had its way women like them would have no history, that therefore it was important, no, urgent, that they record themselves. "Otherwise," Sunny said, "we will *all* have been writ on water." Writ on water . . . in what other plea had she used that phrase? She couldn't remember, and felt lost all over again. Then she heard the applause, saw Sarah clapping harder than anyone. "That little 'oh,' " Sarah had said, and been so proud.

Charlotte had cancelled out of the TV program at the last minute, privately admitting to an attack of nerves, publicly claiming a sore throat. It was just as well. Charlotte's brittle manner, that increasing tendency to throw back her head and laugh at things that weren't funny, might have made Sunny even more self-conscious than she already was: one of a stiff semi-circle of "women in the arts"—including a composer, a painter, and a poet—arranged in floodlit armchairs in an otherwise dark studio, with cameras blinking overhead. Still it was easier than facing a live audience, or an inquisitive interviewer. Gradually as the program went on, she relaxed, as if no one did exist except these other women and herself. She listened to them telling their histories, histories that soon turned out to be a familiar litany of professional slights and insults which had once convinced them they were crazy, just as she had once thought she was crazy too. Now it was her turn. How freely could *she* speak, considering her special circumstance of being maried to a well-known writer? But didn't she owe it to herself as well as to them to be honest? The impersonal outer blackness of the studio finally persuaded her that it was all right. She began to tell how male writer "friends" had handed over her books to their wives to read, how she had once been sure that what she wrote about couldn't possibly be important. (Naturally, she didn't name names. Anyway, in her heart, she was really speaking to Sarah.) "I guess I still feel like a bird with a bruised wing," Sunny said. "I fly, but the thing keeps dragging." She paused—she had never said such a thing before, not even thought it—and instinctively turned to the poet next to her for affirmation. The poet nodded with great sweetness. She had a sad, heart-shaped face and long black hair. She was a widow. Afterwards, they promised to see each other.

The program ended late. Ninth Avenue was dark and deserted when they all came out of the studio to look for cabs, but Sunnny felt strangely fearless, heady with freedom, as one by one they wished each other goodnight. Women, maybe there was the answer, the company of good women. At home she slid quietly into bed beside David, wanting not to wake him, wanting not to jar the perfect equilibrium of the moment. It was like being in love. With what? It didn't matter. The whole world, maybe.

David and Sarah were sitting in the dinette having cereal when she awoke. She joined them with a shy smile. They looked up, then silence. David asked Sarah to bring him a cup of coffee.

"I'll do it," Sunny said brightly, then sat down again. David had buried himself in the *Times*. "Did you watch?" she asked Sarah, who nodded, with a quick furtive glance at David. It reminded her of Charlotte. Did two women with a man around always act as if he were their jailer, Sunny wondered, losing that glow, that feeling of being in love.

"Let's talk later, Ma," Sarah said. "Have to run."

She gave David and Sunny each a quick kiss, and was off. Sunny got up and poured herself some more coffee, then asked David for a piece of the newspaper, any piece.

"Okay," David said with a sigh, handing it over. "I fell asleep. I had a bad headache."

"I see."

"Well, how interested am I supposed to be in a bunch of bored women complaining about their husbands?"

"That's not what it was about."

"It's a movement of idle bourgeois females who haven't anything better to do with their time. They're stirring up trouble just to get their names in the papers."

"You can't stir up trouble if it's not there already."

"Come off it. None of you is concerned with anything serious. Poverty, politics—these are—"

"You don't think women are concerned with such things?"

"Not the ones who run around publicly parading their psyches. Why not admit it? You're all ruthlessly ambitious."

"And you?"

"I just want to write certain books," David said. ". . . Look, I won't be home for dinner. I have to meet with some graduate students." He gathered up his briefcase and was gone.

David just wanted to write certain books. And what did she want? The same thing. So how could she be "ruthlessly ambitious," and he—what? Some selfless seeker after truth? Didn't even he see the irony of it?

The phone rang and kept ringing. Amanda, Joe Farber who said it was terrific publicity, Thorndike mothers, people she hadn't heard from in years, Ricky, who hadn't seen the program at all, but was calling for another reason—she told him no. Late in the morning, Charlotte, who said Sunny had been absolutely *marvelous*, the best one on the panel. Sunny hung up in the middle. Charlotte, Carlotta, the "sad wicked Empress Carlotta." She had finally figured it out. Was she really surprised? No. Angry? Yes, furious. Though David had probably made a beeline for all of her friends over the years anyway, with the possible exception of Bessie Cohen. She took a walk to clear her head. On Broadway, several women stopped her to say how much what she had said on TV meant to them, especially the wounded bird part. She thanked them, grateful for their compliments, and walked on. It was like being a celebrity, a movie star, and Sarah, when she got her alone, would be proud. But it wasn't the same happiness as last night. Last night she had felt at one with the world; she had soared, bruised wing and all. This morning . . . oh, the hell with Charlotte. She joined a small crowd gathered at the window of a TV discount store to look at a replay of the second moon landing. The first moon shot a couple of years ago had been poetic, a miracle. This one was dull and prosy. Everyone seemed to take it for granted: two astronauts in silvery padded suits and helmets taking robot steps on a lumpy surface. They had flown to the moon, but they looked as earthbound as she.

The telephone was ringing again as she walked in. Her heart sank as she heard Natalia's brusque voice on the other end.

"Sunny, David isn't in his studio. Where is he?"

"I don't know."

"You don't know? All right, I'll try to find him somewhere. Izzy's dead."

"What? Oh, my God. Natalia, I'm sorry."

"He didn't know what was going on with him," Natalia said, and hung up.

Sunny held on to the receiver, not knowing what to do. She tried David at his studio also, but there was no answer. Tillie and the cousin didn't answer either. Should she call Sarah at school, tell her about her grandfather? No, better to talk to

David first. Poor Izzy, poor little Izzy, so bewildered, so eager to please even at the end. She thought of him trying to amuse Sarah when she was a baby, accusing her of having stolen his hair. Of his surprise and happiness when Sarah laughed. In a while, David walked in.

"Darling—"

"I know. Natalia told me."

"Oh, sweetheart." She reached out to him, but he shook her off and walked into the bedroom, where he removed his shirt, threw it on the floor, took a fresh one from his bureau drawer. "Okay, I'll see you later."

"Where are you going?"

"To the funeral parlor. Natalia's already there with my mother."

"Wait a minute," Sunny said. "I'll go with you."

David looked at her peculiarly, as if she had nothing to do with this family matter.

"David, please. Sit down. You can have some coffee while I change."

"I don't want anything."

She brought him the coffee anyway, and also a sandwich. He was sitting numbly on the bed and had turned on the TV. He picked up the sandwich automatically, chewing and watching, just as Sarah used to when she was little. The news came on. David looked at the astronauts.

"They're walking on the moon," David said.

"I know."

He turned to her, bewildered, the clown lines back on his face.

"Men walk on the moon," David said, as if demanding an explanation. "Men walk on the moon. But my father is dead."

⌐∥ 2 ⌐∥

The session with Dr. Brill had been absolutely pointless. The sessions with Dr. Brill were generally pointless now and had been for a long time. She couldn't remember how long—maybe since Izzy's funeral over a year ago, though the connection was obscure. But she was tired of trotting out her personal problems week after week in that office which was as impersonal as a motel room. They were getting nowhere.

"Why do you think that is?"

"I told you. I just think it's all superficial, what we talk about here. I think David was right all along."

"Have you heard from Ricky lately, or the two architects?"

"They were superficial too. They no longer interest me."

"What does?"

"*Sarah*. And Sarah's going away."

"How about your work? The new novel."

"It will never get off the ground," Sunny said defiantly—Dr. Brill specialized in writer's block—and was glad the hour was over.

Putting Dr. Brill behind her, she walked resolutely into Goldfarb's florist shop, where she found herself unable to decide between the pink sweetheart roses and the American beauties. The American beauties were gorgeous, deep red, long-stemmed, expensive. But she really leaned toward the small pink sweethearts. Would Sarah think they were too girlish, too sentimental? No, Sarah might shake her head and smile, but she would understand. "Two dozen," Sunny said, "and baby's breath too." She would not take them with her. She wanted them delivered that afternoon. In a long white box, nestled in tissue paper.

She crossed Fifth Avenue and in the brilliant June sunshine walked home through the Park, heedless of guitar players, sailing

Frisbees, lovers sprawled on the grass. Why didn't Dr. Brill understand that right now nothing mattered but Sarah? Why did he keep bringing up Ricky, whom she hadn't given a thought to since that morning she had been so thrilled with herself and her silly triumph on TV? Cradle-snatching, Charlotte had delightedly called it, when she was not invoking Colette. But now her real baby, the grace note of her life, was about to leave home. "What are you carrying on about?" David said, though he was prepared to miss Sarah as much as she did. "She's not dying, only going to Harvard." Nevertheless, she was ridden with anxiety. No more waking up to hear Sarah cheerfully chattering away in the dinette, no more Chinese dinners when David was away and maybe a movie too, no more girlfriends giggling in Sarah's room, no more curling up together on the couch glued to the same magazine, nobody to laugh with, nobody to be proud of who was also proud of her. Did no one understand that a whole part of her life was over, the only part that had been consistently and wholly sweet? She walked the windy block from West End Avenue to Riverside Drive, fighting off tears as she thought of the little roses and all she had been trying to say with them. Upstairs—she wiped her eyes quickly— Sarah was in a tizzy as she got ready for her graduation. She had just discovered that the hem of her white dress was torn.

"I'll fix it," Sunny said, taking it from her. "Go ahead and wash your hair meanwhile."

"Oh, Mama, thank you," Sarah said fervently. "If I trip going up those steps, I'll die." And immediately ran off to the shower.

Sunny sat down on the couch with Sarah's dress bunched in her lap. First she had trouble threading the needle, then she jabbed it into her finger after a few stitches and had to stop and suck the blood so that it wouldn't drip on the white organdy. She had always sewn badly, though Willie Mae had tried her best to teach her; actually Sarah was better at this sort of thing than she was. But she was determined not to make a botch of it. She wondered what that group of "women in the arts" would say about her present conviction that sewing a hem equalled mother love. Never mind. It was Sarah's dress and she was going to make it all right for her. The white organdy reminded her that one day Sarah would get married. She put the dress down for a moment, then resolutely went on sewing. Just as she was taking the last stitch, the messenger from the florist arrived. Sunny set the big white box down on the coffee table and stood looking at it. Sarah came in, rubbing her head with a towel.

"They're for you," Sunny said.

Sarah opened the lid, and there they were, pink sweetheart roses and baby's breath. "Oh, Mama," Sarah said, "oh, Mama." She looked at Sunny and tears sprang into her eyes.

"I guess they're silly," Sunny said. "Not your thing, really."

"Oh, Mama," Sarah said, understanding. She had been right, Sarah always understood.

Suddenly Sarah grabbed at the towel around her head. "Would you take care of them?" she said. "The way you always do? Put aspirin in the water, or something? I forget."

"Sure." Sunny handed her the dress. Sarah ran off to dry her hair and get ready. On her way out, an angel in white, she called, "See you at graduation. Don't forget to tell Daddy to look handsome." She looked down at the flowers, which were still beautiful and poised in the box, gave Sunny a kiss and was gone.

During the ceremony, the hem began to fall down again. But Sarah, flushed and proud, standing on the platform as part of the Thorndike School Chorus, was oblivious. As their final number they were singing a setting of William Blake's "Jerusalem," all of them beautiful overgrown babies, heads thrown back, voices sweet. Sunny looked down at the drooping hem and laughed. As usual, she had underestimated Thorndike's famous sophistication. The boy standing next to Sarah had bare feet.

In the fall, they installed Sarah in Adams House and in silence drove back, Sunny wondering how she would live without Sarah, David in some dark world of his own. They sat at the dinner table like stone statues, exactly as his father had sat with Tillie.

"Well, she does seem very happy there," Sunny said finally, to break the ice. "I guess Harvard agrees with her."

David nodded.

A dangerous subject, Harvard. She had forgotten how hurt his feelings still were that they had rejected him. Was that why he looked so miserable? Or had he been thinking about Izzy too? She was sorry about Izzy, also. Terribly. She had loved him. But she and David still had everything to live for. Their work, their health, a wonderful daughter. Even Gloria wasn't really so bad.

"You know, this could be a great time for us too," Sunny said with a tentative smile. "I mean—alone at last, that sort of thing?"

David sighed. "You still think happiness lies in personal relationships."

"Well, doesn't it? Is there any greater joy than love?"

"You don't understand," David said, getting up abruptly. "I've found God."

God? She stared at him openmouthed. What new obsession was this? It had been bad enough when, as Bessie said, he saw himself and Jesus as two only children.

She waited for him to bring up the subject again, but he didn't, except to sit in the maid's room after dinner occasionally studying a copy of the Bible, Old and New testaments both. Otherwise, his mood seemed to have lightened considerably. It was even okay to go to the movies again. And the weekends when Sarah brought a college friend home, David was always on his best behavior, cordial, charming, courteous to his daughter, deferential to his wife. The Harvard friends were suitably impressed, even when David prefaced his remarks with a smiling, "I know all about Harvard. I've lectured there." It was clear that Sarah hadn't been telling too many tales away from home. Good old Sarah, Sunny thought, she's as eager as I am to believe that this time everything will be all right. And maybe it would—this time.

Now, on a Sunday evening, after Sarah had gone back to school, they sat on the living room couch side by side, looking at highlights of the Watergate hearings on the new TV, David watching with the same intent, propietary air as he had watched Kennedy's assassination. "The emperor has no clothes," Sunny had been about to say when the doorbell rang and David, absorbed, waved her to answer it. Not that Nixon had ever been her idea of an emperor. It was David oddly who had once contemplated voting for Nixon because Noam Chomsky had suggested it as a wily political move, for reasons which escaped her. Still, it was incredible to see that story of deceit and corruption unravel itself day after day, to see . . . Annoyed by having had to tear herself away, she opened the door to find Gloria, and a friend.

Why didn't the girl ever call in advance? They hadn't even heard from her in ages. It was her mother who had told them about Gloria's abortive trip to Cuba to cut sugar cane, and that on her return, disillusioned, to the United States she had hitchhiked out to Oregon to work on an underground newspaper. Another fiasco, evidently, for here she was, hugging Sunny and then an unreceptive David who abruptly turned off the television set.

"This is Dorothy," Gloria said. Dorothy briskly shook hands. Gloria was in her usual baggy camouflage outfit. Dorothy wore tailored pants and a short-sleeved shirt. Her brown hair was cut short and neatly parted on the side.

"We were just watching the Watergate hearings," Sunny said.

"Yeah, beautiful." Gloria shrugged.

"Well, tell us about your travels. Your mother said you might want to settle in Oregon."

"No way," Gloria said. "It's a macho trip. They can keep it."

" 'Can any of you chicks type?' " Dorothy said, with a tight little smile.

Gloria gazed at her fondly.

"And so you're disillusioned with the movement," David said.

"Movements aren't where it's at anymore."

"Oh? What is?" David asked.

"I'll tell you some other time."

"Sunny, isn't there anything to eat around here?" David said testily.

Gloria and Dorothy exchanged quick knowing smiles. "Don't let us keep you," Gloria said. ". . . No, we won't have anything. We're on our way to Women's Veg, over on Columbus. You ought to try it sometime, Sunny." She put her arm through Dorothy's, and let herself out.

"Well, I hope you're satisfied," David said, when Sunny had closed the door after them. "Your stepdaughter's a dyke."

"Satisfied? Why should that satisfy me? Anyway, I don't think it's true. She's just baiting you again."

"But all your pals are dykes, aren't they? And you're a dyke too, aren't you?"

"What in God's name are you talking about?"

"Your love affair with the lady poet on TV."

"*Love* affair? I haven't even seen her since that program."

"That's not what I heard."

"From whom?" Sunny said furiously. "Who's your ventriloquist this time? Why don't you just give me her phone number? I'm tired of talking to the dummy."

"Now I'm a dummy?"

"You get all your ideas from your girlfriends. There's always some pitiful stupid bitch whispering in your ear."

"Then why don't you *leave* me?" David cried, and pointed a finger. "I'll tell you why. Because you're afraid to live alone, that's why. Why don't you admit it? You don't stay with me because you love me. You haven't loved me for years. You don't want me. I repel you. You stay because you're a goddamn coward!"

Sunny ran away from him into the bedroom. She looked out the window at the purple and silver river, the little lights dotting the dusky New Jersey shore, the small boats serenely plying the waters. All so heartbreakingly beautiful, near and yet utterly distant. But it wasn't true that she stayed with David only because she was afraid. Of course she was afraid of life without him. Sometimes the thought of poor Bessie Cohen these days turned her to jelly. But she still *loved* him, if he would only believe that she did, if he would only let her, and stop destroying everything they had. Oh, what was the use? She had heard David slam the door and leave. Now, as she turned, he walked back into the bedroom. He gave her a rueful smile, then held her tight, as if they had just gone through a crisis together. Then he led her into the living room where he put on the television set again and offered her some cold cuts he had bought at Zabars.

She had called Joe Farber on impulse. David was off to the Midwest to give a reading, so at least she knew where he was. He had even kissed her goodbye and given her a number where he could be reached. There was no need to worry now about his mood when he came back. In any case, she wanted to talk to Joe about the new novel, get some feedback from him about whether it was worth doing at all, a love story but with elements of fantasy. She was now convinced that if she could only get back to work everything else would resolve itself, she would manage the other ups and downs. She had meant to drop by the office. It was Joe who had suggested dinner, delighted she had called. His wife was away, his huge Fifth Avenue apartment was being redecorated. "So you see, love? Serendipity," Joe said, repeating it as he sat opposite her, impeccably groomed as always, in the Rainbow Room. Sipping their champagne, they admired the spectacular view, city lights scattered like diamonds. She had already tried several times to bring up her novel, but it had never seemed quite the right moment. Each time Joe had refilled her glass, then his own. They were both probably a bit tight by now, but if so Joe showed no signs of it, except maybe for a slight slurring of his speech, remarks that were a bit more cryptic than usual, a growing ruddiness of the cheeks. He was a gentleman somewhat in his cups, that was all. There would be no sudden rages from Joe, crazy accusations from out of nowhere. "Joe, about the fantasy element—"

But he was asking her if she cared to dance. She followed him a bit unsteadily to the dance floor. She hadn't danced in ages with anyone who knew how. David was a determined hand-pumper, anxious to get it over with. But Joe, as she had expected, was firm, graceful, expert. She gave up worrying and leaned her head against Joe's chin. The music was lovely, ". . . *you are the promised kiss of springtime . . .*" "A penny for your thoughts, Madam," Joe said into her ear. "I was just wishing that life could always be like this." "Like what, love?" "I don't know, old-fashioned, elegant, civilized." "It can," he said, turning her gracefully about. At the end of the set he led them back to their table. With their coffee, he ordered brandy.

"To my favorite lady," Joe said, toasting her with the snifter.

"And to my favorite gentleman," Sunny said. She took a sip and laughed. "That is, after I got over being scared of you."

"Scared of me?" Joe said. "Saw you that first time going into Eleanor's office. Thought, my God, what a sexy woman."

"Did you really?"

"Sexy now."

Joe kissed her hand, and then called for the check. They smiled at each other in the elevator going down. A beautiful evening. Too bad it was almost over. She would call him at the office tomorrow. In the deserted streets around Rockefeller Plaza, she helped him find his Mercedes. He had completely forgotten where he had parked it. Wonderful Joe, wonderful even in his British absentmindedness.

After several false turnings he finally found a street going uptown. "Apartment being redecorated," Joe remarked, settling back behind the wheel. "Entire place a shambles. Will be for days."

"That's too bad. Are you staying in a hotel, then?" Sunny said.

"No, love. Tonight with you."

"Joe, are you nuts?" Sunny said, suddenly stone sober. "You're planning to spend the night with me because your apartment's being redecorated?"

" '21' for a nightcap first? More dancing? Anything you want, my darling."

"I don't think you understand why I called you," Sunny said. "Maybe you'd better just take me home."

"Take you home," Joe said, patting her hand approvingly, then tried to concentrate on his driving the rest of the way. He parked in front of her house, after having lost his way several more times, and came around to let her out. He was very calm and collected. So calm it would have seemed impolite to protest his going up in the elevator, rude to stop him from taking the keys out of her hand and opening the door.

"Where's your loo, darling?" Joe asked before she could say anything.

She pointed it out down the hall and went into the kitchen to put on some coffee. Coffee would sober them both up, allow her to explain that—but he had come up behind her at the stove, taken her in his arms with the same expertise as on the dance floor, kissed her. Her mind ticked away with awful clarity. Had she ever wanted this? Maybe once. But not now. She was cold as ice. And it had all been so lovely. "Excuse me," Sunny said, undoing Joe's arms. "I'll be back in a minute." She escaped to the study and sat on the daybed, regarding her typewriter and pondering the situation. After the coffee she would explain that fond as she was of him, she saw him as an editor, not a lover, that she did not want to risk losing him altogether by . . . should she explain about mixing apples and oranges? . . . that she sincerely hoped . . . Oh, Charlotte would have had a picnic with this one.

"*My God*," Sunny said, coming back into the kitchen. Joe was standing there, stark naked.

He kissed her again, then padded off down the hall. Not a pretty sight. He was chunky. From the bedroom she heard him calling, "Right side or the left, darling?"

"What?"

"Do you sleep on the right side or the left?"

She turned off the burner and put away the can of coffee. Good old Joe Farber, courteous to the end. "It doesn't matter," Sunny said.

It didn't matter. That was the curious part of it. In the morning they had breakfast like an old married couple, though she was in her bathrobe and Joe, having helped himself to David's razor and shaving lotion, sat formally dressed in his English suit. She offered Joe a section of the *Times*. Politely refusing it, he remarked, though his eyes drifted elsewhere, that she was as beautiful in the morning as she was at night. He also repeated his offer to take her to the 21 Club, to charter a plane and fly her to Bermuda, but it was all quite vague. He left early to check on the decorators.

Oddly, she did not hear from Joe again, although she had rather imagined dozens of long-stemmed red roses, lavish arrangements of orchids that she would have to explain away to David. But after that it was easy. Why not? Suddenly, there were other men who seemed to have been waiting in the wings the whole time and who knew to call her when David was out, who approached her at parties, aroused by something about her—as if she were a dog in heat, she thought uncomfortably. Most of them were editors. (Though Hymie too asked her to dinner one time; she refused.) She slept with a few and didn't love any of them. Not one could really hold a candle to David. What did David get out of sleeping with women who didn't hold a candle to *her*?

Still, David remarked that she was easier to live with, and she supposed she was. She no longer hung on his every word, trembled at his frown. Why should she, when there were those others wanting to be nice to her, flatter her in bed, even if after bed there was nothing? "But I've become a whore," she told Dr. Brill. "You're not a whore." She laughed nervously. "They're editors. Who knows if they're fucking me or David?" "They're not fucking David." Well, at least she made sure that David never knew about these little affairs, one-night stands, most of

them, never brought them home to him, certainly never repeated a lover's opinion as her own. She took a ridiculous pride
in that.

One evening, she and David went to a book party at the
Century Club, at one of the rare times when ladies were admitted. Aside from the gentleman's club setting, it was the usual
literary party with the usual guests. She wandered about, accepting a drink from a waiter, helping herself to some canapés,
looking at an exhibit of bad paintings in one of the ground floor
reception rooms, saying hello to a few friends, and then, as
always, went to look for David. She found him in the center
of a small group of men, talking to them intensely. As she
approached, he warned her off with a quick shake of his head
and a self-important little frown, a gentleman among gentlemen. She kept her distance, ticking off each one in her mind:
Don Hoppé, from Colophon Press, Alan Peters from Sterling
Books, Joe Farber—and, of course, David. Poor David, Sunny
thought idly, I've slept with all of them.

3

But David, too, had become easier to live with. In the past few months, much easier. She had never known him to be so, well, *nice*. A little distracted perhaps, but exceedingly thoughtful and considerate. He called now when he thought he might be late for dinner. He inquired about the progress of her book, though not in a prying manner, accepting sympathetically that there were certain technical difficulties. He asked her opinion of Barbara Pym and once, even of Anne Sexton. On Sunday mornings, he had taken to bringing her coffee in bed. "Oh, David," she had said this Sunday morning, thinking that when David was nice there was no one nicer. When she got up, the living room looked radiant, awash with early May sunshine. They sat together in their bathrobes comfortably reading the papers while outside seagulls cawed, swooping by from the river. He had even given her the *Book Review* to look at first, though she returned it quickly, still feeling it was his by rights. Cups and saucers, other sections of the *New York Times* cluttered the sunlit coffee table. They might have been just recently married.

"Well, it sure is unraveling fast," Sunny remarked, glancing up from an article on the missing Watergate tapes. She waited for David to pronounce an authoritative opinion, and instead found him looking at her with a sudden expression of concern. Actually he had looked a bit like that too when he brought her the coffee, as if she were very ill and didn't know it.

"Your hair's all golden. You're a beautiful woman," David said. "I wish you believed that."

"Oh, David, really." She laughed.

"No, it's true." He picked up the *Book Review* again, and read a few pages. ". . . Say, did you see this article on women novelists?"

"I glanced at it," she said warily.

"Your name's mentioned."

"I know."

She was sorry he had noticed, and waited for a withering comment. But David merely pursed his lips and nodded, as if much impressed. Unfortunately, she herself hadn't been impressed at all. The reference was to old work, and the new work was still faltering badly. Maybe she was written out, had nothing more to say. Or maybe the problem was in ultimately having to show it to Joe, though Joe said there was no problem. A perfect gentleman, he had accepted her decision that, although she didn't regret the night of the Rainbow Room, it mustn't ever happen again. And, though he was still happy to remain her editor at Dunbarton and Farber, if she preferred someone else. . . . There had been no bad feelings, no scene. In a way she wished there had. Of course, if she had been dealing with David. . . . She looked across at him and smiled. Ah yes, David had accustomed her to passionate exchanges about everything. Except that right now, David too was pleasantly dispassionate. In fact, he was eyeing her speculatively.

"By the way," he said, "Santa Barbara wants me for a year."

"Santa Barbara? Really? Are you considering it?"

"Why not?"

"It's California."

"So?"

She considered a moment. Well, why not try it again? They were getting along. Maybe they would get along even better in Santa Barbara. They had learned from past mistakes, and it would certainly be beautiful there. And hadn't they in a sense come to the end of their lives in New York?

"They want me to start in September." David said.

"September? Oh, my God, will I be able to get ready so soon, sublet this place, find us a decent house this time?"

David said nothing, but just sat there looking at her worriedly. There was something else, something he hadn't told her.

"David, when did all this come up?"

"Yesterday. They called me at school."

"Yesterday was Saturday, you weren't teaching."

"Friday, then. What is this, the third degree?"

David on the attack was David lying. The matter hadn't come up in the last day or two, universities didn't work like that. No, David must have known about the offer for months, all the time he was being so nice.

"You've already accepted, haven't you?"

"What if I have?"

"Shouldn't you at least have consulted me first?"

"There was nothing to consult you about," David said shortly. Sunny stared at him.

He came over and sat beside her on the sofa, putting a hand over hers. "Oh, Sunny, Sunnoo, don't make a scene, please. We both need a break from each other, you've said so yourself many times. You hate California, you were miserable there the last time. And you don't want to be a whole continent away from Sarah. I understand that."

"I don't know if I want to be a whole continent away from you, either," Sunny said.

"Oh, come off it," David said, with a joshing laugh. "You're dying to get rid of me for a while and you know it."

"How long a while?"

"I don't know." He got up, seeming to breathe easier. "Join me whenever you feel like it."

A short friendly separation? Was that what David was suggesting? Well, maybe he was right. They had certainly torn each other to tatters. Maybe it was time to heal. Maybe it was even brave of David to force the issue. *She* would never have had the courage, God knew. But David was often brave in that way, charging ahead, sometimes like a bull in a china shop, but nevertheless charging ahead. She thought for a moment.

"Why don't we say a month or so for you to find us something, and me to make arrangements here?"

"Whatever you like."

He had agreed too quickly. His relief was too palpable.

"When do you plan to leave?"

"As soon as I'm through at NYU."

"But that's in a couple of weeks."

"So what?" David said.

"Nothing," Sunny said quickly. "Nothing." Because if they were to part for a little while, and she had just agreed that they should, she wanted it to be on the sweetest, least rancorous terms. She went behind his chair and put her arms around his neck, kissing his hair, which was now completely silver gray. She thought of him at Izzy's ghastly funeral. Just a few old Bronx cronies in an almost empty chapel, a rabbi who had never known Izzy, Tillie in hysterics, Natalia shutting her up, David trying to muster a few shreds of dignity. She tightened her arms around him, suddenly afraid of losing him forever.

The month became two months. At first she had merely intended to wait and spend some time with Sarah when she came home from Harvard. But Sarah was home only long enough to dump her stuff, do some laundry, and then take off for her old summer camp where she would be a senior counselor. The apartment was full of dark corners after Sarah left. Sunny called David, but he pointed out, concerned, that all he had been able to find was a temporary one-room studio. There was no place for Sunny to work. Maybe in the fall. . . . If she wanted company couldn't she at least get away for the weekend? She didn't explain why that was impossible. Yes, Amanda had asked her to spend a few days in Vermont but that involved too many terrible memories. Geraldine Marx, whom she ran into one day at the Whitney looking at a show of American primitives, suggested she rent a little house on the Cape. "Be a bachelor girl," Geraldine said laughingly. The phrase turned Sunny's blood to ice. The Hamptons were out too. She hated that jazzy, literary crowd, the same New York crush, only more so. And she certainly had no desire to buddy up again with false Charlotte, though how false she would probably never know. No, work was the answer. It had sustained her before, it would sustain her again. Each day she sat down at her typewriter, turned on the fan in the study, felt her mind turn to putty. She had abandoned the fantasy idea, but what remained was lifeless, wooden. She didn't know these people. She got up, promised herself to come back later in the day, looked at the silent telephone. Where was everyone? Bessie Cohen, stuck in town on account of her job, had invited her to brunch one Sunday, and that was it. She must stop calling her Cohen, though. Now that Manny had remarried, a gorgeous young Japanese who had the personality of a geisha but came from Oregon, Bessie had resumed her maiden name of Finklestein—as if that mattered. She was still in the same apartment, raising her daughters single-handed, so what had her divorce accomplished except to make her more careworn than ever? She would invite Bessie back one of these days. Meanwhile, what about all the men who had seemed to be waiting only for David to depart?—not that she wanted to see them either. Now that David had actually departed had they lost interest? Or without David had *she* lost interest? (Ricky, with his usual youthful instincts had called the very day David left for California, but she had told him firmly it was over.) There weren't even any parties. The summer wasn't a publishing season. Finally, a badly printed little blue postcard came in the mail from the Gotham Book Mart, the kind of invitation she and David always threw away, this time to celebrate an collection of verse by a poet no one had ever heard of. Dr. Brill was also away, taking off the month of August like all the other psychiatrists, but she knew he would have told her to go. Well, what had she to lose? She didn't need to stay long, and afterward she could treat herself to dinner and an aircon-ditioned movie.

Outside, the August heat hit her like a blow to the stomach. The sky was greenish blue and hazy, the smell from the quick food places on Broadway nauseating. All the local freaks had come out on the street too, emerged from wherever they hid in the winter, bleached-blond Negro transvestites, mad old ladies shouting to the heavens, hookers in red hot pants, bedraggled youngsters carrying blaring radios. The air in the Broadway bus was unbreathable, the passengers irritable and sweaty. She walked east on Forty-seventh Street, and inside the entrance to the

Gotham Book Mart started upstairs to the room where the party clearly was being held. The deafening noise from above made her reconsider. But then she looked at the photograph that hung at the top of the stairs and was reassured: a huge blowup of a group of famous poets when they were young—Auden, Delmore, Muriel, Randall, the whole lot of them. The party room was not only mobbed, as she had expected, but mobbed with strangers. She took a quick look around. Was it possible that she could be at a literary party, any literary party, and not know anyone? Of course it was a peculiarly young crowd, most of them scruffy and bohemian. Nevertheless . . . She had turned to leave again when she realized that a woman of her own age, standing by the door, was half-smiling at her. Sunny smiled back, puzzled, somewhat uneasy. . . . Could it be? Oh, God, of all people, Mary Jane!

"How are you, Sunny?" Mary Jane said, still smiling that faintly unnerving smile. Her southern accent sounded more pronounced, but otherwise, allowing for the passage of sixteen or seventeen years—was it that long?—she seemed unchanged, black hair still unruly, white cotton dress dowdy.

"I'd like you to meet my husband," Mary Jane said, introducing the genial little man with eyeglasses who stood beside her. "Dr. Harold Weinstein, Sunny Mansfield—excuse me, Sunny Harvey."

"How do you do, Doctor Weinstein," Sunny said, ignoring the dig. She turned to Mary Jane, who was still smiling. "I heard from someone, maybe Muffy, that you'd gone back to Louisville. I didn't know you'd married."

"Well, I did," Mary Jane said. "I married a psychiatrist. Not mine, I hasten to add."

The genial little man laughed. Was he really a psychiatrist?

"Are you alone?" Mary Jane said.

"Well, David is in California at the moment. I stayed behind in New York to work."

"I meant, are you at this party alone."

"I'm on my way somewhere else," Sunny said quickly. She told Mary Jane to be sure to let her know the next time she was in town—the smile took on a bitter edge—and caught a taxi home, forgetting about the dinner and the airconditioned movie. Inside the apartment, she took a deep breath, as if she had just escaped from danger, and looked at her watch. Seven P.M. here. Four o'clock in the afternoon in California. Maybe David would be at home. He was.

"Oh, darling," Sunny said, sighing with relief.

"What's the matter?"

"Nothing. I just missed you, that's all. It's hot as hell in New York."

"It's hot in Santa Barbara," David said.

"But there are flowers, trees, swimming pools, the Pacific—what if I just grab a plane and come out?"

"There's nowhere for you to work," David said, worriedly.

"I'm sure there's some corner."

"Oh, Sunny, you say that now, but the minute you get here—I know you."

"I suppose you're right," Sunny said. "I suppose the sane thing to do would be to dig in now and when I've earned a holiday—"

"Whenever you want," David said.

He asked about Sarah, complaining that he had not heard from her in some time, cautioned Sunny to keep the check book up to date, and said yes, of course he missed her too. She hung up, telling herself it was foolish to feel so uneasy. David had made the right noises. What more did she want? It was the run-in with Mary Jane that had unnerved her, the irony of finding Mary Jane with a husband when she herself was husbandless. But she wasn't really husbandless. That was merely a temporary situation. She heard David's voice in her mind, friendly, agreeable, saying what she wanted to hear. Yes, the right words. But not the music.

Sarah came home right after Labor Day, a short-lived blessing since soon it was time for her to leave again. Despite Sarah's insistence that it wasn't necessary, Sunny drove her up to Cambridge, wanting to be with her a while longer. But the nearer they got to Harvard, the harder it was to keep up the pretense that everything was all right. Who was it? Who was it this time? Why did she know that this time it was serious?

"Oh, Mama," Sarah said finally, who hadn't been fooled anyway. "Why don't you just go out to California and join him?"

"Do you really think I should?" Sunny asked, grasping at this slimmest of straws for a moment. "No, I really have to work. So does he."

"Oh, go ahead, You know you're dying to see him. You're just moping at the typewriter anyway. It will be like old times. You'll fight and scream, and the neighbors will complain, and then you'll both wind up in bed, as usual."

"Sarah, honestly!"

"Well, it's just all foreplay, isn't it? Kinky, if you ask me. But if that's what you're into—"

Sunny laughed. Harvard had catapulted Sarah into even higher realms of sophistication than Thorndike. Still, maybe her suggestion made sense. "I'll think about it," Sunny said, and turned to her. "Maybe for Christmas you could come out and join us." Sarah stared ahead and didn't answer. "There's a pool where Daddy lives. You could swim every day, and we could travel around, maybe even go back to Hollywood. Wouldn't that be fun? The three of us."

Sarah gave a thin little smile but still didn't answer. She was tan from the summer, lean, muscular in her short-sleeved white shirt, so very put together. But she's a woman, Sunny thought, I should be talking to her like a woman. My friend.

"Oh, Sarah, how will I live without you?" Sunny said.

They were entering Cambridge and Sarah gave her a pleading look.

"I'm sorry," Sunny said.

"You *could* make it on your own, you know," Sarah said. "If you'd only believe it, if you weren't so male-oriented. Instead of which, you torture yourself and everyone around you."

"I've been torturing everyone around me?" Sunny said.

But they had already arrived at Harvard Yard, and Sarah's expression had changed completely. She was a kid again, her face had lit up, and she was bolting out of the car to meet up with some old friends on the sidewalk. They hugged, slapped each other on the back, burst into laughter at some joke Sunny couldn't hear. She sat in the car, waiting for Sarah to come back and help unload the stuff from the trunk, and thought of the beautiful poem by William Snodgrass about his daughter on a swing. How did that line go again? Something like, *I pull her toward me only to push her away.*

She had promised to see her mother on the way back from Cambridge, though it would probably be a pointless visit. Grace was almost always drunk these days. She had even been tipsy at David's father's funeral, tripping over the crowded tombstones in the Workman's Circle plot, giggling apologies as if she were at a Westport cocktail party. William had pretended as usual that nothing was wrong—though really what else could he have done?—while David, curiously, had not been angry but solicitous, even in his grief. Still there were times when Grace was sober and perhaps she would be today.

Sitting on the chintz sofa in the living room, sipping a cup of coffee, Grace did seem to be in control, though her face was puffy and her white hair fuzzy and unkempt. She was wearing old jeans and a gray sweatshirt, which didn't become her and had never been her style. No, Mother should be charming, elegant, wear a black dress and furs, a simple strand of pearls around her neck. Who was this dowdy woman with the lusterless eyes? Why had she destroyed lovely gay Grace Mansfield? Well, at least she *was* drinking coffee.

"And how is our darling Sarah?" Grace said, taking a sip, settling down for a chat. "Glad to be back at Harvard?"

"Too glad."

"Oh, well, it's always that way, isn't it? One day you can't get them out from underfoot and the next day they can't wait to get rid of you. But she's such a lovely girl. Always so kind, so considerate."

"I don't know," Sunny said. "I'm beginning to think that David and I made her life a hell when she was growing up and we didn't even know it. She never even complained. I wish there were some way to make it up to her, but there isn't. It's too late now. Everything seems too late now."

"My goodness," Grace said, laughing. "Why are you so hard on yourself? Sarah seems happy enough to me. . . ." She went over to the bar, absently carrying her cup. "Would you like something?"

"Oh, Mother, must you?"

"What's come over you today, darling?" Grace said.

"Nothing," Sunny said. ". . . Oh, damn it, why didn't you and Daddy at least *try* to stop me?"

"Stop you from what, darling?"

"Marrying David."

Grace laughed again and, abandoning all pretense, poured herself a stiff one into the coffee cup. "Isn't it a little late in the day to wonder about that? You've been married how long?"

"Twenty years—legally." Really, twenty-two. Half her life, she suddenly realized. "But you knew he was difficult. You knew he was older and divorced and had a child. Why didn't you say anything?"

"Would it have stopped you?"

"No."

"Anyway," Grace said, "David isn't difficult, he just has an artistic temperament. Isn't that to be expected of a man of his talents?"

"What about my talents? Do they give me carte blanche to behave as I please too?"

Grace shook her head and smiled indulgently. "Darling, I hope you're not turning into one of those competitive females. They're so unattractive. Daddy and I are very proud of all your accomplishments, as you well know, but—"

"But you're afraid you'll lose your wonderful, famous, distinguished son-in-law."

"We can't lose David," Grace said, astonished. "He's the father of our grandchild. Besides, we've always been very fond of each other."

"I think David has a new girlfriend," Sunny said. "And I feel in my bones that this one means trouble."

"Has he said he wants to leave you?"

"No. Maybe he's waiting for me to leave him." The thought made her shiver. "Never mind. You wouldn't understand. How could you? Daddy would never—"

Grace smiled brightly, though tears had welled up in her blue eyes. She looked like a little bird again, forlorn, flitting about, with no solid branch to light on.

"Oh, God," Sunny said, finally admitting to herself what she had probably always known. "Even from the beginning?"

"I wish I knew what you were talking about," Grace said, suddenly very drunk, her face unfocussed, her hand trembling as it lifted the cup.

"I don't care," Sunny said, defiantly. "It's a different world for women now. We don't have to—"

Grace held out her arms and without thinking Sunny clung to her. But it was hard to tell any longer who was the mother and who the baby.

4

Soon after sunset, the Orthodox Jewish family returned home from Yom Kippur services to break their fast. She passed them on the corner in their holiday outfits, father and son in dark suits and black fedoras, mother and daughter in new fall dresses but carrying no pocketbooks, all of them wearing sneakers. How mystical those sneakers and the absence of pocketbooks had seemed when Bessie first explained about them, how beautiful the celebration of the birth of the universe each fall. Now she couldn't even remember what those quarrels with David concerning her conversion had been about. In the end none of it had mattered in the least. She had never been accepted into the fold. That Jewish family would have thought she was crazy if she told them she was one of them. Only Bessie Cohen still faithfully sent her Jewish New Year cards, only Bessie Cohen would have invited her over tonight for the holiday meal. . . . No, not Cohen, Finklestein, Sunny reminded herself, thinking again as she entered Bessie's apartment, how little else had changed. They were still sitting down at the same old oval table, spread with Bessie's best damask cloth, adorned with silver candlesticks, a braided challah, a ceremonial dish of apples and honey to sweeten the year. The same people too—Bessie's brother and sister-in-law, and their three children, Bessie's two girls— with the surprising addition of a friendly man named Milton, who, however, looked enough like Manny to be a clone, told the same jokes, and was also connected with some Jewish organization. More than anything, there was that same nagging sense as the meal progressed of being an impostor. They were all talking about the service, which she hadn't heard, about fasting, which she hadn't done. So what right had she to be here now? When dinner was over, and the others had been shooed off to rest themselves, including a reluctant Milton, who wanted to help, Sunny joined Bessie in the kitchen, trying at least to make herself useful.

"Well, this is just like old times, isn't it?" Sunny said, scraping dirty plates into the garbage. "Almost as if nothing's changed."

"Everything's changed," Bessie said sharply.

"Yes, well I really didn't get a chance to talk to Milton," Sunny said. "But I'm sure he's—"

"The salt of the earth. You should only be so lucky. Do you need a good lawyer?"

"A lawyer? What makes you think I need a lawyer?"

"You need to protect yourself, bubbeleh. Believe me, I'm speaking from experience."

"Bessie, I don't think you understand. David is merely out in California while I—"

"You better make sure he doesn't have money stashed away somewhere. Maybe a Swiss bank account."

"A Swiss bank account?" Sunny burst into laughter. "David wouldn't even know what one was. He's never concerned himself with money . . ."

Bessie had wrung out a dishcloth and was reaching for the kosher soap.

". . . I mean of course he worries about it sometimes, but that's only because he was so poor when he was growing up. It was the Depression." She paused, remembering the holiday, for some reason wanting Bessie to think well of him. "Actually, he says he's found God."

"Great." Bessie slid her glasses back up her nose with a damp forefinger. "Now if God finds him he'll be in business. . . . Listen, if you want a lawyer, call me. Unless breadlines interest you too."

On the way home, Sunny shook her head over Bessie's dour advice; the idea of David making secret investments was particularly ludicrous. The only brokerage house David had probably ever heard of was Merrill Lynch, and only because James Merrill, son of one of the partners, happened to be a poet. Well, yes, of course, when Gloria was young, David had resented paying child support, since Gertrude kept driving him up the wall with her whining demands. But he would never behave that way toward Sunny and Sarah. Never. No, what she had told Bessie was true. David had always had been far more obsessed with God than with Mammon. But what God? He was rereading Saint Paul, David had mentioned in one of his infrequent letters. She hadn't pursued the matter, afraid that he was flirting with Catholicism again, as he had in the fifties when it was so much in vogue among intellectuals. If only there were a God for both of them, a God who would unite them. Knowing in advance it was useless, she dug up one of the old pamphlets she had studied from during her conversion. Dog-eared, pages missing, it was very vague and disheartening. Only the obligations and responsibilities involved in practicing Judaism with a capital J were stressed. ("Jud-ah-ism," as David had been fond of saying, mimicking Rabbi Binder.) There was nothing to suggest exaltation, fervor. She tried to remember the prayer that Jews recited every day of their lives. . . . "I believe. . . ." Believe what? . . . "I believe with a perfect faith that the Messiah will come, and though He tarry . . ." What if her Messiah had already come and gone?

Nevertheless, when the Jewish holidays were over, Sunny called Rabbi Binder. "How's your famous husband?" he said. "Fine," she heard herself saying, "couldn't be better." "Sunny, I see your name in the paper too these days. How about coming over and giving us a little speech . . . ?"

Thoroughly depressed, Sunny went downstairs and wandered into Riverside Park, made even more depressed by the bright autumn foliage, the sight of young mothers walking along the shining river pushing strollers. It was like seeing a movie of her own life. She ached for Sarah. Where had it all gone, that happy time? If only there were some sign that happiness would return. Please, God, I know I haven't been faithful. I know I have believed in You imperfectly. But if You would just give me a sign. Suddenly a chill wind rustled a shower of dry leaves to the ground, a cloud slid over the sun, and the day turned gray. Then the cloud slid away and the sun came out again, hazy and golden, and there in front of her, like a character in one of his own stories, stood Hymie Shapiro. Neat, punctilious, eyeglasses polished, he looked like an angel in the guise of a CPA.

"Oh, Hymie! I haven't seen you for ages."

"You look great," Hymie said.

"I do?"

"You're a very attractive woman."

"I wish I felt like one."

Hymie shook his head impatiently. "What are you working on?"

"A novel, as usual."

"What else can we do?" Hymie said with a sigh. He regarded her thoughtfully.

"Keep it up, Sunny. Your work has a lot of wit, and charm, and delicacy. A special quality no one else has."

"Really? You think that?"

"I want to see more of it," Hymie said.

"Oh, Hymie."

He vanished as swiftly as he had appeared. She ran home from the park to call David. David would appreciate this mystical encounter.

"*You* sound happy," David said.

"I just ran into Hymie. He looked like an angel from one of his own stories. He spoke like an angel too. He said the most beautiful things about my work. But the point is that the clouds parted, and a ray of sunshine came through just as he—"

"He's a sweet man," David said. "Listen, have you been keeping a record of all the checks you've written?"

"I sent you a list on Monday."

"Oh, okay."

There was a pause. She heard David take a deep sigh.

"Sunny," he said finally. "You're not going overboard, are you? I'm worried."

"Oh, darling," Sunny said, laughing. "I never go overboard. Maybe that's been my real problem all along."

"What are you talking about?"

"What are *you* talking about?"

"*Money!*" David burst out hysterically. "*Money!*"

She sat down in the lawyer's office, already positive she had made a terrible mistake letting Bessie scare her into this. Maybe if it had been a sleek modern office, and Ronald Schein a smooth, sophisticated attorney she would have felt she was only being sensible, taking intelligent precautions. But the office, on Upper Broadway, was shabby, and Ronald Schein an aging man with a wrinkled suit and a tired face.

"Actually, I'm not here for anything serious," Sunny said. "Just a little information." She tried to laugh. "Bessie Cohen said a little information couldn't hurt."

"I know. She called me. If you don't mind, I'd like a few facts." He poised his pencil over a lined yellow legal pad.

"Didn't Bessie tell you everything?"

"Refresh my recollection."

"Yes. Well, to begin with, my husband is David Harvey—" She paused. No awed response. "You've heard of him, of course?"

"What is he? Some kind of writer?"

"A poet. A distinguished poet."

"Listen, a lot of very distinguished people have walked through that door," Ronald Schein said, pointing to it for emphasis. "And they don't impress me. . . . You've been married how many years?"

"Twenty—legally." She gave a nervous giggle at the word legally. In fact, twenty-two. Half my life, she wanted to say.

"Children?"

"One. A daughter. Nineteen. That's Sarah. She's in college. Harvard."

"Well, there may be a problem with the school bills—" "No, never." "—but she's probably too old for a custody battle."

"Oh, David would never want custody," Sunny said, wondering how they had wandered onto this subject. "Sarah's always been my responsibility. Though of course he loves her. He's just been very distracted over the years."

Ronald Schein nodded shortly. "What was your last taxable gross?"

"I don't know," Sunny said, twisting in her chair, wanting to flee. "I just sign things."

"Then you better call your accountant. Try to get copies of your returns for the last three years. If he's a nice guy he won't tell Dave."

"David," Sunny said automatically. But what did nice mean in terms of betraying him with an accountant? "I beg your pardon?"

"Are you currently employed?"

"No. That is, I'm a writer too. Of course not nearly so distinguished, though—"

"Who do you write for?"

"I don't know," Sunny said. "Myself and strangers, I suppose."

"Mrs. Harvey," Ronald Schein said, placing his pencil on the yellow legal pad, "I don't mind telling you you're not in a good frame of mind. I'll also tell you what would make the most sense in your case. Your husband's in California? Go out there. Hang around with him a few months. Establish residence. Sue him under the community property law. You'll split everything down the middle. As you can see, I'm not out for business."

"But I couldn't possibly go out to California under false pretenses. Anyway, we have no property. David is opposed to property. He's a poet, his father was a Socialist, he—"

"Okay, okay. Maybe we can get him on abandonment."

"Abandonment? What makes you think he's abandoned me?"

Ronald Schein smiled cannily. "But the guy has abused you, am I correct?"

"Look, I just really came here for information," Sunny said.

"Verbally? Physically?"

"I don't want to talk about it."

"Physical and verbal abuse," Ronald Schein said, making a note, pinky ring shining.

"Please don't write that down. David—"

"Listen, lady, *you* may be afraid of the great David Harvey, whoever the hell he is," Ronald Schein said, "but I don't give a shit. I've dealt with tougher customers. . . . Pardon my French."

She pardoned his French, wondering at the possibility of someone who wasn't scared of David. No, he had merely never met him. She got up, telling Ronald Schein that when she made up her mind she would call. Yes, she would keep an eye out for secret bank accounts. And yes, she understood that if she wanted him to proceed there would be the matter of a retainer. He added it to the yellow legal pad on which their life had already been fractured into ages, dates, dollars and cents.

Had she been crazy to go to that man, Sunny wondered, collapsing into an armchair in the study. How could she even for a minute have considered consulting a divorce lawyer? Even if Ronald Schein had been as smooth and suave as Dr. Brill, equipped to guide her deftly through the pitfalls ahead, it would have been impossible. As it was she could already hear David asking where she had found this ambulance chaser. And she would have to say that Bessie Cohen had poisoned her mind, that Bessie Cohen had almost sent her charging over a precipice. When the phone rang, she grabbed it eagerly, almost dropping the batch of David's mail she was holding in her lap to forward later on.

"Are you okay?" Gertrude said. "You sound funny."

"Oh, Gertrude . . . No, I'm fine. I just got in, that's all."

"Well, you owe me a *mazel tov*. Gloria's getting married."

Sunny sat up. "You're kidding! Gloria's getting *married*? To whom? When? Where? How?"

"They decided a few days ago. A lovely boy. A social worker. She met him through my cousin."

"Oh, Gertrude, that's really marvelous."

She settled down to listen to the details, feeling that a great weight had been lifted from her heart, that Gertrude's call had wiped the slate clean. Suddenly the whole world made sense again, a world that had nothing to do with lawyers, cold facts and cruel figures. No, this was what her and David's life together had truly been about. Children, happiness, shared suffering, love. And now Gloria was getting married. *Imagine.*

"It's so sweet of you to tell me. Does David know yet?"

"Sure, Gloria called him. He's furious."

"Furious?"

"Well, the boy happens to be Orthodox. Very. Extremely. To tell the truth, he's a Lubavitcher. You can imagine David's reaction. He told her she would have been better off with the Moonies. He says he doesn't even think he'll come to the wedding."

"I'm sure he doesn't mean that," Sunny said, wondering why Gloria hadn't called her too.

"Well, you know David. He says Seymour will make Gloria shave her head and throw David out of the house unless he keeps kosher. He says this is all only Gloria's way of getting back at him. Which is ridiculous, naturally. She loves the boy."

"Naturally," Sunny said.

"Well, you know David," Gertrude repeated, adding chummily, "listen, let's have lunch one of these days."

"Sure," Sunny said, though they had never had lunch before. Gertrude said she would keep her posted and hung up. She put the receiver back on its cradle and thoughtfully lit a cigarette from the pack she had bought on her way home from Ronald Schein. (Mild menthol filters, and she could stop any time.) It was stupid to feel rueful that Gloria herself hadn't called about the engagement. In the end, evidently, blood—even, as in this case, bad blood—really was thicker than water. But why hadn't David called her either, if only to complain? And why had Gertrude sounded quite *that* chummy? "You know David," she had kept saying—as if she and Sunny were now in the same boat. Stubbing out the cigarette, Sunny stooped to gather up David's mail, which had fallen to the floor in her excitement. There was nothing very important, circulars and other junk. Also a long white business envelope that had been forwarded from NYU. She stared at the return address—Merrill, Lynch, Pearce, Fenner and Smith—then tore it open, unable to believe the figures in front of her, unable to believe that Bessie and the lawyer had been right all along.

"Look, I really can't tell you anything," Amanda said, looking around uncomfortably. "I'm sorry I said anything the last time."

"The last time," Sunny said.

They were in a glittery new restaurant, dedicated to chic fast food. They had already finished their overpriced salads, asked after each other's children, talked briefly about Sunny's new novel. Now Amanda looked as if all she wanted was to make a fast getaway. It wasn't fair to hold her there, she knew, to keep picking at Amanda like an old wound until the bleeding started again. But she couldn't help it, she would make it up to her some other time, right now she needed to be *sure*.

"Well, you talk to him, don't you?" Amanda said. "How does he sound?"

"Amanda, please." She stared at Amanda, her heart pounding.

"I've just heard some rumors," Amanda said, looking away again.

"What rumors? Another so-called artist?"

"No. I think she teaches."

"At NYU, I suppose."

"Yes."

"In the English department?"

"No, history. I believe she teaches the history of religion."

Religion? . . . Of course. David had found God—in his fashion. She should have guessed.

"Look, I'm sure it's nothing," Amanda said.

"Oh, it's always a nothing. David's specialty. Is she there with him now?"

"I don't know, I don't think so. I understand that the three of them went out there together, but—look, Sunny, I really do have to—"

"The three of them?"

"Well, David, and Natalia, and—whatever her name is. I believe she's Natalia's protegée."

"Oh, no," Sunny said.

"Come on," Amanda said, trying to smile. "It's not that bad."

Bad? It was worse than bad—terrible beyond her wildest imaginings. How could she have forgotten about Natalia? She thought again of David and his aunt shoulder to shoulder at Izzy's funeral, abandoning Tillie to her unseemly hysterics, as if Tillie had never counted, an emotional red herring all along. Yes, Philip Roth, Norman Mailer, all of the braggarts, stand-up comedians, professional bar mitzvah boys, all of them had Jewish mothers like Tillie. But only David had an aunt. An aunt who had taught him that ugly was beautiful, and cruelty clever, that all Jews but her were contemptible, that all women but her existed only to serve him. If the new one was Natalia's protegée then she was the ultimate pathetic professional. The ultimate enemy.

"Don't do anything rash, for goodness sake," Amanda said. "Don't throw away your marriage on account of this."

"You don't understand. David already has."

5

She opened the letter, trembling. She had expected a phone call. Instead, there was this, hastily typed on a yellow second sheet.

NOVEMBER 1, 1973
Santa Barbara, California

Dear Sunny:

Are you mad? Yes, it's clear to me now that you've always been mad. Mad at the world. Mad at anyone more successful than you are. Mad at anyone more literary, more gifted, more intellectually astute.

Well, all I can say is that now that you've found yourself a lawyer, I hope you've also found a job and an apartment that you can afford. Because you're going to need them, baby.

David

The next one was worse. Scrawled on university stationery.

NOVEMBER 10, 1973
Santa Barbara, California

Dear $unny:

No, I will not negotiate. Wild horses couldn't drag me to the bargaining table with you and that greaseball shyster you have dredged up from the legal netherworld. I will go to jail before I negotiate. Please come to your senses before it's too late. But perhaps it is already too late. I have suspected for some time that your brain is as addled as your mother's. But I am not some all-purpose daddy you can hit for all he's worth. I am

not Hymie Shapiro with money to burn. Shame on you. Do
you hear me? Shame on you.

D

"Look, let's call it off," Sunny said to Ronald Schein. "He
doesn't want to negotiate. I really shouldn't have started all this
in the first place. I apologize for wasting your time."
"Don't be foolish. We'll slap him with a summons."
"A summons? You can't do that."
"Watch me," Ronald Schein said.

2 AM!
Santa Barbara

Oh, Sunny, oh my God. How could you have done such a
thing? A divorce suit without any warning, without any rhyme
or reason. Extreme mental cruelty? On whose side? Against
whom? What are you talking about?

Please, please, don't do this to us. I beg you. I can't believe
that it's just money that impels you. Or am I mistaken in this
too, as in so many expectations of you?

The summons is still shaking in my hand. I implore you not
to put me, us, through this. I don't want to fight. I don't want
to drag you through the mud, though I could. You are far from
blameless. But please, cease and desist from this suit. Where is
your sense of proportion in all this? What do you imagine I
ever wanted for us but to live together peacefully? To work
peacefully? I am not competitive toward you. I could not write
a novel if I tried, and I have never tried. . . .

Santa Barbara
California
6 AM

Yes, now I remember. It all comes back to me, how you
once haughtily declared that you didn't want to be treated as
Gracie Allen. (I forget the exact context.) But surely you un-

derstand that Gracie Allen was the major figure in that comedy act. Sunnoo, Sunnoo, fool that I am I had always expected that in spite of everything we would grow together again, even though I've been frightened by the realization that you hate the idea of living with me, that even the sight of me in the morning seems to set your teeth on edge. Oh, Sunnoo, don't you know you've always been "it" to me? My home.

Please, call off your dogs. I would rather miss you, as I do, than not love you. . . .

Not love her? Not love her? What had she done? Rising from a racked and sleepless bed, she put through a call to David.

"Oh, darling," Sunny said, laughing and crying at the same time. "You're home to me too."

There. It was all over. All settled.

"Do you know what time it is?" David said groggily.

"No. Listen, I'll take the first plane out today. I won't even tell anyone if you don't want me to. Nobody understands us anyway, but us."

"Where'd you get the lawyer—?"

"And David, I'll be your girl again. See? I *am* your girl again."

"Goddamn it, why are you always either at my feet or at my throat?" David said, his voice cracking. ". . . Look, I'll call you later. Let me catch my breath. I'm in as much pain as you are, believe me. But I can't afford to go to pieces. Literally."

"David, we love each other."

"Of course we love each other. I'll probably drop dead from us loving each other. But, frankly, Sunny, after the hell you've put us through these past weeks—"

"*I've* put us through hell?"

"Try to get hold of yourself, for God's sake. Stop listening to those false friends who give you lousy advice. Stop listening to that shyster who's only trying to get his hands on what little money there is. You won't find the answer in any of them, believe me."

"What about *your* false friends—not to mention relatives? What about Merrill, Lynch, Pearce, Fenner and Smith?"

"Sunnoo, are you so hysterical you can't hear what I'm saying? How could you let yourself disintegrate so badly? Where's your pride? At least think of Sarah. What do you think would happen if you came out here now? We'd only be scrapping again within a week. We'd be the laughing stock of this community too, as we have of so many others."

"She's still out there, isn't she? I know she is."

"Sunny," David said firmly. "Be your wonderful self again. Be strong."

Strong, strong? Was he mad? All their lives together David had betrayed her with weak sisters, was currently betraying her with Natalia's protegée, the weakest sister of all. But now he wanted her to be strong? It was the worst thing he had ever said to her. "*Chazak, chazak, v'nit chazek* . . . strength, strength, and yet more strength. . . ." The words inscribed on Edmund Wilson's tombstone. "Do me a favor lady," Ronald Schein said. "Don't call him anymore. Don't communicate with him." "He'll communicate with me. I know David. He'll write me more letters." "So don't open them." ". . . I couldn't not open a letter from David," Sunny said.

In fact, she opened them all, one after the other, about three a week—just as in the old days—though they were all the same, typically David, complaining of his pain, his need to catch his breath, his spiritual isolation, the fact that he wasn't made of money no matter what wild ideas she had, and she should get a grip on herself. But underneath he seemed to be demanding an answer. What answer? Even if Ronald Schein hadn't advised against communication, what answer could she possibly give him?

Perhaps she should march in to see Natalia, confront that wicked androgene once and for all, tell her how she had destroyed David's soul, warped and twisted his life, made him unfit to be husband, father, lover, anything. But Natalia would only laugh and tell David his wife was even crazier than she thought. So what? She could fly out to California, shake David by the shoulders, banish the latest pathetic professional, who was probably waiting on him hand and foot, tell him that love, only love mattered, not evil council, not services rendered. He would agree, be moved to tears by her passion, they would believe in each other once more. And then? He would slip out from under again, betray her in all the ways she knew so well by now. It could go on endlessly if she wanted, until they had both destroyed each other permanently. . . . Another man, then? Ricky, who was tender and sweet, but so terribly young. Dick Reeves, a decent guy. They would pick up where they had left off, go back to Paris. But if Dick Reeves was such a decent guy, why would he abandon his wife and children for some will-o-the-wisp affair? And besides, *that* Paris was over now too.

She was sitting alone in the study—her study? David's study? what difference did it make anymore?—watching darkness descend on the Hudson as she did every evening now, when the doorbell rang. She had forgotten that Bessie was coming over.

"What's the matter, bubbeleh?" Bessie said, following her back down the corridor. "You sounded very lousy on the phone."

"He wants me to be strong," Sunny said, sitting down.

"So be strong."

"How? No matter how I look at it life doesn't mean anything without him."

"It's the only game in town, doll."

"Then I don't think I want to play."

"Jews don't talk like that," Bessie said sharply. "Don't act like a kid. You have a kid."

Sarah, Sunny thought wearily. Why did everyone keep bringing up Sarah? Why did Sarah keep calling with concern though she had said repeatedly she was fine? She suddenly realized that the study was foul smelling. Cigarette butts littered the ashtrays—she had not been able to stop smoking after all. David would be furious. But what if—oh, *coraggio!*—he weren't?

"Listen," Bessie said, "your marriage hasn't been worth piss for years. What are you carrying on about? Why are you clinging to some dream?"

"Because dreams are the only thing worth clinging to."

"Whose dreams, his or yours? . . . *Oy, bubbeleh,* let him go already," Bessie said, sighing with sympathy—but for whom? "The guy's old. He's tired."

"You think David is old and tired?"

"He was born like that. They all were. They thought screwing around would rejuvenate them. Now they're looking to be taken care of."

It was true. She thought of Manny's geisha. Even Jimmy Starrett—having gone through how many wives?—had said he was now looking for a wheelchair pusher. And of course, there was David with Natalia's dishrag.

"I don't care," Sunny said. "I want him back. I want it all back."

Bessie sighed again, no longer sympathetically. "You know what? You should get to work."

Work, work. What did Bessie know about it, Sunny thought, pacing the apartment restlessly after Bessie left. She had been right to want to move after Sarah went to college. The rooms were so big and dark and empty. And once they had been bursting with light and life. Cocktail party chatter, arguments, literary infighting. Sarah's friends, poking around the refrigerator, giggling in the back bedroom. Sulky young Gloria, sitting in Sarah's little rocker, and Sarah hopefully bringing her a jigsaw puzzle. David coming in the front door and automatically reaching for his mail on the foyer table, David starting to undress as soon as they came home from an evening out. The constantly ringing telephone, the quarrels, the passionate lovemaking afterwards. The stony visits from Tillie and Izzy. My God, she would even have been glad to see Bloom pop out of some corner and say, "Hullo."

She walked back into her study, opened a window, and put on the light, laughing helplessly at the pile of David's crazy letters on her desk. She pushed them aside and sat down. I want him back, I want him back, I want him back, she thought, knowing in her heart that the only way to have him back now, would be to part with him forever. She looked at her typewriter. "*Chazak, chazak, v'nit chazek,* strength, strength and yet more strength. . . ." Edmund's epitaph. But also the words Jews said when they finished reading the Torah and started all over again. Would she be up to it? Would it be too hard? She could only pray that the conversion had taken, after all.

And start at the beginning, when he had even loved her name.